SINISTER GAMBITS

SINISTER GAMBITS

Chess Stories of
Murder and Mystery

Edited by
RICHARD PEYTON

SOUVENIR PRESS

CONTENTS

INTRODUCTION

Searching for the origins of chess has been described as rather like solving a detective mystery, proceeding from the known to the unknown; generations of writers and players have sought after the elusive beginning of their unique game with the same fervour as have the great fictional sleuths — Auguste Dupin, Sherlock Holmes, Hercule Poirot — pursued their criminal adversaries.

For some time certain authorities clung to a medieval story that chess had been invented by Xerxes, the king of ancient Persia; later, another school of thought supported an ingenious idea that it had been the brain-child of Palamedes at the siege of Troy. Other sources have ascribed the genesis of the game to an Arab of Mahomet's time, named Ladjladj, or to the Greek Pythagoras who evolved it from rhythmomachy; while some enthusiasts of classical myth have even maintained that it was a divine game first played by the gods and later taught to man by the nymph Scacchis. Opponents of chess have, however, condemned it with equal fervour as the handiwork of the Devil himself!

Part of the problem in solving this mystery is the fact that there is so little on record of chess or the playing of the game before the second half of the eighteenth century, although it was undeniably being played by the nobility in the Middle Ages and by the intelligentsia in succeeding centuries. What is beyond doubt is that four ancient civilisations were all clearly associated with its early development — Islam, Persia, India and China — and it was most probably an imaginative genius in one or other of them who was responsible for the stroke of inspiration that formulated this game, as accessible to paupers as to princes. Such a man would surely also have delighted in the problems of reasoning set by crime and mystery stories which, though formulated long before, similarly did not blossom until the 1800s, thanks to the pen of a self-confessed chess player, Edgar Allan Poe.

Chess offers as much mystery in the playing as in its origins, for it can be viewed equally as a war game, a symbol of the social hierarchy, an art form, an organised sport and, perhaps most challengingly of all, as a complex problem of logic. 'The chessboard is the world,' the biologist T.H. Huxley once declared unequivocally, aligning himself with a whole cavalcade of famous writers, from Lewis Carroll to Vladimir Nabokov, who have exploited the game for its colourful imagery and hermetic mystique.

Once a game is in play, it can be said to mimic human beings in various ways: in cunning, power, flight, war, struggle, attack, defence, capture and so on. 'Chess is an attempt to control chaos,' declares one man who really should know, the present world champion, Gary Kasparov.

Perhaps, however, the best summary of all these elements has been provided by the great German fantasy novelist, Hermann Hesse, himself a skilful player, who wrote in the pages of his masterpiece, *The Glass Bead Game* (1945):

> All the insights, noble thoughts and works of art that the human race has produced in its creative eras, all that scholarly periods have reduced to concepts and converted into intellectual property — on all this immense body of intellectual values the player plays like an organist on an organ. Theoretically this instrument is capable of reproducing in the game the entire intellectual content of the universe.

Small wonder, then, with obscurity surrounding both its creation and its essence, that chess should have provided the inspiration for a not inconsiderable number of mystery stories, or that the writers, almost without exception, were or are enthusiastic players, although only a few aspired to be 'top board' contestants. How they came to be assembled in the pages which follow also involves an example of the mysteries of association which I would like to relate.

It began early in 1990, with the first reports of the eagerly awaited world championship contest between Gary Kasparov and Anatoly Karpov which, thanks to the later saturation media coverage (laying great emphasis on the aggression, competitiveness and three million dollars at stake) has done much to push chess even more centre stage in the public consciousness. This was brought home to me vividly in a quite different way during a visit to Australia in August 1990. It was at the time of the beginning of the crisis in the Gulf, and what caught my eye was a front page headline in two-inch type in the *Melbourne Herald*, which read: 'BLOOD CHESS'. The report beneath began: 'In a strategy described as "blood chess" by American military officials, Iraq today began using Westerners as a human shield at key military targets . . .'

Two months after this came an even more bizarre twist to my association of ideas when I read a report in *The Times* about a bomb threat which had allegedly been made to the Kasparov/Karpov world championship. The newspaper's Chess Correspondent, Raymond Keene, wrote:

A firebomb offensive has threatened to ignite the acrimonious relationship between the chess prima donnas, Gary Kasparov and Anatoly Karpov, only days before the start of their world championship in New York. The affair allegedly occurred in Soviet Georgia after one of Kasparov's closest aides declined to accept a $100,000 bribe to disclose the training programme he had devised for his master. In the best traditions of grand master summits, a chess war loomed after Andrew Page, the London businessman who manages Kasparov's affairs, claimed that Zurab Azmaiparashvili refused the sweetener only to discover that the bomb had been slipped through his mother-in-law's mail box. Mr Page said the incident occurred last week and a woman, whom he did not identify, was burned. The Karpov entourage denies any knowledge, but reports continue to circulate in Moscow . . .

Now 'chess for blood' is, of course, a term familiar to players of the game — almost as familiar as those other words derived from chess, exchequer, stalemate and gambit, are in everyday language — and it was the juxtaposition of the terminology and the reports of the 'combat' between Karpov and Kasparov which turned my mind to thoughts of the various strange, mysterious and sinister short stories I had read over the years in which chess appeared as the theme or as a metaphor. As a result I began putting together this book, drawing on the resources of chess libraries and chess-playing friends. And while I would not claim that *Sinister Gambits* contains every one of the stories of this type, it does offer a comprehensive selection of the very best of such writing.

The book is intended not just for those who play chess —

indeed, no knowledge of the game is necessary to enjoy any of the stories — but I should like to think that the ingenuity and excitement they provide might encourage a few readers to take up what has been referred to as the 'Game of Games.'

Napoleon, a man who was used to warfare and was also something of an enthusiast for the game, once commented of chess, 'It is too difficult for a game and not serious enough for a science.' In this book I hope the reader will find stories that are difficult to put down and seriously puzzling enough to engage his or her powers of detection. The first move is yours.

I

GRANDPLAYER'S NIGHTMARES

'My opponent is a creature of darkness. He is not like a human being. He is angry and evil. He represents something alien to the crowd.'

Gary Kasparov,
World Champion, 1991

Gary Kasparov, the current world chess champion, is only the latest in a long line of grand masters, although his frequently overwhelming victories have made him widely considered to be the greatest player of all time. From Wilhelm Steinitz, who first held the laurel from 1886 to 1894, by way of Alexander Alekhine (who was the champion for two periods, 1927-1935 and 1937-1946) and Mikhail Botvinnik (who outdid his predecessor with three 'reigns', 1948-1957, 1958-1960 and 1961-1963), to Boris Spassky (1969-1972) and the brilliant but enigmatic Bobby Fischer (1972-1975), the supreme players of chess have increasingly become household names. Around the world, chess players everywhere have attempted to emulate these masters, some rising to the position of grand master in their own countries, others content to achieve success at regional or local level — all united in their passion for the game and its complexities. The stories in this first section all involve fictional fascination — in some cases, obsession — with chess, and the authors are also men with considerable experience of their subject-matter.

Fritz Leiber, born in 1910 and widely regarded as being one of the twentieth century's supreme writers of fantasy fiction, makes the opening move with a story of obsession which draws on his own knowledge of the game from playing in tournaments all over America. A graduate in psychology and physiology from the University of Chicago, he worked for a time as an editor of *Science Digest* before beginning to write the tales of fantasy and science fiction (including the sub-genre of 'Swords and Sorcery' for which he is credited with coining the title) and in 1975 was named a 'Grand Master of Fantasy'. Fritz Leiber has described chess as being his greatest enthusiasm apart from writing, and declared in 1967 when he had completed the first authorised Tarzan novel written by anyone except Edgar Rice Burroughs, 'After finishing, I took off to play in a chess tournament — I figured that was just about as far away from the jungle as a man could get!' Apart from 'The Dreams of Albert Moreland' published here, Leiber has written two other fine stories featuring chess, 'The 64-Square Madhouse' and a Sherlock Holmes parody, 'The Moriarty Gambit', in which the great detective defeats his arch-enemy over the chessboard.

The second story, 'The Three Sailors' Gambit', is by the Irish nobleman and fantasy writer, Lord Dunsany (1878-1957), who was for a number of years the Chess Champion of his native Ireland and was particularly proud of having played a drawn game with one of the world chess champions, José Raul Capablanca (1921-1927). As a youngster, Dunsany was something of a chess prodigy, being invited to play for Norfolk (where he was at school) when he was just sixteen. In his autobiography, *Patches of Sunlight* (1938), he describes a salutary chess experience in London which I think is well worth quoting.

> I went one day into Simpson's Divan, close to Charing Cross, where masters and other professionals used to play for a shilling a game. You paid sixpence downstairs, which entitled you to a cigar and to go up to the room in which chess was played. Chess was not mentioned where one bought one's ticket, and the cigar was evidently thought to be the more important of the two. In any event, I bought my cigar-ticket and went upstairs, and there was a Frenchman waiting for a game with a tumbler of water before him into which he was dipping a lump of sugar. I had a game with him and won. But the next time I went there I had the black pieces, which move second, not the white pieces as I had the first time; and the professional with whom I played on this occasion played the Evans Gambit against me, of which, like all other openings, I knew nothing; and it was too much for me. This not only prevented me from getting my head turned, but it rather turned it in the other direction and discouraged me from returning to Simpson's.

Dunsany did persevere with his chess elsewhere, however, and by the outbreak of the First World War was a skilled player. He is today remembered as a rather larger-than-life character who went big-game hunting in Africa, was wounded in the Irish Easter Rebellion of 1916, and delighted in the title of 'The Worst Dressed Man in Ireland'! His writing, though, also earned him the more enduring honour of 'Father of the Invented Fantasy World in short story form', and his books like *The Gods of Pegena*

(1905), *Time and the Gods* (1906) and *The Book of Wonder* (1912) have been highly influential on many later fantasy writers. Like Fritz Leiber, this eccentric Irishman wrote several stories about chess and is represented here by the ingenious tale of 'The Three Sailors' Gambit', in which a trio of sailors outwit a group of grand masters.

Another writer who was also a character in every sense of the word was Gerald Kersh (1911-1968), who was employed variously as a baker, nightclub bouncer, cook and wrestler before serving as a Guardsman in the Second World War and emigrating to America where he became a US citizen and full-time writer in 1959. Those who remember him in London recall him as a huge, burly man of immense strength, who loved recounting tall tales in a deep bass voice. For a time he played chess at the famous King's Head pub in Bayswater, and he may well have drawn from there some of the inspiration for the strange tale of the grandplayer Shakmatko and his persecution by 'The Devil that Troubled the Chessboard'.

Stephen Leacock (1869-1944), the Canadian humorist, led a quite different life from Leiber, Dunsany and Kersh, although his writing is injected with a lot of outrageous and often wild humour. His career was spent primarily as a lecturer in economics at McGill University in Toronto, but his name became familiar on both sides of the Atlantic through his humorous essays and books such as *Nonsense Novels* (1911) and *The Garden of Folly* (1924), in which can be found evidence of his love of chess, which he apparently began playing while a student at Toronto University. His story here, 'Pawn to King's Four', about the strange behaviour of a leading member of a chess club, is a mixture of humour and mystery in the inimitable Leacock style.

'The Royal Game' by Stefan Zweig, the Austrian writer noted for the deep psychological insight of his work, is arguably one of the most famous stories featuring chess. Zweig, the son of Jewish parents, left Vienna to live in London before the advent of World War II, and became a devotee of chess, competing against a number of leading players in Britain as well as America and Brazil, where he tragically took his own life in 1942. His story is of particular interest because it was written in the last four months of his life and reveals a great deal about his knowledge of the game. The British novelist, John Fowles, who is a particular admirer of 'The Royal Game', has described it as a 'fine story of a man who outwits the Gestapo and manages, though scarred, to find the courage to go on living.'

Mr Fowles remarks further about the chess element of the narrative:

> We may also see a parallel between the mad, but saving sanctuary the hero finds in 'imaginary' chess and Zweig's own habitual retreat into the imagination (or literary work) when domestic or political reality threatened him too closely. The mystery is how he failed to see that this last fiction, surely one of the most powerful ever based on the imagery of a game, proved the very contrary of what he persisted in believing: that his daimon was gone, he was 'written out'.

The last story in the section, 'End-Game' is an appropriate one to follow Zweig's tale, because the author, J.G. Ballard, was born in Shanghai and spent the Second World War interned in a Japanese civilian POW Camp. Ballard came to Britain in 1946 and, after reading medicine at Cambridge, took to writing a new kind of science fiction utilising his interest in psychology and in the emotional significance of deserted landscapes and wrecked technology. His collections of stories of near-future decadence and disaster, such as *The Terminal Beach* (1946), have since gained him acceptance as a major author and a figurehead of the 'new wave' of SF writers. It is from this book that Ballard's bizarre story of chess, 'End-Game', is taken.

THE DREAMS OF ALBERT MORELAND

Fritz Leiber

I think of the autumn of 1939, not as the beginning of the Second World War, but as the period in which Albert Moreland dreamed the dream. The two events — the war and the dream — are not, however, divorced in my mind. Indeed, I sometimes fear that there is a connection between them, but it is a connection which no sane person will consider seriously, if he is wise.

Albert Moreland was, and perhaps still is, a professional chess-player. That fact has an important bearing on the dream, or dreams. He made most of his scant income at a games arcade in Lower Manhattan, taking on all comers — the enthusiast who gets a kick out of trying to beat an expert, the lonely man who turns to chess as to a drug, or the down-and-outer tempted into purchasing a half hour of intellectual dignity for a quarter.

After I got to know Moreland, I often wandered into the arcade and watched him playing as many as three or four games simultaneously, oblivious to the clicking and whirring of the pinball games and the intermittent reports from the shooting gallery. He got fifteen cents for every win; the house took the extra dime. When he lost, neither got anything.

Eventually I found out that he was a much better player than he needed to be for his arcade job. He had won casual games from internationally famous masters. A couple of Manhattan clubs had wanted to groom him for the big tournaments, but lack of ambition kept him drifting along in obscurity. I got the impression that he thought chess too trivial a business to warrant serious consideration although he was perfectly willing to dribble his life away at the arcade, waiting for something really important to come along, if it ever did. Once in a while he eked out his income by playing on a club team, getting as much as five dollars.

I met him at the old brownstone house where we both had rooms on the same floor, and it was there that he first told me about the dream.

We had just finished a game of chess, and I was idly watching the battle-scarred pieces slide off the board and pile up in a fold of the blanket on his cot. Outside a fretful wind eddied the dry grit. There was a surge of traffic noises, and the buzz of a defective neon sign. I had just lost, but I was glad that Moreland never let me win, as he occasionally did with the players at the arcade, to encourage them. Indeed, I thought myself fortunate in being able to play with Moreland at all, not knowing then that I was probably the best friend he had.

I was saying something obvious about chess.

'You think it a complicated game?' he inquired, peering at me with quizzical intentness, his dark eyes like round windows pushed up under heavy eaves. 'Well, perhaps it is. But I play a game a thousand times more complex every night in my dreams. And the queer thing is that the game goes on night after night. The same game. I never really sleep. Only dream about the game.'

Then he told me, speaking with a mixture of facetious jest and uncomfortable seriousness that was to characterise many of our conversations.

The images of his dream, as he described them, were impressively simple, without any of the usual merging and incongruity. A board so vast he sometimes had to walk out on it to move his pieces. A great many more squares than in chess and arranged in patches of different colours, the power of the pieces varying according to the colour of the square on which they stood. Above and to each side of the board only blackness, but a blackness that suggested starless infinity, as if, as he put it, the scene were laid on the very top of the universe.

When he was awake he could not quite remember all the rules of the game, although he recalled a great many isolated points, including the interesting fact that — quite unlike chess — his pieces and those of his adversary did not duplicate each other. Yet he was convinced that he not only understood the game perfectly while dreaming, but also was able to play it in the highly strategic manner of the master chess player. It was, he said, as though his night mind had many more dimensions of thought than his waking mind, and was able to grasp intuitively complex series of moves that would ordinarily have to be reasoned out step by step.

'A feeling of increased mental power is a very ordinary dream-delusion, isn't it?' he added, peering at me sharply. 'And so I suppose you might say it's a very ordinary dream.'

I did not know quite how to take that last remark, so I prodded him with a question.

'What do the pieces look like?'

It turned out that they were similar to those of chess in that they were considerably stylised and yet suggested the original forms — architectural, animal, ornamental — which had served as their inspiration. But there the similarity ended. The inspiring forms, so far as he could guess at them, were grotesque in the extreme. There were terraced towers subtly distorted out of the perpendicular, strangely asymmetric polygons that made him think of temples and tombs, vegetable-animal shapes which defied classification and whose formalised limbs and external organs suggested a variety of unknown functions. The more powerful pieces seemed to be modelled after life forms, for they carried stylised weapons and other implements, and wore things similar to crowns and tiaras — a little like the king, queen and bishop in chess — while the carving indicated voluminous robes and hoods. But they were in no other sense anthropomorphic. Moreland sought in vain for earthly analogies, mentioning Hindu idols, prehistoric reptiles, futurist sculpture, squids bearing daggers in their tentacles, and huge ants and mantes and other insects with fantastically adapted end-organs.

'I think you would have to search the whole universe — every planet and every dead sun — before you could find the original models,' he said, frowning. 'Remember, there is nothing cloudy or vague about the pieces themselves in my dream. They are as tangible as this rook.' He picked up the piece, clenched his fist around it for a moment, and then held it out toward me on his open palm. 'It is only in what they suggest that the vagueness lies.'

It was strange, but his words seemed to open some dream-eye in my own mind, so that I could almost see the things he described. I asked him if he experienced fear during his dream.

He replied that the pieces one and all filled him with repugnance — those based on higher life forms usually to a greater degree than the architectural ones. He hated to have to touch or handle them. There was one piece in particular which had an intensely morbid fascination for his dream-self. He identified it as 'the archer' because the stylised weapon it bore gave the impression of being able to hurt at a distance; but like the rest it was quite inhuman. He described it as representing a kind of intermediate, warped life form which had achieved more than human intellectual power without losing — but rather gaining — in brute cruelty and malignity. It was one of opposing pieces for which there was no duplicate among his own. The mingled fear and loathing it inspired in him sometimes became so great that they interfered with his strategic grasp of the whole dream-game, and he was afraid his feeling toward it would sometime rise to such a pitch that he would be forced to capture it just to get it off the board, even though such a capture might compromise his whole position.

'God knows how my mind ever cooked up such a hideous entity,' he finished, with a quick grin. 'Five hundred years ago I'd have said the Devil put it there.'

'Speaking of the Devil,' I asked, immediately feeling my flippancy was silly, 'whom do you play against in your dream?'

Again he frowned. 'I don't know. The opposing pieces move by themselves. I will have made a move, and then, after waiting for what seems like an eon, all on edge as in chess, one of the opposing pieces will begin to shake a little and then to wobble back and forth. Gradually the movement increases in extent until the piece gets off balance and begins to rock and career across the board, like a water tumbler on a pitching ship, until it reaches the proper square. Then, slowly as it began, the movement subsides. I don't know, but it always makes me think of some huge, invisible, senile creature — crafty, selfish, cruel. You've watched that trembly old man at the arcade? The one who always drags the pieces across the board without lifting them, his hand constantly shaking? It's a little like that.'

I nodded. His description made it very vivid. For the first time I began to think of how unpleasant such a dream might be.

'And it goes on night after night?' I asked.

'Night after night!' he affirmed with sudden fierceness. 'And always the same game. It has been more than a month now, and my forces are just beginning to grapple with the enemy. It's draining off my mental energy. I wish it would stop. I'm getting so that I hate to go to sleep.' He paused and turned away. 'It seems queer,' he said after a moment in a softer voice, smiling apologetically, 'it seems queer to get so worked up over a dream. But if you've had bad ones, you know how they can cloud your thoughts all day. And I haven't really managed to get over to you the sort of feeling that grips me while I'm dreaming, and while my brain is working at the game and plotting move-sequence after move-sequence and weighing a thousand complex possibilities. There's repugnance, yes, and fear. I've told you that. But the dominant feeling is one of responsibility. I must not lose the game. More than my own personal welfare depends upon it. There are some terrible stakes involved, though I am never quite sure what they are.

'When you were a little child, did you ever worry tremendously about something, with that complete lack of proportion character-istic of childhood? Did you ever feel that everything, literally everything, depended upon your performing some trivial action, some unimportant duty, in just the right way? Well, while I dream, I have the feeling that I'm playing for some stake as big as the fate of mankind. One wrong move may plunge the uni-verse into unending night. Sometimes, in my dream, I feel sure of it.'

His voice trailed off and he stared at the chessmen. I made some remarks and started to tell about an air-raid nightmare I had just had, but it didn't seem very important. And I gave him some vague advice about changing his sleeping habits, which did not seem very important either, although he accepted it with good grace. As I started back to my room he said, 'Amusing to think, isn't it, that I'll be playing the game again as soon as my head hits the pillow?' He grinned and added lightly, 'Perhaps it will be over sooner than I expect. Lately I've had the feeling that my adversary is about to unleash a surprise attack, although he pretends to be on the defensive.' He grinned again and shut the door.

As I waited for sleep, staring at the wavy churning darkness that is more in the eyes than outside them, I began to wonder whether Moreland did not stand in greater need of psychiatric treatment than most chessplayers. Certainly a person without family, friends, or proper occupation is liable to mental aber-rations. Yet be seemed sane enough. Perhaps the dream was a compensation for his failure to use anything like the full poten-tialities of his highly talented mind, even at chess-playing. Cer-tainly it was a satisfyingly grandiose vision, with its unearthly background and its implications of stupendous mental skill.

There floated into my mind the lines from the *Rubaiyat* about the cosmic chess-player who, 'Hither and thither moves and checks, and slays, And one by one back in the Closet lays.'

Then I thought of the emotional atmosphere of his dreams, and the feelings of terror and boundless responsibility, of tremendous duties and cataclysmic consequences — feelings I recognised from my own dreams — and I compared them with the mad, dismal state of the world (for it was October, and sense of utter catastrophe had not yet been dulled) and I thought of the million drifting Morelands suddenly shocked into a realisation of the desperate plight of things and of priceless chances lost forever in the past and of their own ill-defined but certain complicity in the disaster. I began to see Moreland's dream as the symbol of a last-ditch, too-late struggle against the implacable forces of fate and chance. And my night thoughts began to revolve around the fancy that some cosmic beings, neither gods nor men, had created human life long ago as a jest or experiment or artistic form, and had now decided to base the fate of their creation on the result of a game of skill played against one of their creatures.

Suddenly I realised that I was wide awake and that the darkness was no longer restful. I snapped on the light and impulsively decided to see if Moreland was still up.

The hall was as shadowy and funereal as that of most boarding houses late at night, and I tried to minimise the inevitable dry creakings. I waited for a few moments in front of Moreland's door, but heard nothing, so instead of knocking, I presumed upon our familiarity and edged open the door, quietly, in order not to disturb him if he were abed.

It was then that I heard his voice, and so certain was my impression that the sound came from a considerable distance that I immediately walked back to the stair-well and called, 'Moreland, are you down there?'

Only then did I realise what he had said. Perhaps it was the peculiarity of the words that caused them first to register on my mind as merely a series of sounds.

The words were, 'My spider-thing seizes your armour-bearer. I threaten.'

It instantly occurred to me that the words were similar in general form to any one of a number of conventional expressions in chess, such as, 'My rook captures your bishop. I give check.' But there are no such pieces as 'spider-things' or 'armour-bearers' in chess or any other game I know of.

I automatically walked back towards his room, though I still doubted he was there. The voice had sounded much too far away — outside the building or at least in a remote section of it.

But he was lying on the cot, his upturned face revealed by the light of a distant electric advertisement, which blinked on and off at regular intervals. The traffic sounds, which had been almost inaudible in the hall, made the half-darkness restless and irritably alive. The defective neon sign still buzzed and droned insectlike as it had earlier in the evening.

I tiptoed over and looked down at him. His face, more pale than it should have been because of some quality of the intermittent light, was set in an expression of painfully intense concentration — forehead vertically furrowed, muscles around the eye contracted, lips pursed to a line. I wondered if I ought to awaken him. I was acutely aware of the impersonally murmuring city all around us — block on block of shuttling, routined, aloof existence — and the contrast made his sleeping face seem all the more sensitive and vividly individual and unguarded, like some soft though purposefully tense organism which has lost its protective shell.

As I waited uncertainly, the tight lips opened a little without losing any of their tautness. He spoke, and for a second time the impression of distance was so compelling that I involuntarily looked over my shoulder and out the dustily glowing window. Then I began to tremble.

'My coiled-thing writhes to the thirteenth square of the green ruler's domain,' was what he said, but I can only suggest the quality of the voice. Some inconceivable sort of distance had drained it of all richness and throatiness and overtones so that it was hollow and flat and faint and disturbingly mournful, as voices sometimes sound in open country, or from up on a high roof, or when there is a bad telephone connection. I felt I was the victim of some gruesome deception, and yet I knew that ventriloquism is a matter of motionless lips and clever suggestion rather than any really convincing change in the quality of the voice itself. Without volition there rose in my mind visions of infinite space, unending darkness. I felt as if I were being wrenched up and away from the world, so that Manhattan lay below me like a black asymmetric spearhead outlined by leaden waters, and then still farther outward at increasing speed until earth and sun and stars and galaxies were all lost and I was beyond the universe. To such a degree did the quality of Moreland's voice affect me.

I do not know how long I stood there waiting for him to speak again, with the noises of Manhattan flowing around yet not quite touching me, and the electric sign blinking on and off unalterably like the ticking of a clock. I could only think about the game that was being played, and wonder whether Moreland's adversary had yet made an answering move, and whether things were going for or against Moreland. There was no telling from his face; its intensity of concentration did not change. During those moments or minutes I stood there, I believed implicitly in the reality of the game. As if I myself were somehow dreaming, I could not question the rationality of my belief or break the spell which bound me.

When finally his lips parted a little and I experienced again that impression of impossible, eerie ventriloquism — the words this time being, 'My horned-creature vaults over the twisted tower, challenging the archer' — my fear broke loose from whatever controlled it and I stumbled toward the door.

Then came what was, in an oblique way, the strangest part of the whole episode. In the time it took me to walk the length of the corridor back to my room, most of my fear and most of the feeling of complete alienage and other-worldliness which had dominated me while I was watching Moreland's face, receded so swiftly that I even forgot, for the time being, how great they had been. I do not know why that happened. Perhaps it was because the unwholesome realm of Moreland's dream was so grotesquely dissimilar to anything in the real world. Whatever the cause by the time I opened the door to my room I was thinking, 'Such nightmares can't be wholesome. Perhaps he should see a psychiatrist. Yet it's only a dream,' and so on. I felt tired and stupid. Very soon I was asleep.

But some wraith of the original emotions must have lingered, for I awoke next morning with the fear that something had happened to Moreland. Dressing hurriedly, I knocked at his door, but found the room empty, the bedclothes still rumpled. I inquired of the landlady, and she said he had gone out at eight-fifteen as usual. The bald statement did not quite satisfy my vague anxiety. But since my job-hunting that day happened to lie in the direction of the arcade, I had an excuse to wander in. Moreland was stolidly pushing pieces around with an abstracted, tousle-haired fellow of Slavic features, and casually conducting two rapid-fire checker games on the side. Reassured, I went on without bothering him.

That evening we had a long talk about dreams in general, and I found him surprisingly well-read on the subject and scientifically cautious in his attitudes. Rather to my chagrin, it was I who

THE DREAMS OF ALBERT MORELAND 25

introduced such dubious topics as clairvoyance, mental telepathy, and the possibility of strange telescopings and other distortions of time and space during dream states. Some foolish reticence about admitting I had pushed my way into his room last night kept me from telling him what I had heard and seen, but he freely told me he had had another instalment of the usual dream. He seemed to take a more philosophical attitude now that he had shared his experiences with someone. Together we speculated as to the possible daytime sources of his dream. It was after twelve when we said goodnight.

I went away with the feeling of having been let down — vaguely unsatisfied. I think the fear I had experienced the previous night and then almost forgotten must have been gnawing at me obscurely.

And the following evening it found an avenue of return. Thinking Moreland must be tired of talking about dreams, I coaxed him into a game of chess. But in the middle of the game he put back a piece he was about to move, and said, 'You know, that damned dream of mine is getting very bothersome.'

It turned out that his dream adversary had finally loosed the long-threatened attack, and that the dream itself had turned into a kind of nightmare. 'It's very much like what happens to you in a game of chess,' he explained. 'You go along confident that you have a strong position and that the game is taking the right direction. Every move your opponent makes is one you have foreseen. You get to feeling almost omniscient. Suddenly he makes a totally unexpected attacking move. For a moment you think it must be a stupid blunder on his part. Then you look a little more closely and realise that you have totally overlooked something and that his attack is a sound one. Then you begin to sweat.

'Of course, I've always experienced fear and anxiety and a sense of overpowering responsibility during the dream. But my pieces were like a wall, protecting me. Now I can see only the cracks in that wall. At any one of a hundred weak points it might conceivably be broken. Whenever one of the opposing pieces begins to wobble and shake, I wonder whether, when its move is completed, there will flash into my mind the unalterable and unavoidable combination of moves leading to my defeat. Last night I thought I saw such a move, and the terror was so great that everything swirled and I seemed to drop through millions of miles of emptiness in an instant. Yet just in that instant of waking I realised I had miscalculated, and that my position, though perilous, was still secure. It was so vivid that I almost carried with me into my waking thoughts the reason why, but then some of the steps in the train of dream-reasoning dropped out, as if my waking mind were not big enough to hold them all.'

He also told me that his fixation on 'the archer' was becoming increasingly troublesome. It filled him with a special kind of terror, different in quality, but perhaps higher in pitch than that engendered in him by the dream as a whole: a crazy morbid terror, characterised by intense repugnance, nerve-twisting exasperation, and reckless suicidal impulses.

'I can't get rid of the feeling,' he said, 'that the beastly thing will in some unfair and underhanded manner be the means of my defeat.'

He looked very tired to me, although his face was of the compact, tough-skinned sort that does not readily show fatigue, and I felt concern for his physical and nervous welfare. I suggested that he consult a doctor (I did not like to say psychiatrist) and pointed out that sleeping tablets might be of some help.

'But in a deeper sleep the dream might be even more vivid and real,' he answered, grimacing sardonically. 'No I'd rather play out the game under the present conditions.'

I was glad to find that he still viewed the dream as an interesting and temporary psychological phenomenon (what else he could have viewed it as, I did not stop to analyse). Even while admitting to me the exceptional intensity of his emotions, he maintained something of a jesting air. Once he compared his dream to a paranoid's delusions of persecution, and asked whether I didn't think it was good enough to get him admitted to an asylum.

'Then I could forget the arcade and devote all my time to dream-chess,' he said, laughing sharply as soon as he saw I was beginning to wonder whether he had not meant the remark half-seriously.

But some part of my mind was not convinced by his protestations, and when later I tossed in the dark, my imagination perversely kept picturing the universe as a great arena in which each creature is doomed to engage in a losing game of skill against demoniac mentalities which, however long they may play cat and mouse, are always assured of final mastery — or almost assured, so that it would be a miracle if they were beaten. I found myself comparing them to certain chess-players, who if they cannot beat an opponent by superior skill, will capitalise on unpleasant personal mannerisms in order to exasperate him and break down the lucidity of his thinking.

This mood coloured my own nebulous dreams and persisted into the next day. As I walked the streets I felt myself inundated by an omnipresent anxiety, and I sensed taut, nervous misery in each passing face. For once I seemed able to look behind the mask which every person wears and which is so characteristically pronounced in a congested city, and see what lay behind — the egotistical sensitivity, the smouldering irritation, the thwarted longing, the defeat . . . and, above all, the anxiety, too ill-defined and lacking in definite object to be called fear, but nonetheless infecting every thought and action, and making trivial things terrible. And it seemed to me that social, economic, and physiological factors, even Death and the War, were insufficient to explain such anxiety, and that it was in reality an upwelling from something dubious and horrible in the very constitution of the universe.

That evening I found myself at the arcade. Here too I sensed a difference in things, for Moreland's abstraction was not the calculating boredom with which I was familiar, and his tiredness was shockingly apparent. One of his three opponents, after shifting around restlessly, called his attention to a move, and Moreland jerked his head as if he had been dozing. He immediately made an answering move, and quickly lost his queen and the game by a trap that was very obvious even to me. A little later he lost another game by an equally elementary oversight. The boss of the arcade, a big beefy man, ambled over and stood behind Moreland, his heavy-jowled face impassive, seeming to study the position of the pieces in the last game. Moreland lost that too.

'Who won?' asked the boss.

Moreland indicated his opponent. The boss grunted noncommittally and walked off.

No one else sat down to play. It was near closing time. I was not sure whether Moreland had noticed me, but after a while he stood up and nodded at me, and got his hat and coat. We walked the long stretch back to the rooming house. He hardly spoke a word, and my sensation of morbid insight into the world around persisted and kept me silent. He walked as usual with long, slightly stiff-kneed strides hands in his pockets, hat pulled low, frowning at the pavement a dozen feet ahead.

When we reached the room he sat down without taking off his coat and said, 'Of course, it was the dream made me lose those games. When I woke this morning it was terribly vivid, and I almost remembered the exact position and all the rules. I started to make a diagram. . .'

He indicated a piece of wrapping paper on the table. Hasty crisscrossed lines, incomplete, represented what seemed to be the corner of an indefinitely larger pattern. There were about five hundred squares. On various squares were marks and names standing for pieces, and there were arrows radiating out from the pieces to show their power of movement.

'I got that far. Then I began to forget,' he said tiredly, staring at the floor. 'But I'm still very close to it. Like a mathematical puzzle you've not quite solved. Parts of the board kept flashing into my mind all day, so that I felt with a little more effort I would be able to grasp the whole. Yet I can't.'

His voice changed. 'I'm going to lose, you know. It's that piece I call "the archer". Last night I couldn't concentrate on the board; it kept drawing my eyes. The worst thing is that it's the spearhead of my adversary's attack. I ache to capture it. But I must not, for it's a kind of catspaw too, the bait of the strategic trap my adversary is laying. If I capture it, I will expose myself to defeat. So I must watch it coming closer and closer — it has an ugly, double-angled sort of hopping move — knowing that my only chance is to sit tight until my adversary overreaches himself and I can counterattack. But I won't be able to. Soon, perhaps tonight, my nerve will crack and I will capture it.'

I was studying the diagram with great interest, and only half heard the rest — a description of the actual appearance of 'the archer'. I heard him say something about 'a five-lobed head . . . the head almost hidden by a hood . . . appendages, each with four joints, appearing from under the robe . . . an eight-pronged weapon with wheels and levers about it, and little bag-shaped receptacles, as though for poison . . . posture suggesting it is lifting the weapon to aim it . . . all intricately carved in some lustrous red stone, speckled with violet . . . an expression of bestial, supernatural malevolence. . .'

Just then all my attention focused suddenly on the diagram, and I felt a tightening shiver of excitement, for I recognised two familiar names, which I had never heard Moreland mention while awake. 'Spider-thing' and 'green ruler'.

Without pausing to think, I told him of how I had listened to his sleep-talking three nights before, and about the peculiar phrases he had spoken which tallied so well with the entries on the diagram. I poured out my account with melodramatic haste. My discovery of the entries on the diagram, nothing exceptionally amazing in itself, probably made such a great impression on me because I had hitherto strangely forgotten or repressed the intense fear I had experienced when I had watched Moreland sleeping.

Before I was finished, however, I noticed the growing anxiety of his expression, and abruptly realised that what I was saying might not have the best effect on him. So I minimised my recollection of the unwholesome quality of his voice — the overpowering impression of distance — and the fear it engendered in me.

Even so, it was obvious that he had received a severe shock. For a little while he seemed to be on the verge of some serious nervous derangement, walking up and down with fierce, jerky movements, throwing out crazy statements, coming back again and again to the diabolical convincingness of the dream — which my revelation seemed to have intensified for him — and finally breaking down into vague appeals for help.

Those appeals had an immediate effect on me, making me forget any wild thoughts of my own and putting everything on a personal level. All my instincts were now to aid Moreland, and I once again saw the whole matter as something for a psychiatrist to handle. Our roles had changed. I was no longer the half-awed listener, but the steadying friend to whom he turned for advice. That, more than anything, gave me a feeling of confidence and made my previous speculations seem childish and unhealthy. I felt contemptuous of myself for having encouraged his delusive trains of imagination, and I did as much as I could to make up for it.

After a while my repeated reassurances seemed to take effect. He grew calm and our talk became reasonable once more, though every now and then he would appeal to me about some particular point that worried him. I discovered for the first time the extent to which he had taken the dream seriously. During his lonely broodings, he told me, he had sometimes become convinced that his mind left his body while he slept and travelled immeasurable distances to some transcosmic realm where the game was played.

He had the illusion, he said, of getting perilously close to the innermost secrets of the universe and finding they were rotten and evil and sardonic. At times he had been terribly afraid that the pathway between his mind and the realm of the game would 'open up' to such a degree that he would be 'sucked up bodily from the world', as he put it. His belief that loss of the game would doom the world itself had been much stronger than he had ever admitted to me previously. He had traced a frightening relationship between the progress of the game and of the War, and had begun to believe that the ultimate issue of the War — though not necessarily the victory of either side — hung on the outcome of the game.

At times it had got so bad, he revealed, that his only relief had been in the thought that, no matter what happened, he could never convince others of the reality of his dream. They would always be able to view it as a manifestation of insanity or over-wrought imagination. No matter how vivid it became to him he would never have concrete, objective proof.

'It's this way,' he said. 'You saw me sleeping, didn't you? Right here on this cot. You heard me talk in my sleep, didn't you? About the game. Well, that absolutely proves to you that it's all just a dream, doesn't it? You couldn't rightly believe anything else, could you?'

I do not know why those last ambiguous questions of his should have had such a reassuring effect on me of all people, who had only three nights ago trembled at the indescribable quality of his voice as he talked from his dream. But they did. They seemed like the final seal on an agreement between us to the effect that the dream was only a dream and meant nothing. I began to feel rather buoyant and self-satisfied, like a doctor who has just pulled his patient through a dangerous crisis. I talked to Moreland in what I now realise was almost a pompously sympathetic way, without noticing how dispirited were his obedient nods of agreement. He said little after those last questions.

I even persuaded him to go out to a nearby lunchroom for a midnight snack, as if — God help me! — I were celebrating my victory over the dream. As we sat at the not-too-dirty counter, smoking our cigarettes and sipping burningly hot coffee, I noticed that he had begun to smile again, which added to my satisfaction. I was blind to the ultimate dejection and submissive hopelessness that lay behind those smiles. As I left him at the door of his room, he suddenly caught hold of my hand and said, 'I want to tell you how grateful I am for the way you've worked to pull me out of this mess.' I made a deprecating gesture. 'No, wait,' he continued, 'it does mean a lot. Well, anyway, thanks.'

I went away with a contented, almost virtuous feeling. I had no apprehensions whatever. I only mused, in a heavily philosophic way, over the strange forms fear and anxiety can assume in our pitiably tangled civilisation.

As soon as I was dressed next morning, I rapped briskly at his door and impulsively pushed in without waiting for an answer. For once sunlight was pouring through the dusty window.

Then I saw it, and everything else receded.

It was lying on the crumpled bedclothes, half hidden by a fold of blanket, a thing perhaps ten inches high, as solid as any statuette, and as undeniably real. But from the first glance I knew that its form bore no relation to any earthly creature. This fact would have been as apparent to someone who knew nothing of art as to an expert. I also knew that the red, violet-flecked substance from which it had been carved or cast had no classification among the earthly gems and minerals. Every detail was there. The five-lobed head, almost hidden by a hood. The appendages, each with four joints, appearing from under the robe. The eight-pronged weapon with wheels and levers about it, and the little bag-shaped receptacles, as though for poison. Posture suggesting it was lifting the weapon to aim it. An expression of bestial, supernatural malevolence.

Beyond doubting, it was the thing of which Moreland had dreamed. The thing which had horrified and fascinated him, as it now did me, which had rasped unendurably on his nerves, as it now began to rasp on mine. The thing which has been the spearhead and catspaw of his adversary's attack, and whose capture — and it now seemed evident that it had been captured — meant the probable loss of the game. The thing which had somehow been sucked back along an ever-opening path across unimaginable distances from a realm of madness ruling the universe.

Beyond doubting, it was 'the archer'.

Hardly knowing what moved me, save fear, or what my purpose was, I fled from the room. Then I realised that I must find Moreland. No one had seen him leaving the house. I searched for him all day. The arcade. Chess clubs. Libraries.

It was evening when I went back and forced myself to enter his room. The figure was no longer there. No one at the house professed to know anything about it when I questioned them, but some of the denials were too angry, and I know that 'the archer', being obviously a thing of value and having no overly great terrors for those who do not know its history, has most probably found its way into the hands of some wealthy and eccentric collector. Other things have vanished by a similar route in the past.

Or it may be that Moreland returned secretly and took it away with him.

But I am certain that it was not made on earth.

And although there are reasons to fear the contrary, I feel that somewhere — in some cheap boarding house or lodging place, or in some madhouse — Albert Moreland, if the game is not already lost and the forfeiture begun, is still playing that unbelievable game for stakes it is unwholesome to contemplate.

THE THREE SAILORS' GAMBIT

Lord Dunsany

Sitting some years ago in the ancient tavern at Over, one after-noon in spring, I was waiting as was my custom for something strange to happen.

In this I was not always disappointed, for the very curious leaded panes of that tavern, facing the sea, let a light into the low-ceilinged room so mysterious, particularly at evening, that it somehow seemed to affect the events within. Be that as it may, I have seen strange things in that tavern and heard stranger things told.

And as I sat there three sailors entered the tavern just back, as they said, from sea and come with sun-burned skins from a very long voyage to the South; and one of them had a board and chessmen under his arm, and they were complaining that they could find no one who knew how to play chess. This was the year that the Tournament was in England. And a little dark man at a table in a corner of the room, drinking sugar and water, asked them why they wished to play chess; and they said that they would play any man for a pound. They opened their box of chessmen then, a cheap and nasty set, and the man refused to play with such uncouth pieces, and the sailors suggested that perhaps he could find better ones; and in the end he went round to his lodgings nearby and brought his own, and then they sat down to play for a pound a side. It was a consultation game on the part of the sailors, they said all three must play.

Well, the little dark man turned out to be Stavlokratz.

Of course he was fabulously poor, and the sovereign meant more to him than it did to the sailors, but he didn't seem keen to play, it was the sailors that insisted; he had made the badness of the sailors' chessmen an excuse for not playing at all, but the sailors had overruled that, and then he told them straight out who he was, and the sailors had never heard of Stavlokratz.

Well, no more was said after that. Stavlokratz said no more, either because he did not wish to boast or because he was huffed that they did not know who he was. And I saw no reason to enlighten the sailors about him; if he took their pound they had brought it on themselves, and my boundless admiration for his genius made me feel that he deserved whatever might come his way. He had not asked to play, they had named the stakes, he had warned them, and gave them first move; there was nothing unfair about Stavlokratz.

I had never seen Stavlokratz before, but I had played over nearly every one of his games in the World Championship for the last three or four years; he was always, of course, the model chosen by students. Only young chess-players can appreciate my delight at seeing him play first hand.

Well, the sailors used to lower their heads almost as low as the table and mutter together before every move, but they muttered so low that you could not hear what they planned.

They lost three pawns almost straight off, then a knight, and shortly after a bishop; they were playing in fact the famous Three Sailors' Gambit.

Stavlokratz was playing with the easy confidence that they say was usual with him, when suddenly at about the thirteenth move I saw him look surprised; he leaned forward and looked at the board and then at the sailors, but he learned nothing from their vacant faces; he looked back at the board again.

He moved more deliberately after that; the sailors lost two more pawns, Stavlokratz had lost nothing as yet. He looked at me, I thought, almost irritably, as though something would happen that he wished I was not there to see. I believed at first he had qualms about taking the sailors' pound, until it dawned on me that he might lose the game; I saw that possibility in his face, not on the board, for the game had become almost incomprehensible to me. I cannot describe my astonishment. And a few moves later Stavlokratz resigned.

The sailors showed no more elation than if they had won some game with greasy cards, playing amongst themselves.

Stavlokratz asked them where they got their opening. 'We kind of thought of it,' said one. 'It just come into our heads like,' said another. He asked them questions about the ports they had touched at. He evidently thought, as I did myself, that they had learned their extraordinary gambit, perhaps in some old dependency of Spain, from some young master of chess whose fame had not reached Europe. He was very eager to find who this man could be, for neither of us imagined that those sailors had invented it, nor would anyone who had seen them. But he got no information from the sailors.

Stavlokratz could very ill afford the loss of a pound. He offered to play them again for the same stakes. The sailors began to set up the white pieces. Stavlokratz pointed out that it was his turn for first move. The sailors agreed but continued to set up the white pieces and sat with the white before them waiting for him to move. It was a trivial incident, but it revealed to Stavlokratz and myself that none of these sailors was aware that white always moves first.

Stavlokratz played on them his own opening, reasoning of course that as they had never heard of Stavlokratz they would not know of his opening; and with probably a very good hope of getting back his pound he played the fifth variation with its tricky seventh move, at least so he intended, but it turned to a variation unknown to the students of Stavlokratz.

Throughout this game I watched the sailors closely, and I became sure, as only an attentive watcher can be, that the one on their left, Jim Bunion, did not even know the moves.

When I had made up my mind about this I watched only the other two, Adam Bailey and Bill Sloggs, trying to make out which was the master mind; and for a long while I could not. And then I heard Adam Bailey mutter six words, the only words I heard throughout the game, of all their consultations, 'No, him with the horse's head.' And I decided that Adam Bailey did not know what a knight was, though of course he might have been explaining things to Bill Sloggs, but it did not sound like that; so that left Bill Sloggs. I watched Bill Sloggs after that with a certain wonder; he was no more intellectual than the others to look at, though rather more forceful perhaps. Poor old Stavlokratz was beaten again.

Well, in the end I paid for Stavlokratz, and tried to get a game with Bill Sloggs alone; but this he would not agree to, it must be all three or none. And then I went back with Stavlokratz to his lodgings. He very kindly gave me a game: of course it did not last long, but I am more proud of having been beaten by Stavlokratz than of any game that I have ever won. And then we talked for an hour about the sailors, and neither of us could make head or tale of them. I told him what I had noticed about Jim Bunion and Adam Bailey, and he agreed with me that Bill Sloggs was the man, though as to how he had come by that gambit or that variation of Stavlokratz's own opening he had no theory.

I had the sailors' address, which was that tavern as much as anywhere, and they were to be there all that evening. As evening drew in I went back to the tavern, and found there still the three sailors. And I offered Bill Sloggs two pounds for a game with him alone and he refused, but in the end he played me for a drink. And then I found that he had not heard of the *en passant* rule, and believed that the fact of checking the king prevented him from castling, and did not know that a player can have two or more queens on the board at the same time if he queens his pawns, or that a pawn could ever become a knight; and he made as many of the stock mistakes as he had time for in a short game, which I won. I thought that I should have got at the secret then, but his mates who had sat scowling all the while in the corner came up and interfered. It was a breach of their compact apparently for one to play chess by himself; at any rate they seemed angry. So I left the tavern then and came back again next day, and the next day and the day after, and often saw the three sailors, but none were in a communicative mood. I had got Stavlokratz to keep away, and they could get no one to play chess with at a pound a side, and I would not play with them unless they told me the secret.

And then one evening I found Jim Bunion drunk, yet not so drunk as he wished, for the two pounds were spent; and I gave him very nearly a tumbler of whiskey, or what passed for whiskey in that tavern in Over, and he told me the secret at once. I had given the others some whiskey to keep them quiet, and later on in the evening they must have gone out, but Jim Bunion stayed with me by a little table, leaning across it and talking low, right into my face, his breath smelling all the while of what passed for whiskey.

The wind was blowing outside as it does on bad nights in November, coming up with moans from the south, towards which the tavern faced with all its leaded panes, so that none but I was able to hear his voice as Jim Bunion gave up his secret.

They had sailed for years, he told me, with Bill Snyth; and on their last voyage home Bill Snyth had died. And he was buried at sea. Just the other side of the line they buried him, and his pals divided his kit, and these three got his crystal that only they knew he had, which Bill got one night in Cuba. They played chess with the crystal.

And he was going on to tell me about that night in Cuba when Bill had bought the crystal from the stranger, how some folks might think that they had seen thunderstorms, but let them go and listen to that one that thundered in Cuba when Bill was buying his crystal and they'd find that they didn't know what thunder was. But then I interrupted him, unfortunately perhaps, for it broke the thread of his tale and set him rambling awhile, and cursing other people and talking of other lands, China, Port Said and Spain: but I brought him back to Cuba again in the end. I asked him how they could play chess with a crystal; and he said that you looked at the board and looked at the crystal and there was the game in the crystal the same as it was on the board, with all the odd little pieces looking just the same though smaller, horses' heads and what-nots; and as soon as the other man moved the move came out in the crystal, and then your move appeared after it, and all you had to do was to make it on the board. If you didn't make the move that you saw in the crystal things got very bad in it, everything horribly mixed and moving about rapidly, and scowling and making the same move over and over again, and the crystal getting cloudier and cloudier; it was best to take one's eyes away from it then, or one dreamt about it afterwards, and the foul little pieces came and cursed you in your sleep and moved about all night with their crooked moves.

I thought then that, drunk though he was, he was not telling the truth, and I promised to show him to people who played chess all their lives so that he and his mates could get a pound whenever they liked, and I promised not to reveal his secret even to Stavlokratz, if only he would tell me all the truth; and this promise I have kept till long after the three sailors have lost their secret. I told him straight out that I did not believe in the crystal. Well, Jim Bunion leaned forward then, even further across the table, and swore he had seen the man from whom Bill had bought the crystal and that he was one to whom anything was possible. To begin with, his hair was villainously dark, and his features were unmistakable even down there in the South, and he could play chess with his eyes shut, and even then he could beat anyone in Cuba. But there was more than this, there was the bargain he made with Bill that told one who he was. He sold that crystal for Bill Snyth's soul.

Jim Bunion, leaning over the table with his breath in my face, nodded his head several times and was silent.

I began to question him then. Did they play chess as far away as Cuba? He said they all did. Was it conceivable that any man would make such a bargain as Snyth made? Wasn't the trick well known? Wasn't it in hundreds of books? And if he couldn't read books, mustn't he have heard from sailors that that is the Devil's commonest dodge to get souls from silly people?

Jim Bunion had leant back in his own chair quietly smiling at my questions, but when I mentioned silly people he leaned forward again, and thrust his face close to mine and asked me several times if I called Bill Snyth silly. It seemed that these three sailors thought a great deal of Bill Snyth, and it made Jim Bunion angry to hear anything said against him. I hastened to say that the bargain seemed silly, though not, of course, the man who made it; for the sailor was almost threatening, and no wonder, for the whiskey in that dim tavern would madden a nun.

When I said that the bargain seemed silly he smiled again, and then he thundered his fist down on the table and said that no one had ever got the better of Bill Snyth, and that was the worst bargain for himself that the Devil ever made, and that from all he had read or heard of the Devil he had never been so badly had before as the night when he met Bill Snyth at the inn in the thunderstorm in Cuba, for Bill Snyth already had the damnedest soul at sea; Bill was a good fellow, but his soul was damned right enough, so he got the crystal for nothing.

Yes, he was there and saw it all himself, Bill Snyth in the Spanish inn and the candles flaring, and the Devil walking in out of the rain, and then the bargain between those two old hands, and the Devil going out into the lightning, and the thunderstorm raging on, and Bill Snyth sitting chuckling to himself between the bursts of the thunder.

But I had more questions to ask and interrupted this reminiscence. Why did they all three always play together? And a look of something like fear came over Jim Bunion's face; and at first he would not speak. And then he said to me that it was like this; they had not paid for that crystal, but got it as their share of Bill Snyth's kit. If they had paid for it or given something in exchange to Bill Snyth that would have been all right, but they couldn't do that now because Bill was dead, and they were not sure if the old bargain might not hold good. And Hell must be a large and lonely place, and to go there alone must be bad; and so the three agreed that they would all stick together, and use the crystal all three or not at all, unless one died, and then the two would use it and the one that was gone would wait for them. And the last of the three to go would bring the crystal with him, or maybe the crystal would bring him. They didn't think, he said, they were the kind of men for Heaven, and he hoped they knew their place better than that, but they didn't fancy the notion of Hell alone, if Hell it had to be. It was all right for Bill Snyth, he was afraid of nothing. He had known perhaps five men that were not afraid of death, but Bill Snyth was not afraid of Hell. He died with a smile on his face like a child in its sleep; it was drink killed poor Bill Snyth.

This was why I had beaten Bill Sloggs; Sloggs had the crystal on him while we played, but would not use it; these sailors seemed to fear loneliness as some people fear being hurt; he was the only one of the three who could play chess at all, he had learnt it in order to be able to answer questions and keep up their pretence, but he had learnt it badly, as I found. I never saw the crystal, they never showed it to anyone; but Jim Bunion told me that night that it was about the size that the thick end of a hen's egg would be if it were round. And then he fell asleep.

There were many more questions that I would have asked him but I could not wake him up. I even pulled the table away so that he fell to the floor, but he slept on, and all the tavern was dark but for one candle burning; and it was then that I noticed for the first time that the other two sailors had gone; no one remained at all but Jim Bunion and I and the sinister barman of that curious inn, and he too was asleep.

When I saw that it was impossible to wake the sailor I went out into the night. Next day Jim Bunion would talk of it no more; and when I went back to Stavlokratz I found him already putting on paper his theory about the sailors, which became accepted by chess-players, that one of them had been taught their curious gambit and the other two between them had learnt all the defensive openings as well as general play. Though who taught them no one could say, in spite of enquiries made afterwards all along the Southern Pacific.

I never learnt any more details from any of the three sailors, they were always too drunk to speak or else not drunk enough to be communicative. I seem just to have taken Jim Bunion at the flood. But I kept my promise; it was I that introduced them to the Tournament, and a pretty mess they made of established reputations. And so they kept on for months, never losing a game and always playing for their pound a side. I used to follow them wherever they went merely to watch their play. They were more marvellous than Stavlokratz even in his youth.

But then they took to liberties such as giving their queen when playing first-class players. And in the end one day when all three were drunk they played the best player in England with only a row of pawns. They won the game all right. But the ball broke to pieces. I never smelt such a stench in all my life.

The three sailors took it stoically enough, they signed on to different ships and went back again to the sea, and the world of chess lost sight, for ever I trust, of the most remarkable players it ever knew, who would have altogether spoiled the game.

THE DEVIL THAT TROUBLED THE CHESSBOARD

Gerald Kersh

A shocking book might be written about Pio Busto's apartment-house. It stands on a corner not far from Oxford Street. It stands. No doubt Busto, who knows all the laws pertaining to real-estate, has managed to find some loophole in the Law of Gravity; I can think of no other reason to account for the fact that his house has not yet fallen down. Pio Busto knows how to make a living by letting furnished rooms. He puts a sheet of wallboard across a small bedroom and calls it two apartments. His house is furnished with odds and ends raked from the junk-heaps in the Cattle Market. No space is wasted. He sleeps in a subterranean wash-house, and would convert even this into a bed-sitting-room if the coal-cellar were not crammed with spare furniture and bed-linen. He is something of a character, this Busto; he looks like Lorenzo the Magnificent, and sleeps with a savage old dog named Ouif; in case of burglars he keeps a service revolver under his pillow, and a cavalry sabre hung on a bootlace over his head. He keeps evil spirits at bay with a rusty horseshoe, the lower half of a broken crucifix, and a lithograph of the Mona Lisa whom he believes to be the Virgin Mary.

His rooms are dangerous. You sigh; they shake. You sneeze, and down comes a little piece of ceiling. What is more, the walls are full of little holes, bored by tenants of an inquisitive turn of mind. The curiosity of these people is often highly irritating — your view is sometimes obscured by the eye of your neighbour, who is trying to peep back at you. But Busto's tenants rarely stay long. They are mostly rolling stones, and by the time they come down to Busto's house, which is very far from the bottom of things, they have acquired momentum. They come, and they go.

As for me, I lived for more than three months in one of the cheapest of those spy-hole-riddled bedrooms. I completed my education there. Through three or four tiny holes, which must have been bored by some neglected genius of espionage, I watched people when they thought they were alone. I saw things which walls and the darkness were made to conceal; I heard things which no man was ever supposed to hear. It was degrading, but impossible to resist. I stooped. I stooped to the keyhole of hell, and I learned the secrets of the damned.

Among the damned was Shakmatko.

Picture for yourself this terrifying man.

I saw him for the first time in the saloon bar of the 'Duchess of Euoro' — long-drawn-out, sombre, pallid, and mysterious; dressed all in black. He had the unearthly, only partly human appearance of a figure in a Japanese print. I glanced at him, and said to myself, with a sensation of shock: 'Good God, this man is all forehead!' Imagine one of those old-fashioned square felt hats without the brim: his skull was shaped exactly like that. It towered straight upwards, white and glabrous. His forehead conveyed an impression of enormous weight — it seemed to have pressed his face out of shape. You can reproduce something of his aspect if you model a human face in white plasticine, and then foreshorten it by squashing it down on the table. In plasticine that is all very well; but alive, in a public-house, it does not look so good.

And if all this were not enough, his eyes were hidden behind dark-blue spectacles.

As I looked, he rose from his chair, stretching himself out in three jerks, like a telescope, and came towards me and said, in a hushed voice, with a peculiar foreign intonation:

'Can you please give me a match?'

'With pleasure.'

He recoiled from the light of the match-flame, shading his concealed eyes with a gloved hand. I thought of the Devil in Bon-Bon. The tightly clamped mouth parted a little, to let out a puff of smoke and a few more words:

'I find the light hurts my eyes. Will you drink?'

'Oh, thank you.'

He indicated a chair. When we were seated, he asked:

'Pardon me. You live in this vicinity?'

'Almost next door.'

'Ah. In apartments?'

'That would be a polite name for them.'

'You will excuse my asking?'

'Of course. Are you looking for a room?'

'Yes, I am. But it must be cheap.'

'I live on the corner. They have one or two rooms vacant there. They're cheap enough, but — '

'Are there tables?'

'Oh! Yes, I think so.'

'Then I will go there. One thing: I can pay in advance, but I have no references.'

'I don't suppose Busto will mind that.'

'You see, I never stay long at one place.'

'You like variety, I suppose?'

'I detest variety, but I have to move.'

'Ah, landladies are often very difficult to get on with.'

'It is not that. A large number of people live in this house of yours?'

'A good few. Why?'

'I do not like to be alone.' At this, he looked over his shoulder. 'Perhaps you would be kind enough to tell me the address?'

'I'm going that way. Come along with me, if you like.'

'You are far too kind.' He reached down and picked up a great black suitcase which had been standing between his feet. It seemed to drag him down, as if it were full of lead. I said:

'Can I give you a hand?'

'No, no, no, thank you so very much.'

We walked to the house.

'First afloor fronta vacant, thirteen bobs. Very nice aroom. Top floor back aten bob, electric light include. Spotless. No bug,' lied Busto.

'Ten shillings. Is there a table in that room?'

'Corluvaduck! Bess table ina da world. You come up, I soon show you, mister.

'As long as there is a table.'

We went upstairs. Straining at his suitcase, the stranger climbed slowly. It took us a long time to reach the top of the house, where there was a vacant bedroom next to mine. 'Ecco!' said Busto, proudly indicating the misbegotten divan, the rickety old round table, and the cracked skylight, half blind with soot.

'Hokay?'

'It will do. Ten shilling a week; here is a fortnight's rent in advance. If I leave within a week, the residue is in lieu of notice. I have no references.'

'Hokey. What name, in case of letters?'

'There will be no letters. My name is Shakmatko.'

'Good.'

Shakmatko leaned against the door. He had the air of a man dying of fatigue. His trembling hand fumbled for a cigarette. Again he recoiled from the light of the match, and glanced over his shoulder.

Pity took possession of me. I put an arm about his shoulders, and led him to the divan. He sat down, gasping. Then I went back to pick up his suitcase. I stooped, clutched the handle; tensed myself in anticipation of a fifty-six-pound lift; heaved, and nearly fell backwards down the stairs.

The suitcase weighed next to nothing. It was empty except for something that gave out a dry rattling noise. I did not like that.

Shakmatko sat perfectly still. I watched him through the holes in the wallboard partition. Time passed. The autumn afternoon began to fade. Absorbed by the opacity of the skylight, the light of day gradually disappeared. The room filled with shadow. All that was left of the light seemed to be focused upon the naked top of Shakmatko's skull, as he sat with his head hanging down.His face was invisible. He looked like the featureless larva of some elephantine insect. At last, when night had fallen, he began to move. His right hand became gradually visible; it emerged from his sleeve like something squeezed out of a tube. He did not switch the light on, but, standing a little night-light in a saucer, he lit it cautiously. In this vague and sickly circle of orange-coloured light he took off his spectacles, and began to look about him. He turned his back to me. Snick-snick! He opened the suitcase. My heart beat faster. He returned to the table, carrying an oblong box and a large square board. I held my breath.

He drew a chair up to the table, upon which he carefully placed the board. For a moment he hugged the box to his breast, while he looked over his shoulder; then he slid the lid off the box and, with a sudden clatter, shot out on to the board a set of small ivory chessmen. He arranged these, with indescribable haste, sat for a while with his chin on his clenched hands, then began to move the pieces.

I wish I could convey to you the unearthly atmosphere of that room, where, half buried in the shadows, with the back of his head illuminated by a ray of blue moonlight, and his enormous forehead shining yellow in the feeble radiance of the night-light, Shakmatko sat and played chess with himself.

After a while he began to slide forward in his chair, shake his head, and shrug his shoulders. Sometimes in the middle of a move his hand would waver and his head would nod; then he would force himself to sit upright, rub his eyes violently, look wildly round the room, or listen intently with a hand at his ear.

It occurred to me that he was tired — desperately tired — and afraid of going to sleep.

Before getting into bed I locked my door.

It seemed to me that I had not been asleep for more than a minute or so when I was awakened by a loud noise. There was a heavy crash — this, actually, awoke me — followed by the noise of a shower of small, hard objects scattered over a floor. Then Shakmatko's voice, raised in a cry of anguish and terror:

'You again! Have you found me so soon? Go away! Go away!'

His door opened. I opened my door, looked out, and saw him, standing at the top of the stairs, brandishing a small silver crucifix at the black shadows which filled the staircase.

'What is it?' I asked.

He swung round instantly, holding out the crucifix. When he saw me, he caught his breath in relief.

'Ah, you. Did I disturb you? Forgive me. I — I — May I come into your room?'

'Do,' I said.

'Please close the door quickly,' he whispered as he came in.

'Sit down and pull yourself together. Tell me, what's troubling you?'

'I must leave here in the morning,' said Shakmatko, trembling in every limb. 'It has found me again. So soon! It must have followed on my very heels. Then what is the use? I can no longer escape it, even for a day. What can I do? Where can I go? My God, my God, I am surrounded!'

'What has found you? What are you trying to run away from?' I asked.

He replied: 'An evil spirit.'

I shivered. There are occasions when the entire fabric of dialectical materialism seems to go phut before the forces of nightmarish possibilities.

'What sort of evil spirit?' I asked.

'I think they call them Poltergeists.'

'Things that throw — that are supposed to throw furniture about?'

'Not all my furniture. Only certain things.'

'Such as — '

'Chess-pieces, and things connected with the game of chess. Nothing else. I am a chess-player. It hates chess. It follows me. It follows me from place to place. It waits until I am asleep, and then it tries to destroy my chess-pieces. It has already torn up all my books and papers. There is nothing left but the board and the pieces; they are too strong for it, and so it grows increasingly violent.'

'Good heavens!'

'Perhaps you think that I am mad?'

'No, no. If you had told me that you had merely been seeing things I might have thought so. But if one's chessboard flies off the table, that is another matter.'

'Thank you. I know I am not mad. My name may be unfamiliar to you. Are you interested in chess?'

'Not very. I hardly know the moves.'

'Ah. If you were you would have heard of me. I beat Paolino, in the tournament at Pressburg. My game on that occasion has gone down in history. I should certainly have been world champion but for that Thing.'

'Has it been troubling you for long?'

'My dear sir, it has given me no peace for twenty years. Conceive; twenty years! It visited me, first of all, when I was in Paris, training with Ljubljana. I had been working very hard. I think I had been working nearly all night. I took a hasty lunch, and then lay down and went to sleep. When I woke up I had a feeling that something was wrong: a malaise. I went quickly into my study. What did I see? Chaos!

'All my books on chess had been taken out of the bookcase and dashed to the floor, so violently that the bindings were broken. A photograph of myself in a group of chess-players had been hurled across the room, torn out of the frame, and crumpled into a ball. My chess-pieces were scattered over the carpet. The board had disappeared: I found it later, stuffed up the chimney.

'I rushed downstairs and complained to the concierge. He swore that nobody had come up. I thought no more of it; but two days later it happened again.'

'And didn't you ever see it?'

'Never. It is a coward. It waits until nobody is looking.'

'So what did you do?'

'I ran away. I packed my things, and left that place. I took another flat, in another quarter of Paris. I thought that the house, perhaps, was haunted. I did not believe in such things; but how is it possible to be sure? From the Rue Blanche, I moved to the Boulevard du Temple. There, I found that I had shaken it off. I sighed with relief, and settled down once again to my game.

'And then, when I was once again absorbed, happy, working day and night, it came again.

'My poor books! Torn to pieces! My beautiful notes — savagely torn to shreds! My beloved ivory pieces — scattered and trampled. Ah, but they were too strong for it. It could destroy books and papers; it could destroy thought; it could destroy the calm detachment and peace of mind necessary to my chess — but my ivory pieces and my inlaid ebony board; those, it has never been able to destroy!'

'But what happened then?'

'I ran away again. I found that by moving quickly and suddenly, I could avoid it. I took to living in streets which were difficult to find; complicated turnings, remote back-alleys. And so I often managed to lose it for a while. But in the end, it always found me out. Always, when I thought I had shaken it off for ever; when I settled down to calm work and concentration; there would come a time when I would awake, in horror, and find my papers fluttering in tiny fragments; my pieces in chaos.

'For years and years I have had no permanent home. I have been driven from place to place like a leaf on the wind. It has driven me all over the world. It has become attached to me. It has learned my scent. The time has come when it does not have to look long for my track. Two days, three days, then it is with me. My God, what am I to do?'

'Couldn't you, perhaps, consult the Psychical Research people?'

'I have done so. They are interested. They watch. Needless to say, when they watch, it will not come. I, myself, have sat up for nights and nights, waiting for it. It hides itself. And then — the moment comes when I *must* sleep — and in that moment —

'Coward! Devil! Why won't it show its face? How can I ask anybody for help? How can I dare? Nobody would believe. They would lock me up in an asylum. No, no, there is no help for me.

'No help. Look, I ran away from it last night. I came here

today. Yet it found me, this evening. There is no escape. It has caught up with me. It is on my heels. Even at this moment, it is sitting behind me. I am tired of running away. I must stay awake, but I long for sleep. Yet I dare not go to sleep. If I do, it will creep in. And I am tired out.

'Oh my God, what can I do? It is with me now. This very night. If you don't believe me, come and see.'

Shakmatko led me out, to the door of his room. There, clinging to my arm, he pointed.

The chessboard lay in the fireplace. The pieces were scattered about the room, together with hundreds of pieces of paper, torn as fine as confetti.

'What *can* I do?' asked Shakmatko.

I picked up the chessmen, and, replacing the board on the table, arranged them in their correct positions. Then, turning to Shakmatko, I said:

'Listen. You're tired. You've got to get some sleep. You come and sleep in my bed. I'll watch.'

'You are a man of high courage,' said Shakmatko. 'God will bless you. And *you*, damned spirit of anarchy — ' He shook his fist at the empty room.

I took him back, and covered him with my blanket. Poor old man, he must have been nearly dead for want of rest! He gave a deep sigh, and was asleep as soon as his head touched the pillow.

I tiptoed to his room and sat down. I did not really believe in ghosts; but, for all that, I kept my eye on the chessboard, and turned up the collar of my coat so as to protect my ears in the event of flying bishops.

An hour must have passed.

Then I heard a sound.

It was unmistakably a footstep. I clenched my fists and fixed my eyes on the door. My heart was drumming like rain on a tin roof. A floorboard creaked. The handle of the door turned, and the door opened.

I had already steeled myself to the expectation of something white, something shadowy, or some awful invisibility. What I actually saw proved to be far more horrible.

It was Shakmatko. His eyes were wide open, but rolled up so that only the bloodshot white parts were visible. His face was set in a calm expression. His hands were held out in front of him: he was walking in his sleep.

I leapt up. I meant to cry out: 'Shakmatko!' but my tongue refused to function. I saw him walk steadily over to the table, sweep the pieces off the board with a terrific gesture, and fling the board itself against the opposite wall.

The crash awoke him. He gave a start which shook him from head to foot. His eyes snapped back to their normal positions, and blinked, in utter terror, while his voice broke out:

'Damn you! Have you found me out again? Have you hunted me down again so soon? Accursed — '

'Shakmatko,' I cried, 'you've been walking in your sleep.'

He looked at me. His large, whitish eyes dilated. He brandished a skinny fist.

'You!' he said to me, 'you! Are you going to say that too?'

'But you were,' I said. 'I saw you.'

'They all say that,' said Shakmatko, in a tone of abject hopelessness. 'They all say that. Oh, God, what am I to do? What *am* I to do?'

I returned to my room. For the rest of the night there was complete quiet. But it was nearly dawn before I managed to fall asleep.

I awoke at seven. I was drawn, as by a magnet, to Shakmatko's room. I dressed, went to his door, and tapped very gently. There was no answer. It occurred to me that he had run away. I opened the door and looked in. Shakmatko was lying in bed. His head and one arm hung down.

He looked too peaceful to be alive.

I observed, among the chessmen on the floor, a little square bottle labelled *Luminal*.

In that last sleep Shakmatko did not walk.

PAWN TO KING'S FOUR

Stephen Leacock

'Pawn to King's Four,' I said as I sat down to the chess-table.

'Pawn to King's Four, eh?' said Letherby, squaring himself comfortably to the old oak table, his elbows on its wide margin, his attitude that of the veteran player. 'Pawn to King's Four,' he repeated. 'Aha, let's see!'

It's the first and oldest move in chess, but from the way Letherby said it you'd think it was as new as yesterday . . . Chess-players are like that . . . 'Pawn to King's Four,' he repeated. 'You don't mind if I take a bit of a think over it?'

'No, no,' I said, 'not at all. Play as slowly as you like. I want to get a good look round this wonderful room.'

It was the first time I had ever been in the Long Room of the Chess Club — and I sat entranced with the charm and silence of the long wainscotted room — its soft light, the blue tobacco smoke rising to the ceiling, the open grate fires burning, the spaced-out tables, the players with bent heads, unheeding our entry and our presence . . . all silent except here and there a little murmur of conversation, that rose only to hush again.

'Pawn to King's Four' — repeated Letherby — 'let me see!'

It was, I say, my first visit to the Chess Club; indeed I had never known where it was except that it was somewhere down town, right in the heart of the city, among the big buildings. Nor did I know Letherby himself very well, though I had always understood he was a chess-player. He looked like one. He had the long, still face, the unmoving eyes, the leathery, indoor complexion that marks the habitual chess-player anywhere.

So, quite naturally, when Letherby heard that I played chess he invited me to come round some night to the Chess Club. . . . 'I didn't know you played,' he said. 'You don't look like a chess-player — I beg your pardon, I didn't mean to be rude.'

So there we were at the table. The Chess Club, as I found, was right down town, right beside the New Commercial Hotel; in fact, we met by agreement in the rotunda of the hotel . . . a strange contrast — the noise, the lights, the racket of the big rotunda, the crowding people, the call of the bellboys — and this unknown haven of peace and silence, somewhere just close above and beside it.

I have little sense of location and direction so I can't say just how you get to the Club — up a few floors in the elevator and along a corridor (I think you must pass out of the building here), and then up a queer little flight of stairs, up another little stairway and with that all at once you come through a little door, a sort of end-corner door in the room and there you are in the Long Room. . . .

'Pawn to King's Four,' said Letherby, decided at last, moving the piece forward. . . . 'I thought for a minute of opening on the Queen's side, but I guess not.'

All chess-players think of opening on the Queen's side but never do. Life ends too soon.

'Knight to Bishop's Three,' I said.

'Knight to Bishop's Three, aha!' exclaimed Letherby, 'oho!' and went into a profound study. . . . It's the second oldest move in chess; it was old three thousand years ago in Persepoliz . . . but to the real chess-player it still has all the wings of the morning.

So I could look round again, still fascinated with the room.

'It's a beautiful room, Letherby,' I said.

'It is,' he answered, his eyes on the board, 'yes . . . yes . . . It's really part of the old Roslyn House that they knocked down to make the New Commercial. . . . It was made of a corridor and a string of bedrooms turned into one big room. That's where it got the old wainscotting and those old-fashioned grate fires.'

I had noticed them, of course, at once — the old-fashioned grates, built flat into the wall, the coal bulging and glowing behind bars, with black marble at the side and black marble for the mantel above. . . . There were three of them, one at the side, just near us, one down the room and one across the end. . . . But from none of them came noise or crackle — just a steady warm glow. Beside the old-fashioned grate stood the long tongs, and the old-fashioned poker with the heavy square head that went with it.

'Pawn to Queen's Third,' said Letherby.

Nor in all the room was there a single touch of equipment that

was less than of fifty years ago, a memory of a half century. . . .
Even the swinging doors, panelled with Russian leather, the
main entrance on the right hand at the farthest end, swung
soundlessly on their hinges as each noiseless member entered,
with a murmured greeting.

'Your move,' said Letherby. 'Bishop to Bishop's Four? Right.'

Most attractive of all, perhaps, was a little railed-in place at the
side near the fire-place, all done in old oak . . . something
between a bar and a confessional with coffee over low blue
flames, and immaculate glasses on shelves . . . lemons in a
bag. . . . Round it moved a waiter, in a dinner jacket, the quiet-
est, most unobtrusive waiter one ever saw . . . coffee to this
table . . . cigars to that . . . silent work with lemons behind the
rails . . . a waiter who seemed to know what the members
wanted without their asking. . . . This must have been so, for he
came over to our table presently and set down long glasses of
Madeira — so old, so brown, so aromatic that there seemed to
go up from it with the smoke clouds a vision of the sunny
vineyards beside Funchal. . . . Such at least were the fancies that
my mind began to weave round this enchanted place. . . . And
the waiter, too, I felt there must be some strange romance about
him; no one could have a face so mild, yet with the stamp of
tragedy upon it. . . .

I must say — in fact, I said to Letherby — I felt I'd like to join
the club, if I could. He said, oh, yes, they took in new members.
One came in only three years ago.

'Queen's Knight to Bishop's Third,' said Letherby with a deep
sigh. I knew he had been thinking of something that he daren't
risk. All chess is one long regret.

We played on like that for — it must have been half an hour —
anyway we played four moves each. To me, of course, the peace
and quiet of the room was treat enough . . . but to Letherby, as
I could see, the thing was not a sensation of peace but a growing
excitement, nothing still or quiet about it; a rush, struggle — he
knew that I meant to strike in on the King's side. Fool! he was
thinking that he hadn't advanced the Queen's Pawn another
square . . . he had blocked his Bishop and couldn't castle. . . .
You know, if you are a chess-player, the desperate feeling that
comes with a blocked Bishop. . . . Look down any chess room

for a man who's hands are clenched and you'll know that he can't castle.

So it was not still life for Letherby, and for me, perhaps after a while I began to feel that it was perhaps just a little *too* still. . . . The players moved so little . . . they spoke so seldom, and so low . . . their heads so grey under the light . . . especially, I noticed, a little group at tables in the left-hand corner.

'They don't seem to talk much there,' I said.

'No,' Letherby answered without even turning his head, 'they're blind. Pawn to Queen's Four.'

Blind! Why, of course, Why not? Blind people, I realised, play chess as easily as any other people when they use little pegged boards for it. . . . Now that I looked I could see — the aged fingers lingering and rambling on the little pegs.

'You take the Pawn?' said Letherby.

'Yes,' I said and went on thinking about the blind people . . . and how quiet they all were. . . . I began to recollect a play that was once in New York — people on a steamer, wasn't it? People standing at a bar . . . and you realised presently they were all dead. . . . It was a silly idea, but somehow the Long Room began to seem like that . . . at intervals I could even hear the ticking of the clock on the mantel.

I was glad when the waiter came with a second glass of Madeira. It warmed one up. . . .

'That man seem's a wonderful waiter,' I said.

'Fred?' said Letherby. 'Oh, yes, he certainly is. . . . He looks after everything — he's devoted to the club.'

'Been here long?'

'Bishop to Bishop's Four,' said Letherby.

He didn't speak for a little while. Then he said, 'Why practically all his life — except, poor fellow, he had a kind of tragic experience. He put in ten years in jail.'

'For what?' I asked, horrified.

'For murder,' said Letherby.

'For murder?'

'Yes,' repeated Letherby, shaking his head, 'poor fellow, murder. . . . Some sudden, strange impulse that seized him . . . I shouldn't say jail. He was in the Criminal Lunatic Asylum. Your move.'

'Criminal Asylum!' I said. 'What did he do?'

'Killed a man; in a sudden rage. . . . Struck him over the head with a poker.'

'Good Lord!' I exclaimed. 'When was that? In this city?'

'Here in the club,' said Letherby, 'in this room.'

'What?' I gasped. 'He killed one of the members?'

'Oh, no!' Letherby said reassuringly. 'Not a member. The man was a guest. Fred didn't know him . . . just an insane impulse. . . . As soon as they let him out, the faithful fellow came right back here. That was last year. Your move.'

We played on. I didn't feel so easy. . . . It must have been several moves after that that I saw Fred take the poker and stick its head into the coals and leave it there. I watched it gradually turning red. I must say I didn't like it.

'Did you see that?' I said. 'Did you see Fred stick the poker in the coals?'

'He does it every night,' said Letherby, 'at ten; that means it must be ten o'clock. . . . You can't move that; you're in check.'

'What's it for?' I asked.

'I take your Knight,' Letherby said. Then there was a long pause — Letherby kept his head bent over the board. Presently he murmured, 'Mulled beer,' and then looked up and explained. 'This is an old-fashioned place — some of the members like mulled beer — you dip the hot poker in the tankard. Fred gets it ready at ten — your move.'

I must say it was a relief. . . . I was able to turn to the game again and enjoy the place . . . or I would have done so except for a sort of commotion that there was presently at the end of the room. Somebody seemed to have fallen down . . . others were trying to pick him up. . . . Fred had hurried to them. . . .

Letherby turned half round in his seat.

'It's all right,' he said. 'It's only poor old Colonel McGann. He gets these fits . . . but Fred will look after him; he has a room in the building. Fred's devoted to him; he got Fred out of the Criminal Asylum. But for him Fred wouldn't be here tonight. Queen's Rook to Bishop's Square.'

I was not sure just how grateful I felt to Colonel McGann. . . .

A few moves after that another little incident bothered me, or perhaps it was just that my nerves were getting a little affected . . . one fancied things . . . and the infernal room, at once after the little disturbance, settled down to the same terrible quiet . . . it felt like eternity. . . .

Anyway — there came in through the swinging doors a different kind of man, brisk alert, and with steel blue eyes and a firm mouth. . . . He stood looking up and down the room, as if looking for someone.

'Who is he?' I asked.

'Why, that's Dr Allard.'

'What?' I said. 'The alienist?'

'Yes, he's the head of the Criminal Lunatic Asylum. . . . He's a member here; comes in every night; in fact, he goes back and forward between this and the Asylum. He says he's making comparative studies. Check.'

The alienist caught sight of Letherby and came to our table. Letherby introduced me. Dr Allard looked me hard and straight in the eyes; he paused before he spoke. 'Your first visit here?' he said.

'Yes . . . ' I murmured, 'that is, yes.'

'I hope it won't be the last,' he said. Now what did he mean by that?

Then he turned to Letherby.

'Fred came over to see me today,' he said. 'Came of his own volition. . . . I'm not quite sure. . . . We may not have been quite wise.' The doctor seemed thinking . . . 'However, no doubt he's all right for a while apart from sudden shock . . . just keep an eye. . . . But what I really came to ask is, has Joel Linton been in tonight?'

'No. . . . '

'I hope he doesn't come. He'd better not. . . . If he does, get someone to telephone to me.' And with that the doctor was gone.

'Joel Linton.' I said. 'Why, he's arrested.'

'Not yet . . . they're looking for him. You're in check.'

'I beg your pardon,' I said. Of course I'd read — everybody had — about the embezzlement. But I'd no idea that a man like Joel Linton could be a member of the Chess Club — I always thought, I mean people said, that he was the sort of desperado type.

'He's a member?' I said, my hand on the pieces.

'You can't move that, you're still in check. Yes, he's a member though he likes mostly to stand and watch. Comes every night. Somebody said he was coming here tonight just the same. He says he's not going to be taken alive. He comes round at half past ten. It's about his time . . . that looks like mate in two moves.'

My hands shook on the pieces. I felt that I was done with the Chess Club. . . . Anyway I like to get home early . . . so I was just starting to say . . . that I'd abandon the game, when what happened happened so quickly that I'd no more choice about it.

'That's Joel Linton now,' said Letherby, and in he came through the swing doors, a hard-looking man, but mighty determined. . . . He hung his overcoat on a peg, and as he did so, I was sure I saw something bulging in his coat pocket — eh? He nodded casually about the room. And then started moving among the tables, edging his way towards ours.

'I guess, if you don't mind,' I began. . . . But that is as far as I got. That was when the police came in, two constables and an inspector.

I saw Linton dive his hand towards his pocket.

'Stand where you are, Linton,' the inspector called. . . . Then right at that moment I saw the waiter, Fred, seize the hand-grip of the poker. . . .

'Don't move, Linton,' called the inspector; he never saw Fred moving towards him.

Linton didn't move. But I did. I made a quick back bolt for the little door behind me . . . down the little stairway . . . and down the other little staircase, and along the corridor and back into the brightly lighted hotel rotunda, just the same as when I left it — noise and light and bellboys, and girls at the news-stand selling tobacco and evening papers . . . just the same, but oh, how different! For peace of mind, for the joy of life — give me a rotunda, and make it as noisy as ever you like.

I read all about it next morning in the newspapers. Things always sound so different in the newspaper, beside a coffee pot and a boiled egg. Tumults, murders, floods — all smoothed out. So was this. *Arrest Made Quietly at Chess Club*, it said. *Linton Offers No Resistance.* . . . *Members Continue Game Undisturbed.* Yes, they *would*, the damned old gravestones. . . . Of Fred it said nothing. . . . .

A few days later I happened to meet Letherby. 'Your application is all right,' he said. 'They're going to hurry it through. You'll get in next year. . . . '

But I've sent a resignation in advance. I'm joining the Badminton Club and I want to see if I can't get into the Boy Scouts or be a Girl Guide.

THE ROYAL GAME

Stefan Zweig

The big liner, due to sail from New York to Buenos Aires at midnight, was filled with the activity and bustle incident to the last hour. Visitors who had come to see their friends off pressed hither and thither, page-boys with caps smartly cocked slithered through the public rooms shouting names snappily, baggage, parcels and flowers were being hauled about, inquisitive children ran up and down companion-ways, while the deck orchestra provided persistent accompaniment. I stood talking to an acquaintance on the promenade deck, somewhat apart from the hubbub, when two or three flash-lights sprayed sharply near us, evidently for press photos of some prominent passenger at a last-minute interview. My friend looked in that direction and smiled.

'You have a queer bird on board, that Czentovic.'

And as my face must have revealed that the statement meant nothing to me he added, by way of explanation, 'Mirko Czentovic, the world chess champion. He has just finished off the USA in a coast-to-coast exhibition tour and is on his way to capture Argentina.'

This served to recall not only the name of the young world champion but also a few details relating to his rocket-like career; my friend, a more observant newspaper reader than I, was able to eke them out with a string of anecdotes. At a single stroke, about a year ago, Czentovic had aligned himself with the solidest Elder Statesmen of the art of chess, such as Alekhin, Capablanca, Tartakover, Lasker, Boguljobov; not since the appearance of the nine-year-old prodigy, Reshevsky, in New York in 1922, had a newcomer crashed into the famed guild to the accompaniment of such widespread interest. It seems that Czentovic's intellectual equipment, at the beginning, gave small promise of so brilliant a career. The secret soon seeped through that in his private capacity this champion wasn't able to write a single sentence in any language without misspelling a word, and that, as one of his vexed colleagues, wrathfully sarcastic, put it, 'He enjoys equal ignorance in every field of culture.' His father, a poverty-stricken Yugoslavian boatman on the Danube, had been run down in his tiny vessel one night by a grain steamer, and the orphaned boy, then twelve, was taken in charge by the pastor of their obscure village out of pity. The good man did his level best to instil into the indolent, slow-speaking, low-browed child at home what he seemed unable to grasp in the village school.

But all efforts proved vain. Mirko stared blankly at the writing exercise just as if the strokes had not already been explained a hundred times; his lumbering brain lacked every power to grasp even the simplest subjects. At fourteen he still counted with his fingers, and it was only by dint of great strain that he could read in a book or newspaper. Yet none could say that Mirko was unwilling or disobedient. Whatever he was told to do he did: fetched water, split wood, worked in the field, washed up the kitchen, and he could be relied upon to execute — even if with exasperating slowness — every service that was demanded. But what grieved the kindly pastor most about the blockhead was his total lack of co-operation. He performed no deed unless specially directed, asked no questions, never played with other lads, and sought no occupation of his own accord; after Mirko had concluded his work about the house, he would sit idly with that empty stare one sees with grazing sheep, without participating in the slightest in what might be going on. Of an evening, while the pastor sucked at his long peasant pipe and played his customary three games of chess with the police-sergeant, the fair-haired dull-wit squatted silent alongside them, staring and indifferent, at the chequered board.

One winter evening, while the two men were absorbed in their daily game, a rapid crescendo of bells gave notice of a quickly approaching sleigh. A peasant his cap covered with snow, stamped in hastily to tell the pastor that his mother lay dying and to ask his immediate attendance in the hope that there was still time to administer extreme unction. The priest accompanied him at once. The police-sergeant, who had not yet finished his beer, lighted a fresh pipe preparatory to leaving, and was about to draw on his heavy sheepskin boots when he noticed how immovably Mirko's gaze was fastened on the board with its interrupted game.

'Well, do you want to finish it?' he said jocularly, fully convinced that the sleepyhead had no notion of how to move a single piece. The boy looked up shyly, nodded assent, and took the pastor's place. After fourteen moves the sergeant was beaten and he had to concede that his defeat was in no wise attributable to avoidable carelessness. The second game resulted similarly.

'Balaam's ass!' cried the astounded pastor upon his return, explaining to the policeman, a lesser expert in the Bible, that two thousand years ago there had been a like miracle of a dumb being suddenly endowed with the speech of wisdom. The late hour notwithstanding, the good man could not forgo challenging his half-illiterate helper to a contest. Mirko beat him too, with ease. He played toughly, slowly, deliberately, never once raising his bowed broad brow from the board. But he played with irrefutable certainty, and in the days that followed neither the priest nor the policeman was able to win a single game.

The priest, best able to assess his ward's various shortcomings, now became curious as to the manner in which this one-sided singular gift would resist a severer test. After Mirko had been made somewhat presentable by the efforts of the village barber, he drove him in his sleigh to the nearby town where he knew that many chess-players — a cut above him in ability, he was aware from experience — were always to be found in the café on the main square. The pastor's entrance, as he steered the straw-haired, red-cheeked fifteen-year-old before him, created no small stir in the circle; the boy, in his sheepskin jacket (woollen side in) and high boots, eyes shyly downcast, stood aside until summoned to a chess-table.

Mirko lost the first encounter because his master had never employed the Sicilian defence. The next game, with the best player of the lot, resulted in a draw. But in the third game and the fourth and all that came after he slew them, one after the other.

It so happens that little provincial towns of Yugoslavia are seldom the theatre of exciting events; consequently, this first appearance of the peasant champion before the assembled worthies became no less than a sensation. It was unanimously decided to keep the boy in town until the next day for a special gathering of the chess club and, in particular, for the benefit of Count Simczic of the castle, a chess fanatic. The priest, who now regarded his ward with quite a new pride, but whose joy of discovery was subordinate to the sense of duty which called him home to his Sunday service, consented to leave him for further tests. The chess group put young Czentovic up at the local hotel, where he saw a water-closet for the first time in his life.

The chess-room was crowded to capacity on Sunday afternoon. Mirko faced the board immobile for four hours, spoke no word, and never looked up; one player after another fell before him. Finally a multiple game was proposed; it took a while before they could make clear to the novice that he had to play against several contestants at one and the same time. No sooner had Mirko grasped the procedure than he adapted himself to it, and trod slowly with heavy, creaking shoes from table to table, eventually winning seven of the eight games.

Grave consultations now took place. True, strictly speaking, the new champion was not of the town, yet the innate national pride had received a lively fillip. Here was a chance, at last, for this town, so small that its existence was hardly suspected, to put itself on the map by sending a great man into the world. A vaudeville agent named Koller, who supplied the local garrison cabaret with talent, offered to obtain professional training for the youth from a Viennese expert whom he knew, and to see him through for a year if the deficit were made good. Count Simczic, who in his sixty years of daily chess had never encountered so remarkable an antagonist, signed the guarantee promptly. That day marked the opening of the astonishing career of the Danube boatman's son.

It took only six months for Mirko to master every secret of chess technique, though with one odd limitation which later became apparent to the votaries of the game and caused many a sneer. He never was able to memorise a single game or, to use the professional term, to play blind. He lacked completely the ability to conceive the board in the limitless space of the imagination. He had to have the field of sixty-four black and white squares and the thirty-two pieces tangibly before him; even when he had attained international fame he carried a folding pocket board with him in order to be able to reconstruct a game or work on a problem by visual means. This defect, in itself not important, betrayed a want of imaginative power and provoked animated discussions among chess enthusiasts similar to those in musical circles when it discovers that an outstanding virtuoso or conductor is unable to play or direct without a score. This singularity, however, was no obstacle to Mirko's stupendous rise. At seventeen he already possessed a dozen prizes, at eighteen he won the Hungarian mastery, and finally, at twenty, the championship of the world. The boldest experts, every one of them immeasurably his superior in brains, imagination, and audacity, fell before his tough, cold logic as did Napoleon before the clumsy Kutusov and Hannibal before Fabius Cunctator, of whom Livy records that his traits of phlegm and imbecility were already conspicuous in his childhood. Thus it occurred that the illustrious gallery of chess masters, which included eminent representatives of widely varied intellectual fields — philosophers, mathematicians, constructive, imaginative, and often creative talents — was invaded by a complete outsider, a heavy, taciturn peasant from whom not even the cunningest journalists were ever able to extract a word that would help to make a story. Yet, however he may have deprived the newspapers of polished phrases, substitutes in the way of anecdotes about his person were numerous, for, inescapably, the moment he arose from the board at which he was the incomparable master, Czentovic became a grotesque, an almost comic figure. In spite of his correct dress, his fashionable cravat with its too ostentatious pearl tiepin, and his carefully manicured nails, he remained in manners and behaviour the narrow-minded lout who was accustomed to sweeping out the priest's kitchen. He utilised his gift and his fame to squeeze out all the money they would yield, displaying petty and often vulgar greed, always with a shameless clumsiness that aroused his professional colleagues' ridicule and anger. He travelled from town to town, stopped at the cheapest hotels, played for any club that would pay his fee, sold the advertising rights in his portrait to a soap manufacturer, and oblivious of his competitors' scorn — they being aware that he hardly knew how to write — attached his name to a *Philosophy of Chess* that had been written by a hungry Galician student for a business-minded publisher. As with all leathery dispositions, he was wanting in any appreciation of the ludicrous; from the time he became champion he regarded himself as the most important man in the world, and the consciousness of having beaten all those clever, intellectual, brilliant speakers and writers in their own field and of earning more than they, transformed his early unsureness into a cold and awkwardly flaunted pride.

'And how can one expect that such rapid fame should fail to befuddle so empty a head?' concluded my friend who had just advanced those classic examples of Czentovic's childish lust for rank. 'Why shouldn't a twenty-one-year-old lad from the Banat be afflicted with a frenzy of vanity if, suddenly, by merely shov-

ing figures around on a wooden board, he can earn more in a
week than his whole village does in a year by chopping down
trees under the bitterest conditions? Besides, isn't it damned easy
to take yourself for a great man if you're not burdened with the
slightest suspicion that a Rembrandt, a Beethoven, a Dante, a
Napoleon, ever even existed? There's just one thing in that
immured brain of his — the knowledge that he hasn't lost a game
of chess for months, and as he happens not to dream that the
world holds other values than chess and money, he has every
reason to be infatuated with himself.'

The information communicated by my friend could not fail to
excite my special curiosity. I have always been fascinated by all
types of monomania, by persons wrapped up in a single idea;
for the stricter the limits a man sets for himself, the more clearly
he approaches the eternal. Just such seemingly world-aloof persons create their own remarkable and quite unique world-in-
little, and work, termite-like, in their particular medium. Thus I
made no bones about my intention to examine this specimen of
one-track intellect under a magnifying glass during the twelve-
day journey to Rio.

'You'll be out of luck,' my friend warned me. 'So far as I know,
nobody has succeeded in extracting the least bit of psychological
material from Czentovic. Underneath all his abysmal limitations
this sly farmhand conceals the wisdom not to expose himself.
The procedure is simple: except with such compatriots of his own
sphere as he contrives to meet in ordinary taverns he avoids all
conversation. When he senses a person of culture he retreats into
his shell; that's why nobody can plume himself on having heard
him say something stupid or on having sounded the presumably
bottomless depths of his ignorance.'

As a matter of fact, my friend was right. It proved utterly
impossible to approach Czentovic during the first few days of
the voyage, unless by intruding rudely, which, of course, isn't
my way. He did, sometimes, appear on the promenade deck,
but then always with hands clasped behind his back in a posture
of dignified self absorption, like Napoleon in the familiar painting; and, at that, those peripatetic exhibitions were carried off in
such haste and so jerkily that to gain one's end one would have
had to trot after him. The lounges, the bar, the smoking-room;
saw nothing of him. A steward of whom I made confidential
inquiries revealed that he spent the greater part of the day in his

cabin with a large chessboard on which he recapitulated games or worked out new problems.

After three days it angered me to think that his defence tactics were more effective than my will to approach him. I had never before had a chance to know a great chess-player personally, and the more I now sought to familiarise myself with the type, the more incomprehensible seemed a lifelong brain activity that rotated exclusively about a space composed of sixty-four black and white squares. I was well aware from my own experience of the mysterious attraction of the royal game, which among all games contrived by man rises superior to the tyranny of chance and bestows its palm only on mental attainment, or rather on a definite form of mental endowment. But is it not an offensively narrow construction to call chess a game? Is it not a science, a technique, an art, that sways among these categories as Mahomet's coffin does between heaven and earth, at once a union of all contradictory concepts: primeval yet ever new; mechanical in operation yet effective only through the imagination; bounded in geometric space though boundless in its combinations; ever-developing yet sterile; thought that leads to nothing; mathematics that produce no result; art without works; architecture without substance, and nevertheless, as proved by evidence, more lasting in its being and presence than all books and achievements; the only game that belongs to all peoples and all ages; of which none knows the divinity that bestowed it on the world, to slay boredom, to sharpen the senses, to exhilarate the spirit. One searches for its beginning and for its end. Children can learn its simple rules, duffers succumb to its temptation, yet within this immutable tight square it creates a particular species of master not to be compared with any other — persons destined for chess alone, specific geniuses in whom vision, patience, and technique are operative through a distribution no less precisely ordained than in mathematicians, poets, composers, but merely united on a different level. In the heyday of physiognomical research a Gall would perhaps have dissected the brains of such masters of chess to establish whether a particular coil in the grey matter of the brain, a sort of chess muscle or chess bump, was more conspicuously developed than in other skulls. How a physiognomist would have been fascinated by the case of a Czentovic where that which is genius appears interstratified with an absolute inertia of the intellect, like a single vein of gold in a ton of dead rock! It stands to reason that so unusual a game, one touched with genius, must create out of itself fitting matadors. This I always knew, but what was difficult and almost impossible to conceive of was the life of a mentally alert person whose world contracts to a narrow, black-and-white one-way street; who seeks ultimate triumphs in the two pieces; a being who, by a new opening in which the knight is preferred to the pawn, apprehends greatness and the immortality that goes with casual mention in a chess handbook — of a man of spirit who, escaping madness, can unremittingly devote all of his mental energy during ten, twenty, thirty, forty years to the ludicrous effort to corner a wooden king on a wooden board!

And here, for the first time, one of these phenomena, one of these singular geniuses (or shall I say puzzling fools?) was close to me, six cabins distant, and I, unfortunate, for whom curiosity about mental problems manifested itself in a kind of passion, seemed unable to effect my purpose. I conjured up the absurdest ruses: should I tickle his vanity by the offer of an interview in an important paper, or engage his greed by proposing a lucrative exhibition tour of Scotland? Finally it occurred to me that the hunter's never-failing practice is to lure the woodcock by imitating its mating cry, so what more successful way was there of attracting a chess master's attention to myself than by playing chess?

At no time had I ever permitted chess to absorb me seriously, for the simple reason that it meant nothing to me but a pastime; if I spend an hour at the board it is not because I want to subject myself to a strain but, on the contrary, to relieve mental tension. I 'play' at chess in the literal sense of the word, whereas to real devotees it is serious business. Chess, like love, cannot be played alone, and up to that time I had no idea whether there were other chess lovers on board. In order to attract them from their lairs I set a primitive trap in the smoking-room in that my wife (whose game is even weaker than mine) and I sat at a chessboard as a decoy. Sure enough, we had made no more than six moves before one passer-by stopped, another asked permission to watch, and before long the desired partner materialised. MacIver was his name; a Scottish foundation-engineer who, I learned, had made a large fortune boring for oil in California. He was a robust specimen with an almost square jaw and strong teeth, and a rich complexion pronouncedly rubicund as a result, at least in part surely, of copious indulgence in whisky. His conspicuously broad, almost vehemently athletic shoulders made them-

selves unpleasantly noticeable in his game, for this MacIver typi-
fied those self-important worshippers of success who regard
defeat in even a harmless contest as a blow to their self-esteem.
Accustomed to achieving his ends ruthlessly, and spoiled by
material success, this massive self-made man was so thoroughly
saturated with his sense of superiority that opposition of any
kind became undue resistance if not insult. After losing the first
round he sulked and began to explain in detail, and dictatorially,
that it would not have happened but for a momentary oversight;
in the third he ascribed his failure to the noise in the adjoining
room; never would he lose a game without at once demanding
revenge. This ambitious crabbedness amused me at first, but as
time went on I accepted it as the unavoidable accompaniment to
my real purpose — to tempt the master to our table.

By the third day it worked — but only half-way. It may be that
Czentovic observed us at the chessboard through a window from
the promenade deck or that he just happened to be honouring
the smoking-room with his presence; anyway, as soon as he
perceived us interlopers toying with the tools of his trade, he
involuntarily stepped a little nearer and, keeping a deliberate
distance, cast a searching glance at our board. It was MacIver's
move. This one move was sufficient to apprise Czentovic how
little a further pursuit of our dilettantish striving was worthy of
his expert interest. With the same matter-of-course gesture with
which one of us disposes of a poor detective story that has been
proffered in a library — without even thumbing its pages — he
turned away from our table and left the room. 'Weighed in the
balance and found wanting,' I thought, slightly stung by the
cool, contemptuous look, and to give vent to my ill-humour in
some fashion, I said to MacIver, 'Your move didn't seem to
impress the master.'

'Which master?'

I told him that the man who had just walked by after glancing
disapprovingly at our game was Czentovic, international chess
champion. I added that we would be able to survive it without
taking his contempt too greatly to heart; the poor have to cook
with water. But to my astonishment these idle words of mine
produced quite an unexpected result. Immediately he became
excited, forgot our game, and his ambition took to an almost
audible throbbing. He had no notion that Czentovic was on
board: Czentovic simply had to give him a game; the only time
he had ever played with a champion was in a multiple game

when he was one of forty; even that was fearfully exciting, and he had come quite near winning. Did I know the champion personally? — I didn't. — Would I not invite him to join us? — I declined on the ground that I was aware of Czentovic's reluctance to make new acquaintances. Besides, what charm would intercourse with third-rate players hold for a champion?

It would have been just as well not to say that about third-rate players to a man of MacIver's brand of conceit. Annoyed, he leaned back and declared gruffly that, as for himself, he couldn't believe that Czentovic would decline a gentleman's courteous challenge; he'd see to that. Upon getting a brief description of the master's person he stormed out, indifferent to our unfinished game, uncontrollably impatient to intercept Czentovic on the deck. Again I sensed that there was no holding the possessor of such broad shoulders once his will was involved in an undertaking.

I waited, somewhat tensed. Some ten minutes elapsed and MacIver returned, not in too good humour, it seemed to me.

'Well?' I asked.

'You were right,' he answered, a bit annoyed. 'Not a very pleasant gentleman. I introduced myself and told him who I am. He didn't even put out his hand. I tried to make him understand that all of us on board would be proud and honoured if he'd play the lot of us. But he was cursed stiff-necked about it; said he was sorry but his contract obligations to his agent definitely precluded any game during his entire tour except for a fee. And his minimum is $250 per game.'

I had to laugh. The thought would never have come to me that one could make so much money by pushing figures from black squares to white ones. 'Well, I hope you took leave of him with courtesy equal to his.'

MacIver, however, remained perfectly serious. 'The match is to come off at three tomorrow afternoon. Here in the smoking-room. I hope he won't make mincemeat of us easily.'

'What! You promised him the $250?' I cried, quite taken aback.

'Why not? It's his business. If I had a toothache and there happened to be a dentist aboard, I wouldn't expect him to extract my tooth for nothing. The man's right to ask a fat price; in every line the big shots are the best traders. So far as I'm concerned, the less complicated the business, the better. I'd rather pay in cash than have your Mr Czentovic do me a favour and in the end have to say "thank you". Anyway, many an evening at the club has cost me more than $250 without giving me a chance to play a world champion. It's no disgrace for a third-rate player to be beaten by a Czentovic.'

It amused me to note how deeply I injured MacIver's self-love with that 'third-rate'. But as he was disposed to foot the bill it was not for me to remark on his wounded ambition which promised at last to afford me an acquaintance with my odd fish. Promptly we notified the four or five others who had revealed themselves as chess-players of the approaching event and reserved not only our own table but the adjacent ones so that we might suffer the least possible disturbance from passengers strolling by.

Next day all our group was assembled at the appointed hour. The centre seat opposite that of the master was allotted to MacIver as a matter of course; his nervousness found outlet in the smoking of strong cigars, one after another, and in restlessly glancing ever and again at the clock. The champion let us wait a good ten minutes — my friend's tale prompted the surmise that something like this would happen — thus heightening the impressiveness of his entry. He approached the table calmly and imperturbably. He offered no greeting. 'You know who I am and I'm not interested in who you are' was what his discourtesy seemed to imply, but he began in a dry, businesslike way to lay down the conditions. Since there were not enough boards on the ship for separate games he proposed that we should play against him collectively. After each of his moves he would retire to the end of the room so that his presence might not affect our consultations. As soon as our countermove had been made we were to strike a glass with a spoon, no table-bell being available. He proposed, if it pleased us, ten minutes as the maximum time for each move. Like timid pupils we accepted every suggestion unquestioningly. Czentovic drew black at the choice of colours; while still standing he made the first countermove, then turned at once to go to the designated waiting-place, where he reclined lazily while carelessly examining an illustrated magazine.

There is little point in reporting the game. It ended, as it could not but end, in our complete defeat, and by the twenty-fourth move at that. There was nothing particularly astonishing about an international champion wiping off half a dozen mediocre or sub-mediocre players with his left hand; what did disgust us, though, was the lordly manner with which Czentovic caused us to feel, all too plainly, that it was with his left hand that we had been disposed of. Each time he would give a quick, seemingly

careless look at the board, and would look indolently past us as
if we ourselves were dead wooden figures; and this impertinent
proceeding reminded one irresistibly of the way one throws a
mangy dog a morsel without taking the trouble to look at him.
According to my way of thinking, if he had any sensitivity he
might have shown us our mistakes or cheered us up with a
friendly word. Even at the conclusion this sub-human chess
automaton uttered no syllable, but, after saying 'mate,' stood
motionless at the table waiting to ascertain whether another game
was desired. I had already risen with the thought of indicating
by a gesture — helpless as one always remains in the face of
thick-skinned rudeness — that as far as I was concerned the
pleasure of our acquaintance was ended now that the dollars-
and-cents part of it was over, when, to my anger, MacIver, next
to me, spoke up hoarsely: 'Revanche!'

The note of challenge startled me; MacIver at this moment
seemed much more like a pugilist about to put up his fists than
a polite gentleman. Whether it was Czentovic's disagreeable
treatment of us that affected him or merely MacIver's own pathological irritable ambition, suffice it that the latter had undergone
a complete change. Red in the face up to his hair, his nostrils
taut from inner pressure, he breathed hard, and a sharp fold
separated the bitten lips from his belligerently projected jaw. I
recognised with disquiet that flicker of the eyes that connotes
uncontrollable passion, such as seizes players at roulette when
the right colour fails to come after the sixth or seventh success-
ively doubled stake. Instantly I knew that this fanatical climber
would, even at the cost of his entire fortune, play against Czentovic and play and play and play, for simple or doubled stakes,
until he won at least a single game. If Czentovic stuck to it,
MacIver would prove a gold-mine that would yield him a nice
few thousands by the time Buenos Aires came in sight.

Czentovic remained unmoved. 'If you please,' he responded
politely. 'You gentlemen will take black this time.'

There was nothing different about the second game except that
our group became larger because of a few added onlookers, and
livelier, too. MacIver stared fixedly at the board as if he willed
to magnetise the chessmen to victory; I sensed that he would
have paid a thousand dollars with delight if he could but shout
'Mate' at our cold-snouted adversary. Oddly enough, something
of his sullen excitement entered unconsciously into all of us.
Every single move was discussed with greater emotion than

before; always we would wrangle up to the last moment before agreeing to signal Czentovic to return to the table. We had come to the seventeenth move and, to our own surprise, entered on a combination which seemed staggeringly advantageous because we had been enabled to advance a pawn to the last square but one; we needed but to move it forward to c1 to win a second queen. Not that we felt too comfortable about so obvious an opportunity; we were united in suspecting that the advantage which we seemed to have wrested could be no more than bait dangled by Czentovic, whose vision enabled him to view the situation from a distance of several moves. Yet in spite of common examination and discussion, we were unable to explain it as a feint. At last, at the limit of our ten minutes, we decided to risk the move. MacIver's fingers were on the pawn to move it to the last square when he felt his arm gripped and heard a voice low and impetuous, whisper, 'For God's sake! Don't!'

Involuntarily we all turned about. I recognised in the man of some forty-five years, who must have joined the group during the last few minutes in which we were absorbed in the problem before us, one whose narrow sharp face had already arrested my attention on deck strolls because of its extraordinary, almost chalky pallor. Conscious of our gaze, he continued rapidly:

'If you make a queen he will immediately attack with the bishop, then you'll take it with your knight. Meantime, however, he moves his pawn to d7, threatens your rook, and even if you check with the knight you're lost and will be wiped out in nine or ten moves. It's practically the constellation that Alekhin introduced when he played Boguljobov in 1922 at the championship tournament at Pistany.'

Astonished, MacIver released the pawn and, like the rest of us, stared amazedly at the man who had descended in our midst like a rescuing angel. Anyone who can reckon a mate nine moves ahead must necessarily be a first-class expert, perhaps even a contestant now on his way to the tournament to seize the championship, so that his sudden presence, his thrust into the game at precisely the critical moment, partook almost of the supernatural.

MacIver was the first to collect himself. 'What do you advise?' he asked suppressedly.

'Don't advance yet; rather a policy of evasion. First of all, get the king out of the danger line from g8 to h7. Then he'll probably transfer his attack to the other flank. Then you parry that with the rook, c8 to c4; two moves and he will have lost not only a pawn but his superiority, and if you maintain your defensive properly you may be able to make it a draw. That's the best you can get out of it.'

We gasped, amazed. The precision no less than the rapidity of his calculations dizzied us; it was as if he had been reading the moves from a printed page. For all that, this unsuspected turn by which, thanks to his cutting in, the contest with a world champion promised a draw, worked wonders. Animated by a single thought, we moved aside so as not to obstruct his observation of the board.

Again MacIver inquired: 'The king, then; to h7?'

'Surely. The main thing is to duck.'

MacIver obeyed and we rapped on the glass. Czentovic came forward at his habitual even pace, his eyes swept the board and took in the countermove. Then he moved the pawn h2 to h4 on the king's flank exactly as our unknown aid had predicted. Already the latter was whispering excitedly:

'The rook forward, the rook, to c4; then he'll first have to cover the pawn. That won't help him, though. Don't bother about his pawns but attack with the knight c3 to d5, and the balance is again restored. Press the offensive instead of defending.'

We had no idea of what he meant. He might have been talking Chinese. But once under his spell MacIver did as he had been bidden. Again we struck the glass to recall Czentovic. This was the first time that he made no quick decision; instead he looked fixedly at the board. His eyebrows contracted involuntarily. Then he made his move, the one which our stranger had said he would, and turned to go. Yet before he started off something novel and unexpected happened. Czentovic raised his eyes and surveyed our ranks; plainly he wanted to ascertain who it was that offered such unaccustomed energetic resistance.

From this moment our excitement grew immeasurably. Thus far we had played without genuine hope, but now every pulse beat hotly at the thought of breaking Czentovic's cold disdain. Without loss of time our new friend had directed the next move and we were ready to call Czentovic back. My fingers trembled as I hit the spoon against the glass. And now we registered our first triumph. Czentovic, who hitherto had executed his purpose standing, hesitated, hesitated and finally sat down. He did this slowly and heavily, but that was enough to cancel — in a physical sense if in no other — the difference in levels that had previously obtained. We had necessitated his acknowledgment of equality, spatially at least. He cogitated long, his eyes resting immovably on the board so that one could scarcely discern the pupils under the heavy lids, and under the strained application his mouth opened gradually, which gave him a rather foolish look. Czentovic reflected for some minutes, then made a move and rose. At once our friend said half audibly:

'A stall! Well thought out! But don't yield to it! Force an exchange, he's got to exchange, then we'll get a draw and not even the gods can help him.'

MacIver did as he was told. The succeeding manoeuvres between the two men — we others had long since become mere supernumeraries — consisted of a back-and-forth that we were unable to comprehend. After some seven moves Czentovic looked up after a period of silence and said, 'Draw.'

For a moment a total stillness reigned. Suddenly one heard the rushing of the waves and the jazzing radio in the adjacent drawing-room; one picked out every step on the promenade outside and the faint thin susurration of the wind that carried through the window-frames. None of us breathed; it had come upon us too abruptly and we were nothing less than frightened in the face of the impossible: that this stranger should have been able to force his will on the world champion in a contest already half lost. MacIver shoved himself back and relaxed, and his suppressed breathing became audible in the joyous 'Ah' that passed his lips. I took another look at Czentovic. It had already seemed to me during the later moves that he grew paler. But he understood how to maintain his poise. He persisted in his apparent imperturbability and asked, in a negligent tone, the while he pushed the figures off the board with a steady hand:

'Would you like to have a third game, gentlemen?'

The question was matter-of-fact, just business. What was noteworthy was that he ignored MacIver and looked straight and intently into the eyes of our rescuer. Just as a horse takes a new rider's measure by the firmness of his seat, he must have become cognisant of who was his real, in fact his only, opponent. We could not help but follow his gaze and look eagerly at the unknown. However, before he could collect himself and formulate an answer, MacIver, in his eager excitement, had already cried to him in triumph:

'Certainly, no doubt about it! But this time you've got to play him alone! You against Czentovic!'

What followed was quite extraordinary. The stranger, who

curiously enough was still staring with a strained expression at the bare board, became affrighted upon hearing the lusty call and perceiving that he was the centre of observation. He looked confused.

'By no means, gentlemen,' he said haltingly, plainly perplexed. 'Quite out of the question. You'll have to leave me out. It's twenty, no, twenty-five years since I sat at a chess-board and . . . and I'm only now conscious of my bad manners in crashing into your game without so much as a by your leave . . . Please excuse my presumption. I don't want to interfere further.' And before we could recover from our astonishment he had left us and gone out.

'But that's just impossible!' boomed the irascible MacIver, pounding with his fist. 'Out of the question that this fellow hasn't played chess for twenty-five years. Why, he calculated every move, every countermove, five or six in advance. You can't shake that out of your sleeve. Just out of the question — isn't it?'

Involuntarily, MacIver turned to Czentovic with the last question. But the champion preserved his unalterable frigidity.

'It's not for me to express an opinion. In any case there was something queer and interesting about the man's game; that's why I purposely left him a chance.'

With that he rose lazily and added, in his objective manner: 'If he or you gentlemen should want another game tomorrow, I'm at your disposal from three o'clock on.'

We were unable to suppress our chuckles. Every one of us knew that the chance which Czentovic had allowed his nameless antagonist had not been prompted by generosity and that the remark was no more than a childish ruse to cover his frustration. It served to stimulate the more actively our desire to witness the utter humbling of so unshakable an arrogance. All at once we peaceable, indolent passengers were seized by a mad, ambitious will to battle, for the thought that just on our ship, in mid ocean, the palm might be wrested from the champion — a record that would be flashed to every news agency in the world — fascinated us challengingly. Added to that was the lure of the mysterious which emanated from the unexpected entry of our saviour at the crucial instant, and the contrast between his almost painful modesty and the rigid self-consciousness of the professional. Who was this unknown? Had destiny utilised this opportunity to command the revelation of a yet undiscovered chess phenomenon? Or was it that we were dealing with an expert who, for some undisclosed reason, craved anonymity? We discussed these various possibilities excitedly; the most extreme hypotheses were not sufficiently extreme to reconcile the stranger's puzzling shyness with his surprising declaration in the face of his demonstrated mastery. On one point, however, we were of one mind: to forgo no chance of a renewal of the contest. We resolved to exert ourselves to the limit to induce our godsend to play Czentovic the next day, MacIver pledging himself to foot the bill. Having in the meantime learned from the steward that the unknown was an Austrian, I, as his compatriot, was delegated to present our request.

Soon I found our man reclining in his deck-chair, reading. In the moment of approach I used the opportunity to observe him. The sharply chiselled head rested on the cushion in a posture of slight exhaustion; again I was struck by the extraordinary colourlessness of the comparatively youthful face framed at the temples by glistening white hair, and I got the impression, I cannot say why, that this person must have aged suddenly. No sooner did I stand before him than he rose courteously and introduced himself by a name that was familiar to me as belonging to a highly respected family of old Austria. I remembered that a bearer of that name had been an intimate friend of Schubert, and that one of the old Emperor's physicians-in-ordinary had belonged to the same family. Dr B was visibly dumbfounded when I stated our wish that he should take Czentovic on. It proved that he had no idea that he had stood his ground against a champion, let alone the most famous one in the world at the moment. For some reason this news seemed to make a special impression on him, for he inquired once and again whether I was sure that his opponent was truly a recognised holder of international honours. I soon perceived that this circumstance made my mission easier, but sensing his refined feelings, I considered it discreet to withhold the fact that MacIver would be a pecuniary loser in case of an eventual defeat. After considerable hesitation Dr B at last consented to a match, but with the proviso that my fellow-players be warned against putting extravagant hope in his expertness.

'Because,' he added with a clouded smile, 'I really don't know whether I have the ability to play the game according to all the rules. I assure you that it was not by any means false modesty that made me say that I hadn't touched a chessman since my college days, say more than twenty years. And even then I had no particular gifts as a player.'

This was said so simply that I had not the slightest doubt of its truth. And yet I could not but express wonderment at his accurate memory of the details of positions in games by many different masters; he must, at least, have been greatly occupied with chess theory. Dr B smiled once more in that dreamy way of his.

'Greatly occupied! Heaven knows, it's true enough that I have occupied myself with chess greatly. But that happened under quite special, I might say unique, circumstances. The story of it is rather complicated and it might go as a little chapter in the story of our agreeable epoch. Do you think you would have patience for half an hour. . . ?'

He waved towards the deck-chair next to his. I accepted the invitation gladly. There were no near neighbours. Dr B removed his reading spectacles, laid them to one side, and began.

'You were kind enough to say that, as a Viennese, you remembered the name of my family. I am pretty sure, however, that you could hardly have heard of the law office which my father and I conducted — and later I alone — for we had no cases that got into the papers and we avoided new clients on principle. In truth, we no longer had a regular law practice but confined ourselves exclusively to advising, and mainly to administering the fortunes of the great monasteries with which my father, once a Deputy of the Clerical Party, was closely connected. Besides — in this day and generation I am no longer obliged to keep silence about the Monarchy — we had been entrusted with the investment of the funds of certain members of the Imperial family. These connections with the Court and the Church — my uncle had been the Emperor's household physician, another was an abbot in Seitenstetten — dated back two generations; all we had to do was to maintain them, and the task allotted to us through this inherited confidence — a quiet, I might almost say a soundless, task — really called for little more than strict discretion and dependability, two qualities which my late father possessed in full measure; he succeeded, in fact, through his prudence in preserving considerable values for his clients through the years of inflation as well as the period of collapse. Then, when Hitler seized the helm in Germany and began to raid the properties of churches and cloisters, certain negotiations and transactions initiated from the other side of the frontier with a view to saving at least the movable valuables from confiscation, went through our hands and we two knew more about sundry secret trans-actions between the Curia and the Imperial house than the public will ever learn of. But the very inconspicuousness of our office — we hadn't even a sign on the door — as well as the care with which both of us almost ostentatiously kept out of Monarchist circles, offered the safest protection from officious investigations. In fact, no Austrian official had ever suspected that during all those years the secret couriers of the Imperial family delivered and fetched their most important mail in our unpretentious fourth floor office.

'It happened that the National Socialists began, long before they armed their forces against the world, to organise a different but equally schooled and dangerous army in all contiguous coun-tries — the legion of the unprivileged, the despised, the injured. Their so-called "cells" nested themselves in every office, in every business; they had listening-posts and spies in every spot, right up to the private chambers of Dollfuss and Schuschnigg. They had their man, as alas! I learned only too late, even in our insignificant office. True, he was nothing but a wretched, ungifted clerk whom I had engaged, on the recommendation of a priest, for no other purpose than to give the office the appear-ance of a going concern; all that we really used him for was innocent errands, answering the telephone, and filing papers, that is to say papers of no real importance. He was not allowed to open the mail. I typed important letters myself and kept no copies. I took all essential documents to my home, and I held private interviews nowhere but in the priory of the cloister or in my uncle's consultation-room. These measures of caution pre-vented the listening-post from seeing anything that went on; but some unlucky happening must have made the vain and ambitious fellow aware that he was mistrusted and that interesting things were going on behind his back. It may have been that in my absence one of the couriers made a careless reference to "His Majesty" instead of the stipulated "Baron Fern", or that the rascal opened letters surreptitiously. Whatever the reason, before I had so much as suspected him, he managed to get a mandate from Berlin or Munich to watch us. It was only much later, long after my imprisonment began, that I remembered how his early laziness at work had changed in the last few months to a sudden eagerness when he frequently offered, almost intrusively, to post my letters. I cannot acquit myself of a certain amount of imprudence, but after all, haven't the greatest diplomats and generals of the world too been out-manoeuvred by Hitler's cunning? Just how precisely and lovingly the Gestapo had long been directing its attention to me was manifested tangibly by the fact that the SS people arrested me on the evening of the very day of Schuschnigg's abdication, and a day before Hitler entered Vienna. Luckily I had been able to burn the most important documents upon hearing Schuschnigg's farewell address over the radio, and the other papers, along with the indispensable vouchers for the securities held abroad for the cloisters and two archdukes, I concealed in a basket of laundry which my faithful housekeeper took to my uncle. All of this almost literally in the last minute before the fellows stove my door in.'

Dr B interrupted himself long enough to light a cigar. I noticed by the light of the match a nervous twitch at the right corner of his mouth that had struck me before and which, as far as I could observe, recurred every few minutes. It was merely a fleeting vibration, hardly stronger than a breath, but it imparted to the whole face a singular restlessness.

'I suppose you expect that I'm going to tell you about the concentration camp to which all who held faith with our old Austria were removed; about the degradations, martyrings and tortures that I suffered there. Nothing of the kind happened. I was in a different category. I was not put with those luckless ones on whom they released their accumulated resentment by corporal and spiritual degradation, but rather was assigned to that small group out of which the National Socialists hoped to squeeze money or important information. My obscure person in itself meant nothing to the Gestapo, of course. They must have guessed, though, that we were the dummies, the administrators and confidants, of their most embittered adversaries, and what they expected to compel from me was incriminating evidence, evidence against the monasteries to support charges of violation by those who had selflessly taken up the cudgels for the Monarchy. They suspected, and not without good reason, that a substantial portion of the funds that we handled was still secreted and inaccessible to their lust for loot — hence their choice of me on the very first day in order to force the desired information by their trusted methods. That is why persons of my sort, to whom they looked for money or significant evidence, were not dumped into a concentration camp but were sorted out for special hand-

ling. You will recall that our Chancellor, and also Baron Roths-
child, from whose family they hoped to extort millions, were not
planted behind barbed wire in a prison camp but, ostensibly
privileged, were lodged in individual rooms in a hotel, the Metro-
pole, which happened to be the Gestapo headquarters. The same
distinction was bestowed on my insignificant self.

'A room to oneself in a hotel — sounds pretty decent, doesn't
it? But you may believe me that they had not in mind a more
decent but a more crafty technique when, instead of stuffing us
"prominent" ones in blocks of twenty into icy barracks, they
housed us in tolerably heated hotel rooms, each by himself.
For the pressure by which they planned to compel the needed
testimony was to be exerted more subtly than through common
beating or physical torture: by the most conceivably complete
isolation. They did nothing to us; they merely deposited us in
the midst of nothing, knowing well that of all things the most
potent pressure on the soul of man is nothingness. By placing
us singly, each in an utter vacuum, in a chamber that was her-
metically closed to the world without, it was calculated that the
pressure created from inside, rather than cold and the scourge,
would eventually cause our lips to spring apart.

'The first sight of the room allotted to me was not at all repel-
lent. There was a door, a table, a bed, a chair, a wash-basin, a
barred window. The door, however, remained closed night and
day; the table remained bare of book, newspaper, pencil, paper;
the window gave on a brick wall; my ego and my physical self
were contained in a structure of nothingness. They had taken
every object from me: my watch, that I might not know the hour;
my pencil, that I might not make a note; my pocket-knife, that I
might not sever a vein; even the slight narcotic of a cigarette was
forbidden me. Except for the warder, who was not permitted to
address me or to answer a question, I saw no human face, I heard
no human voice. From dawn to night there was no sustenance for
eye or ear or any sense; I was alone with myself with my body
and four or five inanimate things, rescuelessly alone with table,
bed, window, and basin. One lived like a diver in his bell in the
black ocean of this silence — like a diver, too, who is dimly aware
that the cable to safety has already snapped and that he never
will be raised from the soundless depths. There was nothing to
do, nothing to hear, nothing to see; about me, everywhere and
without interruption, there was nothingness, emptiness without
space or time. I walked to and fro, and with me went my

thoughts, to and fro, to and fro, ever again. But even thoughts, insubstantial as they seem, require an anchorage if they are not to revolve and circle around themselves; they too weigh down under nothingness. One waited for something from morn to eve and nothing happened. Nothing happened. One waited, waited, waited; one thought, one thought, one thought until one's temples smarted. Nothing happened. One remained alone. Alone. Alone.

'That lasted for a fortnight, during which I lived outside of time, outside the world. If war had broken out then I would never have discovered it, for my world comprised only table, door, bed, basin, chair, window and wall, every line of whose scalloped pattern embedded itself as with a steel graver in the innermost folds of my brain every time it met my eye. Then, at last, the hearings began. Suddenly I received a summons; I hardly knew whether it was day or night. I was called and led through a few corridors, I knew not whither; then I waited and knew not where it was, and found myself standing at a table behind which some uniformed men were seated. Piles of papers on the table, documents of whose contents I was in ignorance; and then came the questions, the real ones and the false, the simple and the cunning, the catch questions and the dummy questions; and whilst I answered, strange and evil fingers toyed with papers whose contents I could not surmise, and strange evil fingers wrote a record and I could not know what they wrote. But the most fearsome thing for me at those hearings was that I never could guess or figure out what the Gestapo actually knew about the goings on in my office and what they sought to worm out of me. I have already told you that at the last minute I gave my housekeeper the really incriminating documents to take to my uncle. Had he received them? Had he not received them? How far had I been betrayed by that clerk? Which letters had they intercepted and what might they not already have screwed out of some clumsy priest at one of the cloisters which we represented?

'And they heaped question on question. What securities had I bought for this cloister, with which banks had I corresponded, do I know Mr So-and-so or do I not, had I corresponded with Switzerland and with God-knows-where? And not being able to divine what they had already dug up, every answer was fraught with danger. Were I to admit something that they didn't know I might be unnecessarily exposing somebody to the axe. If I denied too much I harmed myself.

'The worst was not the examination. The worst was the return from the examination to my void, to the same room with the same table, the same bed, the same basin, the same wall-paper. No sooner was I by myself than I tried to recapitulate, to think of what I should have said and what I should say next time so as to divert any suspicion that a careless remark of mine might have aroused. I pondered, I combed through, I probed, I appraised every single word of testimony before the examining officers. I restated their every question and every answer that I made. I sought to sift out the part that went into the protocol, knowing well that it was all incalculable and unascertainable. But these thoughts, once given rein in empty space, rotated in my head unceasingly, always starting afresh in ever-changing combinations and insinuating themselves into my sleep.

'After every hearing by the Gestapo my own thoughts took over no less inexorably the martyrising questions, searchings and torments, and perhaps even more horribly, for the hearings at least ended after an hour, but this repetition, thanks to the spiteful torture of solitude, ended never. And always the table, chest, bed, wall-paper, window; no diversion, not a book or magazine, not a new face, no pencil with which to jot down an item, not a match to toy with — nothing, nothing, nothing. It was only at this point that I apprehended how devilishly intelligently, with what murderous psychology, this hotel-room system was conceived. In a concentration camp one would, perhaps, have had to wheel stones until one's hands bled and one's feet froze in one's boots; one would have been packed in stench and cold with a couple of dozen others. But one would have seen faces, would have had space, a tree, a star, something, anything, to stare at, while here everything stood before one unchangeably the same, always the same, maddeningly the same. There was nothing here to switch me off from my thoughts, from my delusive notions, from my diseased recapitulating. That was just what they purposed: they wanted me to gag and gag on my thoughts until they choked me and I had no choice but to spit them out at last, to admit — admit everything that they were after, finally to yield up the evidence and the people.

'I gradually became aware of how my nerves were slacking under the grisly pressure of the void and, conscious of the danger, I tensed myself to the bursting point in an effort to find or create any sort of diversion. I tried to recite or reconstruct everything I had ever memorised in order to occupy myself —

the folk songs and nursery rhymes of childhood, the Homer of my high-school days, clauses from the Civil Code. Then I did problems in arithmetic, adding or dividing, but my memory was powerless without some integrating force. I was unable to concentrate on anything. One thought flickered and darted about: how much do they know? What is it that they don't know? What did I say yesterday — what ought I to say next time?

'This simply indescribable state lasted four months. Well, four months; easy to write, just about a dozen letters! Easy to say, too: four months, a couple of syllables. The lips can articulate the sound in a quarter of a second: four months. But nobody can describe or measure or demonstrate, not to another or to himself, how long a period endures in the spaceless and timeless, nor can one explain to another how it eats into and destroys one, this nothing and nothing and nothing that is all about, everlastingly this table and bed and basin and wall-paper, and always that silence, always the same warder who shoves the food in without looking at one, always those same thoughts that revolve around one in the nothingness, until one becomes insane.

'Small signs made me disturbedly conscious that my brain was not working right. Early in the game my mind had been quite clear at the examinations; I had testified quietly and deliberately; my twofold thinking — what should I say and what not? — had still functioned. Now I could no more than articulate haltingly the simplest sentences, for while I spoke my eyes were fixed in a hypnotic stare on the pen that sped recordingly across the paper as if I wished to race after my own words. I felt myself losing my grip, I felt that the moment was coming closer and closer when, to rescue myself, I would tell all I knew and perhaps more; when, to elude the strangling grip of that nothingness, I would betray twelve persons and their secrets without deriving any advantage myself but the respite of a single breath.

'One evening I really reached that limit: the warder had just served my meal at such a moment of desperation when I suddenly shrieked after him: "Take me to the Board! I'll tell everything! I want to confess! I'll tell them where the papers are and where the money is! I'll tell them everything! Everything!" Fortunately he was far enough away not to hear me. Or perhaps he didn't want to hear me.

'An event occurred in this extremest need, something unforeseeable, that offered rescue, rescue if only for a period. It was late in July, a dark, ominous, rainy day: I recall these details quite definitely because the rain was rattling against the windows of the corridor through which I was being led to the examination. I had to wait in the ante-room of the audience chamber. Always one had to wait before the session; the business of letting one wait was a trick of the game. They would first rip one's nerves by the call, the abrupt summons from the cell in the middle of the night, and then, by the time one was keyed to the ordeal with will and reason tensed to resistance, they caused one to wait, meaningless meaningful waiting, an hour, two hours, three hours before the trial, to weary the body and humble the spirit. And they caused me to wait particularly long on this Thursday, the 27th of July; twice the hour struck while I attended, standing, in the ante-room; there is a special reason, too, for my remembering the date so exactly.

'A calendar hung in this room — it goes without saying that they never permitted me to sit down; my legs bored into my body for two hours — and I find it impossible to convey to you how my hunger for something printed, something written, made me stare at these figures, these few words, "27 July", against the wall; I wolfed them into my brain. Then I waited some more and waited and looked to see when the door would open at last, meanwhile reflecting on what my inquisitors might ask me this time, knowing well that they would ask me something quite different from that for which I was schooling myself. Yet in the face of all that, the torment of the waiting and standing was nevertheless a blessing, a delight, because this room was, after all, a different one from my own, somewhat larger and with two windows instead of one, and without the bed and without the basin and without that crack in the window-sill that I had regarded a million times. The door was painted differently, a different chair stood against the wall, and to the left stood a filing cabinet with documents as well as a clothes-stand on which three or four wet military coats hung — my torturers' coats. So that I had something new, something different to look at, at last something different for my starved eyes, and they clawed greedily at every detail.

'I took in every fold of those garments; I observed, for example, a drop suspended from one of the wet collars and, ludicrous as it may sound to you, I waited in an inane excitement to see whether the drop would eventually detach itself and roll down or whether it would resist gravity and stay put; truly, this drop held me breathless for minutes, as if my life had been at stake.

It rolled down after all, and then I counted the buttons on the coat again, eight on one, eight on another, ten on the third, and again I compared the rank marks; all of these absurd and unimportant trifles toyed with, teased, and pinched my hungry eyes with an avidity which I forgo trying to describe. And suddenly I saw something that paralysed my gaze. I had discovered a slight bulge in the side-pocket of one of the coats. I moved closer to it and thought that I recognised, by the rectangular shape of the protrusion, what this swollen pocket harboured: a book! My knees trembled: a *book!*

'I hadn't had a book in my hand for four months, so that the mere idea of a book in which words appear in orderly arrangement, of sentences, pages, leaves, a book in which one could follow and stow in one's brain new, unknown, diverting thoughts, was at once intoxicating and stupefying. Hypnotised, my eyes rested on the little swelling which the book inside the pocket formed; they glowered at the spot as if to burn a hole in the coat. The moment came when I could no longer control my greed; involuntarily I edged nearer. The mere thought that my hands might at least feel the book through the cloth made the nerves of my fingers tingle to the nails. Almost without knowing what I did, I found myself getting closer to it.

'Happily the warder ignored my singular behaviour; indeed, it may have seemed to him quite natural that a man wanted to lean against a wall after standing erect for two hours. And then I was quite close to the coat, my hands purposely clasped behind me so as to be able to touch the coat unnoticed. I felt the stuff and the contact confirmed that here was something square, something flexible, and that it crackled softly — a book, a book ! And then a thought went through me like a shot: steal the book ! If you can turn the trick, you can hide the book in your cell and read, read, read — read again at last. The thought, hardly lodged in me, operated like a strong poison; at once there was a singing in my ears, my heart hammered, my hands froze and resisted my bidding. But after that first numbness I pressed myself softly and insinuatingly against the coat; I pressed — always fixing the warder with my eye — the book up out of the pocket, higher and higher, with my artfully concealed hands. Then: a tug, a gentle, careful pull, and in no time the little book was in my hand. Not until now was I frightened at my deed. Retreat was no longer possible. What to do with it? I shoved the book under my trousers at the back just far enough for the belt to hold it, then gradually to the hip so that while walking I could keep it in place by holding my hands on the trouser-seams, military fashion. I had to try it out, so I moved a step from the clothes-stand, two steps, three steps. It worked. It was possible to keep the book in place while walking if I but kept pressing firmly against my belt.

'Then came the hearing. It demanded greater attention than ever on my part, for while answering I concentrated my entire effort on securing the book inconspicuously rather than on my testimony. Luckily this session proved to be a short one and I got the book safely to my room, though it slipped into my trousers most dangerously while in the corridor on my way back and I had to simulate a violent fit of coughing as an excuse for bending over to get it under my belt again. But what a moment, that, as I bore it back into my inferno, alone at last yet no longer alone !

'You will suppose, of course, that my first act was to seize the book, examine it and read it. Not at all! I wanted, first of all, to savour the joy of possessing a book; the artificially prolonged and nerve-inflaming desire to day-dream about the kind of book I would wish this stolen one to be: above all, very small type, narrowly spaced, with many, many letters, many, many thin leaves so that it might take long to read. And then I wished to myself that it might be one that would demand mental exertion, nothing smooth or light; rather somethig from which I could learn and memorise, preferably — oh, what an audacious dream — Goethe or Homer. At last I could no longer check my greed and my curiosity. Stretched on the bed so as to arouse no suspicion in case the warder might open the door without warning, tremblingly I drew the volume from under my belt.

'The first glance produced not merely disappointment but a sort of bitter vexation, for this booty, whose acquirement was surrounded with such monstrous danger and such glowing hope, proved to be nothing more than a chess anthology, a collection of one hundred and fifty championship games. Had I not been barred, locked in, I would, in my first rage, have thrown the thing through an open window; for what was to be done — what could be done — with nonsense of the kind? Like most of the other boys at school, I had now and then tried my hand at chess to kill time. But of what use was this theoretical stuff to me? You can't play chess alone, and certainly not without chessmen and a board. Annoyed, I thumbed the pages, thinking to discover reading matter of some sort, an introduction, a manual; but, besides the bare rectangular reproductions of the various master games with their symbols — a1-a2, Kt-f1-Kt-g3, etc — to me then unintelligible, I found nothing. All of it appeared to me as a kind of algebra the key to which was hidden. Only gradually I puzzled out that the letters a, b, c stood for the vertical rows, the figures 1 to 8 for the rows across, and indicated the current position of each figure; thus these purely graphic expressions did, nevertheless, attain to speech.

'Who knows, I thought, if I were able to devise a chessboard in my cell I could follow these games through; and it seemed like a sign from heaven that the weave of my bedspread disclosed a coarse chequer-work. With proper manipulation it yielded a field of sixty-four squares. I tore out the first leaf and concealed the book under my mattress. Then from bits of bread that I sacrificed, I began to mould king, queen and the other figures (with ludicrous results, of course), and after no end of effort I was finally able to undertake on the bedspread the reproduction of the positions pictured in the chess book. But my absurd bread-crumb figures, half of which I had covered with dust to differentiate them from "white" ones, proved utterly inadequate when I tried to pursue the printed game. I was all confusion in those first days; I would have to start a game afresh five times, ten times, twenty times. But who on earth had so much unused and useless time as I, slave of emptiness, and who commanded so much immeasurable greed and patience!

'It took me six days to play the game to the end without an error, and in a week after that I no longer required the chessmen to comprehend the relative positions, and in just one more week I was able to dispense with the bedspread; the printed symbols, a1, a2, c7, c8, at first abstractions to me, automatically transformed themselves into visual plastic positions. The transposition had been accomplished perfectly. I had projected the chessboard and its figures within myself and, thanks to the bare rules, observed the immediate set-up just as a practised musician hears all instruments singly and in combination upon merely glancing at a printed score.

'It cost me no effort, after another fortnight, to play every game in the book from memory or, in chess language, blind; and only then did I begin to understand the limitless benefaction which my impertinent theft constituted. For I had acquired an occupation — a senseless, a purposeless one if you wish — yet one that negated the nothingness that enveloped me; the one hundred and fifty championship games equipped me with a weapon against the strangling monotony of space and time.

'From then on, to conserve the charm of this new interest without interruption, I divided my day precisely: two games in the morning, two in the afternoon, a quick recapitulation in the evening. That served to fill my day which previously had been as shapeless as jelly; I had something to do that did not tire me, for a wonderful feature of chess is that through confining mental energy to a strictly bounded field the brain does not flag even under the most strained concentration; rather it makes more acute its agility and energy. In the course of time the repetition of the master games, which had at first been mechanical, awakened an artistic, a pleasurable comprehension in me. I learned to understand the refinements, the tricks and feints in attack and defence; I grasped the technique of thinking ahead, planning combinations and riposting, and soon recognised the personal note of each champion in his individual method as infallibly as one spots a particular poet on hearing only a few lines. That which began as a mere time-killing occupation became a joy, and the personalities of such great chess strategists as Alekhin, Lasker, Boguljobov and Tartakover entered into my solitude as beloved comrades.

'My silent cell was constantly and variously peopled, and the very regularity of my exercises restored my already impaired intellectual capacity; my brain seemed refreshed and, because of constant disciplined thinking, even keenly whetted. My ability to think more clearly and concisely manifested itself, above all, at the hearings; unconsciously I had perfected myself at the chessboard in defending myself against false threats and masked dodges; from this time on I gave them no openings at the sessions and I even harboured the thought that the Gestapo men began, after a while, to regard me with a certain respect. Possibly they asked themselves, seeing so many others collapse, from what secret sources I alone found strength for such unshakable resistance.

'This period of happiness in which I played through the one hundred and fifty games in that book systematically, day by day, continued for about two and a half to three months. Then I arrived unexpectedly at a dead point. Suddenly I found myself once more facing nothingness. For by the time that I had played through each one of these games innumerable times, the charm of novelty and surprise was lost, the exciting and stimulating power was exhausted. What purpose did it serve to repeat again and again games whose every move I had long since memorised? No sooner did I make an opening move than the whole thing unravelled of itself; there was no surprise, no tension, no problem. At this point I would have needed another book with more games to keep me busy, to engage the mental effort that had become indispensable to divert me. This being totally impossible, my madness could take but one course: instead of the old games I had to devise new ones myself. I had to try to play the game with myself or, rather, against myself.

'I have no idea to what extent you have given thought to the intellectual status of this game of games. But one doesn't have to reflect deeply to see that if pure chance can determine a game of calculation, it is an absurdity in logic to play against oneself. The fundamental attraction of chess lies, after all, in the fact that its strategy develops in different wise in two different brains, that in this mental battle Black, ignorant of White's immediate manoeuvres, seeks constantly to guess and cross them, while White, for his part, strives to penetrate Black's secret purposes and to outstrip and parry them. If one person tries to be both Black and White you have the preposterous situation that one and the same brain at once knows something and yet does not know it; that, functioning as White's partner, it can instantly obey a command to forget what, a moment earlier as Black's partner, it desired and plotted. Such cerebral duality really implies a complete cleavage of the conscious, a lighting up or dimming of the brain function at pleasure as with a switch; in short, to want to play against oneself at chess is about as paradoxical as to want to jump over one's own shadow.

'Well, briefly, in my desperation I tried this impossibility, this absurdity, for months. There was no choice but this nonsense if I was not to become quite insane or slowly to disintegrate mentally. The fearful state that I was in compelled me at least to attempt this split between Black ego and White ego so as not to be crushed by the horrible nothingness that bore in on me.'

Dr B relaxed in his deck-chair and closed his eyes for a minute. It seemed as if he were exerting his will to suppress a disturbing recollection. Once again the left corner of his mouth twitched in that strange and evidently uncontrollable manner. Then he settled himself a little more erectly.

'Well then, I hope I've made it all pretty intelligible up to this point. I'm sorry, but I doubt greatly that the rest of it can be pictured quite as clearly. This new occupation, you see, called for so unconditional a harnessing of the brain as to make any simultaneous self-control impossible. I have already intimated my opinion that a chess contest with oneself spells nonsense, but there is a minimal possibility for even such an absurdity if a real chessboard is present, because the board, being tangible, affords a sense of distance, a material extra-territoriality. Before a real chessboard with real chessmen you can stop to think things over, and you can place yourself physically first on this side of the table, then on the other, to fix in your eyes how the scene looks to Black and how it looks to White. Obliged as I was to conduct these contests against myself — or with myself, as you please — on an imaginary field, so I was obliged to keep fixedly in mind the current set-up on the sixty-four squares and, besides, to make advance calculations as to the possible further moves open to each player, which meant — I know how mad this must sound to you — imagining doubly, triply, no, imagining sextuply, duodecibly for each one of my egos, always four or five moves in advance.

'Please don't think that I expect you to follow through the involutions of this madness. In these plays in the abstract space of fantasy I had to figure out the next four or five moves in my capacity of White, likewise as Black, thus considering every possible future combination with two brains, so to speak, White's brain and Black's brain. But even this auto-cleaving of personality was not the most dangerous aspect of my abstruse experiment; rather it was that with the need to play independently I lost my foothold and fell into a bottomless pit. The mere replaying of championship games, which I had been indulging in during the preceding weeks, had been, after all, no more than a feat of repetition, a straight recapitulation of given material and, as such, no greater strain than to memorise poetry or learn sections of the Civil Code by heart; it was a delimited, disciplined function and thus an excellent mental exercise. My two morning games, my two in the afternoon, represented a definite task that I was able to perform coolly; it was a substitute for normal occupation and, moreover, if I erred in the progress of a game or forgot the next move, I always had recourse to the book. It was only because the replaying of others' games left my self out of the picture that this activity served to soothe and heal my shattered nerves; it was all one to me whether Black or White was victor, for was it not Alekhin or Boguljobov who sought the palm, while my own person, my reason, my soul derived satisfaction as observer, as fancier of the niceties of those jousts as they worked out. From the moment at which I tried to play against myself I began, unconsciously, to challenge myself. Each of my egos, my Black ego and my White ego, had to contest against the other and become the centre, each on its own, of an ambition, an impatience to win, to conquer; after each move that I made as Ego Black I was in a fever of curiosity as to what Ego White would do. Each of my egos felt triumphant when the other made a bad move and likewise suffered chagrin at similar clumsiness of its own.

'All that sounds senseless, and in fact such a self-produced schizophrenia, such a split consciousness with its fund of dangerous excitement, would be unthinkable in a person under normal conditions. Don't forget, though, that I had been violently torn from all normality, innocently charged and behind bars, for months martyrised by the refined employment of solitude — a man seeking an object against which to discharge his long-accumulated rage. And as I had nothing else than this insane, match with myself, that rage, that lust for revenge, canalised itself fanatically into the game. Something in me wanted to justify itself, but there was only this other self with which I could wrestle; so while the game was on, an almost maniac excitement waxed in me. In the beginning my deliberations were still quiet and composed; I would pause between one game and the next so as to recover from the effort; but little by little my frayed nerves forbade all respite. No sooner had Ego White made a move than Ego Black feverishly plunged a piece forward; scarcely had a game ended but I challenged myself to another, for each time, of course, one of my chess-egos was beaten by the other and demanded satifaction.

'I shall never be able to tell, even approximately, how many games I played against myself during those months in my cell as a result of this crazy insatiability; a thousand perhaps, perhaps more. It was an obsession against which I could not arm myself; from dawn to night I thought of nothing but knights and pawns, rooks and kings, and a and b and c, and "Mate!" and "Castle"; my entire being and every sense embraced the chequered board. The joy of play became a lust for play; the lust for play became a compulsion to play, a frenetic rage, a mania which saturated not only my waking hours but eventually my sleep, too. I could think only in terms of chess, only in chess moves, chess problems; sometimes I would wake with a damp brow and become aware that a game had unconsciously continued in my sleep, and if I dreamt of persons it was exclusively in the moves of the bishop, the rook, in the advance and retreat of the knight's move.

'Even when I was brought before the examining Board I was no longer able to keep my thoughts within the bounds of my responsibilities; I'm inclined to think that I must have expressed myself confusedly at the last sessions, for my judges would glance at one another strangely. Actually I was merely waiting, while they questioned and deliberated, in my cursed eagerness to be led back to my cell so that I could resume my mad round, to start a fresh game, and another and another. Every interruption disturbed me; even the quarter-hour in which the warder cleaned up the room, the two minutes in which he served my meals, tortured my feverish impatience; sometimes the midday meal stood untouched on the tray at evening because the game made me forgetful of food. The only physical sensation that I experienced was a terrible thirst; the fever of this constant thinking and playing must already have manifested itself then; I emptied the bottle in two swallows and begged the warder for more, and nevertheless felt my tongue dry in my mouth in the next minute.

'Finally my excitement during the games rose — by that time I did nothing else from morning till night — to such a height that I was no longer able to sit still for a minute; uninterruptedly, while cogitating on a move, I would walk to and fro, quicker and quicker, to and fro, to and fro, and the nearer the approach to the decisive moment of the game the hotter my steps; the lust to win, to victory, to victory over myself increased to a sort of rage; I trembled with impatience, for the one chess-ego in me was always too slow for the other. One would whip the other forward and, absurd as this may seem to you, I would call angrily, "Quicker, quicker!" or "Go on, go on!" when the one self in me failed to riposte to the other's thrust quickly enough. It goes without saying that I am now fully aware that this state of mine was nothing less than a pathological form of overwrought mind for which I can find no other name than one not yet known to medical annals: chess poisoning.

'The time came when this monomania, this obsession, attacked my body as well as my brain. I lost weight, my sleep was restless and disturbed, upon waking I had to make great efforts to compel my leaden lids to open; sometimes I was so weak that when I grasped a glass I could scarcely raise it to my lips, my hands trembled so; but no sooner did the game begin than a mad power seized me: I rushed up and down, up and down with fists clenched, and I would sometimes hear my own voice as through a reddish fog, shouting hoarsely and angrily at myself, "Check!" or "Mate!"

'How this horrible, indescribable condition reached its crisis is something that I am unable to report. All that I know is that I woke one morning and the waking was different from usual. My body was no longer a burden, so to speak; I rested softly and easily. A tight, agreeable fatigue, such as I had not known for months, lay on my eyelids; the feeling was so warm and benignant that I couldn't bring myself to open my eyes. For minutes I lay awake and continued to enjoy this heavy soddenness, this tepid reclining in agreeable stupefaction. All at once I seemed to hear voices behind me, living human voices, low whispering voices that spoke words; and you can't possibly imagine my delight, for months had elapsed, perhaps a year, since I had heard other words than the hard, sharp, evil ones from my judges. "You're dreaming," I said to myself. "You're dreaming! Don't, in any circumstances, open your eyes. Let the dream last or you'll again see the cursed cell about you, the chair and washstand and the table and the wall-paper with the eternal pattern. You're dreaming — keep on dreaming!"

'But curiosity held the upper hand. Slowly and carefully I raised my lids. A miracle! It was a different room in which I found myself, a room wider and more ample than my hotel cell. An unbarred window admitted light freely and permitted a view of trees, green trees swaying in the wind, instead of my bald brick partition; the walls shone white and smooth, above me a high white ceiling. I lay in a new and unaccustomed bed and — surely, it was no dream — human voices whispered behind me.

'In my surprise I must have made an abrupt, involuntary movement, for at once I heard an approaching step. A woman came softly, a woman with a white head-dress, a nurse, a Sister. A delighted shudder ran through me: I had seen no woman for a year. I stared at the lovely apparition, and it must have been a glance of wild ecstasy, for she admonished me, "Quiet, don't move." I hung only on her voice, for was not this a person who talked! Was there still somebody on earth who did not interrogate me, torture me? And to top it all — ungraspable wonder! — a soft, warm, almost tender woman's voice. I stared hungrily at her mouth, for the year of inferno had made it seem to me impossible that one person might speak kindly to another. She smiled at me — yes, she smiled; then there still were people who could smile benevolently — put a warning finger to her lips, and went off noiselessly. But I could not obey her order; I was not yet sated with the miracle. I tried to wrench myself into a sitting posture so as to follow with my eyes this wonder of a human being who was kind. But when I reached out to support my weight on the edge of the bed something failed me. In place of my right hand, fingers, and wrist I became aware of something foreign — a thick, large, white cushion, obviously a comprehensive bandage. At first I gaped uncomprehendingly at this bulky object, then slowly I began to grasp where I was and to reflect on what could have happened to me. They must have injured me, or I had done some damage to my hand myself. The place was a hospital.

'The physician, an amiable elderly man, turned up at noon. He knew my family and made so genial an allusion to my uncle, the Imperial household doctor, as to create the impression that he was well disposed towards me. In the course of conversation he put all sorts of questions, one of which, in particular, astonished me: Was I a mathematician or a chemist? I answered in the negative.

' "Strange," he murmured. "In your fever you cried out such unusual formulas, c3, c4. We could make nothing of it."

'I asked him what had happened to me. He smiled oddly.

' "Nothing too serious. An acute irritation of the nerves," and added in a low voice, after looking carefully around, "and quite intelligible, of course. Let's see, it was March 13, wasn't it!"

I nodded.

' "No wonder, with that system," he admitted. "You're not the first. But don't worry." The manner of his soothing speech and sympathetic smile convinced me that I was in a safe haven.

'A couple of days thereafter the doctor told me quite of his own accord what had taken place. The warder had heard shrieks from my cell and thought, at first, that I was disputing with somebody who had broken in. But no sooner had he shown himself at the door than I made for him, shouted wildly something that sounded like "Aren't you ever going to move, you rascal, you coward?" grasped at his windpipe, and finally attacked him so ferociously that he had to call for help. Then when they were dragging me, in my mad rage, for medical examination, I had suddenly broken loose and thrust myself against the window in the corridor, thereby lacerating my hand — see this deep scar. I had been in a sort of brain fever during the first few days in the hospital, but now he found my perceptive faculties quite in order. "To be sure," said he under his voice, "its just as well that I don't report that higher up or they may still come and fetch you back there. Depend on me, I'll do my best."

'Whatever it was that this benevolent doctor told my torturers about me is beyond my knowledge. In any case, he achieved what he sought to achieve: my release. It may be that he declared me irresponsible, or it may be that my importance to the Gestapo had diminished, for Hitler had since occupied Bohemia, thus liquidating the case of Austria. I had merely to sign an undertaking to leave the country within a fortnight, and this period was so filled with the multitude of formalities that now surround a journey — military certificate, police, tax and health certificates, passport, visas — as to leave me no time to brood over the past. Apparently one's brain is controlled by secret, regulatory powers which automatically switch off whatever may annoy or endanger the mind, for every time I wanted to ponder on my imprisonment the light in my brain seemed to go off; only after many weeks, indeed only now, on this ship, have I plucked up enough courage to pass in review all that I lived through.

'After all this you will understand my unbecoming and perhaps strange conduct to your friends. It was only by chance that I was strolling through the smoking-room and saw them sitting at the chessboard; my feet seemed rooted where I stood from astonishment and fright. For I had totally forgotten that one can play chess with a real board and real figures, forgotten that two physically separate persons sit opposite each other at this game. Truly, it took me a few minutes before I remembered that what those men were playing was what I had been playing, against myself during the months of my helplessness. The cipher-code which served me in my worthy exercises was but a substitute, a symbol for these solid figures; my astonishment that this pushing about of pieces on the board was the same as the imaginary fantastics in my mind must have been like that of an astronomer who, after complicated paper calculations as to the existence of a new planet, eventually really sees it in the sky as a clear, white, substantial body. I stared at the board as if magnetised and saw there my set-up, knight, rook, king, queen, and pawns, as genuine figures carved out of wood. In order to get the hang of the game I had voluntarily to transmute it from my abstract realm of numbers and letters into the movable figures. Gradually I was overcome with curiosity to observe a real contest between two players. Then followed that regrettable and impolite interference of mine with your game. But that mistaken move of your friend's was like a stab at my heart. It was pure instinct that made me hold him back, a quite impulsive grasp like that with which one involuntarily seizes a child leaning over a banister. It was not until afterwards that I became conscious of the impropriety of my intrusiveness.'

I hastened to assure Dr B that we were all happy about the incident to which we owed his acquaintance and that, after what he had confided in me, I would be doubly interested in the opportunity to see him at tomorrow's improvised tournament.

'Really, you mustn't expect too much. It will be nothing but a test for me — a test whether I — whether I'm at all capable of dealing with chess in a normal way, in a game with a real board with substantial chessmen and a living opponent — for now I doubt more than ever that those hundreds, they may have been thousands, of games that I played were real games according to the rules and not merely a sort of dream-chess, fever-chess, a delirium in which, as always in dreams, one skips intermediate steps. Surely you do not seriously believe that I would measure myself against a champion, that I expect to give tit for tat to the greatest one in the world. What interests and fascinates me is nothing but the posthumous curiosity to discover whether what went on in my cell was chess or madness, whether I was then at the dangerous brink or already beyond it — that's all, nothing else.'

At this moment the gong summoning passengers to dinner was heard. The conversation must have lasted almost two hours, for Dr B had told me his story in much greater detail than that in which I assemble it. I thanked him warmly and took my leave. I had hardly covered the length of the deck when he was alongside me, visibly nervous, saying with something of a stutter:

'One thing more. Will you please tell your friends beforehand, so that it should not later seem discourteous, that I will play only one game. . . . The idea is merely to close an old account — a final settlement, not a new beginning. . . . I can't afford to sink back a second time into that passionate play-fever that I recall with nothing but horror. And besides — besides, the doctor warned me, expressly warned me. Everyone who has ever succumbed to a mania remains for ever in jeopardy, and a sufferer from chess poisoning — even if discharged as cured — had better keep away from a chessboard. You understand, then — only this one experimental game for myself and no more.'

We assembled in the smoking-room the next day promptly at the appointed hour, three o'clock. Our circle had increased by yet two more lovers of the royal game, two ship's officers who had obtained special leave from duty to watch the tourney. Czentovic, too, not as on the preceding days, was on time. After the usual choice of colours there began the memorable game of this *homo obscurissimus* against the celebrated master.

I regret that it was played for thoroughly incompetent observers like us, and that its course is as completely lost to the annals of the art of chess as are Beethoven's improvisations to music. True, we tried to piece it together from our collective memory on the following afternoons, but in vain; very likely, in the passion of the moment, we had allowed our interest to centre on the players rather than on the game. For the intellectual contrast between the contestants became physically plastic according to their manner as the play proceeded. Czentovic, the creature of routine, remained the entire time as immobile as a block, his eyes unalterably fixed on the board; thinking seemed to cost him almost physical effort that called for extreme concentration on the part of every organ. Dr B on the other hand, was completely slack and unconstrained. Like the true dilettante, in the best sense of the word, to whom only the play in play — the *diletto* — gives joy, he relaxed fully, explained moves to us in easy conversation during the early intervals, lighted a cigarette carelessly, and glanced at the board for a minute only when it came his turn to play. Each time it seemed as if he had expected just the move that his antagonist made.

The perfunctory moves came off quite rapidly. It was not until the seventh or eighth that something like a definite plan seemed to develop. Czentovic prolonged his periods of reflection; by that we sensed that the actual battle for the lead was setting in. But, to be quite frank, the gradual development of the situation represented to us lay observers, as usually in tournament games, something of a disappointment. The more the pieces wove themselves into a singular design the more impenetrable became the real lie of the land. We could not discern what one or the other rival purposed or which of the two had the advantage. We noticed merely that certain pieces insinuated themselves forward like levers to undermine the enemy front, but since every move of these superior players was part of a combination that comprised a plan for several moves ahead, we were unable to detect the strategy of their back-and-forth.

An oppressive fatigue took possession of us, largely because of Czentovic's interminable cogitation between moves, which eventually produced visible irritation in our friend too. I observed uneasily how, the longer the game stretched out, he became increasingly restless, moving about in his chair, nervously lighting a succession of cigarettes, occasionally seizing a pencil to make a note. He would order mineral water and gulp it down, glass after glass; it was plain that his mind was working a hundred times faster than Czentovic's. Every time the latter, after endless reflection, decided to push a piece forward with his heavy hand, our friend would smile like one who encounters something long expected and make an immediate riposte. In his nimble mind he must have calculated every possibility that lay open to his opponent; the longer Czentovic took to make a decision the more his impatience grew, and during the waiting his lips narrowed into an angry and almost inimical line. Czentovic, however, did not allow himself to be hurried. He deliberated, stiff and silent, and increased the length of the pauses the more the field became denuded of figures. By the forty-second move, after one and a half hours, we sat limply by, almost indifferent to what was going on in the arena. One of the ship's officers had already departed, another was reading a book and would look up only when a piece had been moved. Then suddenly, at a move of Czentovic's, the unexpected happened. As soon as Dr B perceived that Czentovic took hold of the bishop to move it, he crouched like a cat about to spring. His whole body trembled and Czentovic had no sooner executed his intention than he pushed his queen forward and said loudly and triumphantly, 'There ! That's done with!', fell back in his chair, his arms crossed over his breast, and looked challengingly at Czentovic. As he spoke his pupils gleamed with a hot light.

Impulsively we bent over the board to figure out the significance of the move so ostentatiously announced. At first blush no direct threat was observable. Our friend's statement, then, had reference to some development that we short-thoughted amateurs could not prefigure. Czentovic was the only one among us who had not stirred at the provocative call; he remained as still as if the insulting 'done with' had glanced off him unheard. Nothing happened. Everybody held his breath and at once the ticking of the clock that stood on the table to measure the moves became audible. Three minutes passed, seven minutes, eight minutes — Czentovic was motionless, but I thought I noticed an inner tension that became manifest in the greater distension of his thick nostrils.

This silent waiting seemed to be as unbearable to our friend as to us. He shoved his chair back, rose abruptly and began to traverse the smoking-room, first slowly, then quicker and quicker. Those present looked at him wonderingly, but none with greater uneasiness than I, for I perceived that in spite of his vehemence this pacing never deviated from a uniform span; it was as if, in this awful space, he would each time come plump against an invisible cupboard that obliged him to reverse his steps. Shuddering, I recognised that it was an unconscious reproduction of the pacing in his erstwhile cell; during those months of incarceration it must have been exactly thus that he rushed to and fro, like a caged animal; his hands must have been clenched and his shoulders hunched exactly like this; it must have been like this that he pelted forward and back a thousand times there, the red lights of madness in his paralysed though feverish stare. Yet his mental control seemed still fully intact, for from time to time he turned impatiently towards the table to see if Czentovic had made up his mind. But time stretched to nine, then ten minutes.

What occurred then, at last, was something that none could have predicted. Czentovic slowly raised his heavy hand, which, until then, had rested inert on the table. Tautly we all watched for the upshot. Czentovic, however, moved no piece, but instead, with the back of his hand pushed, with one slow determined sweep, all the figures from the board. It took us a moment to comprehend: he gave up the game. He had capitulated in order that we might not witness his being mated. The impossible had come to pass: the champion of the world, victor at innumerable tournaments, had struck his colours before an unknown man, who hadn't touched a chessboard for twenty or twenty-five years. Our friend, the anonymous, the ignotus, had overcome the greatest chess master on earth in open battle.

Automatically, in the excitement, one after another rose to his feet; each was animated by the feeling that he must give vent to the joyous shock by saying or doing something. Only one remained stolidly at rest: Czentovic. After a measured interval he lifted his head and directed a stony look at our friend.

'Another game?' he asked.

'Naturally,' answered Dr B with an enthusiasm that was disturbing to me, and he seated himself, even before I could remind him of his own stipulation to play only once, and began to set up the figures in feverish haste. He pushed them about in such heat that a pawn twice slid from his trembling fingers to the floor; the pained discomfort that his unnatural excitement had already produced in me grew to something like fear. For this previously calm and quiet person had become visibly exalted; the twitching of his mouth was more frequent and in every limb he shook as with fever.

'Don't,' I said softly to him. 'No more now; you've had enough for today. It's too much of a strain for you.'

'Strain! Ha!' and he laughed loudly and spitefully. 'I could have played seventeen games during that slow ride. The only strain is for me to keep awake. Well, aren't you ever going to begin?'

These last words had been addressed in an impetuous, almost rude tone to Czentovic. The latter glanced at him quietly and evenly, but there was something of a clenched fist in that adamantine, stubborn glance. On the instant a new element had entered: a dangerous tension, a passionate hate. No longer were they two players in a sporting way; they were two enemies sworn to destroy each other. Czentovic hesitated long before making the first move, and I had a definite sensation that he was delaying on purpose. No question but that this seasoned tactician had long since discovered that just such dilatoriness wearied and irritated his antagonist. He used no less than four minutes for the normal, the simplest of openings, moving the king's pawn two spaces. Instantly our friend advanced his king's pawn, but again Czentovic was responsible for an eternal, intolerable pause; it was like waiting with beating heart for the thunder-clap after a streak of fiery lightning, and waiting — with no thunder forthcoming. Czentovic never stirred. He meditated quietly, slowly, and as I felt, increasingly, maliciously slowly — which gave me plenty of time to observe Dr B. He had just about consumed his third glass of water; it came to my mind that he had spoken of his feverish thirst in his cell. Every symptom of abnormal excitement was plainly present: I saw his forehead grow moist and the scar on his hand become redder and more sharply out-

lined. Still, however, he held himself in rein. It was not until the
fourth move, when Czentovic again pondered exasperatingly,
that he forgot himself and exploded with, 'Aren't you ever going
to move?'

Czentovic looked up coldly. 'As I remember it, we agreed on
a ten-minute limit. It is a principle with me not to make it less.'

Dr B bit his lips. I noticed under the table the growing restlessness with which he lifted and lowered the sole of his shoe, and
I could not control the nervousness that overcame me because
of the oppressive prescience of some insane thing that was boiling
in him. As a matter of fact, there was a second encounter at
the eighth move. Dr B, whose self-control diminished with the
increasing periods of waiting, could no longer conceal his tension;
he was restless in his seat and unconsciously began to drum on
the table with his fingers. Again Czentovic raised his peasant
head.

'May I ask you not to drum. It disturbs me. I can't play with
that going on.'

'Ha, ha,' answered Dr B with a short laugh, 'one can see that.'

Czentovic flushed. 'What do you mean by that?' he asked,
sharply and evilly.

Dr B gave another curt and spiteful laugh. 'Nothing except that
it's plain that you're nervous.'

Czentovic lowered his head and said nothing. Seven minutes
elapsed before he made his move, and that was the funereal
tempo at which the game dragged on. Czentovic became corre-
spondingly stonier; in the end he utilised the maximum time
before determining on a move, and from interval to interval the
conduct of our friend became stranger and stranger. It appeared
as if he no longer had any interest in the game but was occupied
with something quite different. He abandoned his excited pacing
and remained seated motionlessly. Staring into the void with
a vacant and almost insane look, he uninterruptedly muttered
unintelligible words; either he was absorbed in endless combinations or — and this was my inner suspicion — he was working
out quite other games, for each time that Czentovic got to the
point of making a move he had to be recalled from his absent
state. Then it took a minute or two to orientate himself. My
conviction grew that he had really forgotten all about Czentovic
and the rest of us in this cold aspect of his insanity which might
at any instant discharge itself violently. Surely enough, at the
nineteenth move the crisis came. No sooner had Czentovic

executed his play than Dr B giving no more than a cursory look at the board, suddenly pushed his bishop three spaces forward and shouted so loudly that we all started

'Check! Check, the king!'

Every eye was on the board in anticipation of an extraordinary move. Then, after a minute, there was an unexpected development. Very slowly Czentovic tilted his head and looked — which he had never done before — from one face to another. Something seemed to afford him a rich enjoyment, for little by little his lips gave expression to a satisfied and scornful smile. Only after he had savoured to the full the triumph which was still unintelligible to us did he address us, saying with mock deference:

'Sorry — but I see no check. Perhaps one of you gentlemen can see my king in check?'

We looked at the board and then uneasily over at Dr B. Czentovic's king was fully covered against the bishop by a pawn — a child could see that — thus the king could not possibly be in check. We turned one to the other. Might not our friend in his agitation have pushed a piece over the line, a square too far one way or the other? His attention arrested by our silence, Dr B now stared at the board and began, stutteringly:

'But the king ought to be on f7 — that's wrong, all wrong — Your move was wrong! All the pieces are misplaced — the pawn should be on g5 and not on g4. Why, that's quite a different game — that's — '

He halted abruptly. I had seized his arm roughly, or rather I had pinched it so hard that even in his feverish bewilderment he could not but feel my grip. He turned and looked at me like a somnambulist.

'What — what do you want?'

I only said 'Remember!' at the same time lightly drawing my finger over the scar on his hand. Automatically he followed my gesture, his eyes fixed glassily on the blood-red streak. Suddenly he began to tremble and his body shook.

'For God's sake,' he whispered with pale lips. 'Have I said or done something silly? Is it possible that I'm again . . .?'

'No' I said, in a low voice, 'but you have to stop the game at once. It's high time. Recollect what the doctor said.'

With a single movement Dr B was on his feet. 'I have to apologise for my stupid mistake,' he said in his old, polite voice, inclining himself to Czentovic. 'What I said was plain nonsense, of course. It goes without saying that the game is yours.' Then to us: 'My apologies to you gentlemen, also. But I warned you beforehand not to expect too much from me. Forgive the disgrace — it is the last time that I yield to the temptation of chess.'

He bowed and left in the same modest and mysterious manner in which he had first appeared before us. I alone knew why this man would never again touch a chessboard, while the others, a bit confused, stood around with that vague feeling of having narrowly escaped something uncomfortable and dangerous. 'Damned fool,' MacIver grumbled in his disappointment.

Last of all, Czentovic rose from his chair, half glancing at the unfinished game.

'Too bad,' he said generously. 'The attack wasn't at all badly conceived. The man certainly has lots of talent for an amateur.'

END-GAME

J.G. Ballard

After his trial they gave Constantin a villa, an allowance and an executioner. The villa was small and high-walled, and had obviously been used for the purpose before. The allowance was adequate to Constantin's needs — he was never permitted to go out and his meals were prepared for him by a police orderly. The executioner was his own. Most of the time they sat on the enclosed veranda overlooking the narrow stone garden, playing chess with a set of large well-worn pieces.

The executioner's name was Malek. Officially he was Constantin's supervisor, and responsible for maintaining the villa's tenuous contact with the outside world, now hidden from sight beyond the steep walls, and for taking the brief telephone call that came promptly at nine o'clock every morning. However, his real role was no secret between them. A powerful, doughy-faced man with an anonymous expression, Malek at first intensely irritated Constantin, who had been used to dealing with more subtle sets of responses. Malek followed him around the villa, never interfering — unless Constantin tried to bribe the orderly for a prohibited newspaper, when Malek merely gestured with a slight turn of one of his large hands, face registering no disapproval, but cutting off the attempt as irrevocably as a bulkhead — nor making any suggestions as to how Constantin should spend his time. Like a large bear, he sat motionlessly in the lounge in one of the faded arm chairs, watching Constantin.

After a week Constantin tired of reading the old novels in the bottom shelf of the bookcase — somewhere among the grey well-thumbed pages he had hoped to find a message from one of his predecessors — and invited Malek to play chess. The set of chipped mahogany pieces reposed on one of the empty shelves of the bookcase, the only item of decoration or recreational equipment in the villa. Apart from the books and the chess set the small six-roomed house was completely devoid of ornament.

There were no curtains or picture rails, bedside tables or standard lamps, and the only electrical fittings were the lights recessed behind thick opaque bowls into the ceilings. Obviously the chess set and the row of novels had been provided deliberately, each representing one of the alternative pastimes available to the temporary tenants of the villa. Men of a phlegmatic or philosophical temperament, resigned to the inevitability of their fate, would choose to read the novels, sinking backwards into a self-anaesthetised trance as they waded through the turgid prose of those nineteenth-century romances.

On the other hand, men of a more volatile and extrovert disposition would obviously prefer to play chess, unable to resist the opportunity to exercise their Machiavellian talents for positional manoeuvre to the last. The games of chess would help to maintain their unconscious optimism and, more subtly, sublimate or divert any attempts at escape.

When Constantin suggested that they play chess Malek promptly agreed, and so they spent the next long month as the late summer turned to autumn. Constantin was glad he had chosen chess; the game brought him into immediate personal involvement with Malek, and like all condemned men he had soon developed a powerful emotional transference on to what effectively was the only person left in his life.

At present it was neither negative nor positive; but a relationship of acute dependence — already Malek's notional personality was becoming overlayed by the associations of all the anonymous but nonetheless potent figures of authority whom Constantin could remember since his earliest childhood: his own father, the priest at the seminary he had seen hanged after the revolution, the first senior commissars, the party secretaries at the ministry of foreign affairs and, ultimately, the members of the central committee themselves. Here, where the anonymous faces had crystallised into those of closely observed colleagues and rivals, the process seemed to come full circle, so that he himself was identified with those shadowy personas who had authorised his death and were now represented by Malek.

Constantin had also, of course, become dominated by another obsession, the need to know: *when*? In the weeks after the trial and sentence he had remained in a curiously euphoric state, too stunned to realise that the dimension of time still existed for him, he had already died *a posteriori*. But gradually the will to live, and his old determination and ruthlessness, which had served him so well for thirty years, reasserted themselves, and he realised that a small hope still remained to him. How long exactly in terms of time he could only guess, but if he could master Malek his survival became a real possibility.

The question remained: When?

Fortunately he could be completely frank with Malek. The first point he established immediately.

'Malek,' he asked on the tenth move one morning, when he had completed his development and was relaxing for a moment. 'Tell me, do you know — when?'

Malek looked up from the board, his large almost bovine eyes gazing blandly at Constantin. 'Yes, Mr Constantin, I know when.' His voice was deep and functional, as expressionless as a weighing machine's.

Constantin sat back reflectively. Outside the glass panes of the verandah the rain fell steadily on the solitary fir tree which had maintained a precarious purchase among the stones under the wall. A few miles to the south-west of the villa were the outskirts of the small port, one of the dismal so-called 'coastal resorts' where junior ministry men and party hacks were sent for their bi-annual holidays. The weather, however, seemed peculiarly inclement, the sun never shining through the morose clouds, and for a moment, before he checked himself, Constantin felt glad to be within the comparative warmth of the villa.

'Let me get this straight,' he said to Malek. 'You don't merely know in a general sense — for example, after receiving an instruction from so-and-so — but you know *specifically* when?'

'Exactly.' Malek moved his queen out of the game. His chess was sound but without flair or a personal style, suggesting that he had improved merely by practice — most of his opponents, Constantin realised with sardonic amusement, would have been players of a high class.

'You know the *day* and the *hour* and the *minute*,' Constantin pressed. Malek nodded slowly, most of his attention upon the game, and Constantin rested his smooth sharp chin in one hand, watching his opponent. 'It could be within the next ten seconds, or again, it might not be for ten years?'

'As you say.' Malek gestured at the board. 'Your move.'

Constantin waved this aside. 'I know, but don't let's rush it.

These games are played on many levels, Malek. People who talk about three-dimensional chess obviously know nothing about the present form.' Occasionally he made these openings in the hope of loosening Malek's tongue, but conversation with him seemed to be impossible.

Abruptly he sat forward across the board, his eyes searching Malek's. 'You alone know the date, Malek, and as you have said, it might not be for ten years — or twenty. Do you think you can keep such a secret to yourself for so long?'

Malek made no attempt to answer this, and waited for Constantin to resume play. Now and then his eyes inspected the corners of the verandah, or glanced at the stone garden outside. From the kitchen came the occasional sounds of the orderly's boots scraping the floor as he lounged by the telephone on the deal table.

As he scrutinised the board Constantin wondered how he could provoke any response whatever from Malek; the man had shown no reaction at the mention of ten years, although the period was ludicrously far ahead. In all probability their real game would be a short one. The indeterminate date of the execution, which imbued the procedure with such a bizarre flavour, was not intended to add an element of torture or suspense to the condemned's last days, but simply to obscure and confuse the very fact of his exit. If a definite date were known in advance there might be a last-minute rally of sympathy, an attempt to review the sentence and perhaps apportion the blame elsewhere, and the unconscious if not conscious sense of complicity in the condemned man's crimes might well provoke an agonised reappraisal and, after the execution of the sentence, a submerged sense of guilt upon which opportunists and intriguers could play to advantage.

By means of the present system, however, all these dangers and unpleasant side-effects were obviated, the accused was removed from his place in the hierarchy when the opposition to him was at its zenith and conveniently handed over to the judiciary, and thence to one of the courts of star chamber whose proceedings were always held in camera and whose verdicts were never announced.

As far as his former colleagues were concerned, he had disappeared into the endless corridor world of the bureaucratic purgatories, his case permanently on file but never irrevocably closed. Above all, the fact of his guilt was never established and confirmed. As Constantin was aware, he himself had been convicted upon a technicality in the margins of the main indictment against him, a mere procedural device, like a bad twist in the plot of a story, designed solely to bring the investigation to a close. Although he knew the real nature of his crime, Constantin had never been formally notified of his guilt; in fact the court had gone out of its way to avoid preferring any serious charges against him whatever.

This ironic inversion of the classical Kafkaesque situation, by which, instead of admitting his guilt to a non-existent crime, he was forced to connive in a farce maintaining his innocence of offences he knew full well he had committed, was preserved in his present situation at the execution villa.

The psychological basis was more obscure but in some way far more threatening, the executioner beckoning his victim towards him with a beguiling smile, reassuring him that all was forgiven. Here he played upon, not those unconscious feelings of anxiety and guilt, but that innate conviction of individual survival, that obsessive preoccupation with personal immortality which is merely a disguised form of the universal fear of the image of one's own death. It was this assurance that all was well, and the absence of any charges of guilt or responsibility, which had made so orderly the queues into the gas chambers.

At present the paradoxical face of this diabolical device was worn by Malek, his lumpy amorphous features and neutral but ambiguous attitude making him seem less a separate personality than the personification of the apparat of the state. Perhaps the sardonic title of 'supervisor' was nearer the truth than had seemed at first sight, and that Malek's role was simply to officiate, or at the most serve as moderator, at a trial by ordeal in which Constantin was his own accused, prosecutor and judge.

However, he reflected as he examined the board, aware of Malek's bulky presence across the pieces, this would imply that they had completely misjudged his own personality, with its buoyancy and most gallic verve and panache. He, of all people, would be the last to take his own life in an orgy of self-confessed guilt. Not for him the neurotic suicide so loved of the Slav. As long as there were a way out he would cheerfully shoulder any burden of guilt, tolerant of his own weaknesses, ready to shrug them off with a quip. This insouciance had always been his strongest ally.

His eyes searched the board, roving down the open files of the queens and bishops, as if the answer to the pressing enigma were to be found in these polished corridors.

When? His own estimate was two months. Almost certainly, (and he had no fear here that he was rationalising) it would not be within the next two or three days, nor even the next fortnight. Haste was almost unseemly, quite apart from violating the whole purpose of the exercise. Two months would see him safely into limbo, and be sufficiently long for the suspense to break him down and reveal any secret allies, sufficiently brief to fit his particular crime.

Two months? Not as long as he might have wished. As he translated his queen's bishop into play Constantin began to map out his strategy for defeating Malek. The first task, obviously, was to discover when Malek was to carry out the execution, partly to give him peace of mind, but also to allow him to adjust the context of his escape. A physical leap to freedom over the wall would be pointless. Contacts had to be established, pressure brought to bear at various sensitive points in the hierarchy, paving the way for a reconsideration of his case. All this would take time.

His thoughts were interrupted by the sharp movement of Malek's left hand across the board, followed by a guttural grunt. Surprised by the speed and economy with which Malek had moved his piece as much by the fact that he himself was in check, Constantin sat forward and examined his position with more care. He glanced with grudging respect at Malek, who had sat back as impassively as ever, the knight he had deftly taken on the edge of the table in front of him. His eyes watched Constantin with their usual untroubled calm, like those of an immensely patient governess, his great shoulders hidden within the bulky suiting. But for a moment, when he had leaned across the board, Constantin had seen the powerful extension and flexion of his shoulder musculature.

Don't look so smug, my dear Malek, Constantin said to himself with a wry smile. At least I know now that you are left-handed. Malek had taken the knight with one hand, hooking the piece between the thick knuckles of his ring and centre fingers, and then substituting his queen with a smart tap, a movement not easily performed in the centre of the crowded board. Useful though the confirmation was — Constantin had noticed Malek apparently trying to conceal his left-handedness during their meals and when opening and closing the windows — he found this sinistral aspect of Malek's personality curiously disturbing, an indication that there would be nothing predictable about his opponent, or the ensuing struggle of wits between them. Even Malek's apparent lack of sharp intelligence was belied by the astuteness of his last move.

Constantin was playing white, and had chosen the Queen's Gambit, assuming that the fluid situation invariably resulting from the opening would be to his advantage and allow him to get on with the more serious task of planning his escape. But Malek had avoided any possible errors, steadily consolidating his position, and had even managed to launch a counter-gambit, offering a knight-to-bishop exchange which would soon undermine Constantin's position if he accepted.

'A good move, Malek,' he commented. 'But perhaps a little risky in the long run.' Declining the exchange, he lamely blocked the checking queen with a pawn.

Malek stared stolidly at the board, his heavy policeman's face, with its almost square frame from one jaw angle to the other, betraying no sign of thought. His approach, Constantin reflected as he watched his opponent, would be that of the pragmatist, judging always by immediate capability rather than by any concealed intentions. As if confirming this diagnosis, Malek simply returned his queen to her former square, unwilling or unable to exploit the advantage he had gained and satisfied by the captured piece.

Bored by the lower key on to which the game had descended, and the prospect of similar games ahead, Constantin castled his king to safety. For some reason, obviously irrational, he assumed that Malek would not kill him in the middle of a game, particularly if he, Malek, were winning. He recognised that this was an unconscious reason for wanting to play chess in the first place, and had no doubt motivated the many others who had also sat with Malek on the verandah listening to the late summer rain. Suppressing a sudden pang of fear, Constantin examined Malek's powerful hands protruding from his cuffs like two joints of meat. If Malek wanted to, he could probably kill Constantin with his bare hands.

That raised a second question, almost as fascinating as the first.

'Malek, another point.' Constantin sat back, searching in his pockets for imaginary cigarettes (none were allowed him). 'For-

give my curiosity, but I am an interested party, as it were — '
He flashed Malek his brightest smile, a characteristically incisive
thrust modulated by ironic self-deprecation which had been so
successful with his secretaries and at ministry receptions, but the
essay at humour failed to move Malek. 'Tell me, do you
know . . . how — ?' Searching for some euphemism, he repeated:
'Do you know how you are going to . . . ?' and then gave up the
attempt, cursing Malek to himself for lacking the social grace to
rescue him from his awkwardness.

Malek's chin rose slightly, a minimal nod. He showed no signs
of being bored or irritated by Constantin's laboured catechism,
or of having noticed his embarrassment.

'What is it, then?' Constantin pressed, recovering himself.
'Pistol, pill or — ' with a harsh laugh he pointed through the
window ' — do you set up a guillotine in the rain? I'd like to
know.'

Malek looked down at the chessboard, his features more gluti-
nous and dough-like than ever. Flatly, he said: 'It has been
decided.'

Constantin snorted. 'What on earth does *that* mean?' he snapped belligerently. 'Is it painless?'

For once Malek smiled, a thin smear of amusement hung fleet-
ingly around his mouth. 'Have you ever killed anything, Mr
Constantin?' he asked quietly. 'Yourself, personally, I mean.'

'Touché,' Constantin granted. He laughed deliberately, trying
to dispel the tension. 'A perfect reply.' To himself he said: I
mustn't let curiosity get the upper hand, the man was laughing
at me.

'Of course,' he went on, 'death is always painful. I merely
wondered whether, in the legal sense of the term, it would be
humane. But I can see that you are a professional, Malek, and
the question answers itself. A great relief, believe me. There are
so many sadists about, perverts and the like — ' again he watched
carefully to see if the implied sneer provoked Malek ' — that one
can't be too grateful for a clean curtain fall. It's good to know. I
can devote these last days to putting my affairs in order and
coming to terms with the world. If only I knew how long there
was left I could make my preparations accordingly. One can't be
forever saying one's last prayers. You see my point?'

Colourlessly, Malek said: 'The Prosecutor-General advised you
to make your final arrangements immediately after the trial.'

'But what does that mean?' Constantin asked, pitching his

voice a calculated octave higher. 'I'm a human being, not a book-keeper's ledger that can be totted up and left to await the audi-tor's pleasure. I wonder if you realise, Malek, the courage this situation demands from me? It's easy for you to sit there — '

Abruptly Malek stood up, sending a shiver of terror through Constantin. With a glance at the sealed windows, he moved around the chess table towards the lounge. 'We will postpone the game,' he said. Nodding to Constantin, he went off towards the kitchen where the orderly was preparing lunch.

Constantin listened to his shoes squeaking faintly across the unpolished floor, then irritably cleared the pieces off the board and sat back with the black king in his hand. At least he had provoked Malek into leaving him. Thinking this over, he won-dered whether to throw caution to the winds and begin to make life intolerable for Malek — it would be easy to pursue him around the villa, arguing hysterically and badgering him with neurotic questions. Sooner or later Malek would snap back, and might give away something of his intentions. Alternatively, Con-stantin could try to freeze him out, treating him with contempt as the hired killer he was, refusing to share a room or his meals with him and insisting on his rights as a former member of the central committee. The method might well be successful. Almost certainly Malek was telling the truth when he said he knew the exact day and minute of Constantin's execution. The order would have been given to him and he would have no discretion to advance or delay the date to suit himself. Malek would be reluc-tant to report Constantin for difficult behaviour — the reflection on himself was too obvious and his present post was not one from which he could graciously retire — and in addition not even the Police-President would be able to vary the execution date now that it had been set without convening several meetings. There was then the danger of re-opening Constantin's case. He was not without his allies, or at least those who were prepared to use him for their own advantage.

But despite these considerations, the whole business of play-acting lacked appeal for Constantin. His approach was more serpentine. Besides, if he provoked Malek, uncertainties were introduced, of which there were already far too many.

He noticed the supervisor enter the lounge and sit down quietly in one of the grey armchairs, his face, half-hidden in the shadows, turned towards Constantin. He seemed indifferent to the normal pressures of boredom and fatigue (luckily for himself, Constantin reflected — an impatient man would have pulled the trigger on the morning of the second day), and content to sit about in the armchairs, watching Constantin as the grey rain fell outside and the damp leaves gathered against the walls. The difficulties of establishing a relationship with Malek — and some sort of relationship was essential before Constantin could begin to think of escape — seemed insuperable, only the games of chess offering an opportunity.

Placing the black king on his own king's square, Constantin called out: 'Malek, I'm ready for another game, if you are.'

Malek pushed himself out of the chair with his long arms, and then took his place across the board. For a moment he scrutinised Constantin with a level glance, as if ascertaining that there would be no further outbursts of temper, and then began to set up the white pieces, apparently prepared to ignore the fact that Constantin had cleared the previous game before its completion.

He opened with a stolid Ruy Lopez, an over-analysed and uninteresting attack, but a dozen moves later, when they broke off for lunch, he had already forced Constantin to castle on the queen's side and had established a powerful position in the centre.

As they took their lunch together at the card table behind the sofa in the lounge, Constantin reflected upon this curious element which had been introduced into his relationship with Malek. While trying to check any tendency to magnify an insignificant triviality into a major symbol, he realised that Malek's proficiency at chess and his ability to produce powerful combinations out of pedestrian openings, was symptomatic of his concealed power over Constantin.

The drab villa in the thin autumn rain, the faded furniture and unimaginative food they were now mechanically consuming, the whole grey limbo with its slender telephone connection with the outside world were, like his chess, exact extensions of Malek's personality, yet permeated with secret passages and doors. The unexpected thrived in such an ambience. At any moment, as he shaved, the mirror might retract to reveal the flaming muzzle of a machine pistol, or the slightly bitter flavour of the soup they were drinking might be other than that of lentils.

These thoughts preoccupied him as the afternoon light began to fade in the east, the white rectangle of the garden wall illuminated against this dim backdrop like a huge tabula rasa. Excusing himself from the chess game, Constantin feigned a headache and retired to his room upstairs.

The door between his room and Malek's had been removed, and as he lay on the bed he was conscious of the supervisor sitting in his chair with his back to the window. Perhaps it was Malek's presence which presented him from gaining any real rest, and when he rose several hours later and returned to the verandah he felt tired and possessed by a deepening sense of foreboding.

With an effort he rallied his spirits, and by concentrating his whole attention on the game was able to extract what appeared to be a drawn position. Although the game was adjourned without comment from either player, Malek seemed to concede by his manner that he had lost his advantage, lingering for a perceptible moment over the board when Constantin rose from the table.

The lesson of all this was not lost to Constantin the following day. He was fully aware that the games of chess were not only taxing his energies but providing Malek with a greater hold upon himself than he upon Malek. Although the pieces stood where they had left them the previous evening, Constantin did not suggest that they resume play. Malek made no move towards the board, apparently indifferent to whether the game was finished or not. Most of the time he sat next to Constantin by the single radiator in the lounge, occasionally going off to confer with the orderly in the kitchen. As usual the telephone rang briefly each morning, but otherwise there were no callers or visitors to the villa. To all intents it remained suspended in a perfect vacuum.

It was this unvarying nature of their daily routines which Constantin found particularly depressing. Intermittently over the next few days he played chess with Malek, invariably finding himself in a losing position, but the focus of his attention was elsewhere, upon the enigma cloaked by Malek's expressionless face. Around him a thousand invisible clocks raced onwards towards their beckoning zeros, a soundless thunder like the drumming of apocalyptic hoof-irons.

His mood of foreboding had given way to one of mounting fear, all the more terrifying because, despite Malek's real role, it seemed completely sourceless. He found himself unable to concentrate for more than a few minutes upon any task, left his meals unfinished and fidgeted helplessly by the verandah

window. The slightest movement by Malek would make his
nerves thrill with anguish; if the supervisor left his customary
seat in the lounge to speak to the orderly Constantin would find
himself almost paralysed by the tension, helplessly counting the
seconds until Malek returned. Once, during one of their meals,
Malek started to ask him for the salt and Constantin almost
choked to death.

The ironic humour of this near-fatality reminded Constantin
that almost half of his two-month sentence had elapsed. But his
crude attempts to obtain a pencil from the orderly and later,
failing this, to mark the letters in a page torn from one of the
novels were intercepted by Malek, and he realised that short of
defeating the two policemen in single-handed combat he had no
means of escaping his ever more imminent fate.

Latterly he had noticed that Malek's movements and general
activity around the villa seemed to have quickened. He still sat
for long periods in the armchair, observing Constantin, but his
formerly impassive presence was graced by gestures and incli-
nations of the head that seemed to reflect a heightened cerebral
activity, as if he were preparing himself for some long-awaited
denouement. Even the heavy musculature of his face seemed to
have relaxed and grown sleeker, his sharp mobile eyes, like those
of an experienced senior inspector of police, roving constantly
about the rooms.

Despite his efforts, however, Constantin was unable to galvan-
ise himself into any defensive action. He could see clearly that
Malek and himself had entered a new phase in their relationship,
and that at any moment their outwardly formal and polite
behaviour would degenerate into a gasping ugly violence, but he
was nonetheless immobilised by his own state of terror. The days
passed in a blur of uneaten meals and abandoned chess games,
their very identity blotting out any sense of time or progression,
the watching figure of Malek always before him.

Every morning, when he woke after two or three hours of
sleep to find his consciousness still intact, a discovery almost
painful in its relief and poignancy, he would be immediately
aware of Malek standing in the next room, then waiting discreetly
in the hallway as Constantin shaved in the bathroom (also without its door) following him downstairs to breakfast, his careful

reflective tread like that of a hangman descending from his gallows.

After breakfast Constantin would challenge Malek to a game of chess, but after a few moves would begin to play wildly, throwing pieces forwards to be decimated by Malek. At times the supervisor would glance curiously at Constantin, as if wondering whether his charge had lost his reason, and then continue to play his careful exact game, invariably winning or drawing. Dimly Constantin perceived that by losing to Malek he had also surrendered to him psychologically, but the games had now become simply a means of passing the unending days.

Six weeks after they had first begun to play chess, Constantin more by luck than skill succeeded in an extravagant pawn gambit and forced Malek to sacrifice both his centre and any possibility of castling. Roused from his state of numb anxiety by the temporary victory, Constantin sat forward over the board, irritably waving away the orderly who announced from the door of the lounge that he would serve lunch.

'Tell him to wait, Malek. I musn't lose my concentration at this point, I've very nearly won the game.'

'Well . . . ' Malek glanced at his watch, then over his shoulder at the orderly, who, however, had turned on his heel and returned to the kitchen. He started to stand up. 'It can wait. He's bringing the — '

'No!' Constantin snapped. 'Just give me five minutes, Malek. Damn it, one adjourns on a move, not half-way through it.'

'Very well.' Malek hesitated, after a further glance at his watch. He climbed to his feet. 'I will tell him.'

Constantin concentrated on the board, ignoring the supervisor's retreating figure, the scent of victory clearing his mind. But thirty seconds later he sat up with a start, his heart almost seizing inside his chest.

Malek had gone upstairs! Constantin distinctly remembered him saying he would tell the orderly to delay lunch, but instead he had walked straight up to his bedroom. Not only was it extremely unusual for Constantin to be left unobserved when the orderly was otherwise occupied, but the latter had still not brought in their first luncheon course.

Steadying the table, Constantin stood up, his eyes searching the open doorways in front and behind him. Almost certainly the orderly's announcement of lunch was a signal, and Malek had found a convenient pretext for going upstairs to prepare his execution weapon.

Faced at last by the nemesis he had so long dreaded, Constantin listened for the sounds of Malek's feet descending the staircase. A profound silence enclosed the villa, broken only by the fall of one of the chess pieces to the tiled floor. Outside the sun shone intermittently in the garden, illuminating the broken flagstones of the ornamental pathway and the bare face of the walls. A few stunted weeds flowered among the rubble, their pale colours blanched by the sunlight, and Constantin was suddenly filled by an overwhelming need to escape into the open air for the few last moments before he died. The east wall, lit by the sun's rays, was marked by a faint series of horizontal grooves, the remnants perhaps of a fire escape ladder, and the slender possibility of using these as hand-holds made the enclosed garden, a perfect killing ground, preferable to the frantic claustrophobic nexus of the villa.

Above him, Malek's measured tread moved across the ceiling to the head of the staircase. He paused there and then began to descend the stairs, his steps chosen with a precise and careful rhythm.

Helplessly, Constantin searched the verandah for something that would serve as a weapon. The french windows on to the garden were locked, and a slotted pinion outside secured the left-hand member of the pair to the edge of the sill. If this were raised there was a chance that the windows could be forced outwards.

Scattering the chess-pieces onto the floor with a sweep of his hand, Constantin seized the board and folded it together, then stepped over to the window and drove the heavy wooden box through the bottom pane. The report of the bursting glass echoed like a gun shot through the villa. Kneeling down, he pushed his hand through the aperture and tried to lift the pinion, jerking it up and down in its rusty socket. When it failed to clear the sill he forced his head through the broken window and began to heave against it helplessly with his thin shoulders, the fragments of broken glass falling on to his neck.

Behind him a chair was kicked back, and he felt two powerful hands seize his shoulders and pull him away from the window. He struck out hysterically with the chess box, and then was flung head-first to the tiled floor.

His convalescence from this episode was to last most of the following week. For the first three days he remained in bed, recovering his physical identity, waiting for the sprained muscles of his hands and shoulders to repair themselves. When he felt sufficiently strong to leave his bed he went down to the lounge and sat at one end of the sofa, his back to the windows and the thin autumn light.

Malek still remained in attendance, and the orderly prepared his meals as before. Neither of them made any comment upon Constantin's outburst of hysteria, or indeed betrayed any signs that it had taken place, but Constantin realised that he had crossed an important rubicon. His whole relationship with Malek had experienced a profound change. The fear of his own imminent death, and the tantalising mystery of its precise date which had so obsessed him, had been replaced by a calm acceptance that the judicial processes inaugurated by his trial would take their course and that Malek and the orderly were merely the local agents of this distant apparat. In a sense his sentence and present tenuous existence at the villa were a microcosm of life itself, with its inherent but unfeared uncertainties, its inevitable quietus to be made on a date never known in advance. Seeing his role at the villa in this light Constantin no longer felt afraid at the prospect of his own extinction, fully aware that a change in the political wind could win him a free pardon.

In addition, he realised that Malek, far from being his executioner, a purely formal role, was in fact an intermediary between himself and the hierarchy, and in an important sense a potential ally of Constantin's. As he reformed his defence against the indictment preferred against him at the trial — he knew he had been far too willing to accept the *fait accompli* of his own guilt — he calculated the various ways in which Malek would be able to assist him. There was no doubt in his mind that he had misjudged Malek. With his sharp intelligence and commanding presence, the supervisor was very far from being a hatchet-faced killer — this original impression had been the result of some cloudiness in Constantin's perceptions, an unfortunate myopia which had cost him two precious months in his task of arranging a re-trial.

Comfortably swathed in his dressing-gown, he sat at the card-table in the lounge (they had abandoned the verandah with the colder weather, and a patch of brown paper over the window reminded him of that first circle of purgatory) concentrating on the game of chess. Malek sat opposite him, hands clasped on one knee, his thumbs occasionally circling as he pondered a move. Although no less reticent than he had ever been, his manner seemed to indicate that he understood and confirmed Constantin's reappraisal of the situation. He still followed Constantin around the villa, but his attentions were noticeably more perfunctory, as if he realised that Constantin would not try again to escape.

From the start, Constantin was completely frank with Malek.

'I am convinced, Malek, that the Prosecutor-General was misdirected by the Justice Department, and that the whole basis of the trial was a false one. All but one of the indictments were never formally presented, so I had no opportunity to defend myself. You understand that, Malek? The selection of the capital penalty for one count was purely arbitrary.'

Malek nodded, moving a piece. 'So you have explained, Mr Constantin. I am afraid I do not have a legalistic turn of mind.'

'There's no need for you to,' Constantin assured him. 'The point is obvious. I hope it may be possible to appeal against the court's decision and ask for a re-trial' Constantin gestured with a piece. 'I criticise myself for accepting the indictments so readily. In effect I made no attempt to defend myself. If only I had done so I am convinced I should have been found innocent.'

Malek murmured non-committally, and gestured towards the board. Constantin resumed play. Most of the games he consistently lost to Malek, but this no longer troubled him and, if anything, only served to reinforce the bonds between them.

Constantin had decided not to ask the supervisor to inform the Justice Department of his request for a re-trial until he had convinced Malek that his case left substantial room for doubt. A premature application would meet with an automatic negative from Malek, whatever his private sympathies. Conversely, once Malek was firmly on his side he would be prepared to risk his reputation with his seniors, and indeed his championing of Constantin's cause would be convincing proof in itself of the latter's innocence.

As Constantin soon found from his one-sided discussions with Malek, arguing over the legal technicalities of the trial, with their infinitely subtle nuances and implications, was an unprofitable method of enlisting Malek's support and he realised that he would have to do so by sheer impress of personality, by his manner, bearing and general conduct, and above all by his confidence of his innocence in the face of the penalty which might at any moment be imposed upon him. Curiously, this latter pose was not as difficult to maintain as might have been expected; Constantin already felt a surge of conviction in his eventual escape from the villa. Sooner or later Malek would recognise the authenticity of this inner confidence.

To begin with, however, the supervisor remained his usual phlegmatic self. Constantin talked away at him from morning to evening, every third word affirming the probability of his being found 'innocent', but Malek merely nodded with a faint smile and continued to play his errorless chess.

'Malek, I don't want you to think that I challenge the competence of the court to try the charges against me, or that I hold it in disrespect,' he said to the supervisor as they played their usual morning board some two weeks after the incident on the verandah. 'Far from it. But the court must make its decisions within the context of the evidence presented by the prosecutor. And even then, the greatest imponderable remains — the role of the accused. In my case I was, to all intents, not present at the trial, so my innocence is established by *force majeure*. Don't you agree, Malek?'

Malek's eyes searched the pieces on the board, his lips pursing thinly. 'I'm afraid this is above my head, Mr Constantin. Naturally I accept the authority of the court without question.'

'But so do I, Malek. I've made that plain. The real question is simply whether the verdict was justified in the light of the new circumstances I am describing.'

Malek shrugged, apparently more interested in the end-game before them. 'I recommend you to accept the verdict, Mr Constantin. For your peace of mind, you understand.'

Constantin looked away with a gesture of impatience. 'I don't agree, Malek. Besides, a great deal is at stake.' He glanced up at the windows which were drumming in the cold autumn wind. The casements were slightly loose, and the air lanced around them. The villa was poorly heated, only the single radiator in the lounge warming the three rooms downstairs. Already Constantin dreaded the winter. His hands and feet were perpetually cold and he could find no means of warming them.

'Malek, is there any chance of obtaining another heater?' he asked. 'It's none too warm in here. I have a feeling it's going to be a particularly cold winter.'

Malek looked up from the board, his bland grey eyes regarding Constantin with a flicker of curiosity, as if this last remark were one of the few he had heard from Constantin's lips which contained any overtones whatever.

'It is cold,' he agreed at last. 'I will see if I can borrow a heater. This villa is closed for most of the year.'

Constantin pestered him for news of the heater during the following week — partly because the success of his request would have symbolised Malek's first concession to him — but it failed to materialise. After one palpably lame excuse Malek merely ignored his further reminders. Outside, in the garden, the leaves whirled about the stones in a vortex of chilling air, and overhead the low clouds raced seaward. The two men in the lounge hunched over their chessboard by the radiator, hands buried in their pockets between moves.

Perhaps it was this darkening weather which made Constantin impatient of Malek's slowness in seeing the point of his argument, and he made his first suggestions that Malek should transmit a formal request for a re-trial to his superiors at the Department of Justice.

'You speak to someone on the telephone every morning, Malek,' he pointed out when Malek demurred. 'There's no difficulty involved. If you're afraid of compromising yourself — though I would have thought that a small price to pay in view of what is at stake — the orderly can pass on a message.'

'It's not feasible, Mr Constantin.' Malek seemed at last to be tiring of the subject. 'I suggest that you — '

'Malek!' Constantin stood up and paced around the lounge. 'Don't you realise that you must? You're literally my only means of contact, if you refuse I'm absolutely powerless, there's no hope of getting a reprieve!'

'The trial has already taken place, Mr Constantin,' Malek pointed out patiently.

'It was a mis-trial! Don't you understand, Malek, I accepted that I was guilty when in fact I was completely innocent!'

Malek looked up from the board, his eyebrows lifting. '*Completely* innocent Mr Constantin?'

Constantin snapped his fingers. 'Well, virtually innocent. At least in terms of the indictment and trial.'

'But that is merely a technical difference, Mr Constantin. The Department of Justice is concerned with absolutes.'

'Quite right, Malek. I agree entirely.' Constantin nodded approvingly at the supervisor and privately noted his quizzical expression, the first time Malek had displayed a taste for irony.

He was to notice this fresh leit-motiv recurringly during the next days; whenever he raised the subject of his request for a re-trial Malek would counter with one of his deceptively naïve queries, trying to establish some minor tangential point, almost as if he were leading Constantin on to a fuller admission. At first Constantin assumed that the supervisor was fishing for infor-mation about other members of the hierarchy which he wished to use for his own purposes, but the few titbits he offered were ignored by Malek, and it dawned upon him that Malek was genuinely interested in establishing the sincerity of Constantin's conviction of his own innocence.

He showed no signs, however, of being prepared to contact his superiors at the Department of Justice, and Constantin's impatience continued to mount. He now used their morning and afternoon chess sessions as an opportunity to hold forth at length on the subject of the shortcomings of the judicial system, using his own case as an illustration, and hammered away at the theme of his innocence, even hinting that Malek might find himself held responsible if by any mischance he was not granted a reprieve.

'The position I find myself in is really most extraordinary,' he told Malek almost exactly two months after his arrival at the villa. 'Everyone else is satisfied with the court's verdict, and yet I alone know that I am innocent. I feel very like someone who is about to be buried alive.'

Malek managed a thin smile across the chess-pieces. 'Of course, Mr Constantin, it is possible to convince oneself of any-thing, given a sufficient incentive.'

'But Malek, I assure you,' Constantin insisted, ignoring the board and concentrating his whole attention upon the supervisor, 'this is no death-cell repentance. Believe me, I know. I have examined the entire case from a thousand perspectives, ques-tioned every possible motive. There is no doubt in my mind. I may once have been prepared to accept the possibility of my guilt but I realise now that I was entirely mistaken — experience encourages us to take too great a responsibility for ourselves, when we fall short of our ideals we become critical of ourselves and ready to assume that we are at fault. How dangerous that can be, Malek, I now know. Only the truly innocent man can really understand the meaning of guilt.'

Constantin stopped and sat back, a slight weariness overtaking him in the cold room. Malek was nodding slowly, a thin and not altogether unsympathetic smile on his lips as if he understood everything Constantin had said. Then he moved a piece, and with a murmured 'excuse me' left his seat and went out of the room.

Drawing the lapels of the dressing-gown around his chest, Constantin studied the board with a desultory eye. He noticed that Malek's move appeared to be the first bad one he had made in all their games together, but he felt too tired to make the most of his opportunity. His brief speech to Malek, confirming all he believed, now left nothing more to be said. From now on whatever happened was up to Malek.

'Mr Constantin.'

He turned in his chair and, to his surprise, saw the supervisor standing in the doorway, wearing his long grey overcoat.

'Malek — ?' For a moment Constantin felt his heart gallop, and then controlled himself. 'Malek, you've agreed at last, you're going to take me to the Department?'

Malek shook his head, his eyes staring sombrely at Constantin. 'Not exactly. I thought we might look at the garden, Mr Constantin. A breath of fresh air, it will do you good.'

'Of course, Malek, it's kind of you.' Constantin rose a little unsteadily to his feet, and tightened the cord of his dressing-gown. 'Pardon my wild hopes.' He tried to smile at Malek, but the supervisor stood by the door, hands in his overcoat pockets, his eyes lowered fractionally from Constantin's face.

They went out on to the verandah towards the french windows. Outside the cold morning air whirled in frantic circles around the small stone yard, the leaves spiralling upwards into the dark sky. To Constantin there seemed little point in going out into the garden, but Malek stood behind him, one hand on the latch.

'Malek.' Something made him turn and face the supervisor. 'You do understand what I mean, when I say I am absolutely innocent. I *know* that.'

'Of course, Mr Constantin.' The supervisor's face was relaxed and almost genial. 'I understand. When you know you are innocent, then you are guilty.'

His hand opened the verandah door on to the whirling leaves.

II

BIZARRE CHESSMEN

Chess is like war on a board. The object is to crush the other man's mind. I like to see them squirm.

Bobby Fischer,
World Champion, 1972-1975

From the time when chess began to evolve, its pieces have been made in many different sizes and styles, including weird and wonderful figures and creatures. There was one enormous set which was described by an Arab historian writing in AD 950. 'By far the most frequent use of ivory is for the manufacture of men for chess,' he stated. 'Several of the chessmen are figures of men and animals, a span high and big, or even more. During the game a man stands by, specially to carry the men from one square to another.'

Nor is this just an ancient phenomenon, for in the Victorian era a number of giant-size sets were produced in an attempt to make the game more of a 'spectator sport'. According to a report in the Daily Telegraph of 1884, 'These gigantic men are fitted to serve in carrying out a suggestion made for equipping public parks with chessboards of such size that spectators on an elevated mall could follow the game.'

The idea was also tried in America in the 1930s, when pieces the size of a small man were carved from wood to be played on square paving stones which could be set into any suburban lawn and form a playing surface of grass and stone about twenty feet across. Other examples of this kind have also been reported more recently in Russia, Italy, Spain and Australia.

Chessmen which come to life are featured in the first story, 'The Queen of the Red Chessmen' by Lucretia Peabody Hale (1820-1900), the American author of the children's classic, The Peterkin Papers (1880) and sister of the famous preacher and novelist, Edward Everett Hale, who wrote The Man Without a Country (1863). Miss Hale was something of a pioneer female chess-player in the United States and was apparently fascinated by the allegorical sets that were made in the nineteenth century, on such themes as Good versus Evil, the Church versus the Devil, and the Court of Love versus the Court of Mephistopheles. It was this which inspired her to write 'The Queen of the Red

Chessmen', which was published in *Atlantic Monthly* magazine in February 1858 and has not been reprinted since.

It is interesting to note that many chess sets have been made over the years based on warring nations: in England, for instance, pieces resembling Roman soldiers and others representing Crusaders were popular in the eighteenth century, while in France chessmen depicting Napoleon's campaigns in Egypt were much admired by players a hundred years ago. Even as I write, a special edition of the Waterloo Chess Set, with the pieces crafted in pewter and layered with 22 carat gold and sterling silver, their pedestal bases embellished with a circular band of blue for the French and scarlet for the Allies, is being marketed to commemorate the 175th anniversary of the 'battle that shaped the modern world'.

The fiction of talking chess-pieces leads conveniently to the fact of real people being used as chessmen — a phenomenon which once again can be found recorded in chess history, particularly during the first half of this century. Indeed, there was something of a vogue for 'live chess' in Britain, France and America; a vogue which the Hollywood film-makers took up and utilised in a number of musical films.

Among the most famous games of this kind was an annual event in the city of Prague in Czechoslovakia, where the Battle of Kuttenberg on January 6, 1422, was re-enacted by human chess-pieces. Unfortunately, this was halted by the outbreak of the First World War. In 1931, a similar grand game of living chess was staged at the Colonial Exhibition in Paris, with black soldiers taking the parts of the black chessmen!

The innocently titled story 'A Game of Chess' is actually about a very deadly game of living chess, and the enthusiast who brought it to my attention wondered if the author's inspiration might have been the appalling games played by an Algerian bey who ordered his human chessmen to be beheaded as soon as they were captured! The author of the tale, Robert Barr (1850-1912) was a prolific journalist, a world traveller, and co-editor with the great Jerome K. Jerome of the pioneer humour magazine, *The Idler*. He is also remembered in the history of the detective story genre as the author of *The Triumphs of Eugene Valmont* (1906), about a pernickety little French sleuth believed by some experts to have inspired Agatha Christie's Hercule Poirot.

There is, sadly, nothing on record about Robert Barr's own

involvement in chess, although the details in his story indicated that he must have had more than a passing interest in the game. The plot of 'A Game of Chess' has been described by the American Fantasy authority, Sam Moskowitz, as 'a unique tale of murder by an ingenious scientific method approaching science fiction', and it has certainly lost nothing of its ability to shock in the ninety years since it was first published in *Pearson's Magazine* of March 1900.

'A Set of Chessmen' is an equally innocuous-sounding title, disguising a chilling story of some pieces which once belonged to a deceased chess fiend who still continues to play games 'through' them. It is another first class tale from Richard Marsh (1857-1915), the author of *The Beetle* (1897), a horror novel about a female who can turn into a large insect, which has been compared by several experts to Bram Stoker's classic, *Dracula*. Marsh was apparently a collector of chess sets, and pride of place in his study was given to a set from America carved in the shapes of animals, ranging from lions as Kings to horses as Queens and dogs as pawns. There is no evidence, however, that he owned anything quite as sinister as the set in his story, which was first published in 1901.

Research had produced even less evidence about the background to 'The Haunted Chessmen' by Ernest Robertson Punshon (1872-1956). Punshon was a British playwright and mystery story writer who contributed to a number of the best known horror magazines in the Thirties, including *Weird Tales* and *Ghost Stories*. He may well have known all about chessmen made from ivory, wood, even solid silver and porcelain — but pieces made from *human bone*? For in his story a set made from human remains is the centrepiece of the action which concerns a man compelled to play, literally, for his life . . .

Fate also hangs in the balance in 'Bishop's Gambit' by August Derleth (1909-1971), the famous American regional writer and promoter of the works of H.P. Lovecraft. Derleth, who grew up in rural Sauk City, Wisconsin, started playing chess at the University of Winconsin, and later competed in state chess tournaments when his duties as writer and publisher permitted. 'Bishop's Gambit' pits a youngster against his mother's hated lover in a chess game for her affections — a contest he seems destined to lose until a totally unexpected chessmaster intervenes.

The title of the final story, 'The Immortal Game', will need no introduction to the keen chess-player, for it refers to the famous contest between Adolf Anderssen and Lionel Kieseritsky. But thanks to the imagination of Paul Anderson (1926-), one of today's leading writers of fantasy and science fiction, it has been used as the basis for a quite extraordinary tale which links the evolution of chess in the ancient civilisations with its possibilities in modern technology. Anderson, who has a degree in physics and a special interest in scientific numeracy, also brings to his tale an affection and knowledge of chess which makes it one of the most thought-provoking in the book.

THE QUEEN OF THE RED CHESSMEN

Lucretia Peabody Hale

The box of chessmen had been left open all night. That was a great oversight! For everybody knows that the contending chessmen are but too eager to fight their battles over again by midnight, if a chance is only allowed them.

It was at the Willows – so called, not because the house is surrounded by willows, but because a little clump of them hangs over the pond close by. It is a pretty place, with its broad lawn in front of the door-way, its winding avenue hidden from the road by high trees. It is a quiet place, too; the sun rests gently on the green lawn, and the drooping leaves of the willows hang heavily over the water.

No one would imagine what violent contests were going on under the still roof, this very night. It was the night of the first of May. The moon came silently out from the shadows; the trees were scarcely stirring. The box of chessmen had been left on the balcony steps by the drawing-room window, and the window, too, that warm night, had been left open. So, one by one, all the chessmen came out to fight over again their evening's battles.

It was a famously carved set of chessmen. The bishops wore their mitres, the knights, pranced on spirited steeds, the castles rested on the backs of elephants – even the pawns mimicked the private soldiers of an army. The skilful carver had given to each piece, and each pawn, too, a certain individuality. That night there had been a close contest. Two well-matched players had guided the game, and it had ended with leaving a deep irritation on the conquered side.

It was Isabella, the Queen of the Red Chessmen, who had been obliged to yield. She was young and proud, and it was she, indeed, who held the rule; for her father, the old Red King, had grown too imbecile to direct affairs; he merely bore the name of sovereignty. And Isabella was loved by knights, pawns, and all; the bishops were willing to die in her cause, the castles would have crumbled to earth for her. Opposed to her, stood the detested White Queen. All the Whites, of course, were despised by her; but the haughty, self-sufficient queen angered her most.

The White Queen was reigning during the minority of her only son. The White Prince had reached the age of nineteen, but the strong mind of his mother had kept him always under restraint. A simple youth, he had always yielded to her control. He was pure-hearted and gentle, but never ventured to make a move of his own. He sought shelter under cover of his castles, while his more energetic mother went forth at the head of his army. She was dreaded by her subjects – never loved by them. Her own pawn, it is true, had ventured much for her sake, had often with his own life redeemed her from captivity; but it was loyalty that bound even him – no warmer feeling of devotion or love.

The Queen Isabella was the first to come out from her prison.

'I will stay here no longer,' she cried; 'the blood of the Reds grows pale in this inactivity.'

She stood upon the marble steps; the May moon shone down upon her. She listened a moment to a slight murmuring within the drawing-room window. The Spanish lady, the Murillo-painted Spanish lady, had come down from her frame that bound her against the wall. Just for this one night in the year, she stepped out from the canvas to walk up and down the rooms majestically. She would not exchange a word with anybody; nobody understood her language. She could remember when Murillo looked at her, watched over her, created her with his pencil. She could have nothing to say to little paltry shepherd-esses, and other articles of *virtu*, that came into grace and motion just at this moment.

The Queen of the Red Chessmen turned away, down into the avenue. The May moon shone upon her. Her feet trod upon unaccustomed ground; no black or white square hemmed her in; she felt a new liberty.

'My poor old father!' she exclaimed, 'I will leave him behind; better let him slumber in an ignoble repose than wander over the board, a laughing-stock for his enemies. We have been conquered – the foolish White Prince rules!'

A strange inspiration stole upon her; the breath of the May night hovered over her; the May moon shone upon her. She could move without waiting for the will of another; she was free. She passed down the avenue; she had left her old prison behind.

Early in the morning, – it was just after sunrise, – the kind

Doctor Lester was driving home, after watching half the night
out with a patient. He passed the avenue to the Willows, but
drew up his horse just as he was leaving the entrance. He saw
a young girl sitting under the hedge. She was without any
bonnet, in a red dress, fitting closely and hanging heavily about
her. She was so very beautiful, she looked so strangely lost and
out of place here at this early hour, that the doctor could not
resist speaking to her.

'My child, how came you here?'

The young girl rose up, and looked round with uncertainty.

'Where am I?' she asked.

She was very tall and graceful, with an air of command, but
with a strange, wild look in her eyes.

'The young woman must be slightly insane,' thought the
doctor; 'but she cannot have wandered far.'

'Let me take you home,' he said aloud. 'Perhaps you come
from the Willows?'

'Oh, don't take me back there!' cried Isabella, 'they will im-
prison me again! I had rather be a slave than a conquered queen!'

'Decidedly insane!' thought the doctor. 'I must take her back
to the Willows.'

He persuaded the young girl to let him lift her into his chaise.
She did not resist him; but when he turned up the avenue, she
leaned back in despair. He was fortunate enough to find one of
the servants up at the house, just sweeping the steps of the hall-
door. Getting out of his chaise, he said confidentially to the
servant,

'I have brought back your young lady.'

'Our young lady!' exclaimed the man, as the doctor pointed
out Isabella.

'Yes, she is a little insane, is she not?'

'She is not our young lady,' answered the servant; we have
nobody in the house just now, but Mr and Mrs Fogerty, and Mrs
Fogerty's brother, the old geologist.

'Where did she come from?' inquired the doctor.

'I never saw her before,' said the servant, 'and I certainly
should remember. There's some foreign folks live down in the
cottage, by the railroad; but they are not the like of her!'

The doctor got into his chaise again, bewildered.

'My child,' he said, 'you must tell me where you came from.'

'Oh, don't let me go back again!' said Isabella, clasping her
hands imploringly. 'Think how hard it must be never to take a

move of one's own! To know how the game might be won, then see it lost through folly! Oh, that last game, lost through utter weakness! There was that one move! Why did he not push me down to the king's row? I might have checkmated the White Prince, shut in by his own castles and pawns – it would have been a direct checkmate! Think of his folly! he stopped to take the queen's pawn with his bishop, and within one move of a checkmate!'

'Quite insane!' repeated the doctor. 'But I must have my breakfast. She seems quiet; I think I can keep her till after breakfast, and then I must try and find where the poor child's friends live. I don't know what Mrs Lester will think of her.'

They rode on. Isabella looked timidly round.

'You don't quite believe me,' she said, at last. 'It seems strange to you.'

'It does,' answered the doctor, 'seem very strange.'

'Not stranger than to me,' said Isabella – 'it is so very grand to me! All this motion! Look down at that great field there, not cut up into squares! If I only had my knights and squires there! I would be willing to give her as good a field, too; but I would show her where the true bravery lies. What a place for the castles, just to defend that pass!'

The doctor whipped up his horse.

Mrs Lester was a little surprised at the companion her husband had brought home to breakfast with him.

'Who is it?' she whispered.

'That I don't know – I shall have to find out,' he answered, a little nervously.

'Where is her bonnet?' asked Mrs Lester; this was the first absence of conventionality she had noticed.

'You had better ask her,' answered the doctor.

But Mrs Lester preferred leaving her guest in the parlour while she questioned her husband. She was somewhat disturbed when she found he had nothing more satisfactory to tell her.

'An insane girl! and what shall we do with her?' she asked.

'After breakfast I will make some inquiries about her,' answered the doctor.

'And leave her alone with us? that will never do! You must take her away directly – at least to the Insane Asylum – somewhere! What if she should grow wild while you were gone? She might kill us all! I will go in and tell her that she cannot stay here.'

On returning to the parlour, she found Isabella looking dreamily out of the window. As Mrs Lester approached, she turned.

'You will let me stay with you a little while, will you not?'

She spoke in a quiet tone, with an air somewhat commanding. It imposed upon nervous little Mrs Lester. But she made a faint struggle.

'Perhaps you would rather go home,' she said.

'I have no home now,' said Isabella; 'some time I may recover it; but my throne has been usurped.'

Mrs Lester looked round in alarm, to see if the doctor were near.

'Perhaps you had better come in to breakfast,' she suggested.

She was glad to place the doctor between herself and their new guest.

Celia Lester, the only daughter, came downstairs. She had heard that her father had picked up a lost girl in the road. As she came down in her clean morning dress, she expected to have to hold her skirts away from some little squalid object of charity. She started when she saw the elegant-looking young girl who sat at the table. There was something in her air and manner that seemed to make the breakfast equipage, and the furniture of the room about her, look a little mean and poor. Yet the doctor was very well off, and Mrs Lester fancied she had everything quite in style. Celia stole into her place, feeling small in the presence of the stranger.

After breakfast, when the doctor had somewhat refreshed himself by its good cheer from his last night's fatigue, Isabella requested to speak to him.

'Let me stay with you a little while,' she asked, beseechingly; 'I will do everything for you that you desire. You shall teach me anything; I know I can learn all that you will show me, all that Mrs Lester will tell me.'

'Perhaps so – perhaps that will be best,' answered the doctor, 'until your friends inquire for you; then I must send you back to them.'

'Very well,very well,' said Isabella, relieved. 'But I must tell you they will not inquire for me. I see you will not believe my story. If you only would listen to me, I could tell it all to you.'

'That is the only condition I can make with you,' answered the doctor, 'that you will not tell your story – that you will never even think of it yourself. I am a physician. I know that it is not good for you to dwell upon such things. Do not talk of them to me, nor to my wife or daughter. Never speak of your story to anyone who comes here. It will be better for you.'

'Better for me,' said Isabella, dreamily, 'that no one should know! Perhaps so. I am, in truth, captive to the White Prince; and if he should come and demand me – I should be half afraid to try the risks of another game.'

'Stop, stop!' exclaimed the doctor, 'you are already forgetting the condition. I shall be obliged to take you away to some retreat, unless you promise me — '

'Oh, I will promise you anything,' interrupted Isabella; 'and you will see that I can keep my promise.'

Meanwhile Mrs Lester and Celia had been holding a consultation.

'I think she must be someone in disguise,' suggested Celia.

Celia was one of the most unromantic of persons. Both she and her mother had passed their lives in an unvarying routine of duties. Neither of them had ever found time from their sewing even to read. Celia had her books of history laid out, that she meant to take up when she should get through her work; but it seemed hopeless that this time would ever come. It had never come to Mrs Lester, and she was now fifty years old. Celia had never read any novels. She had tried to read them, but never was interested in them. So she had a vague idea of what romance was, conceiving of it only as something quite different from her everyday life. For this reason the unnatural event that was taking place this very day was gradually appearing to her something possible and natural. Because she knew there was such a thing as romance, and that it was something quite beyond her comprehension, she was the more willing to receive this event quietly from finding it incomprehensible.

'We can let her stay here today, at least,' said Mrs Lester. 'We will keep John at work in the front door-yard, in case we should want him. And I will set Mrs Anderson's boy to weeding in the border; we can call him, if we should want to send for help.'

She was quite ashamed of herself, when she had uttered these words, and Isabella walked into the room, so composed, so refined in her manners.

'The doctor says I may stay here a little while, if you will let me,' said Isabella, as she took Mrs Lester's hands.

'We will try to make you comfortable,' replied Mrs Lester.

'He says you will teach me many things – I think he said, how to sew.'

'How to sew! Was it possible she did not know how to sew?' Celia thought to herself. 'How many servants she must have had, never to have learned how to sew herself!'

And this occupation was directly provided, while the doctor set forth on his day's duties, and at the same time to inquire about the strange apparition of the young girl. He was so convinced that there was a vein of insanity about her, that he was very sure that questioning her only excited her the more. Just as he had parted from her, some compunction seized her, and she followed him to the door.

'There is my father,' said she.

'Your father! where shall I find him?' asked the doctor.

'Oh, he could not help me,' she replied; 'it is a long time since he has been able to direct affairs. He has scarcely been conscious of my presence, and will hardly feel my absence, his mind is so weak.'

'But where can I find him?' persisted the doctor.

'He did not come out,' said Isabella; 'the White Queen would not allow it, indeed.'

'Stop, stop!' exclaimed the doctor, 'we are on forbidden ground.'

He drove away.

'So there is insanity in the family,' he thought to himself. 'I am quite interested in this case. A new form of monomania! I should be quite sorry to lose sight of it. I shall be loath to give her up to her friends.'

But he was not yet put to that test. No one could give him any light with regard to the strange girl. He went first to the Willows, and found there so much confusion that he could hardly persuade any one to listen to his questions. Mrs Fogerty's brother, the geologist, had been riding that morning, and had fallen from his horse and broken his leg. The doctor arrived just in time to be of service in setting it. Then he must linger some time to see that the old gentleman was comfortable, so that he was obliged to stay nearly the whole morning. He was much amused at the state of disturbance in which he left the family. The whole house was in confusion, looking after some lost chessmen.

'There was nothing,' said Mrs Fogerty, apologetically, 'that would soothe her brother so much as a game of chess. That, perhaps, might keep him quiet. He would be willing to play chess with Mr Fogerty by the day together. It was so strange! they had a game the night before, and now some of the pieces could not be found. Her brother had lost the game, and today he was so eager to take his revenge!'

'How absurd!' thought the doctor; 'what trifling things people interest themselves in! Here is this old man more disturbed at losing his game of chess than he is at breaking his leg! It is different in my profession, where one deals with life and death. Here is this young girl's fate in my hands, and they talk to me of the loss of a few paltry chessmen!'

The 'foreign people' at the cottage knew nothing of Isabella. No one had seen her the night before, or at any time. Dr Lester even drove ten miles to Dr Giles' Retreat for the Insane, to see if it were possible that a patient could have wandered away from there. Dr Giles was deeply interested in the account Dr Lester gave. He would very gladly take such a person under his care.

'No,' said Dr Lester, 'I will wait awhile. I am interested in the young girl. It is not possible but that I shall in time find out from her, by chance, perhaps, who her friends are, and where she came from. She must have wandered away in some delirium of fever – but it is very strange, for she appears perfectly calm now. Yet I hardly know in what state I shall find her.'

He returned to find her very quiet and calm, learning from his wife and daughter how to sew. She seemed deeply interested in this new occupation, and had given all her time and thought to it. Celia and her mother privately confided to the doctor their admiration of their strange guest. Her ways were so graceful and beautiful! All that she said seemed so new and singular! The doctor, before he went away, had exhorted Mrs Lester and Celia to ask her no questions about her former life, and everything had gone on very smoothly. And everything went on as smoothly for some weeks. Isabella seemed willing to be as silent as the doctor, upon all exciting subjects. She appeared to be quite taken up with her sewing, much to Mrs Lester's delight.

'She will turn out quite as good a seamstress as Celia,' said she to the doctor. 'She sews steadily all the time, and nothing seems to please her so much as to finish a piece of work. She will be able to do much more than her own sewing, and may prove quite a help to us.'

'I shall be very glad,' said the doctor, 'if anything can be a help, to prevent you and Celia from working yourselves to death. I shall be glad if you can ever have done with that eternal sewing. It is time that Celia should do something about cultivating her mind.'

'Celia's mind is so well regulated,' interrupted Mrs Lester.

'We won't discuss that,' continued the doctor – 'we never come to an agreement there. I was going on to say that I am becoming so interested in Isabella, that I feel towards her as if she were my own. If she is of help to the family, that is very well – it is the best thing for her to be able to make herself of use. But I don't care to make any profit to ourselves out of her help. Somehow I begin to think of her as belonging to us. Certainly she belongs to nobody else. Let us treat her as our own child. We have but one, yet God has given us means enough to care for many more. I confess I should find it hard to give Isabella up to anyone else. I like to find her when I come home – it is pleasant to look at her.'

'And I, too, love her,' said Mrs Lester. 'I like to see her as she sits quietly at her work.'

So Isabella went on learning what it was to be one of the family, and becoming, as Mrs Lester remarked, a very experienced seamstress. She seldom said anything as she sat at her work, but seemed quite occupied with her sewing; while Mrs Lester and Celia kept up a stream of conversation, seldom addressing Isabella, as, indeed, they had few topics in common.

One day, Celia and Isabella were sitting together.

'Have you always sewed?' asked Isabella.

'Oh yes,' answered Celia – 'since I was quite a child.'

'And do you remember when you were a child?' asked Isabella, laying down her work.

'Oh yes, indeed,' said Celia; 'I used to make all my doll's dresses myself.'

'Your doll's dresses!' repeated Isabella.

'Oh, yes,' replied Celia – 'I was not ashamed to play with doll's in that way.'

'I should like to see some dolls,' said Isabella.

'I will show you my large doll,' said Celia; 'I have always kept it, because I fitted it out with such a nice set of clothes. And I keep it for children to play with.'

She brought her doll, and Isabella handled it and looked at it with curiosity.

'So you dressed this, and played with it,' said Isabella, inquiringly, 'and moved it about as one would move a piece at chess?'

Celia started at this word 'chess'. It was one of the forbidden words. But Isabella went on:

'Suppose this doll should suddenly have begun to speak, to move, and walk round, would not you have liked it?'

'Oh, no!' exclaimed Celia. 'What! a wooden thing speak and move! It would have frightened me very much.'

'Why should it not speak, if it has a mouth, and walk, if it has feet?' asked Isabella.

'What foolish questions you ask!' exclaimed Celia, 'of course it has not life.'

'Oh, life – that is it!' said Isabella. 'Well, what is life?'

'Life! why it is what makes us live,' answered Celia. 'Of course you know what life is.'

'No, I don't know,' said Isabella, 'but I have been thinking about it lately, while I have been sewing – what it is.'

'But you should not think, you should talk more, Isabella,' said Celia. 'Mamma and I talk while we are at work, but you are always very silent.'

'But you think sometimes?' asked Isabella.

'Not about such things,' replied Celia. 'I have to think about my work.'

'But your father thinks, I suppose, when he comes home and sits in his study alone?'

'Oh, he reads when he goes into his study – he reads books and studies them,' said Celia.

'Do you know how to read?' asked Isabella.

'Do I know how to read!' cried Celia angrily.

'Forgive me,' said Isabella, quickly, 'but I never saw you reading. I thought perhaps – women are so different here!'

She did not finish her sentence, for she saw Celia was really angry. Yet she had no idea of hurting her feelings. She had tried to accommodate herself to her new circumstances. She had observed a great deal, and had never been in the habit of asking questions. Celia was disturbed at having it supposed that she did not know how to read; therefore it must be a very important thing to know how to read, and she determined she must learn. She applied to the doctor. He was astonished at her entire ignorance, but he was very glad to help her. Isabella gave herself up to her reading, as she had done before to her sewing. The doctor was now the gainer. All the time he was away, Isabella sat in his study, poring over her books; when he returned, she had a famous lesson to recite to him. Then he began to tell her of books that he was interested in. He made Celia come in, for a history class. It was such a pleasure to him to find Isabella interested in what he could tell her of history!

'All this really happened,' said Isabella to Celia once – 'these people really lived!'

'Yes, but they died,' responded Celia, in an indifferent tone – 'and ever so long ago, too!'

'But did they die,' asked Isabella, 'if we can talk about them, and imagine how they looked? They live for us as much as they did then.'

'That I can't understand,' said Celia. 'My uncle saw Napoleon when he was in Europe, long ago. But I never saw Napoleon. He is dead and gone to me, just as much as Alexander the Great.'

'Well, who does live, if Alexander the Great, if Napoleon, and Columbus do not live?' asked Isabella impatiently.

'Why, papa and mama live,' answered Celia, 'and you – '

'And the butcher,' interrupted Isabella, 'because he brings you meat to eat; and Mr Spool, because he keeps the thread store. Thank you for putting me in, too! Once — '

'Once!' answered Celia, in a dignified tone, 'I suppose once you lived in a grander circle, and it appears to you we have nobody better than Mr Spool and the butcher.'

Isabella was silent, and thought of her 'circle', her former circle. The circle here was large enough, the circumference not very great, but there were as many points in it as in a larger one. There were pleasant, motherly Mrs Gibbs, and her agreeable daughters – the Gresham boys, just in from college – the Misses Tarletan, fresh from a New York boarding-school – Mr Lovell, the young minister – and the old Misses Pendleton, that made raspberry jam – together with Celia's particular friends, Anna and Selina Mountfort, who had a great deal of talking with Celia in private, but not a word to say to anybody in the parlour. All these, with many others in the background, had been speculating upon the riddle that Isabella presented – 'Who was she? and where did she come from?'

Nobody found any satisfactory answer. Neither Celia nor her mother would disclose anything. It is a great convenience in keeping a secret, not to know what it is. One can't easily tell what one does not know.

'The doctor really has a treasure in his wife and daughter,' said Mrs Gibbs, 'they keep his secrets so well! Neither of them will lisp a word about this handsome Isabella.'

'I have no doubt she is the daughter of an Italian refugee,' said one of the Misses Tarletan. 'We saw a number of Italian refugees in New York.'

This opinion became prevalent in the neighbourhood. That Dr Lester should be willing to take charge of an unknown girl did not astonish those who knew of his many charitable deeds. It was not more than he had done for his cousin's child. He had adopted Lawrence Egerton, educated him, sent him to college, and was giving him every advantage in his study of the law. In the end Lawrence would probably marry Celia and the pretty property that the doctor would leave behind for his daughter.

'She is one of my patients,' the doctor would say, to anyone who asked him about her.

The tale that she was the daughter of an Italian refugee became more rife after Isabella had begun to study Italian. She liked to have the musical Italian words linger on her tongue. She quoted Italian poetry, read Italian history. In conversation, she generally talked of the present, rarely of the past or of the future. She listened with wonder to those who had a talent for reminiscence. How rich their past must be, that they should be willing to dwell in it! Her own she thought very meagre. If she wanted to live in the past, it must be in the past of great men, not in that of her own little self. So she read of great painters and great artists, and because she read of them she talked of them. Other people, in referring to bygone events, would say 'When I was in Trenton last summer,' – 'In Cuba the spring that we were there'; but Isabella would say, 'When Raphael died, or when Dante lived.' Everybody liked to talk with her – laughed with her at her enthusiasm. There was something inspiring, too, in this enthusiasm; it compelled attention, as her air and manner always attracted notice. By her side, the style and elegance of the Misses Tarletan faded out; here was a moon that quite extinguished the light of their little tapers. She became the centre of admiration; the young girls admired her, as they are prone to admire some one particular star. She never courted attention, but it was always given.

'Isabella attracts everybody,' said Celia to her mother. 'Even the old Mr Spencers, who have never been touched by woman before, follow her, and act just as she wills.'

Little Celia who had been quite a belle hitherto, sunk into the shade by the side of the brilliant Isabella. Yet she followed willingly in the sunny wake that Isabella left behind. She expanded somewhat, herself, for she was quite ashamed to know nothing of all that Isabella talked about so earnestly. The sewing gave place to a little reading, to Mrs Lester's horror. The Mountforts and the Gibbses met with Isabella and Celia to read and study, and went into town with them to lectures and to concerts.

A winter passed away and another summer came. Still Isabella was at Dr Lester's; and with the lapse of time the harder did it become for the doctor to question her of her past history – the more, too, was she herself weaned from it.

The young people had been walking in the gardens one evening.

'Let me sit by you here in the porch,' said Lawrence Egerton to Celia – 'I want rest, for body and spirit. I am always in a battle-field when I am talking with Isabella. I must either fight with her or against her. She insists on my fighting all the time. I have to keep my weapons bright, ready for use, every moment. She will lead me, too, in conversation, sends me here, orders me there. I feel like a poor knight in chess, under the sway of a queen —'

'I don't know anything about chess,' said Celia, curtly.

'It is a comfort to have you a little ignorant,' said Lawrence. 'Please stay in bliss awhile. It is repose, it is refreshment. Isabella drags one into the company of her heroes, and then one feels completely ashamed not to be on more familiar terms with them all. Her Mazzinis, her Tancreds, heroes false and true – it makes no difference to her – put one into a whirl between history and story. What a row she would make in Italy, if she went back there!'

'What could we do without her?' said Celia. 'It was so quiet and commonplace before she came!'

'That is the trouble,' replied Lawrence, 'Isabella won't let anything remain commonplace. She pulls everything out of its place – makes a hero or heroine out of a piece of clay. I don't want to be in heroics all the time. Even Homer's heroes ate their suppers comfortably. I think it was a mistake in your father, bringing her here. Let her stay in her sphere queening it, and leave us poor mortals to our bread and butter.'

'You know you don't think so,' expostulated Celia; 'you worship her shoe-tie, the hem of her garment.'

'But I don't want to,' said Lawrence — 'it is a compulsory worship. I had rather be quiet.'

'Lazy Lawrence!' cried Celia, 'it is better for you. You would be the first to miss Isabella. You would find us quite flat without her brilliancy, and would be hunting after some other excitement.'

'Perhaps so,' said Lawrence. 'But here she comes to goad us on again. Queen Isabella, when do the bull-fights begin?'

'I wish I were Queen Isabella!' she exclaimed. 'Have you read the last accounts from Spain? I was reading them to the doctor today. Nobody knows what to do there. Only think what an opportunity for the Queen to show herself such a queen! Why will not she make of herself such a queen as the great Isabella of Castile was?'

'I can't say,' answered Lawrence.

'Queens rule in chess,' said Horace Gresham. 'I always wondered that the king was made such a poor character there. He is not only ruled by his cabinet, bishops, and knights, but his queen is by far the more warlike character.'

'Whoever plays the game rules – you or Mr Egerton,' said Isabella, bitterly; 'it is not the poor queen. She must yield to the power of the moving hand. I suppose it is so with us women. We see a great aim before us, but have not the power.'

'Nonsense!' exclaimed Lawrence, 'it is just the reverse. With some women – for I won't be personal – the aim, as you call it, is very small – a poor amusement, another dress, a larger house — '

'You may stop,' interrupted Isabella, 'for you don't believe this. At least, keep some of your flings for the women that deserve them; Celia and I don't accept them.'

'Then we'll talk of the last aim we were discussing – the ride tomorrow.'

The next winter was passed by Mrs Lester, her daughter, and Isabella in Cuba. Lawrence Egerton accompanied them thither, and the doctor hoped to go for them in the spring. They went on Mrs Lester's account. She had worn herself out with her household labours – very uselessly, the doctor thought – so he determined to send her away from them. Isabella and Celia were very happy all this winter and spring. With Isabella Spanish took the place of Italian studies. She liked talking in Spanish. They made some friends among the residents, as well as among the strangers, particularly the Americans. Of these last, they enjoyed most the society of Mrs Blanchard and her son, Otho, who were at the same hotel with them.

The opera, too, was a new delight to Isabella, and even Celia was excited by it.

'It is a little too absurd, to see the dying scene of Romeo and

Juliet sung out in an opera!' remarked Lawrence Egerton, one morning; 'all the music of the spheres could not have made that scene, last night, otherwise than supremely ridiculous.'

'I am glad you did not sit by us, then,' replied Celia; 'Isabella and I were crying.'

'I dare say,' said Lawrence. 'I should be afraid to take you to see a tragedy well acted. You would both be in hysterics before the killing was over.'

'I should be really afraid,' said Celia, 'to see Romeo and Juliet finely performed. It would be too sad.'

'It would be much better to end it up comfortably,' said Lawrence. 'Why should not Juliet marry her Romeo in peace?'

'It would be impossible!' exclaimed Isabella – 'impossible to bring together two such hostile families! Of course the result must be a tragedy.'

'In romances,' answered Lawrence, 'that may be necessary; but not in real life.'

'Why not in real life?' asked Isabella. 'When two thunder-clouds meet, there must be an explosion.'

'But we don't have such hostile families arrayed against each other now-a-days,' said Lawrence. 'The Bianchi and the Neri have died out; unless the feud lives between the whites and the blacks of the present day.'

'Are you sure that it has died out everywhere?' asked Isabella.

'Certainly not,' said Otho Blanchard; 'my mother, Bianca Bianco, inherits her name from a long line of ancestry, and with it come its hatreds as well as its loves.'

'You speak like an Italian or Spaniard,' said Lawrence. 'We are cold-blooded Yankees, and in our slow veins such passions do die out. I should have taken you for an American from your name.'

'It is our name Americanised; we have made Americans of ourselves, and the Bianchi have become the Blanchards.'

'The romance of the family, then,' persisted Lawrence, 'must needs become Americanised too. If you were to meet a lovely young lady of the enemy's race, I think you would be willing to bury your sword in the sheath for her sake.'

'I hope I should not forget the honour of my family,' said Otho. 'I certainly never could, as long as my mother lives; her feelings on the subject are stronger even than mine.'

'I cannot imagine the possibility of such feelings dying out,' said Iasbella. 'I cannot imagine such different elements amalgamating. It would be like fire and water uniting. Then there would be no longer any contest; the game of life would be over.'

'Why will you make out life to be a battle always?' exclaimed Lawrence; 'won't you allow us any peace? I do not find such contests all the time – never, except when I am fighting with you.'

'I had rather fight with you than against you,' said Iasbella, laughing. 'But when one is not striving, one is sleeping.'

'That reminds me that it is time for our siesta,' said Lawrence; 'so we need not fight any longer.'

Afterwards Isabella and Celia were talking of their new friend Otho.

'He does not seem to me like a Spaniard,' said Celia, 'his complexion is so light; then, too, his name sounds German.'

'But his passions are quick,' replied Isabella. 'How he coloured up when he spoke of the honour of his family!'

'I wonder that you like him,' said Celia; 'when he is with his mother, he hardly ventures to say his soul is his own.'

'I don't like his mother,' said Isabella; 'her manner is too imperious and unrefined, it appears to me. No wonder that Otho is ill at ease in her presence. It is evident that her way of talking is not agreeable to him. He is afraid that she will commit herself in some way.'

'But he never stands up for himself,' answered Celia; 'he always yields to her. Now I should not think you would like that.'

'He yields because she is his mother,' said Isabella; 'and it would not be becoming to contradict her.'

'He yields to you, too,' said Celia; 'how happens that?'

'I hope he does not yield to me more than is becoming,' answered Isabella, laughing; 'perhaps that is why I like him. After all, I don't care to be always sparring, as I am with Lawrence Egerton. With Otho I find that I agree wonderfully in many things. Neither of us yields to the other, neither of us is obliged to convince the other.'

'Now I should think you would find that stupid,' said Celia. 'What becomes of this desire of yours never to rest, always to be struggling after something?'

'We might strive together, we might struggle together,' responded Isabella.

She said this musingly, not in answer to Celia, but to her own thoughts – as she looked away, out from everything that surrounded her. The passion for ruling had always been upper-most in her mind; suddenly there dawned upon her the pleasure of being ruled. She became conscious of the pleasure of conquer-ing all things for the sake of giving all to another. A new sense of peace stole upon her mind. Before, she had felt herself alone, even in the midst of the kindness of the home that had been given her. She had never dared to think or to speak of the past, and as little of the future. She had gladly flung herself into the details of everyday life. She had given her mind to the study of all that it required. She loved the doctor, because he was always leading her on to fresh fields, always exciting her to a new knowledge. She loved him, too, for himself, for his tenderness and kindness to her. With Mrs Lester and Celia she felt herself on a different footing. They admired her, but they never came near her. She led them, and they were always behind her.

With Otho she experienced a new feeling. He seemed, very much as she did herself, out of place in the world just around him. He was a foreigner – was not yet acclimated to the society about him. He was willing to talk of other things than everyday events. He did not talk of 'things', indeed, but he speculated, as though he lived a separate life from that of mere eating and drinking. He was not content with what seemed to everyday people possible, but was willing to believe that there were things not dreamed of in their philosophy.

'It is a satisfaction,' said Lawrence once to Celia, 'that Isabella has found somebody who will go high enough into the clouds to suit her. Besides, it gives me a little repose.'

'And a secret jealousy at the same time; is it not so?' asked Celia. 'He takes up too much of Isabella's time to please you.'

'The reason he pleases her,' said Lawrence, 'is because he is more womanly than manly, and she thinks women ought to rule the world. Now if the world were made up of such as he, it would be very easily ruled. Isabella loves power too well to like to see it in others. Look at her when she is with Mrs Blanchard! It is a splendid sight to see them together!'

'How can you say so? I am always afraid of some outbreak.'

These families were, however, so much drawn together, that, when the doctor came to summon his wife and daughter and Isabella home, Mrs Blanchard was anxious to accompany them to New England. She wondered if it were not possible to find a country seat somewhere near the Lesters, that she could occupy for a time. The doctor knew that the Willows was to be vacant this spring. The Fogertys were all going to Europe, and would be very willing to let their place.

So it was arranged after their return. The Fogertys left for Europe, and Mrs Blanchard took possession of the Willows. It was a pleasant walking distance from the Lesters, but it was several weeks before Isabella made her first visit there. She was averse to going into the house, but, in company with Celia, Lawrence and Otho, walked about the grounds. Presently they stopped near a pretty fountain that was playing in the midst of the garden.

'That is a pretty place for an Undine,' said Otho.

'The idea of an Undine makes me shiver,' said Lawrence. 'Think what a cold-blooded, unearthly being she would be!'

'Not after she had a soul!' exclaimed Isabella.

'An Undine with a soul!' cried Lawrence. 'I conceive of them as malicious spirits, who live and die as the bubbles of water rise and fall.'

'You talk as if there were such things as Undines,' said Celia. 'I remember once trying to read the story of Undine, but I never could finish it.'

'It ends tragically,' remarked Otho.

'Of course all such stories must,' responded Lawrence; 'of course it is impossible to bring the natural and the unnatural together.'

'That depends upon what you call the natural,' said Otho.

'We should differ, I suppose,' said Lawrence, 'if we tried to explain what we each call the natural. I fancy your "real life" is different from mine.'

'Pictures of real life,' said Isabella, 'are sometimes pictures of horses and dogs, sometimes of children playing, sometimes of fruits of different seasons heaped upon one dish, sometimes of watermelons cut open.'

'That is hardly your picture of real life,' said Lawrence, laughing – 'a watermelon cut open! I think you would rather choose the picture of the Water Fairies from the Dusseldorf Gallery.'

'Why not?' said Isabella. 'The life we see must be very far from being the only life that is.'

'That is very true,' answered Lawrence; 'but let the fairies live their life by themselves, while we live our life in our own way. Why should they come to disturb our peace, since we cannot comprehend them, and they certainly cannot comprehend us?'

'You do not think it well, then,' said Isabella, stopping in their

walk, and looking down – 'you do not think it well that beings
of different natures should mingle?'

'I do not see how they can,' replied Lawrence. 'I am limited
by my senses; I can perceive only what they show me. Even my
imagination can picture to me only what my senses can paint.'

'Your senses!' cried Otho, contemptuously – 'it is very true, as
you confess, you are limited by your senses. Is all this beauty
around you created merely for you – and the other insects about
us? I have no doubt it is filled with invisible life.'

'Do let us go in!' said Celia. 'This talk, just at twilight, under
the shade of this shrubbery, makes me shudder. I am not afraid
of the fairies. I never could read fairy stories when I was a child;
they were tiresome to me. But talking in this way makes one
timid. There might be strollers or thieves under all these hedges.'

They went into the house, through the hall, and different
apartments, till they reached the drawing-room. Isabella stood
transfixed upon the threshold. It was all so familiar to her! Everything as she had known it before! Over the mantelpiece hung
the picture of the scornful Spanish lady; a heavy bookcase stood
in one corner; comfortable chairs and couches were scattered
round the room; beautiful landscapes against the wall seemed
like windows cut into foreign scenery. There was an air of ease
in the room, an old-fashioned sort of ease, such as the Fogertys
must have loved.

'It is a pretty room, is it not?' said Lawrence. 'You look at it
as if it pleased you. How much more comfort there is about it
than in the fashionable parlours of the day! It is solid, substantial
comfort.'

'You look at it as if you had seen it before,' said Otho to
Isabella. 'Do you know the room impressed me in that way, too?'

'It is singular,' said Lawrence, 'the feeling, that "all this has
been before", that comes over one at times. I have heard it
expressed by a great many people.'

'Have you, indeed, ever had this feeling?' asked Isabella.

'Certainly,' replied Lawrence; 'I say to myself sometimes, "I
have been through all this before!" and I can almost go on to tell
what is to come next – it seems so much a part of my past
experience.'

'It is strange it should be so with you – and with you too,' she
said, turning to Otho.

'Perhaps we are all more alike than we have thought,' said
Otho.

Otho's mother appeared, and the conversation took another turn.

Isabella did not go to the Willows again, until all the Lester family were summoned there to a large party that Mrs Blanchard gave. She called it a house-warming, although she had been in the house some time. It was a beautiful evening. A clear moon-light made it as brilliant outside on the lawn as the lights made the house within. There was a band of music stationed under the shrubbery, and those who chose could dance. Those who were more romantic wandered away down the shaded walks, and listened to the dripping of the fountain.

Lawrence and Isabella returned from a walk through the grounds, and stopped a moment on the terrace in front of the house. Just then a dark cloud appeared in the sky, threatening the moon. The wind, too, was rising, and made a motion among the leaves of the trees.

'Do you remember,' asked Lawrence, 'that child's story of the Fisherman and his Wife? how the fisherman went down to the sea-shore, and cried out,

'O man of the sea,
Come listen to me!
For Alice, my wife,
The plague of my life,
Has sent me to beg a boon of thee!'

The sea muttered and roared – do you remember? There was always something impressive to me in the descriptions, in the old story, of the changes in the sea, and of the tempest that rose up, more and more fearful, as the fisherman's wife grew more ambitious and more and more grasping in her desires, each time that the fisherman went down to the sea-shore. I believe my first impression of the sea came from that. The coming on of a storm is always associated with it. I always fancy that it is bringing with it something beside the tempest – that there is something ruinous behind it.'

'That is more fanciful than you usually are,' said Isabella; 'but, alas! I cannot remember your story, for I never read it.'

'That is where your education and Celia's were fearfully neglec-ted,' said Lawrence; 'you were not brought up on fairy stories and Mother Goose. You have not needed the first, as Celia has; but Mother Goose would have given a tone to your way of thinking, that is certainly wanting.'

A little while afterwards, Isabella stood upon the balcony steps leading from the drawing-room. Otho was with her. The threatening clouds had driven almost every one into the house. There was distant thunder and lightning; but through the cloud-rifts, now and then, the moonlight streamed down. Isabella and Otho had been talking earnestly – so earnestly, that they were quite unobservant of the coming storm, of the strange lurid light that hung around.

'It is strange that this should take place here!' said Isabella – 'that just here I should learn that you love me! Strange that my destiny should be completed in this spot!'

'And this spot has its strange associations with me,' said Otho, 'of which I must some time speak to you. But now I can think only of the present. Now, for the first time, do I feel what life is – now that you have promised to be mine!'

Otho was interrupted by a sudden cry. He turned to find his mother standing behind him.

'You are here with Isabella! She has promised herself to you!' she exclaimed. 'It is a fatality, a terrible fatality! Listen, Isabella! You are the Queen of the Red Chessmen; and he, Otho, is the King of the White Chessmen – and I, their Queen. Can there be two queens? Can there be a marriage between two hostile families? Do you not see, if there were a marriage between the Reds and the Whites, there were no game? Look! I have found our old prison! The pieces would all be here – but we, we are missing! Would you return to the imprisonment of this poor box – to your old mimic life? No, my children, go back! Isabella, marry this Lawrence Egerton, who loves you. You will find what life is, then. Leave Otho, that he may find this same life also.'

Isabella stood motionless.

'Otho, the White Prince! Alas! where is my hatred? But life without him! Even stagnation were better! I must needs be captive to the White Prince!'

She stretched out her hand to Otho. He seized it passionately. At this moment there was a grand crash of thunder. A gust of wind extinguished at once all the lights in the drawing-room. The terrified guests hurried into the hall, into the other rooms.

'The lightning must have struck the house!' they exclaimed.

A heavy rain followed; then all was still. Everybody began to recover his spirits. The servants relighted the candles. The drawing-room was found untenanted. It was time to go; yet there was a constraint upon all the party, who were eager to find their hostess and bid her good-bye.

But the hostess could not be found! Isabella and Otho, too, were missing! The doctor and Lawrence went every where, calling for them, seeking them in the house, in the grounds. They were nowhere to be found – neither that night, nor the next day, nor even afterwards!

The doctor found in the balcony a box of chessmen fallen down. It was nearly filled; but the red queen, and the white king and queen, were lying at a little distance. In the box was the red king, his crown fallen from his head, himself broken in pieces. The doctor took up the red queen, and carried it home.

'Are you crazy?' asked his wife.

'What are you going to do with that red queen?'

But the doctor placed the figure on his study-table, and often gazed at it wistfully.

Whenever, afterwards, as was often the case, anyone suggested a new theory to account for the mysterious disappearance of Isabella and the Blanchards, the doctor looked at the carved image on his table and was silent.

A GAME OF CHESS

Robert Barr

Here follows a rough translation of the letter which Henri Drumont wrote in Boukrah, two days before his death, to his uncle, Count Ferrand in Paris. It explains the incidents which led up to the situation hereinafter to be described.

My dear Uncle,

You will have gathered from former letters of mine, that when one gets east of Budapest, official corruption becomes rampant to an extent hardly believable in the West. Goodness knows, things are bad enough in Paris, but Paris official life is comparatively clean when brought into contrast with Boukrah. I was well aware before I left France that much money would have to be secretly spent if we were to secure the concession for lighting Boukrah with electricity, but I was unprepared for the exactions that were actually levied upon me. It must be admitted that the officials are rapacious enough, but once bought, they remain bought, or, at least, such has been my experience of them.

There is, however, a horde of hangers-on, who seem even more insatiable than the governing body of the town, and the worst of these is one Schwikoff, editor of the leading paper here, the *Boukrah Gazette*, which is merely a daily blackmailing sheet. He has every qualification needed by an editor of a paper in Eastern Europe, which may be summed up by saying that he is demoniacally expert with the rapier, and a dead shot with a pistol. He has said time and again that his scurrilous paper could wreck our scheme, and I believe there is some truth in his assertion. Be that as it may, I have paid him at different times large sums of money, but each payment seems but the precursor of a more outrageous demand. At last I was compelled to refuse further contributions to his banking account, and the young man smiled, saying he hoped my decision was not final, for, if it was, I should regret it. Although Schwikoff did not know it, I had the concession signed and completed at that moment, which document I sent to you yesterday morning. I expected Schwikoff would be very angry when he learned of this, but such did not appear to be the case.

He met me last night in the smoking-room of the Imperial Club, and shook hands with great apparent cordiality, laughing over his discomfiture, and assuring me that I was one of the shrewdest businessmen he had ever met. I was glad to see him take it in this way, and later in the evening when he asked me to have a game of chess with him, I accepted his invitation, thinking better for the Company that he should be a friend, if he were so disposed.

We had not progressed far with the game, when he suddenly accused me of making a move I had no right to make. I endeavoured to explain, but he sprang up in an assumed rage and dashed a glass of wine in my face. The room was crowded with officers and gentlemen. I know you may think me foolish for having sent my seconds on such a man as Schwikoff, who is a well known blackmailer, but, nevertheless, he comes of a good family, and I, who have served in the French Army, and am of your blood, could not accept tamely such an insult. If what I hear of his skill as a swordsman is true, I enter the contest well aware that I am outclassed, for I fear I have neglected the training of my right arm in my recent pursuit of scientific knowledge. Whatever may be the outcome, I have the satisfaction of knowing that the task given me has been accomplished. Our Company has now the right to establish its plant and lay its wires in Boukrah, and the people here have such an Eastern delight in all that is brilliant and glittering, that I feel certain our project will be a financial success.

Schwikoff and I will meet about the time you receive this letter, or, perhaps a little earlier, for we fight at daybreak, with rapiers, in the large room of the Fencing School of Arms in this place.

Accept, my dear uncle, the assurance of my most affectionate consideration. — Your unworthy nephew'

Henri.

The old man's hand trembled as he laid down the letter after reading it, and glanced up at the clock. It was the morning of the duel, and daylight came earlier at Boukrah than at Paris.

Count Ferrand was a member of an old French family that had been impoverished by the Revolution. Since then, the Ferrand family had lived poorly enough until the Count, as a young man, had turned his attention towards science, and now, in his old age, he was supposed to possess fabulous wealth, and was known to be the head of one of the largest electric manufacturing companies in the environs of Paris. No one at the works was aware that the young man, Henri Drumont, who was given employ in the manufactory after he had served his time in the army, was the nephew of the old Count, for the head of the company believed that the young man would come to a more accurate knowledge of the business if he had to take the rough with the smooth, and learn his trade from the bottom upwards.

The glance at the clock told the old Count that the duel, whatever its result, had taken place. So there was nothing to be done but await tidings. It was the manager of the works who brought them in.

'I am sorry to inform you, sir,' he said, 'that the young man, Henri Drumont, who we sent to Boukrah, was killed this morning in a duel. His assistant telegraphs for instructions. The young man has no relatives here that I know of, so I suppose it would be as well to have him buried where he died.'

The manager had no suspicion that he was telling his Chief of the death of his heir.

'The body is to be brought back to France,' said the Count quietly.

And it was done. Later, when the question arose of the action to be taken regarding the concession received from Boukrah, the Count astonished the directors by announcing that, as the concession was an important one, he himself would take the journey to Boukrah, and remain there until the electric plant, already forwarded, was in position, and a suitable local manager found.

The Count took the Orient Express from Paris, and, arriving in Boukrah, applied himself with an energy hardly to be expected from one of his years, to the completion of the work which was to supply the city with electricity.

Count Ferrand refused himself to all callers until the electric plant was in operation, and the interior of the building he had bought, completed to his satisfaction. Then, practically the first man admitted to his private office was Schwikoff, editor of the *Boukrah Gazette*. He had sent in his card with a request, written in passable French, for information regarding the electrical installation, which would be of interest, he said, to the readers of the *Gazette*. Thus Schwikoff was admitted to the presence of Count Ferrand, whose nephew he had killed, but the journalist, of course, knew nothing of the relationship between the two men, and thought, perhaps, he had done the courteous old gentleman a favour, in removing from the path of his advancement the young man who had been in the position now held by this grey-haired veteran.

The ancient noble received his visitor with scrupulous courtesy, and the blackmailer, glancing at his hard, inscrutable face, lined with experience, thought that here, perhaps, he had a more difficult victim to bleed than the free-handed young fellow whom he had so deferentially removed from existence, adhering strictly to the rules of the game, himself acquitted of all guilt by the law of his country, and the custom of his city, passing unscathed into his customary walk of life, free to rapier the next man who offended him. Count Ferrand said politely that he was ready to impart all the information in his possession for the purposes of publication. The young man smiled and shrugged his shoulders slightly.

'To tell you the truth, sir, at once and bluntly, I do not come so much for the purpose of questioning you regarding your business, as with the object of making some arrangement concerning the Press, with which I have the great honour to be connected. You may be aware, sir, that much of the success of your company will depend on the attitude of the Press towards you. I thought, perhaps, you might be able to suggest some method by which all difficulties would be smoothed away; a method that would result in our mutual advantage.'

'I shall not pretend to misunderstand you,' replied the Count, 'but I was led to believe that large sums had already been disbursed, and that the difficulties, as you term them, had already been removed.'

'So far as I am concerned,' returned the blackmailer, 'the sums paid to me were comparatively trivial, and I was led to hope that when the company came into active operation, as, thanks to your energy, is now the case, it would deal more liberally with me.'

The Count in silence glanced at some papers he took from a pigeonhole, then made a few notes on the pad before him. At last he spoke.

'Am I right in stating that an amount exceeding ten thousand francs was paid to you by my predecessor, in order that the influence of your paper might be assured?'

Schwikoff again shrugged his shoulders.

'It may have been something like that,' he said carelessly. 'I do not keep my account of these matters.'

'It is a large sum,' persisted Ferrand.

'Oh! a respectable sum; but still you must remember what you got for it. You have the right to bleed for ever all the inhabitants of Boukrah.'

'And that gives you the right to bleed us?'

'Oh! if you like to put it that way, yes. We give you *quid pro quo* by standing up for you when complaints of your exactions are made.'

'Precisely. But I am a businessman, and would like to see where I am going. You would oblige me, then, by stating a definite sum, which would be received by you in satisfaction of all demands.'

'Well, in that case, I think twenty thousand francs would be a moderate amount.'

'I cannot say that moderation is the most striking feature of your proposal,' said the Count dryly, 'still we shall not trouble about that, if you will be reasonable in the matter of payment. I propose to pay you in instalments of a thousand francs a month.'

'That would take nearly two years,' objected Schwikoff. 'Life is uncertain. Heaven only knows where we shall be two years from now.'

'Most true; or even a day hence. Still, we have spent a great deal of money on this establishment, and our income has not yet begun; therefore, on behalf of the company, I must insist on easy payments. I am willing, however, to make it two thousand francs a month, but beyond that I should not care to go without communicating with Paris.'

'Oh, well,' swaggered Schwikoff, with the air of a man making great concessions, 'I suppose we may call that satisfactory, if you make the first payment now.'

'I do not keep such a sum in my office, and, besides, I wish to impose further terms. It is not my intention to make an arrangement with any but the leading paper of this place, which I understand the *Gazette* to be.'

'A laudable intention. The *Gazette* is the only paper that has any influence in Boukrah.'

'Very well; then I must ask you, for your own sake as for mine, to keep this matter a strict secret; even to deny that you receive a subsidy, if the question should come up.'

'Oh, certainly, certainly.'

'You will come for payment, which will be in gold, after office hours, on the first of each month. I shall be here alone to receive you. I should prefer that you came in by the back way, where your entrance will be unseen, and so we shall avoid comment, because, when I refuse the others, I should not care for them to know that one of their fellows has been an advantage over them. I shall take the money from the bank before it closes. What hour, therefore, after six o'clock will be most convenient for you?'

'That is immaterial — seven, eight, or nine, or even later, if you like.'

'Eight o'clock will do; by that time everyone will have left the building but myself. I do not care for late hours, even if they occur but once a month. At eight o'clock precisely you will find the door at the back ajar. Come in without announcement, so that we may not be taken by surprise. The door is self-locking, and you will find me here with the money. Now, that I may be able to obtain the gold in time, I must bid you adieu.'

At eight o'clock precisely Count Ferrand, standing in the passage, saw the back door shoved open and Schwikoff enter, closing it behind him.

'I hope I have not kept you waiting,' said Schwikoff.

'Your promptitude is exceptional,' said the other politely. 'As a businessman, I must confess I like punctuality. I have left the money in the upper room. Will you have the goodness to follow me?'

They mounted four pairs of stairs, all lighted by incandescent lamps. Entering a passageway on the upper floor, the Count closed the big door behind him; then opening another door, they came to a large oblong room, occupying nearly the whole of the top storey, brilliantly lighted by an electric lustre depending from the ceiling.

'That is my experimenting laboratory,' said the old man as he closed the second door behind him.

It was certainly a remarkable room, entirely without windows. On the wall at the right hand near the entrance, were numerous switches in shining brass and copper and steel.

From the door onward were perhaps ten feet of ordinary flooring, then across the whole width of the room extended a gigantic chessboard, the squares yellow and grey, made alternately of copper and steel; beyond that again was another ten feet of plain flooring, which supported a desk and some chairs. Schwikoff's eyes glittered as he saw a pile of gold on the desk. Near the desk was a huge open fireplace, constructed like no fireplace Schwikoff had ever seen before. The centre, where the grate should have been, was occupied by what looked like a great earthenware bathtub, some six or seven feet long.

'That,' said the electrician, noticing the other's glance at it, 'is an electric furnace of my own invention, probably the largest electric furnace in the world. I am convinced there is a great future before carbide of calcium, and I am carrying on some experiments drifting towards the perfection of the electric crucible.'

'Carbide of calcium?' echoed Schwikoff, 'I have never heard of it.'

'Perhaps it would not interest you, but it is curious from the fact that it is a rival of the electric light, and yet only through the aid of electricity is carbide of calcium made commercially possible.'

'Electricity creates its own rival, you mean; most interesting I am sure. And is this a chessboard let into the floor?'

'Yes, another of my inventions. I am a devotee of chess.'

'So am I.'

'Then we shall have to have a game together. You don't object to high stakes I hope?'

'Oh, no, if I have the money.'

'Ah, well, we must have a game with stakes high enough to make the contest interesting.'

'Where are your chessmen? They must be huge.'

'Yes, this board was arranged so that living chessmen might play on it. You see, the alternate squares are of copper, the others of steel. That black line which surrounds each square is hard rubber, which does not allow the electricity to pass form one square to another.'

'You use electricity, then, in playing.'

'Oh, electricity is the motive power of the game; I will explain it all to you presently; meanwhile, would you oblige me by counting the gold on the desk? I think you will find there exactly two thousand francs.'

The old man led the way across the metal chessboard. He proffered a chair to Schwikoff, who sat down before the desk.

Count Ferrand took the remaining chair, carried it over the metal platform, and sat down near the switch, having thus the huge chessboard between him and his guest. He turned a lever from one polished knob to another, the transit causing a wicked, vivid flash to illuminate the room with the venomous glitter of blue lightning. Schwikoff gave a momentary start at the crackle and the blinding light. Then he continued his counting in silence. At last he looked up and said, 'This amount is quite correct.'

'Please do not move from your chair,' commanded the Count. 'I warn you that the chessboard is now a broad belt of death between you and me. On every disc the current is turned, and a man stepping anywhere on the board will receive into his body two thousand volts, killing him instantly as with a stroke of lightning, which, indeed, it is.'

'Is this a practical joke?' asked Schwikoff, turning a little pale about the lips, sitting still, as he had been ordered to do.

'It is practical enough, and no joke, as you will learn when you know more about it. You see this circle of twenty-four knobs at my hand, with each knob of which, alternatively, this lever communicates when I turn it.'

As the Count spoke he moved the lever, which went crackling past a semi-circle of knobs, emitting savage gleams of steel-like fire as it touched each metal projection.

'From each of these knobs,' explained the Count, as if he were giving a scientific lecture, 'electricity is turned on to a certain combination of squares before you. When I began speaking the whole board was electrified; now, a man might walk across the board, and his chances of reaching this side alive would be as three to one.'

Schwikoff sprang suddenly to his feet, terror in his face, and seemed about to make a dash for it. The old man pushed the lever back into its former position.

'I want you to understand,' said the Count suavely, 'that upon any movement on your part, I shall instantly electrify the whole board. And please remember that, although I can make the chessboard as safe as the floor, a push on this lever and the metal becomes a belt of destruction. You must keep a cool head on your shoulders, Mr Schwikoff, otherwise you have no chance for your life.'

Schwikoff, standing there, stealthily drew a revolver from his hip pocket. The Count continued in even tones:

'I see you are armed, and I know you are an accurate marksman. You may easily shoot me dead as I sit here. I have thought that all out in the moments I have given to the consideration of this business. On my desk downstairs is a letter to the manager, saying that I am called suddenly to Paris, and that I shall not return for a month. I ask him to go on with the work, and tell him on no account to allow anyone to enter this room. You might shout till you were hoarse, but none outside would hear you. The walls and ceiling and floor have been deadened so effectively that we are practically in a silent, closed box. There is no exit except up through the chimney, but if you look at the crucible to which I called your attention you will see that is now white hot, so there is no escape that way. You will, therefore, be imprisoned here until you starve to death, or until despair causes you to commit suicide by stepping on the electrified floor.'

'I can shatter your switchboard from here with bullets.'

'Try it,' said the old man calmly. 'The destruction of the switch-board merely means that the electricity comes permanently on the floor. If you shatter the switchboard, it will then be out of my power to release you, even if I wished to do so, without going down stairs and turning off the electricity at the main. I assure you that all these things have had my most earnest consideration, and while it is possible that something may have been overlooked, it is hardly probable that you, in your now excited state of mind, will chance upon that omission.'

Schwikoff sank back in his chair.

'Why do you wish to murder me?' he asked. 'You may retain your money, if that is what you want, and I shall keep quiet about you in the paper.'

'Oh, I care nothing for the money nor the paper.'

'It is because I killed your predecessor.'

'My predecessor was my nephew and my heir. Through his duel with you, I am now a childless old man, whose riches are but an incumbrance to him, and yet those riches would buy me freedom were I to assassinate you in broad daylight in the street. Are you willing now to listen to the terms I propose to you?'

'Yes.'

'Very good. Throw your pistol into the corner of the room beside me; its possession will do you no good.'

After a moment's hesitation, Schwikoff flung his pistol across the metal floor into the corner. The old man turned the lever to still another knob.

'Now,' he said, 'you have a chance of life again; thirty-two of the squares are electrified, and thirty-two are harmless. Stand, I beg of you, on the square which belongs to the Black King.'

'And meet my death.'

'Not on that square, I assure you. It is perfectly safe.'

But the young man made no movement to comply. 'I ask you to explain your intention.'

'You shall play the most sinister game of chess you have ever engaged in; Death will be your opponent. You shall have the right to the movements of the King — one square in any direction that you choose. You will never be in a position in which you have not the choice of at least two squares upon which you can step with impunity; in fact, you shall have at each move the choice of eight squares on which to set your foot, and as a general thing, four of those will mean safety, and the other four death, although sometimes the odds will be more heavily against you, and sometimes more strongly in your favour. If you reach this side unscathed you are then at liberty to go, while if you touch one of the electric squares, your death will be instantaneous. Then I shall turn off the current, place your body in that electrical furnace, turn on the current again, with the result that for a few moments there will be thick, black smoke from the chimney, and a handful of white ashes in the crucible.'

'And you run no danger?'

'No more than you did when you stood up against my nephew, having previously unjustly insulted him.'

'The duel was carried out according to the laws of the code.'

'The laws of my code are more generous. You have a chance for your life. My nephew had no such favour shown to him; he was doomed from the beginning, and you knew it.'

'He had been an officer in the French Army.'

'He allowed his sword arm to get out of practice, which was wrong, of course, and he suffered for it. However, we are not discussing him; it is your fate that is in question. I give you now two minutes in which to take your stand on the King's square.'

'And if I refuse?'

'If you refuse, I turn the electricity on the whole board, and then I leave you. I will tear up the letter which is on my desk below, return here in the morning, give the alarm, say you broke in to rob me of the gold which is beside you on the desk, and give you in charge of the authorities, a disgraced man.'

'But what if I tell the truth?'

'You would not be believed, and I have pleasure in knowing that I have money enough to place you in prison for the rest of your life. The chances are, however, that with the electricity fully turned on, this building will be burned down before morning. I fear my installation is not perfect enough to withstand so strong a current. In fact, now that the thought has suggested itself to me, fire seems a good solution of the difficulty. I shall arrange the wires on leaving so that a conflagration will break out within an hour after my departure, and, I assure you, you will not be rescued by the firemen when they understand their danger from live wires in a building for which, I will tell them, it is impossible to cut off the electricity. Now, sir, you have two minutes.'

Schwikoff stood still while Ferrand counted the seconds left to him; finally, as the time was about to expire, he stepped on the King's square, and stood there, swaying slightly, drops of perspiration gathering on his brow.

'Bravo,' cried the Count, 'you see, as I told you, it is perfectly safe. I give you two minutes to make your next move.'

Schwikoff, with white lips, stepped diagonally to the square of the Queen's Pawn, and stood there, breathing hard, but unharmed.

'Two minutes to make the next move,' said the old man, in the unimpassioned tones of a judge.

'No, no!' shouted Schwikoff excitedly, 'I made my last move at once; I have nearly four minutes. I am not to be hurried; I must keep my head cool. I have as you see, superb control over myself.'

His voice had now risen to a scream, and his open hand drew the perspiration down from his brow over his face, streaking it grimly.

'I am calm!' he shrieked, his knees knocking together, 'but this is no game of chess; it is murder. In a game of chess I could take all the time I wanted in considering a move.'

'True, true!' said the old man suavely, leaning back in his chair, although his hand never left the black handle of the lever. 'You are right. I apologise for my infringement of the laws of chess; take all the time you wish, we have the night before us.'

Schwikoff stood there long in the ominous silence, a silence interrupted now and then by a startling crackle from the direction of the glowing electric furnace. The air seemed charged with electricity and almost unbreathable. The time given him, so far from being an advantage, disintegrated his nerve, and as he looked fearfully over the metal chessboard the copper squares seemed to be glowing red hot, and the dangerous illusion that the steel squares were cool and safe became uppermost in his mind.

He curbed with difficulty his desire to plunge, and stood balancing himself on his left foot, cautiously approaching the steel square with his right toe. As the boot neared the steel square Schwikoff felt a strange thrill pass through his body. He drew back his foot quickly with a yell of terror, and stood, his body inclining now to the right, now to the left, like a tall tree hesitating before its fall. To save himself he crouched.

'Mercy! Mercy!' he cried. 'I have been punished enough. I killed the man, but his death was sudden, and not fiendish torture like this. I have been punished enough.'

'Not so,' said the old man. 'An eye for an eye.'

All self control abandoned the victim. From his crouching position he sprang like a tiger. Almost before his out-stretched hands touched the polished metal his body straightened and stiffened with a jerk, and as he fell, with a hissing sound, dead on the chessboard, the old man turned the lever free from the fatal knob. There was no compassion in his hard face for the executed man, but instead his eyes glittered with the scientific fervour of research. He rose, turned the body over with his foot, drew off one of the boots, and tore from the inside a thin sole of cork.

'Just as I thought,' he murmured. 'Oh, the irony of ignorance! There existed, after all, the one condition I had not provided for. I knew he was protected the moment he stepped on the second square, and, if his courage had not deserted him, he would have walked unharmed across the board, as the just, in medieval times, passed through the ordeal of the red-hot plough shares.'

A SET OF CHESSMEN

Richard Marsh

'But, Monsieur, perceive how magnificent they are! There is not in Finistère, there is not in Brittany, nay, it is certain there is not in France so superb a set of chessmen. And ivory! And the carving — observe, for example, the variety of detail.'

They certainly were a curious set of chessmen, magnificent in a way, but curious first of all. As Monsieur Bobineau remarked, holding a rook in one hand and a knight in the other, the care paid to details by the carver really was surprising. But two hundred and fifty francs! For a set of chessmen!

'So, so, my friend. I am willing to admit that the work is good — in a kind of way. But two hundred and fifty francs! If it were fifty, now?'

'Fifty!' Up went Monsieur Bobineau's shoulders, and down went Monsieur Bobineau's head between them, in the fashion of those toys which are pulled by a string. 'Ah, mon Dieu! Monsieur laughs at me!'

And there came another voluble declaration of their merits. They certainly were a curious set. I really think they were the most curious set I ever saw. I would have preferred them, for instance, to anything they have at South Kensington, and they have some remarkable examples there. And, of course, the price was small — I even admit it was ridiculously small. But when one has only five thousands francs a year for everything, two hundred and fifty being taken away — and for a set of chessmen — do leave a vacancy behind.

I asked Bobineau where he got them. Business was slack that sunny afternoon — it seemed to me that I was the only customer he ever had, but that must have been a delusion on my part. Report said he was a warm man, one of Morlaix's warmest men, and his queer old shop in the queer old Grande Rue — Grande Rue! what a name for an alley! — contained many things which were valuable as well as queer. But there, at least, was no other customer in sight just then, so Bobineau told me all the tale.

It seemed there had been a Monsieur Funichon — Auguste Funichon — no, not a Breton, a Parisian, a true Parisian, who had come and settled down in the commune of Plouigneau, over by the *gare*. This Monsieur Funichon was, for example, a little — well, a little — a little *exalted*, let us say. It is true that the country people said he was stark mad, but Bobineau, for his part, said no, no, no! It is not necessary, because one is a little eccentric, that one is mad. Here Bobineau looked at me out of the corner of his eye. Are not the English, of all people, the most eccentric, and yet is it not known to all the world that they are not, necessarily, stark mad? This Monsieur Funichon was not rich, quite the contrary. It was a little place he lived in — the merest cottage, in fact. And in it he lived alone, and, according to report, there was only one thing he did all the day and all night long, and that was, play chess. It appears that he was the rarest and most amiable of imbeciles, a chess-maniac. Is there such a word?

'What a life!' said Monsieur Bobineau. 'Figure it to yourself! To do nothing — nothing! — but play chess! they say' — Monsieur Bobineau looked round him with an air of mystery — 'they say he starved himself to death. He was so besotted by his miserable chess that he forgot — absolutely forgot, this imbecile — to eat.'

That was what Monsieur Bobineau said they said. It required a vigorous effort of the imagination to quite take it in. To what a state of forgetfulness must a man arrive before he forgets to eat! But whether Monsieur Funichon forgot to eat, or whether he didn't, at least he died, and being dead they sold his goods — why they sold them was not quite clear, but at the sale Monsieur Bobineau was the chief purchaser. One of the chief lots was the set of ivory chessmen which had caught my eye. They were the dead man's favourite set, and no wonder! Bobineau was of opinion that if he had had his way he would have had them buried with him in his grave.

'It is said,' he whispered, again with the glance of mystery around, 'that they found him dead, seated at the table, the chessmen on the board, his hand on the white rook, which was giving mate to the adversary's king.'

Either what a vivid imagination had Bobineau, or what odd things the people said! One pictures the old man, seated all alone, with his last breath finishing his game.

Well, I bought the set of ivory chessmen. At this time of day

I freely admit that they are cheap at two hundred and fifty francs — dirt cheap, indeed; but a hundred was all I paid. I knew Bobineau so well — I daresay, he bought them for twenty-five. As I bore them triumphantly away my mind was occupied by thoughts of their original possessor. I was filled by quite a sentimental tenderness as I meditated on the part they had played, according to Bobineau, in that last scene. But St Servan drove all those thoughts away. Philippe Henri de St Servan was rather a difficult person to get on with. It was with him I shared at that time my apartment on the *place*.

'Let us see!' I remarked when I got in, 'what have I here?'

He was seated, his country pipe in his mouth, at the open window, looking down upon the river. The Havre boat was making ready to start — at Morlaix the nautical event of the week. There was quite a bustle on the quay. St Servan just looked round, and then looked back again. I sat down and untied my purchase.

'I think there have been criticisms — derogatory criticisms — passed by a certain person upon a certain set of chessmen. Perhaps that person will explain what he has to say to these.'

St Servan marched up to the table. He looked at them through his half-closed eyelids.

'Toys!' was all he said.

'Perhaps! Yet toys which made a tragedy. Have you ever heard of the name of Funichon?' By a slight movement of his grisly grey eyebrows he intimated that it was possible he had. 'These chessmen belonged to him. He had just finished a game with them when they found him dead — the winning piece, a white rook, was in his hand. Suggest an epitaph to be placed over his grave. There's a picture for a painter — eh?'

'Bah! He was a Communist!'

That was all St Servan said. And so saying, St Servan turned away to look out of the window at the Havre boat again. There was an end of Monsieur Funichon for him. Not that he meant exactly what he said. He simply meant that Monsieur Funichon was not Legitimist — out of sympathy with the gentlemen who met, and decayed, visibly, before the naked eye, at the club on the other side of the *place*. With St Servan not to be Legitimist meant to be nothing at all — out of his range of vision absolutely. Seeing that was so, it is strange he should have borne with me as he did. But he was a wonderful old man.

* * *

We played our fist game with the ivory chessmen when St Servan returned from the club. I am free to confess that it was an occasion for me. I had dusted all the pieces, and had the board all laid when St Servan entered, and when we drew for choice of moves the dominant feeling in my mind was the thought of the dead man sitting all alone, with the white rook in his hand. There was an odour of sanctity about the affair — a whiff of air from the land of the ghosts.

Nevertheless, my loins were girded up, and I was prepared to bear myself as a man in the strife. We were curiously well matched, St Servan and I. We had played two hundred and twenty games, and, putting draws aside, each had scored the same number of wins. He had his days, and so had I. At one time I was eleven games ahead, but since that thrice blessed hour I had not scored a single game. He had tracked me steadily, and eventually had made the scores exactly tie. In these latter days it had grown with him to be an article of faith that as a chess-player I was quite played out — and there was a time when I had thought the same of him!

He won the move, and then, as usual, there came an interval for reflection. The worst thing about St Servan — regardless from a chess-playing point of view — was, that he took such a time to begin. When a man has opened his game it is excusable — laudable, indeed — if he pauses to reflect, a reasonable length of time. But I never knew a man who was so fond of reflection before a move was made. As a rule, that absurd habit of his had quite an irritating effect upon my nerves, but that evening I felt quite cool and prepared to sit him out.

There we sat, both smoking our great pipes, he staring at the board, and I at him. He put out his hand, almost touched a piece, and then, with a start, he drew it back again. An interval — the same pantomime again. Another interval — and a repetition of the pantomime. I puffed a cloud of smoke into the air, and softly sighed. I knew he had been ten minutes by my watch. Possibly the sigh had a stimulating effect, for he suddenly stretched out his hand and moved queen's knight's pawn a single square.

I was startled. He was great at book openings, that was the absurdest part of it. He would lead you to suppose that he was meditating something quite original, and then would perhaps begin with fool's mate after all. He, at least, had never tried queen's knight's pawn a single square before.

I considered a reply. Pray let it be understood — though I would not have confessed it to St Servan for the world — that I am no player. I am wedded to the game for an hour or two at night, or, peradventure, of an afternoon at times; but I shall never be admitted to its inner mysteries — never! not if I outspan Methuselah. I am not built that way. St Servan and I were two children who, loving the sea, dabble their feet in the shallows left by the tide. I have no doubt that there are a dozen replies to that opening of his, but I did not know one then. I had some hazy idea of developing a game of my own, while keeping an eye on his, and for that purpose put out my hand to move the queen's pawn two, when I felt my wrist grasped by — well, by what felt uncommonly like an invisible hand. I was so startled that I almost dropped my pipe. I drew my hand back again, and was conscious of the slight detaining pressure of unseen fingers. Of course it was hallucination, but it seemed so real, and was so expected, that — well I settled my pipe more firmly between my lips — it had all but fallen from my mouth, and took a whiff or two to calm my nerves. I glanced up, cautiously, to see if St Servan noticed my unusual behaviour, but his eyes were fixed stonily upon the board.

After a moment's hesitation — it was absurd! — I stretched out my hand again. The hallucination was repeated, and in a very tangible form. I was distinctly conscious of my wrist being wrenched aside and guided to a piece I had never meant to touch, and almost before I was aware of it, instead of the move I had meant to make, I had made a servile copy of St Servan's opening — I had moved queen's knight's pawn a single square!

To adopt the language of the late Dick Swiveller, that was a staggerer. I own that for an instant I was staggered. I could do nothing else but stare. For at least ten seconds I forgot to smoke. I was conscious that when St Servan saw my move he knit his brows. Then the usual interval for reflection came again. Half unconsciously I watched him. When, as I supposed, he had decided on his move, he stretched out his hand, as I had done, and also, as I had done, he drew it back again. I was a little startled — he seemed a little startled too. There was a momentary pause; back went his hand again, and, by way of varying the monotony, he moved — king's knight's pawn a single square.

I wondered, and held my peace. There might be a gambit

based upon these lines, or there might not; but since I was quite clear that I knew no reply to such an opening I thought I would try a little experiment, and put out my hand, not with the slightest conception of any particular move in my head, but simply to see what happened. Instantly a grasp fastened on my wrist; my hand was guided to — king's knight's pawn a single square.

This was getting, from every point of view, to be distinctly interesting. The chessmen appeared to be possessed of a property of which Bobineau had been unaware. I caught myself wondering if he would have insisted on a higher price if he had known of it. Curiosities nowadays do fetch such fancy sums — and what price for a ghost? They appeared to be automatic chessmen, automatic in a sense entirely their own.

Having made my move, or having had somebody else's move made for me, which is perhaps the more exact way of putting it, I contemplated my antagonist. When he saw what I had done, or what somebody else had done — the things are equal — St Servan frowned. He belongs to the bony variety, the people who would not loll in a chair to save their lives — his aspect struck me as being even more poker-like than usual. He meditated his reply an unconscionable length of time, the more unconscionable since I strongly doubted if it would be his reply after all. But at last he showed signs of action. He kept his eyes fixed steadily upon the board, his frown became pronounced, and he began to raise his hand. I write 'began', because it was a process which took some time. Cautiously he brought it up, inch by inch. But no sooner had he brought it over the board than his behaviour became quite singular. He positively glared, and to my eyes seemed to be having a struggle with his own right hand. A struggle in which he was worsted, for he leaned back in his seat with a curiously discomfited air.

He had moved queen's rook's pawn two squares — the automatic principle which impelled these chessmen seemed to have a partiality for pawns.

It was my turn for reflection. I pressed the tobacco down in my pipe, and thought — or tried to think — it out. Was it an hallucination, and was St Servan the victim of hallucination too? Had I moved those pawns spontaneously, actuated by the impulse of my own free will, or hadn't I? And what was the meaning of the little scene I had just observed? I am a tolerably strong man. It would require no slight exercise of force to compel me to move one piece when I had made up my mind that I would move another piece instead. I have been told, and I believe not altogether untruly told, that the rigidity of my right wrist resembles iron. I have not spent so much time in the tennis-court and fencing-room for nothing. I had tried one experiment. I thought I would try another. I made up my mind that I would move queen's pawn two — stop me who stop can.

I felt that St Servan in his turn was watching me. Preposterously easy though the feat appeared to be as I resolved on it performance, I was conscious of an unusual degree of cerebral excitement — a sort of feeling of do or die. But as, in spite of the feeling, I didn't do, it was perhaps as well I didn't die. Intending to keep complete control over my own muscles, I raised my right hand, probably to the full as cautiously as St Servan had done. I approached the queen's pawn. I was just about to seize the piece when that unseen grasp fastened on my wrist. I paused, with something of the feeling which induces the wrestler to pause before entering on the veritable tug of war. For one thing, I was desirous to satisfy myself as to the nature of the grasp — what it was that seemed to grasp me.

It seemed to be a hand. The fingers went over the back of my wrist, and the thumb beneath. The fingers were long and thin — it was altogether a slender hand. But it seemed to be a man's hand, and an old man's hand at that. The skin was tough and wrinkled, clammy and cold. On the little finger there was a ring, and on the first, about the region of the first joint, appeared to be something of the nature of a wart. I should say that it was anything but a beautiful hand, it was altogether too attenuated and clawlike, and I would have betted that it was yellow with age.

At first the pressure was slight, almost as slight as the touch of a baby's hand, with a gentle inclination to one side. But as I kept my own hand firm, stiff, resolved upon my own particular move, with, as it were, a sudden snap, the pressure tightened and, not a little to my discomfiture, I felt my wrist held as in an iron vice. Then, as it must have seemed to St Servan, who, I was aware, was still keenly watching me, I began to struggle with my own hand. The spectacle might have been fun for him, but the reality was, at that moment, anything but fun to me. I was dragged to one side. Another hand was fastened upon mine. My fingers were forced open — I had tightly clenched my fist to enable me better to resist — my wrist was forced down, my fingers were closed upon a piece, I was compelled to move it forward, my fingers were unfastened to replace the piece upon the board. The move completed, the unseen grasp instantly relaxed, and I was free, or appeared to be free, again to call my hand my own.

I had moved the queen's rook's pawn two squares. This may seem comical enough to read about, but it was anything but comical to feel. When the thing was done I stared to St Servan, and St Servan stared at me. We stared at each other, I suppose, a good long minute, then I broke the pause.

'Anything the matter?' I inquired. He put up his hand and curled his moustache, and, if I may say so, he curled his lip as well. 'Do you notice anything odd about — about the game?' As I spoke about the game I motioned my hand towards my brand-new set of chessmen. He looked at me with hard suspicious eyes.

'Is it a trick of yours?' he asked.

'Is what a trick of mine?'

'If you do not know, then how should I?'

I drew a whiff or two from my pipe, looked at him keenly all the time, then signed toward the board with my hand.

'It's your move,' I said.

He merely inclined his head. There was a momentary pause. When he stretched out his hand he suddenly snatched it back again, and half started from his seat with a stifled execration.

'Did you feel anything upon your wrist?' I asked.

'*Mon Dieu*! It is not what I feel — see that!'

He was eyeing his wrist as he spoke. He held it out under the glare of the lamp. I bent across and looked at it. For so old a man he had a phenomenally white and delicate skin — under the glare of the lamp the impressions of finger-marks were plainly visible upon his wrist. I whistled as I saw them.

'Is it a trick of yours?' he asked again.

'It is certainly no trick of mine.'

'Is there anyone in the room besides us two?'

I shrugged my shoulders and looked round. He too looked round, with something I thought not quite easy in his glance.

'Certainly no one of my acquaintance, and certainly no one who is visible to me!'

With his fair white hand — the left, not the one which had the finger-marks upon the wrist — St Servan smoothed his hugh moustache.

'Someone, or something, has compelled me — yes, from the

first — to move, not as I would have, but — bah! I know not how.'

'Exactly the same thing has occurred to me.'

I laughed. St Servan glared. Evidently the humour of the thing did not occur to him, he being the sort of man who would require a surgical operation to make him see a joke. But the humorous side of the situation struck me forcibly.

'Perhaps we are favoured by the presence of a ghost — perhaps even by the ghost of Monsieur Funichon. Perhaps, after all, he has not yet played his last game with his favourite set. He may have returned — shall we say from — where? — to try just one more set-to with us! If, my dear sir' — I waved my pipe affably, as though addressing an unseen personage — 'it is really you, I bet you will reveal yourself — materialise is, I believe, the expression now in vogue — and show us the sort of ghost you are!'

Somewhat to my surprise, and considerably to my amusement, St Servan rose from his seat and stood by the table, stiff and straight as a scaffold-pole.

'These, Monsieur, are subjects on which one does not jest.'

'Do you, then, believe in ghosts?' I knew he was a superstitious man — witness his fidelity to the superstition of right divine — but this was the first inkling I had of how far his superstition carried him.

'Believe! — In ghosts! In what, then, do you believe? I, Monsieur, am a religious man.'

'Do you believe, then, that a ghost is present with us now — the ghost, for instance, of Monsieur Funichon?'

St Servan paused. Then he crossed himself — actually crossed himself before my eyes. When he spoke there was a peculiar dryness in his tone.

'With your permission, Monsieur, I will retire to bed.'

There was an exasperating thing to say! There must be a large number of men in the world who would give — well, a good round sum, to light even on the trail of a ghost. And here were we in the actual presence of something — let us say apparently curious, at any rate, and there was St Servan calmly talking about retiring to bed, without making the slightest attempt to examine the thing! It was enough to make the members of the Psychical Research Society turn in their graves. The mere suggestion fired my blood.

'I do beg, St Servan, that you at least will finish the game.' I saw he hesitated, so I drove the nail well home. 'Is it possible that you, a brave man, having given proofs of courage upon countless fields, can turn tail at what is doubtless an hallucination after all?'

'Is it that Monsieur doubts my courage?'

I knew the tone — if I was not careful I should have an affair upon my hands.

'Come, St Servan, sit down and finish the game.'

Another momentary pause. He sat down, and — it would not be correct to write that we finished the game, but we made another effort to go on. My pipe had gone out. I refilled and lighted it.

'You know, St Servan, it is really nonsense to talk about ghosts.'

'It is a subject on which I never talk.'

'If something does compel us to make moves which we do not intend, it is something which is capable of a natural explanation.'

'Perhaps Monsieur will explain it, then?'

'I will! Before I've finished! If you only won't turn tail and go to bed! I think it very possible, too, that the influence, whatever it is, has gone — it is quite on the cards that our imagination has played us some subtle trick. It is your move, but before you do anything just tell me what move you mean to make.'

'I will move' — he hesitated — 'I will move queen's pawn.'

He put out his hand, and, with what seemed to me hysterical suddenness, he moved king's rook's pawn two squares.

'So! our friend is still here, then! I suppose you did not change your mind?'

There was a *very* peculiar look about St Servan's eyes.

'I did not change my mind.'

I noticed, too, that his lips were uncommonly compressed.

'It is my move now. *I* will move queen's pawn. We are not done yet. When I put out my hand you grasp my wrist — and we shall see.'

'Shall I come round to you?'

'No, stretch out across the table — now!'

I stretched out my hand; that instant he stretched out his, but spontaneous though the action seemed to be, another, an unseen hand, had fastened on my wrist. He observed it too.

'There appears to be another hand between yours and mine.'

'I know there is.'

Before I had the words well out my hand had been wrenched

aside, my fingers unclosed, and then closed, then unclosed again, and I had moved king's rook's pawn two squares. St Servan and I sat staring at each other — for my part I felt a little bewildered.

'This is very curious! Very curious indeed! But before we say anything about it we will try another little experiment, if you don't mind. I will come over to you.' I went over to him. 'Let me grasp your wrist with both my hands.' I grasped it, as firmly as I could, as it lay upon his knee. 'Now try to move queen's pawn.'

He began to raise his hand, I holding on to his wrist with all my strength. Hardly had he raised it to the level of the table when two unseen hands, grasping mine, tore them away as though my strength were of no account. I saw him give a sort of shudder — he had moved queen's bishop's pawn two squares.

'This is a devil of a ghost!' I said.

St Servan said nothing. But he crossed himself, not once, but half a dozen times.

'There is still one little experiment that I would wish to make.'

St Servan shook his head.

'Not I!' he said.

'Ah but, my friend, this is an experiment which I can make without your aid. I simply want to know if there is nothing tangible about our unseen visitor except his hands. It is my move.' I returned to my side of the table. I again addressed myself, as it were, to an unseen auditor. 'My good ghost, my good Monsieur Funichon — if it is you — you are at liberty to do as you desire with my hand.'

I held it out. It instantly was grasped. With my left hand I made several passes in the air up and down, behind and before, in every direction so far as I could. It met with no resistance. There seemed to be nothing tangible but those invisible fingers which grasped my wrist — and I had moved queen's bishop's pawn two squares.

St Servan rose from his seat.

'It is enough. Indeed it is too much. This ribaldry must cease. It had been better had Monsieur permitted me to retire to bed.'

'Then you are sure it is a ghost — the ghost of Monsieur Funichon, we'll say.'

'This time Monsieur must permit me to wish him a good night's rest.'

He bestowed on me, as his manner was, a stiff inclination of the head, which would have led a stranger to suppose that we had met each other for the first time ten minutes ago, instead of being the acquaintances of twelve good years. He moved across the room.

'St Servan, one moment before you go! You are surely not going to leave a man alone at the post of peril?'

'It were better that Monsieur should come too.'

'Half a second, and I will. I have only one remark to make, and that is to the ghost.'

I rose from my seat. St Servan made a half movement towards the door, then changed his mind and remained quite still.

'If there is any other person with us in the room, may I ask that person to let us hear his voice, or hers? Just to speak one word.'

Not a sound.

'It is possible — I am not acquainted with the laws which govern — eh — ghosts — that the faculty of speech is denied to them. If that be so, might I ask for the favour of a sign — for instance, move a piece while my friend and I are standing where we are?'

Not a sign; not a chessman moved.

'Then, Monsieur Funichon, if it indeed be you, and you are incapable of speech, or even of moving a piece of your own accord, and are only able to spoil our game, I beg to inform you that you are an exceedingly ill-mannered and foolish person, and had far better have stayed away.'

As I said this I was conscious of a current of cold air before my face, as though a swiftly moving hand had shaved my cheek.

'By Jove, St Servan, something has happened at last. I believe our friend the ghost has tried to box my ears!'

St Servan's reply came quietly stern.

'I think it were better that Monsieur came with me.'

For some reason St Servan's almost contemptuous coldness fired my blood. I became suddenly enraged.

'I shall do nothing of the kind! Do you think I am going to be fooled by a trumpery conjuring trick which would disgrace a shilling séance? Driven to bed at this time of day by a ghost! And such a ghost! If it were something like a ghost one wouldn't mind; but a fool of ghost like this!'

Even as the words passed my lips I felt the touch of fingers against my throat. I snatched at them, only to find that there was nothing there.

'Damn you!' I cried. 'Funichon, you old fool, do you think that you can frighten me? You see those chessmen; they are mine, bought and paid for with my money — you dare to try and prevent me doing with them exactly as I please.'

Again the touch against my throat. It made my rage the more. 'As I live, I will smash them all to pieces, and grind them in powder beneath my heel.'

My passion was ridiculous — childish even. But then the circumstances were exasperating — unusually so, one might plead. I was standing three or four feet from the table. I dashed forward. As I did so a hand was fastened on my throat. Instantly it was joined by another. They gripped me tightly. They maddened me. With a madman's fury I still pressed forward. I might as well have fought with fate. They clutched me as with bands of steel, and flung me to the ground.

* * *

When I recovered consciousness I found St Servan bending over me.

'What is the matter?' I inquired, when I found that I was lying on the floor.

'I think you must have fainted.'

'Fainted! I never did such a thing in my life. It must have been a curious kind of faint, I think.'

'It was a curious kind of faint.'

With his assistance I staggered to my feet. I felt bewildered. I glanced round. There were the chessmen still upon the board, the hanging lamp above. I tried to speak. I seemed to have lost the use of my tongue. In silence he helped me to the door. He half led, half carried me — for I seemed to have lost the use of my feet as well as that of my tongue — to my bedroom. He even assisted me to undress, never leaving me till I was between the sheets. All the time not a word was spoken. When he went I believe he took the key outside and locked the door.

That was a night of dreams. I know not if I was awake or sleeping, but all sorts of strange things presented themselves to my mental eye. I could not shut them from my sight. One figure was prominent in all I saw — the figure of a man. I knew, or thought I knew, that it was Monsieur Funichon. He was a lean old man, and what I noticed chiefly were his hands. Such ugly hands! In some fantastical way I seemed to be contending with them all through the night.

And yet in the morning when I woke — for I did wake up, and that from as sweet refreshing sleep as one might wish to have — it was all gone. It was bright day. The sun was shining into the great, ill-furnished room. As I got out of bed and began to dress, the humorous side of the thing had returned to me again. The idea of there being anything supernatural about a set of ivory chessmen appeared to me to be extremely funny.

I found St Servan had gone out. It was actually half-past ten! His *table d'hôte* at the Hôtel de Bretagne was at eleven, and before he breakfasted he always took a *petit verre* at the club. If he had locked the door overnight he had not forgotten to unlock it before he started. I went into the rambling barnlike room which served us for a *salon*. The chessmen had disappeared. Probably St Servan had put them away — I wondered if the ghost had interfered with him. I laughed to myself as I went out — fancy St Servan contending with a ghost.

The proprietor of the Hôtel de Bretagne is Legitimist, so all the aristocrats go there — of course, St Servan with the rest. Presumably the landlord's politics is the point, to his cooking they are apparently indifferent — I never knew a worse table in my life! The landlord of the Hôtel de l'Europe may be a Communist for all I care — *his* cooking is first-rate, so I go there. I went there that morning. After I had breakfasted I strolled off towards the Grande Rue, to Monsieur Bobineau.

When he saw me Monsieur was all smirks and smiles — he *must* have got those chessmen for *less* than five-and-twenty francs! I asked him if he had any more of the belongings of Monsieur Funichon.

'But certainly! Three other sets of chessmen.'

I didn't want to look at those, apparently one set was quite enough for me. Was that all he had?

'But no! There was an ancient bureau, very magnificent, carved' —

I thanked him — nor did I want to look at that. In the Grande Rue at Morlaix old bureaux carved about the beginning the fifteenth century — if you listen to the vendors — are as plentiful as cobble-stones.

'But I have all sorts of things of Monsieur Funichon. It was I who bought them nearly all. Books, papers and' — '

Monsieur Bobineau waved his hands towards a multitude of books and papers which crowded the shelves at the side of his shop. I took a volume down. When I opened it I found it was in manuscript.

'That work is unique!' explained Bobineau. 'It was the intention of Monsieur Funichon to give it to the world, but he died before his purpose was complete. It is the records of all the games of chess he ever played — in fifty volumes. Monsieur will perceive it is unique.'

I should think it was unique! In fifty volumes! The one I held was a large quarto, bound in leather, containing some six or seven hundred pages, and was filled from cover to cover with matter in a fine, clear handwriting, written on both sides of the page. I pictured the face of the publisher to whom it was suggested that *he* should give to the world such a work as that.

I opened the volume at the first page. It was, as Bobineau said, apparently the record, the comments, of an interminable series of games of chess. I glanced at the initial game. Here are the opening moves, just as they were given there:

White	Black
Queen's Knight's Pawn, one square.	Queen's Knight's Pawn, one square.
King's Knight's Pawn, one square.	King's Knight's Pawn, one square.
Queen's Rook's Pawn, two squares.	Queen's Rook's Pawn, two squares.
King's Rook's Pawn, two squares.	King's Rook's Pawn, two squares.

They were exactly the moves of the night before. They were such peculiar moves, and made under such peculiar circumstances, that I was scarcely likely to mistake them. So far as we had gone, St Servan and I, assisted by the unseen hand, had reproduced Monsieur Funichon's initial game in the first volume of his fifty — and a very peculiar game it seemed to be. I asked Bobineau what he would take for the volume which I held.

'Monsieur perceives that to part them would spoil the set, which is unique. Monsieur shall have the whole fifty' — I shuddered. I imagine Bobineau saw I did, he spoke so very quickly — 'for a five-franc piece, which is less than the value of the paper and the binding.'

I knew then that he had probably been paid for carting the rubbish away. However, I paid him his five-franc piece, and marched off with the volume under my arm, giving him to understand, to his evident disappointment, that at my leisure I would give him instructions as to the other forty-nine.

As I went along I thought the matter over. Monsieur Funichon seemed to have been a singular kind of man — he appeared to have carried his singularity even beyond the grave. Could it have been the cold-blooded intention of his ghost to make us play the whole contents of the fifty volumes through? What a fiend of a ghost his ghost must be!

I opened the volume and studied the initial game. The people were right who had said that the man was mad. None but an imbecile would have played such a game — his right hand against his left! — and none but a raving madman would have recorded his imbecility in black and white, as though it were a thing to be proud of! Certainly none but a criminal lunatic would have endeavoured to foist his puerile travesty of the game and study of chess upon two innocent men.

Still the thing was curious. I flattered myself that St Servan would be startled when he saw the contents of the book I was carrying home. I resolved that I would instantly get out the chessmen and begin another game — perhaps the ghost of Monsieur Funichon would favour us with a further exposition of his ideas of things. I even made up my mind that I would communicate with the Psychical Research Society. Not at all improbably they might think the case sufficiently remarkable to send down a member of their body to inquire into the thing upon the spot. I almost began to hug myself on the possession of a ghost, a ghost, too, which might be induced to perform at will — almost on the principle of 'drop a coin into the slot and the figures move'! It was cheap at a hundred francs. What a stir those chessmen still might make! What vexed problems they might solve! Unless I was much mistaken, the expenditure of those hundred francs had placed me on the royal road to immortality.

Filled with such thoughts I reached our rooms. I found that St Servan had returned. With him, if I may say so, he had brought his friends. Such friends! Ye Goths! When I opened the door the first thing which greeted me was a strong, not to say suffocating, smell of incense. The room was filled with smoke. A fire was blazing on the hearth. Before it was St Servan, on his knees, his hands clasped in front of him, in an attitude of prayer. By him stood a priest, in his robes of office. He held what seemed a pestle and mortar, whose contents he had thrown by handfuls on to the flames, muttering some doggerel to himself the while.

Behind him were two acolytes, 'with nice clean faces, and nice white stoles', who were swinging censers — hence the odour which filled the room. I was surprised when I beheld all this. They appeared to be holding some sort of religious service — and I had not bargained for that sort of thing when I had arranged with St Servan to share the rooms with him. In my surprise I unconsciously interrupted the proceedings.

'St Servan! Whatever is the meaning of this?'

St Servan looked up, and the priest looked round — that was all the attention they paid to me. The acolytes eyed me with what I conceived to be a grin upon their faces. But I was not to be put down like that.

'I must ask you, St Servan, for an explanation.'

The priest turned the mortar upside down, and emptied the remainder of its contents into the fire.

'It is finished,' he said.

St Servan rose from his knees and crossed himself.

'We have exorcised the demon,' he observed.

'You have what?' I asked.

'We have driven out the evil spirit which possessed the chessmen.'

I gasped. A dreadful thought struck me.

'You don't mean to say that you have dared to play tricks with my property?'

'Monsieur,' said the priest, 'I have ground it into dust.'

He had. That fool of a St Servan had actually fetched his parish priest and his acolytes and their censers, and between them they had performed a comminatory service made and provided for the driving out of demons. They had ground my ivory chessmen in the pestle and mortar, and then burned them in the fire. And this in the days of the Psychical Research Society! And they had cost me a hundred francs! And that idiot of a ghost had never stretched out a hand or said a word!

THE HAUNTED CHESSMEN

E.R. Punshon

It was in Fred Kerr's rooms that I saw them first. For a wonder Kerr was by himself; he was the most popular man I ever knew, I think, and it was the rarest thing in the world to find him alone. But that I had done so this evening rather pleased me, for I was very full of my success against Jenoure Baume, and very anxious to tell Kerr all about it. Even he had never yet beaten Jenoure Baume.

Of course, Baume isn't a master of chess in the sense that are Lasker and Casablanca. Still, for a common-or-garden player like myself, with a purely local reputation, to beat him is something of an achievement, and I wanted very much to tell Kerr of my success. He was very sympathetic and very interested, and in analysing the game with me he pointed out a move Jenoure Baume might have made which would almost certainly have cost me my queen. Fortunately Baume had not seen it — nor had I for that matter — and I told Kerr he really ought to go in for chess seriously.

'Not enough open air about it for me,' he answered laughingly. 'I'll take it up when I'm sixty.' When I rose to go he mentioned that the date of his wedding had been fixed for the following month.

I congratulated him warmly — Lady Norah was a charming girl, and the match most suitable in every way — and in one of his little confidential outbursts that every one found so charming he told me how happy he was and how fortunate he counted himself.

'And is that one of the wedding-presents?' I asked, nodding towards a set of chessmen standing on a board on a small side-table.

I had noticed them as soon as I entered the room. Of Indian workmanship as I guessed, they were very beautifully carved and polished, and when I looked at them again I was conscious of a curious impression. I cannot define it exactly — but it was almost as though they moved and stirred, as though they all watched eagerly, intently. The idle thought came to me that those inanimate carved pieces of polished bone were watching me as a spider from its web watches a fly hovering near.

Vexed with myself for having such foolish fancies — I remember I thought they were due to the strain of my game with Jenoure Baume — I went over to look at them more closely.

'Awfully fine carving!' I said, picking up one of the white pieces. 'Indian, isn't it? Are they a wedding present?'

'No,' Kerr answered. 'The fact is, I bought them from poor Will Lathbury's widow.'

'Oh, indeed!' I said.

I had only met Lathbury once or twice, but, of course, I knew him well by reputation as a sound, steady player, and the mysterious tragedy that had ended his life had been a great shock to me.

'Those were the pieces they found near him,' Kerr added.

Poor Lathbury had been discovered one morning lying dead across his chessboard on which he had apparently been working out some problem, or analysing a game. The razor with which he had cut his throat was in his hand, and there was no faintest explanation possible of his miserable deed. It was certainly shown in evidence that for a day or two before the end he had seemed slightly worried, and had spoken about some game of chess or problem that appeared to be troubling him. And he had complained of not sleeping very well, a most unusual thing with him. But that was all. The coroner suggested that his mind had become affected by his intense application to his favourite game, but that was all rubbish. However, the jury returned the usual verdict, and there the matter had to rest.

'Are they ivory?' I asked, looking more closely at the piece I was handling.

'Well, the story goes,' answered Kerr, with a touch of hesitation — 'the story goes that they are made from human bones.'

'Oh Lord!' I said, putting down a little quickly the piece I was holding.

'I don't know if it's true,' Kerr added, 'very likely it isn't. It may be just a yarn. But the tale is that an Indian Rajah some time in the Middle Ages captured a hated enemy, killed him, and had these made from his bones.'

'Ugh!' I said. 'What an idea! What on earth made you get them?'

'I hardly know,' he answered. 'Mrs Lathbury wanted to get rid of them — naturally. They hadn't very pleasant associations for her. She asked me what they ought to fetch. I said I would take them if she liked. I thought it was a way to help her, and then it's lovely carving.'

'Rather too lovely for me,' I said, and I could have sworn that the black queen turned her head and shot at me a glance of malignant and deadly hatred.

Of course, the notion was absurd, and when I looked again I saw the piece as immobile as any other bit of carved bone. And yet when I looked a third time I was once more aware of that air of cruel and furtive waiting as of some evil thing lurking patiently which before had seemed to me to hover over those two double rows of carved figures.

Determined to conquer my fancies I picked up the black queen and, examining it more closely, I thought I made out that it was a trick in the arrangement of the eyes which gave the piece that aspect of alert watchfulness I had noticed.

'Carved out of human bone!' I repeated, weighing the piece in my hand. 'What an idea! Well, shall we have a game?'

I thought Kerr looked startled and even a little alarmed. He shook his head quickly without speaking. I felt very relieved; for the idea was powerfully in my mind that it was not against him that I must play, but against some other — some unknown — antagonist.

I said good-night a little hurriedly and took myself off. The fact is, I had wanted to play so badly that I felt that if I stayed there much longer with that black queen in my hand and the pieces drawn up ready, I should find myself making the first move — against Whom, I wondered? Whom or what?

I remember very plainly that as I went out of the room I had a last impression of those pieces drawn up in line as though waiting — waiting with a malign and dreadful patience.

I know my heart was beating faster than usual, and my forehead was a little damp as I came out into the street. The idea was with me that I had escaped some great danger, but what or why I had no idea.

* * *

A week or two passed, and I only remembered my experience of that night to be ashamed of the inexplicable agitation I had felt. Then one day I happened to meet Baume. He knew Kerr fairly well, and declared he was wasting on other pursuits talents that had been meant for chess alone. Then I chanced to mention those curious carved bone chessmen.

'He says they are made of human bone,' I remarked, with a laugh. 'Gruesome idea, isn't it?'

To my surprise Baume looked very grave. Apparently the old man knew those chessmen well — and did not like them. Finally he blurted out:

'You tell you friend to drop them in the river. That is the best for them.'

Going home that night I noticed on the placard of one of the evening papers, 'Mysterious Suicide', and on that of another, 'Strange West End Tragedy'. I paid no attention just then, but the next morning over breakfast I noticed a column headed, 'Mysterious Death of Well-known Sportsman', and, on glancing at it, I saw that it referred to poor Fred Kerr.

He had been found first thing in the morning laying dead with a bullet through his brain. The pistol with which he had committed the miserable deed was still clasped in his right hand, and the account mentioned that the body lay across a chessboard on which the pieces were arranged in what seemed an unfinished game.

It was a frightful shock to me — indeed it must have been so to all who knew Kerr. I could hardly believe that a man so full of life and spirits, so richly dowered with all good gifts, had ended his life in such a way. There was no explanation. At the inquest a verdict of accidental death was returned, the idea being that Kerr had shot himself while cleaning or examining his pistol.

An attempt was made to suggest foul play on the grounds that the position of the pieces on the chessboard showed that a game had just been concluded, that this game must have been played with someone, and that someone had disappeared and was, therefore, under suspicion.

Conclusive evidence showed, however, that the unhappy man had been alone all that evening. Of course, the position of the pieces might be accounted for in many ways. He might have been working out an end-game, or analysing some position. It was not a problem he had been working on, though, as black was winning and, of course, the problem convention is for white to win.

However, not much attention was paid to the chessmen; and as foul play was ruled out and suicide seemed incredible, the jury fell back on the idea of accident, though there was not the least support for such a theory.

Poor Kerr! I called to leave a wreath and express my sympathy. I asked if I might see my old friend for the last time, and they agreed. With feelings of the utmost sadness I looked my last on my friend's face, and as I did so there came upon me slowly, irresistibly, the idea that he had died in terror and anguish of soul and body.

I felt this impression slowly invade and possess my mind, till I shook and trembled with the knowledge that I stood in the presence of unnameable dread. I began to edge slowly away towards the door, very slowly, for I knew that if I went quickly my panic would overcome me, and I should run, and I knew that would be very dangerous, fatal perhaps. By an intense effort of will I kept my face towards the bed in which lay That which I had no longer regarded as the earthly frame of my friend, but felt was changed into something unspeakably horrible and foul. My hair bristled, the flesh crept under my bones, I forced myself to keep my eyes fixed steadily on the still form upon the bed, though I was sure it was watching me with an intent and evil patience as a spider in its web watches the fly fluttering near — the very sensation I had had before.

Somehow or another, I don't know how, I got to the bottom of the stairs. I stood there, a little dizzy, a little faint, trying to recover myself.

Presently I got out into the street however or another, and I know that for some time afterwards I had no liking for the dark and no taste for being alone.

* * *

Poor Kerr had been the owner of a good many curios he had collected, some of them of value, and when I heard after a time that his friends had decided to sell them at auction, I thought I would go and see if I could pick up some little memento of one I had so much admired and liked.

I bought two rather fine carvings by Meryon; very cheap they were, too. I noticed Mark Norand, the captain of our chess club match team, and after speaking a word or two to him, I was thinking of going when the auctioneer put up the carved bone chessmen.

He did not repeat the tale that they were of human bone — perhaps he thought that wouldn't sound very attractive, or he may not have known the story — but he laid great emphasis on the excellence of the carving. Mark Norand made the first bid, and I know I was very startled. Somehow I hadn't thought of anyone actually buying the things. I said to him:

'I wouldn't have them if I were you.'

He looked at me with rather a puzzled and slightly suspicious air.

'Why, do you want them yourself?' he asked.

'Good heavens, no!' I answered, but I could see he did not quite believe me.

In the auction-room everyone is inclined to be suspicious of everyone else. It is a warfare there without quarter and without scruple. Mark Norand was a friend of mine, but he did not mean to be done out of any bargain that was going. He bought the chessmen for three guineas — cheap enough, considering the excellence of the carving.

He was very pleased with himself and his purchase, and his idea that he had got ahead of me. He asked me to go round and play a game with his new possessions. I refused point blank and he laughed. I think he believed I was a little piqued at losing the chessmen.

We got busier than ever at the office, and I was kept very much occupied for some time. I could not even get a spare hour to slip round to the club for a game, and it was quite by accident that I happened to hear someone mention Mark Norand and say that he was looking very ill.

I knew where it was he generally lunched. The place was out of the way for me, and I didn't like the cooking there, but I went the next day. Almost the first man I saw when I entered was Norand. He was sitting at one of the tables with food before him, but he had pushed it away untasted and was pouring over a chessboard.

'Hullo, Norand,' I said, 'working out a problem?'

He looked up at me. I could not help starting. He was greatly altered, but it was not that I noticed so much as the horrid fear I saw peeping out from his bloodshot eyes and lurking in the new lines that had come about his mouth.

'Oh, you?' he said, and to mingle with the fear I read in his eyes there came a fierce dull resentment, so that he looked at me as though he held me for his deadliest enemy.

'You knew, didn't you? Why didn't you tell me?' he demanded.

'Knew what? Tell you what?' I asked.

'Those chessmen,' he muttered, shuddering. He added: 'Why did you let me buy them?'

'I told you not to; I warned you,' I said.

'Told me not to, warned me not to!' he repeated, and gave me a look of deadly hate. 'If you saw a man knocking at the gate of hell without knowing it, would you just tell him not to do that and then walk away?'

'Why, what's the matter?' I asked.

He did not answer, and the waiter came up just then. I ordered the first thing I saw on the bill. Norand had become intent on his game again. I noticed it was a position in the game and not a problem he was working at — and the waiter, who knew him as an old customer, and saw I was a friend, observed to me:

'The gentleman's worrying too much over his chess. He hardly eats anything now.'

'Has he been long like this?' I asked.

'Only about a week, sir,' the man answered.

He brought me what I had ordered, and Norand looked up presently.

'What do you think of this position?' he asked.

'Well, white looks in rather a fix,' I answered. 'Good Lord, what's the matter?'

I really thought he was going to have a fit; he fell back in his seat, panting for breath and ghastly pale. I might have pronounced his death warrant. I jumped up with some vague idea of getting a doctor but he stopped me.

'No, no, I'm all right,' he said — croaked, rather. 'For God's sake, look at the board, and see if you can find any way out!'

'For white?' I asked.

'For white,' he repeated.

I bent over the board. It seemed to me mate was pretty sure to come in three or four moves. I said:

'Is it a game you're playing?'

He nodded.

'Who's your opponent?' I asked.

He did not answer, and I could see well that a secret and terrible agitation possessed him.

'I don't know,' he stammered.

And the idea came to me that he did know but that he dared not say. This seemed to me highly absurd and at the same time quite reasonable.

He wiped his face again.

'You see,' he argued, 'the thing's impossible.'

'I don't know what you mean; I don't know what you are talking about,' I said angrily.

But the idea burnt my mind like fire, that I did know and that I also dared not say.

He leaned across the table, his eyes alight with that mingled desperate fear and deadly hate I had seen in them before.

'You ought to have warned me,' he muttered. 'Mind this, if I lose I will leave you the things in my will.'

I remember it did not seem to any way absurd that he should couple together the ideas of losing the game and of making his will.

I was studying the position of the pieces so intently that I, like him, pushed aside my lunch almost untasted. Gradually there was coming back to me a memory of the move poor Kerr had suggested Jenoure Baume might have tried in the game he lost to me. It seemed to me a variation of Kerr's idea might be effective in Norand's present position.

I explained the move. Norand jumped at the idea. We developed it together and, so far as we could see, an attack pressed on those lines was practically sure to win the game. Norand's relief was tremendous, mine scarcely less so. Then all at once his expression changed. He said:

'Suppose when I play the knight it slips of itself on to some other square when I'm not looking?'

I stared at him and laughed. The suggestion seemed so absurd I could not help it.

'Well, of course,' I said, 'if your pieces do that, I don't see much chance.'

He did not answer, and I left the restaurant and went back to the office, feeling relieved in one way, but a good deal worried about poor Norand at the same. His obvious terror, my own odd impressions, all seemed to me fanciful and even ridiculous in the face of his wild suggestion of pieces that moved of their own volition.

All the same I was not surprised when, a day or two later, I heard that the poor fellow had drowned himself in a small pond that lay at the foot of his garden. The account in the papers said he had been sitting up late at chess and that he must have gone straight from the chessboard to his doom.

* * *

I could not help making some inquiries about the position of the men on the board. I found, as I had half expected, that they indicated the close of a game in which black had just brought off a mate. My informant told me that presumably poor Norand had been analysing some game. He had not been working out a problem as black was the winning side; and he had not been playing with anyone, as the evidence showed conclusively that he had been alone all the evening.

The usual verdict was returned, and I wrote to Norand's solicitor to say that I absolutely refused to accept any legacy he might have left me.

But I did not post the letter. At one time I had the feeling that the whole thing was pure fancy and that it would be foolish and cowardly to refuse the chessmen if he had really left them to me. And then, again, the idea would come to me that it was all true, but that I was forewarned, and forearmed.

As it happened they were delivered one evening while the Vicar was with me. While he was there I opened the parcel and showed him the chessmen. He was mildly interested and mildly shocked when I told him the tale that they were carved from human bone. He thought it a most repulsive idea, but remarked on the excellence of the carving.

'That black queen, for example,' he said, 'what an idea of — of — well, vitality, almost that figure has.'

I agreed, and after I had seen the Vicar to the door I went back to my room. I found those chessmen I had left lying on the table where the Vicar had been looking at them, now all drawn up in position on the board.

No living soul, I knew well, had been in the room during my short absence. I stood for a moment or two on the threshold, a little daunted, a little confused, and as I watched I understood that I was expected to play — I saw, too, a thrill of a sinister impatience run through the drawn-up lines of the pieces.

I sat down in front of them. I could not help myself. Each separate piece, from king to pawn, showed animate, palpitating, ready, one and all a-quiver with desire and greed, like hungry beasts of prey waiting for their living victim to be thrown to them. The impression grew in my mind that I was in a more dreadful and more imminent danger than any other living man that night, and that this danger was one that threatened not my life only.

I would have fled, but flight, I knew well, was no longer possible. I tried to mutter a prayer, but the words would not come. I tried to lift my hand to push board and pieces to the ground, but I seemed to have lost control of my arm. The quivering, eager, evil impatience of the pieces increased; I should not have been surprised to see them break into some wild dance of hideous ritual.

All at once they grew quiet, though still instinct with vivid, hungry eagerness, and I felt come upon me a sudden awe and fear and horror as I realised that my Antagonist was there.

I could see nothing, I heard nothing, only I knew well that he was there, that the had come and was seated opposite.

I understood the game was about to begin.

I could not help myself. Slowly I lifted my hand. I swear I did not touch it, but the king's pawn it had been my thought to move slid forward two squares.

A moment's pause and then the black king's pawn, untouched, moved forward in reply. I made my next move, or rather, when I raised my hand with the intention of doing it, the piece transferred itself untouched to the position I had in my mind. The answering move came almost at once. And so the game was played on.

All the time I never touched a piece; once I had made up my mind and raised my hand the piece I was thinking of immediately took up the position I wished. The black pieces did the same; they moved, advanced, retreated, but all in harmony and all in evident obedience to the will of my unseen, unknown Antagonist.

Invisible, but not unknown.

For I was very sure there sat opposite me a man long dead, with an evil face and cruel eyes and hungry, slobbering mouth, wearing the jewelled robes of an Indian prince, and played with all his skill this game for his master in which the prize was — myself.

I knew that now the game had begun, it had to be finished. I called up all my powers to my aid. I felt my mind grow clear; my nerves were calm and steady. I played my best. I played as

I had never played before; I believe I played that night a game that would not have disgraced a master.

More than once I felt I had my Antagonist in difficulties, but each time he retrieved himself. I won a pawn, but lost it again. Still, I began to believe I had a chance of winning.

I pressed hard. I felt a clearness in my brain, a vividness of thought and clearness of vision I have never know before or since. Once or twice, when I was tempted to make a move that might have been dangerous, it was as thought I heard a secret whisper warning me to be careful. I knew, too, that my Antagonist was troubled, and I understood that my pieces themselves, both black and white, felt this, and were troubled also.

I had begun a hot attack on the black queen. If I could win her I felt the game could be mine. It was not only that the queen is the most powerful piece, but I realised also that in her lay the focus of the opposing power, that from her or through her there radiated a sort of vigour and encouragement all the other pieces felt — and not the black only but my own white as well.

My attack on the queen failed. I was a move too late, and she slipped out of the net I had so nearly drawn around her. The failure left my position less strong, and I found myself attacked in my turn. I rallied my forces, but the pressure grew stronger and stronger.

The critical point was on my left, where I was beginning to plan a counter-attack. It promised well, and I was beginning to make progress when I found a return thrust aimed at me.

I was puzzled, and, on looking, found that the position of my pieces was no longer as it had been, but a much weaker one. I could not understand, for I was sure I had not moved them. As I looked and wondered I was aware that my unseen Antagonist smiled evilly to himself, and the black queen shook with a horrid, secret merriment that spread and spread till every piece upon the board, black and white, was laughing wickedly to itself, rejoicing in the prospect of my defeat.

I realised in a flash that one of my pawns had turned traitor and, when I was not looking, had slipped back from the square where I had placed it to the one behind where it was so much less effective.

* * *

It cost me my bishop before I could re-establish my position, and the small inner voice I had seemed to hear before whispered to me that I must watch closely and unceasingly, or the same thing would happen again. I understood that my Antagonist, smiling evilly to himself, could make any one of my pieces betray me, and that this foul play he kept ever in reserve to help him at need. No wonder that he had always won his games all through the centuries!

I was a piece to the bad now, and I had the double strain of playing and of watching to see that none of my men slipped from the squares on which I had placed them. I set my teeth and played my best. I lost another piece, and my king, hotly attacked, was pinned into one corner. Still I fought on, though my brow was wet and my hands shook and upon me lay the consciousness of impending doom.

I made one last feeble attempt at a counter-attack. I do not think it could possibly have saved me, but it was audacious, a little disconcerting, and meant delay at the least. And that was something, for I knew that if I could hold out till cock-crow I should earn at least a day's respite. That my Antagonist knew also, and he grew, one must suppose, impatient.

I was watching my pieces intently since there was not one of them but would have played the traitor had chance offered. My new attack hinged on the one rook I had remaining, and suddenly I saw it sliding away from where it stood to an adjoining square, where it would have been comparatively useless. It stopped when my eye fell on it, for apparently they had no power to move — or my Antagonist no power to make them move — when I was watching, and then something made me look away again. Instantly the rook slipped off to the adjoining square, and at once again all the other pieces, black and white alike, shook with a passion of secret, evil laughter.

For a moment despair overcame me, for now it was only a question of mate in two moves.

But, as before a tiny voice had whispered to me to be cautious when I had contemplated an unsound move, so now again I head that small, still voice sound clear and vivid in my ear. I knew that my one hope was to do as it advised.

I sprang to my feet.

Pointing at the rook that had moved I cried with a loud voice: 'I appeal.'

I was aware of an instant, fierce commotion all around me; I saw the pieces, black and white, all palpitant; I heard no sound, but I knew that my Antagonist was dismayed and troubled.

Again I cried:

'I appeal.'

The fierce tumult and commotion I was aware of all round, grew yet wilder and more fierce. Though I heard nothing, saw nothing, I knew that all about was fury, dismay, excitement, a hurrying to and fro of strange and evil things, a passage of vast and awful shadows. The pieces were all quivering with hatred and alarm. My dread, long dead Antagonist seemed to me to be screaming hoarsely in an agony of protest and pain. Though still I heard, saw, felt nothing, I was somehow conscious that I stood in the very centre of a chaos of invisible, conflicting powers; that unimaginable forces were aimed against me, but that neverthe-less I stood protected. For the third time I cried out very loudly:

'I appeal.'

That strange and awful tumult passed. All was still and silent, all that had filled my small room so dreadfully fled swiftly far away. The chessmen were no longer animate and palpitant, but were quiet as any other bits of carved bone; I had a vision of my Antagonist, baffled, howling, far in the depths of nethermost space.

I knew I was safe now, and knew also what next I had to do. The still, small voice I had heard before had whispered that to me also, and I hurried to obey. I swept the chessmen into their box, and carrying it carefully in my hands, I went into the garden, out by the side of the gate, and up the lane that leads to the churchyard.

Dawn was grey in the east, the cocks were crowing as I reached it. There amidst the graves, in earth consecrated by holy words for the last resting-place of men, I dug with my bare hands and buried deep the box and the pieces of carved bone it held, deep in the shadows of a cross reared on a grave near by. There I left them to rest for ever; and so, drunk with weariness and terror, went back to my home to rest in peace and thankfulness and safety.

BISHOP'S GAMBIT

August Derleth

On the sixth day of his haphazard investigation of the attic, Albert found his grandmother's board and chessmen. They were locked in a case in a locked trunk, but, being briefly alone in the house, he had no hesitation about breaking both locks. He did it with despatch, knowing no one was likely to come up into the attic for months. Anyway, he had made the attic, with all its boxes, trunks, old furniture, and forgotten toys, his own, a sort of private world which perhaps only a child could understand and enjoy.

Albert had not been looking for the chess-set. It was just that he had been conducting a routine examination of his domain by way of taking inventory. Year after year, the attic yielded surprising and often delightful discoveries, for, as he grew older, he learned to appreciate different things. Now, being seven, the chess-set attracted him. Grandfather Josiah Valliant had been dead only three months, and Albert could remember very clearly the seemingly endless hours which he had whiled away watching the old man at his game. He took the set over to one of the gable windows into the sunlight streaming into the dust-mote atmosphere, and set it up on a little gate-legged table there.

He remembered very clearly every move his grandfather had made. First he took the white king's pawn and moved it out; it seemed to him that he could almost hear the old man's rumbling voice explaining, 'That is the bishop's gambit, Albert.' The next move would come from across the board — the counter opening from the black king. Then the white king's bishop's pawn went out. He grew absorbed, casting his memory back, to his grandfather's sunny room, seeing in his mind's eye the shawled old man, usually so gruff, but with him always patient, seeing himself sitting there, watching fascinated, while the pieces moved under the old man's fingers, and, sometimes, at the behest of a friend come to spend a few hours with Josiah Valliant.

'Albert! Albert Valliant!'

His absorption was broken. He started up in irritation, but he had no impulse to disobey. He got out of the attic before he answered, and, brushing himself, went down the long, dark stairs to the living-room where his mother expected him to give her a report of his activities for the hours during which she had been away.

Mrs Valliant was a vain, foolish woman, pretty in a vapid way, with China-blue eyes and a small mouth which seemed incapable of any but a doll-like expression. She was blonde and much befrilled, and she was not, at the moment, being fawned upon by the tall man with the black moustache, known to him chiefly by his mother's name of 'Dear Perry'. And had Albert behaved himself while she was gone?

'Yes,' said Albert dutifully.

Dust on his clothes, grime on his hands — she observed, she commented. To the bathroom now, quick, to be cleaned for dinner. 'And Albert,' she said, 'guess who's coming to have dinner with us?'

Albert grew sullen. He did not need to guess; he knew. He said nothing.

'Guess, Albert,' said his mother gaily.

Silence answered her.

'My little boy must have lost his tongue,' she said chidingly.

He made an indeterminate sound and marched sturdily to the bathroom.

Her voice followed him, resigned. 'I don't know how you got it into your head that Perry doesn't like you! I'm sure he does. And he wants so much that you should like him. Oh, I know he doesn't pretend to think he can take your poor dead father's place — but I know, I'm positive, if Henry were alive, he'd *want* you to learn to like Perry, just as Perry likes you, and I know . . .'

He closed the bathroom door and enjoyed the beneficence of freedom from her pursuing voice, which had begun to assume that sound of complaint so familiar to him. He wished he could say, like grandfather had said, 'Oh, for God's sake, Verna, stop that damned whining!' But of course, he could not.

Finishing in the bathroom, he opened the door cautiously and peered out. Sounds from the kitchen informed him that his mother was out of range. He slipped from the bathroom and mounted once more into the attic, before the last sunlight had quite withdrawn. It lay redly against the gabled ceiling; it reflected from there with a kind of pale, old rose luminousness to the chessboard below, shrouding the figures in a glowing haze.

He stared at them. What had he done? Moved out the two pawns in the bishop's gambit, yes. Followed out with the pawn to open for the defence from the black king. Then his mother had called. And since then — why, since then someone else must have discovered his game, for there it was, well advanced, with havoc wrought amongst the black pieces, and the king only a few moves from being checkmated, the white pieces inexorably moving in for the final triumph. Albert stood looking at the board with unwavering eyes while the sunlight faded and drew away into a crimson afterglow in the west, and the dusk came up like magic in the attic. Who could have come here? he wondered. Who — when his mother and he were alone in the house, though the cook had now come in, of course. But it might have been the cook, come early. No, that was not possible; she knew nothing about chess.

He went to the board and took his place at white. Even though the twilight had invaded the attic, and the cheery sounds of robins' carols came in from outside, there was enough light to complete the game. Black had two moves, white had three. He made them. Checkmate.

'My game,' said Albert.

'*Our* game,' said somebody else gently.

Albert looked around. There was no one there. There was nothing but a host of shadows which had not been there before. Evening made its own shadows awaiting night and the darkness in which all shadows were but one vastness of black without end. He stood waiting for another sound, but there was nothing. Robins carolled, farther away a meadow-lark sang, the mourning doves cooed sadly under the eaves, and from the street came the muted voices of life: children screaming in play, cars going by, the whistling of policemen directing traffic at the intersection, the clanging of the streetcar.

Resolutely, Albert reset the board. Back went the white pieces, back went the black — back into place in even rows. Now, then — the game waited upon the next day, and would it were now, and that dinner were over, and 'dear Perry' were gone away again.

He went out of the attic and descended dutifully to his room where he waited until his mother called him for dinner.

Perry Cross was tall, urbane, handsome. He had a way with women — so everyone said, and it was certain that he would have his way with so giddy and foolish a woman as Mrs Henry Valliant, now a year widowed and no longer protected even in theory by the influence of her father-in-law. He had dark, snapping eyes; he had a fine black moustache; he had well-pressed clothes and a well-pressed mouth. He owned rings, a cane, bony features; he possessed patience, cunning, fortitude. He was predatory, but suavely so. Women loved him; he loved women — with money; he loved them lavishly, exacting ultimate repayment. He could not possibly have loved anyone so insipid as Verna Valliant for any other reason but money, which she had.

'Good evening, Albert,' she said.

'H-lo,' answered Albert indifferently, appraising the table.

'Were you ever a little boy, Perry?' asked his mother. 'I can't believe you were, really.'

Cross said something in a low voice; his mother giggled.

Albert was disgusted. He looked at them both with the utmost distaste, spurred all the more by the unmistakeable venom for him which he had not failed to notice in Cross's single direct glance.

'Children can be so difficult, can't they?' said Mrs Valliant, and rang for dinner service to begin, having given the cook just enough time to change into another costume. Perry Cross had once said that he appreciated a woman who knew how to save and take care of her money.

'Oh, the right training does wonders,' said Cross, glancing across at Albert with a little smile on his thin lips.

Albert flinched inside.

'Albert, you haven't even told dear Perry how glad you are to see him,' said his mother.

Silence.

'Albert!'

'I'm not.'

'At least he's honest,' said Cross, but the look he turned on Albert belied his appreciation of that honesty.

Now his mother was fluttering, all in a dither for having prodded him until he had said something he should have left unsaid.

The food came. Consommé. A tossed salad in wooden bowls. Lamb chops. Cranberry pudding and coffee. The conversation during the meal was light, ignoring Albert. This suited him. Ever since his mother had permitted 'dear Perry' such frequent access to the house — which was after grandfather Valliant's death — Albert had retreated more and more into his own world, which was select and did not include silly women or sleek men who manifestly hated children. Perry Cross existed on its perimeter. His mother was retreating to the same distance with meteoric rapidity undeterred by the knowledge that she was, after all, his mother.

After dinner, Cross leaned back and surveyed Albert with judicious scrutiny.

'Do you think we ought to tell him, Verna?' he said without taking his eyes off Albert.

'Oh, dear! He'll have to know, won't he?' She turned to Albert. 'How would you like to have dear Perry as your new father, Albert?' she asked, visibly apprehensive.

Albert was horrified. For a moment he wanted to vomit, but on reflection, the cranberry pudding had been too good. He gave Cross a stare of unmistakable contempt, pushed his chair back from the table, and stalked indignantly from the room. He went up the stairs muttering to himself. Father, indeed! His mother's shrill anger rising from below, coupled with Cross's attempts to soothe her, left him as cold as an icicle in the Antarctic.

'I wish my granddaddy was here,' he said into the darkness of his room. 'He'd show that Perry Cross!'

He fell asleep presently to dream dreams of Perry Cross as his new father beating and beating him, filling him full of 'the right training'.

In the morning his mother came querulously to his room, complaining about what a bad boy he had been the night before, and how dear Perry had had his feelings hurt, and how dear Perry only wanted him to love him . . .

'I hate him and he hates me,' said Albert forthrightly.

She slapped him virtuously, but she was sorry immediately, and burst into tears. 'Now see what you've done, you bad boy,' she cried. 'Upsetting me so much I had to hit you — my own little boy.'

'You didn't have to.'

'Albert!'

Sullen silence answered her.

'Albert, you must learn to like Mr Cross.'

Silence prolonged.

'Do you hear me?'

'Yes.'

'There now. You just try, that's all. He'll love you like he loves all the little children.'

'And like he loved all his other wives,' said Albert vindictively.

'Why, Albert!'

'I know. Granddaddy told me. He's been married five times before. And every time he got richer and richer. Sometimes it was the insurance, and sometimes it was just because they were fools . . .'

'Albert Valliant!'

'Like you.'

She stuffed her handkerchief into her mouth and looked at him, wide-eyed. He gazed unwinkingly back at her, his small mouth and chin set and firm. 'You are a bad, bad boy,' she said at last, through her handkerchief, so that it was a distant, half-strangled sound. But she retreated before his burgeoning anger.

After he got up and had his breakfast, he went outside. But he was not satisfied there; so in a little while, he made his way back up to the attic, half expecting to find another marvellous change in the pieces on the chessboard. However, they were not altered; they stood just as he had left them, and he sat down to them with a feeling of relief. Relief was an integral part of being in the attic, for here he was away from every troublesome thing — he did not have to think of Perry Cross or school beginning again in less than a month, or now, of his mother's impending marriage — nothing. This was his world — the sloping walls, the dark room filled with enchanting perfumes and pungences, and two gable windows looking out over all the city, for the Valliant house stood on a little knoll, and from one of its gables at least it was possible to see the ocean and sometimes ships on that blue water, and gulls flying like something fantastic and unreal in a world as distant as a star.

He sat down at the chessboard.

No sooner was he there than he was seized, as before, with the urge to play. He pushed the king's pawn to fourth place. That was the way to begin; that was grandfather Valliant's way. Bishop's gambit. He reached over and brought up the black king's pawn to sit glowering at the white pawn, face to face across the middle of the board. He came back and brought forth the sacrifice — his king's bishop's pawn — to fourth place. He tried to imagine what black ought to do. What if, unlike Grandfather Valliant's game, black did not accept the challenge? What then? But black had to accept or lose his own pawn, of course.

But indeed — was it necessary to take the black pawn or the white, for that matter?

He stretched out his hand to move, and held it there in mid-air above the board.

The black pawn stood in place of his bishop's pawn, and his pawn, instead, lay over at the side of the board. He withdrew his hand, thoughtfully.

'But I didn't do it,' he said aloud.

'No, of course not.'

Ah, but he knew that voice. 'Where are you, Grandpa?'

'Play, boy.'

He looked in vain for that kindly, bearded face with the eyes that could be so fierce and challenging. Once he thought he saw it opposite him, across the chessboard; again it seemed to be at his shoulder, peering intently at the board. It was strange, and yet it was not strange. Bending to play, he found that each time he made the wrong move, something held his hand and guided him to the right move. What fun it was! Almost like old times in grandfather's room, before Perry Cross had moved into his mother's life with such force and determination.

Even in the midst of his game — though his fourth that afternoon — Cross obtruded, and presently he found himself telling Grandfather Valliant all about it; for, though he could never seem to see anything of the old man except a shadowy something from time to time, he could hear those subdued grunts and harrumphs which Grandfather Valliant always gave when he was listening to him.

'And so if he is going to be my new dad, he's going to beat me, he's going to whip me,' said Albert earnestly. 'I know it the way he looks at me, and there won't be anything mama can do to stop him, either, unless she gives him all her money.'

'Humph!'

'I wish you were here all the time, Grandpa; then he wouldn't come every night like this. And I could stay with you if he took mama away.'

'Humph!'

It was not a very satisfactory conversation, but at least Albert had someone who listened to him without interruption, and, unlike his mother, without fidgeting and tears and recriminations.

In the evening he was scolded for having been in the attic again.

His mother was almost incoherent. He mustn't go there again, but if he did, he must wear old clothes and he mustn't get so dirty; good little boys didn't get dirty. He must learn to like 'dear Perry' because 'dear Perry' was going to be his stepfather and that meant he must be just like a son to him. Would he promise?

'Promise what?'

'Will you promise to like Perry?'

No answer.

'Will you try?'

No answer.

'Albert, for the last time, will you promise to try to like Perry somehow?'

'Yes, Mother.'

'Yes, what?'

'I promise to try to like him somehow.'

'And keep out of the attic. You look like a tramp.'

'But right now,' he amended, 'I hate Perry Cross.'

'Oh, you bad boy!'

There were further tears, more recriminations, in the midst of which Perry Cross came, bearing flowers — some roses he had bought at the florist's down the street. However distrait she was, Mrs Valliant cooed and fluttered. And whatever was the matter with her? demanded Perry Cross. He had never seen her eyes so red. Surely not with tears!

'Oh, its that naughty little boy of mine,' she cried. 'He won't stay out of the attic. Every afternoon — lunch till supper — there he is, dirty as a — a tramp! I can't make him obey!'

Cross laughed. From his vantage-point on the stairs, Albert shuddered.

'Some day perhaps you might let me try, darling,' said Cross.

'Oh, would you? I mean, do you think you could?'

'Perhaps he has something up there he doesn't want anyone else to see. We might surprise him.'

'Oh, Perry, you *are* clever.'

Albert crept up the stairs. He remembered as if it were yesterday his grandfather saying kindly, 'Albert, your mother isn't very smart; but she's very sweet and she *is* your mother, and after I'm gone you'll have to watch over her.' He flung himself on to his bed and buried his head in the pillow, sobbing. 'I can't do anything,' he said in miserable impotence, 'I'm too little and he's too big!'

In the next four days Albert played seventeen games of chess. Though he was not aware of it, he used Alekhine's opening and the queen's gambit; he played against Philidor's and the Indian defence; he opened with Ruy Lopez and Reti's; but the bishop's gambit remained his favourite; he felt less strange with it, having been so long accustomed to his grandfather's preference.

He had long and pleasant conversations (if very much one-sided), with his grandfather, and he felt somehow safe in the dusty confines of the attic.

Yet he was aware that Perry Cross and his mother discussed him; he was aware of this as of impending doom, and he expected at any moment that Cross would prevail upon her to let him try his hand with Albert. Still, he believed intuitively that Cross would wait until his mother was securely in his grasp before he tried.

The week passed, and another began.

Late one sunny August afternoon, a board creaked knowingly behind Albert at his game. He turned, his intimate conversation halted abruptly.

Cross stood there, eyeing him speculatively. 'Talking to yourself, Albert?'

No answer.

Cross moved forward peering over Albert's thin shoulders. 'Ah, chess. Imagine that! Can you play?'

Silence.

'But, of course, you can, or you wouldn't be at it — would you?'

He moved around the gate-legged table and sat down on a box on the other side, his back to the window. The box, being small, gave him a hunched appearance; with the light streaming in at his back, he looked malevolent.

Albert was caught in a shell of danger, sensing it all around him. He pushed his chin out, stubbornly, and sat with his small hands clenched.

'Did my mother send you up here?' he demanded.

'She knows I'm here, Albert.'

'I don't believe you.'

In a flash, Cross's hand whipped across the table and fell,

knuckles forward upon one cheek. Albert drew back, his fingers instinctively reaching for the stinging place.

'You should be careful when you suggest people are lying, Albert. That isn't nice.' He smiled, but his eyes did not smile. 'You and I will have to get to know each other better, Albert.'

'I know you,' said Albert thickly. There were tears in his throat, but he was too proud to let them show. 'I know you more than I want to know you,' he said fiercely. 'You can just get out of here. This is my place. Mine — and grandpa's.'

'Oh, there is someone else with you?' Cross made a pretence much exaggerated, of peering about the attic, but his eyes returned to Albert, and from Albert, swung down to the board, which he studied.

'Let us begin with a game of chess, Albert,' he said finally. Without waiting for Albert's acquiescence, he began to reset the board. 'I play a little, too. In a way, Albert, I am a master — at least of pawns, if not of chess.'

'Of women,' said Albert.

Cross looked sharply, angrily at him, but decided that the boy did not know what he had said. Nor did Albert; he had not meant to say it; he had not even thought it at the moment; something inside him had impelled the words from his lips. He felt strange even at the sound of them, for he had wanted to say that no, he would not play chess with Cross, and even now he wanted to withdraw, but something held him, something would not let him go.

'Shall we play?' asked Cross levelly, but his voice was a challenge.

'Yes,' said Albert, but 'No,' rattled in his bewildered brain. And, 'For what stakes?' he asked. This also came from no part of him.

Cross gave a long, studied gaze. 'Well,' he said at last. 'Well, well, Albert — somebody has been teaching you things. Only seven, too. But since you suggest it, I'll take you up. If you lose, you must forget that you don't like me, and if I lose, you may continue to dislike me for a while.'

'No,' said Albert with a mocking sound of contempt alien even to him. 'I'll play for your life or mine.' What am I saying? he thought despairingly, crying out inside of him to Grandfather Valliant.

Cross clucked and chuckled. 'That is to say, we shall agree

that if you lose, I am to do whatever I like to you, and if I lose, you shall do what you like with my life? Is that the stake, Albert?'

'Yes.' The desperate 'No' remained locked within him.

'Very well. Open, Albert,' commanded Cross.

Albert leaned over the board, bewildered and frightened still. He moved the king's pawn forward.

'Ah, bishop's gambit, eh? Relatively common.' Out came the expected counter.

Black to white, the pawns looked across the middle of the board, as over them looked Cross to Albert.

Albert moved once again, the only move he knew; he moved in an agony of apprehension — would Cross accept the challenge?

Leisurely, Cross captured the white bishop's pawn.

Now, suddenly, Albert's apprehension fell away, and, raising his hand to make his third move, he knew that the power which played his game was not his own. And, looking at his hand, as at something strange, it seemed to him that he could see over it, enclosing it, as it were, the gnarled old hand, broad with spatulate fingers, of his Grandfather Valliant.

The game went on, the battle raging to and fro across the board.

But inexorably, inexplicably to Cross, the advantage went steadily to Albert. Cross's first confidence shook, then faded. What was happening was beyond his understanding — that a child could master his game with so simple an opening as the bishop's gambit! But it was taking place despite his most studied moves, and slowly, surely, he was being mated, and as inevitably at last, Albert made his final move.

'Checkmate!' he cried.

Furious, Cross swept the chessmen from the table. The board came flying after. With another blow, he knocked the gate-legged table out of the way. He stood towering over Albert, crouching unmoved before him.

'So — you won, Albert. And what do you suppose you would do with my life even if you could command it?'

'I'd throw it away,' said Albert stoutly.

Something leaned down over Albert, something that was tall and dark as a cloud, something with great, gnarled hands like Grandfather Valliant's, something that picked Cross up as if he were a toy and flung him through the window, shattering the glass, out and up to plummet down three storeys and more to the slope of the back yard below. He fell with an awful sound directly into the alley.

At the precinct station, Captain Molloy called Squad Car Seven.

'Kelly, run out to one-eleven Whitney. A junkman just reported a dead or injured man in the alley there. While you're about it, send Jackson in to make some inquiries of Mrs Valliant at that address. That fellow Cross has been seen there. We've got the autopsy on his fourth wife. Unmistakable trace of arsenic. Pick him up if he's there. That's all.'

Albert stopped only to set up the chessmen once more.

'I'll be back tomorrow, Grandpa,' he said.

He descended to the upper floor. He went on down to the lower floor.

His mother was peering curiously and apprehensively out of the kitchen window, murmuring about the crowd out there. What could have happened?

'Mother?'

She turned. 'Oh, you've been in the attic again . . . '

'I promised about Mr Cross,' he said with intent purpose. 'The way he is now, I like him.'

THE IMMORTAL GAME

Poul Anderson

The first trumpet sounded far and clear and brazen cold, and Rogard the Bishop stirred to wakefulness with it. Lifting his eyes, he looked through the suddenly rustling, murmuring line of soldiers, out across the broad plain of Cinnabar and the frontier, and over to the realm of Leukas.

Away there, across the somehow unreal red-and-black distances of the steppe, he saw sunlight flash on armour and caught the remote wild flutter of lifted banners. *So it is war*, he thought. *So we must fight again.*

Again? He pulled his mind from the frightening dimness of that word. Had they ever fought before?

On his left, Sir Ocher laughed aloud and clanged down the vizard on his gay young face. It gave him a strange, inhuman look, he was suddenly a featureless thing of shining metal and nodding plumes, and the steel echoed in his voice: 'Ha, a fight! Praise God, Bishop, for I had begun to fear I would rust here forever.'

Slowly, Rogard's mind brought forth wonder. 'Were you sitting and thinking — before now?' he asked.

'Why — ' Sudden puzzlement in the reckless tones: 'I think I was . . . Was I?' Fear turning into defiance: 'Who cares'? I've got some Leukans to kill!' Ocher reared in his horse till the great metallic wings thundered.

On Rogard's right, Flambard the King stood, tall in crown and robes. He lifted an arm to shade his eyes against the blazing sunlight. 'They are sending Diomes, the royal guardsman, first,' he murmured. 'A good man.' The coolness of his tone was not matched by the other hand, its nervous plucking at his beard.

Rogard turned back, facing over the lines of Cinnabar to the frontier. Diomes, the Leukan King's own soldier, was running. The long spear flashed in his hand, his shield and helmet threw back the relentless light in a furious dazzle, and Rogard thought he could hear the clashing of iron. Then that noise was drowned in the trumpets and drums and yells from the ranks of Cinnabar, and he had only his eyes.

Diomes leaped two squares before coming to a halt on the frontier. He stopped then, stamping and thrusting against the Barrier which suddenly held him, and cried challenge. A muttering rose among the cuirassed soldiers of Cinnabar, and spears lifted before the flowing banners.

King Flambard's voice was shrill as he leaned forward and touched his own guardsman with his sceptre. 'Go Carlon! Go to stop him!'

'Aye, sire.' Carlon's stocky form bowed, and then he wheeled about and ran, holding his spear aloft, until he reached the frontier. Now he and Diomes stood face to face, snarling at each other across the Barrier, and for a sick moment Rogard wondered what those two had done, once in an evil and forgotten year, that there should be such hate between them.

'Let me go, sire!' Ocher's voice rang eerily from the slit-eyed mask of his helmet. The winged horse stamped on the hard red ground, and the long lance swept a flashing arc. 'Let me go next.'

'No, no, Sir Ocher.' It was a woman's voice. 'Not yet. There'll be enough for you and me to do, later in this day.'

Looking beyond Flambard, the Bishop saw his Queen, Evyan the Fair, and there was something within him which stumbled and broke into fire. Very tall and lovely was the grey-eyed Queen of Cinnabar, where she stood in armour and looked out at the growing battle. Her sun-browned young face was coifed in steel, but one rebellious lock blew forth in the wind, and she brushed at it with a gauntleted hand while the other drew her sword snaking from its sheath. 'Now may God strengthen our arms,' she said, and her voice was low and sweet. Rogard drew his cope tighter about him and turned his mitred head away with a sigh. But there was a bitter envy in him for Columbard, the Queen's Bishop of Cinnabar.

Drums thumped from the Leukan ranks, and another soldier ran forth. Rogard sucked his breath hissingly in, for this man came till he stood on Diomes' right. And the newcomer's face was sharp and pale with fear. There was no Barrier between him and Carlon.

'To his death,' muttered Flambard between his teeth. 'They sent that fellow to his death.'

Carlon snarled and advanced on the Leukan. He had little

choice — if he waited, he would be slain, and his King had not commanded him to wait. He leaped, his spear gleamed, and the Leukan soldier toppled and lay emptily sprawled in the black square.

'First blood!' cried Evyan, lifting her sword and hurling sunbeams from it. 'First blood for us!'

Aye, so, thought Rogard bleakly, *But King Mikillati had a reason for sacrificing that man. Maybe we should have let Carlon die. Carlon the bold, Carlon the strong, Carlon the lover of laughter. Maybe we should have let him die.*

And now the Barrier was down for Bishop Asator of Leukas, and he came gliding down the red squares, high and cold in his glistening white robes, until he stood on the frontier. Rogard thought he could see Asator's eyes as they swept over Cinnabar. The Leukan Bishop was poised to rush in with his great mace should Flambard, for safety, seek to change with Earl Ferric as the Law permitted.

Law?

There was no time to wonder what the Law was, or why it must be obeyed, or what had gone before this moment of battle. Queen Evyan had turned and shouted to the soldier Raddic, guardsman of her own Knight Sir Cupran: 'Go! Halt him!' And Raddic cast her his own look of love, and ran, ponderous in his mail, up to the frontier. There he and Asator stood, no Barrier between them if either used a flanking move.

Good! Oh, good, my Queen! thought Rogard wildly. For even if Asator did not withdraw, but slew Raddic, he would be in Raddic's square, and his threat would be against a wall of spears. *He will retreat, he will retreat —*

Iron roared as Asator's mace crashed through helm and skull and felled Raddic the guardsman.

Evyan screamed, once only. 'And I sent him! I sent him!' Then she began to run.

'Lady!' Rogard hurled himself against the Barrier. He could not move, he was chained here in his square, locked and barred by a Law he did not understand, while his lady ran towards death. 'O Evyan, Evyan!'

Straight as a flying javelin ran the Queen of Cinnabar. Turning, straining after her, Rogard saw her leap the frontier and come to a halt by the Barrier which marked the left-hand bound of the kingdoms, beyond which lay only dimness to the frightful edge of the world. There she wheeled to face the dismayed ranks of Leukas and her cry drifted back like the shriek of a stooping hawk: 'Mikillati! Defend yourself!'

The thunder-crack of cheering from Cinnabar drowned all answer, but Rogard saw, at the very limits of his sight, how hastily King Mikillati stepped from the line of her attack, into the stronghold of Bishop Asator. Now, thought Rogard fiercely, now the white-robed ruler could never seek shelter from one of his Earls. Evyan had stolen his greatest shield.

'Hola, my Queen!' With a sob of laughter, Ocher struck spurs into his horse. Wings threshed, blowing Rogard's cope about him, as the Knight hurtled over the head of his own guardsman and came to rest two squares in front of the Bishop. Rogard fought down his own anger; he had wanted to be the one to follow Evyan. But Ocher was a better choice.

Oh, much better! Rogard gasped as his flittering eyes took in the broad battlefield. In the next leap, Ocher could cut down Diomes, and then between them he and Evyan could trap Mikillati!

Briefly, that puzzlement nagged at the Bishop. Why should men die to catch someone else's King? What was there in the Law that said Kings should strive for mastery of the world and —

'Guard yourself, Queen!' Sir Merkon, King's Knight of Leukas, sprang in a move like Ocher's. Rogard's breath rattled in his throat with bitterness, and he thought there must be tears in Evyan's bright eyes. Slowly, then, the Queen withdrew two squares along the edge, until she stood in front of Earl Ferric's guardsman. It was still a good place to attack from, but not what the other had been.

Boan, guardsman of the Leukan Queen Dolora, moved one square forward, so that he protected great Diomes from Ocher. Ocher snarled and sprang in front of Evyan, so that he stood between her and the frontier: clearing the way for her, and throwing his own protection over Carlon.

Merkon jumped likewise, landing to face Ocher with the frontier between them. Rogard clenched his mace and vision blurred from him; the Leukans were closing in on Evyan.

'Ulfar!' cried the King's Bishop. 'Ulfar, can you help her?'

The stout old yeoman who was guardsman of the Queen's Bishop nodded wordlessly and ran one square forward. His spear menaced Bishop Asator, who growled at him — no Barrier between those two now!

Merkon of Leukas made another soaring leap, landing three squares in front of Rogard. 'Guard yourself!' the voice belled from his faceless helmet. 'Guard yourself, O Queen!'

No time now to let Ulfar slay Asator. Evyan's great eyes looked wildly about her; then, with swift decision, she stepped between Merkon and Ocher. Oh, a lovely move! Out of the fury in his breast, Rogard laughed.

The guardsman of the Leukan King's Knight clanked two squares ahead, lifting his spear against Ocher. It must have taken boldness thus to stand before Evyan herself; but the Queen of Leukas could slay her. 'Get free, Ocher!' she cried. 'Get away!' Ocher cursed and leaped from danger, landing in front of Rogard's guardsman.

The King's Bishop bit his lip and tried to halt the trembling in his limbs. How the sun blazed! Its light was a cataract of dry white fire over the barren red and black squares. It hung immobile, enormous in the vague sky, and men gasped in their armour. The noise of bugles and iron, hoofs and wings and stamping feet, was loud under the small wind that blew across the world. There had never been anything but this meaningless war, there would never be aught else, and when Rogard tried to think beyond the moment when the fight had begun, or the moment when it would end, there was only an abyss of darkness.

Earl Rafaeon of Leukas took one ponderous step toward his King, a towering figure of iron readying for combat. Evyan whooped. 'Ulfar!' she yelled. 'Ulfar, your chance!'

Columbard's guardsman laughed aloud. Raising his spear, he stepped over into the square held by Asator. The white-robed Bishop lifted his mace, futile and feeble, and then he rolled in the dust at Ulfar's feet. The men of Cinnabar howled and clanged sword on shield.

Rogard held aloof from triumph. Asator, he thought grimly, had been expendable anyway. King Mikillati had something else in mind.

It was like a blow when he saw Earl Rafaeon's guardsman run forward two squares and shout to Evyan to guard herself. Raging, the Queen of Cinnabar withdrew a square to her rearward. Rogard saw sickly how unprotected King Flambard was now, the soldiers scattered over the field and the hosts of Leukas marshalling. But Queen Dolora, he thought with a wild clutching hope, Queen Dolora, her tall cold beauty was just as open to a strong attack.

The soldier who had driven Evyan back took a leap across the frontier. 'Guard yourself, O Queen!' he cried again. He was a small, hard-bitten, unkempt warrior in dusty helm and corselet. Evyan cursed, a bouncing soldierly oath, and moved one square forward to put a Barrier between her and him. He grinned impudently in his beard.

It is ill for us, it is a bootless and evil day. Rogard tried once more to get out of his square and go to Evyan's aid, but his will would not carry him. The Barrier held, invisible and uncrossable, and the Law held, the cruel and senseless Law which said a man must stand by and watch his lady be slain, and he railed at the bitterness of it and lapsed into a grey waiting.

Trumpets lifted brazen throats, drums boomed, and Queen Dolora of Leukas stalked forth into battle. She came high and white and icily fair, her face chiselled and immobile in its haughtiness under the crowned helmet and stood two squares in front of her husband, looming over Carlon. Behind her, her own Bishop Sorkas poised in his stronghold, hefting his mace in armoured hands. Carlon of Cinnabar spat at Dolora's feet, and she looked at him from cool blue eyes and then looked away. The hot dry wind did not ruffle her long pale hair; she was like a statue, standing there and waiting.

'Ocher,' said Evyan softly, 'out of my way.'

'I like not retreat, my lady,' he answered in a thin tone.

'Nor I,' said Evyan. 'But I must have an escape route open. We will fight again.'

Slowly, Ocher withdrew, back to his own home. Evyan chuckled once, and a wry grin twisted her young face.

Rogard was looking at her so tautly that he did not see what was happening until a great shout of iron slammed his head around. Then he saw Bishop Sorkas, standing in Carlon's square with a bloodied mace in his hands, and Carlon lay dead at his feet.

Carlon, your hands are empty, life has slipped from them and there is an unending darkness risen in you who loved the world. Goodnight, my Carlon, Goodnight.

'Madam — ' Bishop Sorkas spoke quietly, bowing a little, and there was a smile on his crafty face. 'I regret, madam, that — ah — '

'Yes. I must leave you.' Evyan shook her head, as if she had been struck, and moved a square backwards and sideways. Then, turning, she threw the glance of an eagle down the black squares to Leukas' Earl Aracles. He looked away nervously, as if he would crouch behind the three soldiers who warded him. Evyan drew a deep breath sobbing into her lungs.

Sir Theutas, Dolora's Knight, sprang from his stronghold, to place himself between Evyan and the Earl. Rogard wondered dully if he meant to kill Ulfar the soldier; he could do it now. Ulfar looked at the Knight who sat crouched, and hefted his spear and waited for his own weird.

'Rogard!'

The Bishop leaped, and for a moment there was fire-streaked darkness before his eyes.

'Rogard, to me! To me, and help sweep them from the world!' *Evyan's voice.*

She stood in her scarred and dinted armour, holding her sword aloft, and on that smitten field she was laughing with a new-born hope. Rogard could not shout his reply. There were no words. But he raised his mace and ran.

The black squares slid beneath his feet, footfalls pounding, jarring his teeth, muscles stretching with a resurgent glory and all the world singing. At the frontier, he stopped, knowing it was Evyan's will though he could not have said how he knew. Then he faced about, and with clearing eyes looked back over that field of iron and ruin. Save for one soldier and a knight, Cinnabar was now cleared of Leukan forces, Evyan was safe, a counterblow was readying like the first whistle of hurricane. Before him were the proud banners of Leukas — now to throw them into the dust! Now to ride with Evyan into the home of Mikillati!

'Go to it, sir,' rumbled Ulfar, standing on the Bishop's right and looking boldly at the white Knight who could slay him. 'Give 'em hell from us.'

Wings beat in the sky, and Theutas soared down to land on Rogard's left. In the hot light, the blued metal of his armour was like running water. His horse snorted, curveting and flapping its wings; he sat it easily, the lance swaying in his grasp, the blank helmet turned to Flambard. One more such leap, reckoned Rogard wildly, and he would be able to assail the King of Cinnabar. Or — no — a single spring from here and he would spit Evyan on his lance.

And there is a Barrier beween us!

'Watch yourself, Queen!' The arrogant Leukan voice boomed hollow out of the steel mask.

'Indeed I will, Sir Knight!' There was only laughter in Evyan's tone. Lightly, then, she sped up the row of black squares. She brushed by Rogard, smiling at him as she ran, and he tried to smile back but his face was stiffened. Evyan, Evyan, she was plunging alone into her enemy's homeland!

Iron belled and clamoured. The white guardsman in her path toppled and sank at her feet. One fist lifted strengthlessly, and a dying shrillness was in the dust: 'Curse you, curse you, Mikillati, curse you for a stupid fool, leaving me here to be slain — no, no, no — '

Evyan bestrode the body and laughed again in the very face of Earl Aracles. He cowered back, licking his lips — he could not move against her, but she could annihilate him in one more step. Beside Rogard, Ulfar whooped, and the trumpets of Cinnabar howled in the rear.

Now the great attack was launched! Rogard cast a fleeting glance at Bishop Sorkas. The lean white-coped form was gliding forth, mace swinging loose in one hand, and there was a little sleepy smile on the pale face. No dismay — ? Sorkas halted, facing Rogard, and smiled a little wider, skinning his teeth without humour. 'You can kill me if you wish,' he said softly. 'But do you?'

'For a moment Rogard wavered. To smash that head — !

'Rogard! Rogard, to me!'

Evyan's cry jerked the King's Bishop around. He saw now what her plan was, and it dazzled him so that he forgot all else. Leukas *is ours!*

Swiftly he ran. Diomes and Boan howled at him as he went between them, brushing impotent spears against the Barriers. He passed Queen Dolora, and her lovely face was as if cast in steel, and her eyes followed him as he charged over the plain of Leukas. Then there was no time for thinking, Earl Rafaeon loomed before him, and he jumped the last boundary into the enemy's heartland.

The Earl lifted a meaningless axe. The Law read death for him, and Rogard brushed aside the feeble stroke. The blow of his mace shocked in his own body, slamming his jaws together. Rafaeon crumpled, falling slowly, his armour loud as he struck the ground. Briefly, his fingers clawed at the iron-hard black earth, and then he lay still.

They have slain Raddic and Carlon — we have three guardsmen, a

Bishop, and an Earl — Now we need only be butchers! Evyan, Evyan, warrior Queen, this is your victory!

Diomes of Leukas roared and jumped across the frontier. Futile futile, he was doomed to darkness. Evyan's lithe form moved up against Aracles, her sword flamed and the Earl crashed at her feet. Her voice was another leaping brand: 'Defend yourself, King!'

Turning, Rogard grew aware that Mikillati himself had been right beside him. There was a Barrier between the two men — but Mikillati had to retreat from Evyan, and he took one step forward and sideways. Peering into his face, Rogard felt a sudden coldness. There was no defeat there, it was craft and knowledge and an unbending steel will — *what was Leukas planning?*

Evyan tossed her head, and the wind fluttered the lock of hair like a rebel banner. 'We have them, Rogard!' she cried.

Far and faint, through the noise and confusion of battle, Cinnabar's bugles sounded the command of her King. Peering into the haze, Rogard saw that Flambard was taking precautions. Sir Theutas was still a menace, where he stood beside Sorkas. Sir Cupran of Cinnabar flew heavily over to land in front of the Queen's Earl's guardsman, covering the route Theutas must follow to endanger Flambard.

Wise, but — Rogard looked again at Mikillati's chill white face, and it was as if a breath of cold blew through him. Suddenly he wondered why they fought. For victory, yes, for mastery over the world — but when the battle had been won, what then?

He couldn't think past that moment. His mind recoiled in horror he could not name. In that instant he knew icily that this was not the first war in the world, there had been others before, and there would be others again. *Victory is death.*

But Evyan, glorious Evyan, she could not die. She would reign over all the world and —

Steel blazed in Cinnabar. Merkon of Leukas came surging forth, one tigerish leap which brought him down on Ocher's guardsman. The soldier screamed, once, as he fell under the trampling, tearing hoofs, but it was lost in the shout of the Leukan Knight: 'Defend yourself, Flambard! Defend yourself!'

Rogard gasped. It was like a blow in the belly. He had stood triumphant over the world, and now all in one swoop it was brought toppling about him. Theutas shook his lance, Sorkas his mace, Diomes raised a bull's bellow — somehow, incredibly somehow, the warriors of Leukas had entered Cinnabar and were thundering at the King's own citadel.

'No, no — ' Looking down the long empty row of squares, Rogard saw that Evyan was weeping. He wanted to run to her, hold her close and shield her against the falling world, but the Barriers were around him. He could not stir from his square, he could only watch.

Flambard cursed lividly and retreated into his Queen's home. His men gave a shout and clashed their arms — there was still a chance!

No, not while the Law bound men, thought Rogard, not while the Barriers held. Victory was ashen, and victory and defeat alike were darkness.

Beyond her thinly smiling husband, Queen Dolora swept forward. Evyan cried out as the tall white woman halted before Rogard's terrified guardsman, turned to face Flambard where he crouched, and called to him: 'Defend yourself, King!'

'No — no — you fool!' Rogard reached out, trying to break the Barrier, clawing at Mikillati. 'Can't you see, none of us can win, it's death for us all if the war ends. Call her back!'

Mikillati ignored him. He seemed to be waiting.

And Ocher of Cinnabar raised a huge shout of laughter. It belled over the plain, dancing joyous mirth, and men lifted weary heads and turned to the young Knight where he sat in his own stronghold, for there was youth and triumph and glory in his laughing. Swiftly, then, a blur of steel, he sprang, and his winged horse rushed out of the sky on Dolora herself. She turned to meet him, lifting her sword, and he knocked it from her hand and stabbed with his own lance. Slowly, too haughty to scream, the white Queen sank under his horse's hoofs.

And Mikillati smiled.

'I see,' nodded the visitor. 'Individual computers, each controlling its own robot piece by a tight beam, and all the computers on a given side linked to form a sort of group-mind constrained to obey the rules of chess and make the best possible moves. Very nice. And it's a pretty cute notion of yours, making the robots look like medieval armies.' His glance studied the tiny figures where they moved on the oversized board under one glaring floodlight.

'Oh, that's pure frippery,' said the scientist. 'This is really a serious research project in multiple computer-linkages. By letting them play game after game, I'm getting some valuable data.'

15

'It's a lovely set-up,' said the visitor admiringly. 'Do you realise that in this particular contest the two sides are reproducing one of the great classic games?'

'Why, no. Is that a fact?'

'Yes. It was a match between Anderssen and Kieseritsky, back in — I forget the year, but it was quite some time ago. Chess books often refer to it as the Immortal Game. . . . So your computers must share many of the properties of a human brain.'

'Well, they're complex things, all right,' admitted the scientist. 'Not all their characteristics are known yet. Sometimes my chessmen surprise even me.'

'Hm.' The visitor stooped over the board. 'Notice how they're jumping around inside their squares, waving their arms, batting at each other with their weapons?' He paused, then murmured slowly: 'I wonder — I wonder if your computers may not have consciousness. If they might not have — minds.'

'Don't get fantastic,' snorted the scientist.

'But how do you know?' persisted the visitor. 'Look, your feedback arrangement is closely analogous to a human nervous system. How do you know that your individual computers, even if they are constrained by the group linkage, don't have individual personalities? How do you know that their electronic senses don't interpret the game as, oh, as an interplay of free will and necessity; how do you know they don't receive the data of the moves as their own equivalent of blood, sweat and tears?' He shuddered a little.

'Nonsense,' grunted the scientist. 'They're only robots. Now — hey! Look there! Look at that move!'

Bishop Sorkas took one step ahead, into the black square adjoining Flambard's. He bowed and smiled. 'The war is ended,' he said.

Slowly, very slowly, Flambard looked about him. Sorkas, Merkon, Theutas, they were crouched to leap on him wherever he turned; his own men raged helpless against the Barriers; there was no place for him to go.

He bowed his head. 'I surrender,' he whispered.

Rogard looked across the red and black to Evyan. Their eyes met, and they stretched out their arms to each other.

'Checkmate,' said the scientist. 'That game's over.'

He crossed the room to the switchboard and turned off the computers.

III

BLOOD CHESS

'The game of chess is one of man's bloodiest and most erotic battlegrounds and gives its players an opportunity to live out fantasies of revenge against the all-powerful God-King-Father triad and seeking counter-balancing refuge in the Virgin-Queen-Mother.'

Professor Felix Marti-Ibanez,
The Psychology of Chess, 1960

'Chess for Blood!' is a familiar expression among enthusiasts, and this final part of the book is entirely devoted to stories of bloodshed and death. To make the first move there is probably no more suitable purveyor of murder and mystery than the late Dame Agatha Christie (1890-1976). Appropriately it was her namesake, John Christie, who some two hundred years ago pieced together what is generally regarded as one of the first accounts of the 'bloody' origins of chess. Dame Agatha's contribution likewise presents a tough case of detective work for her redoubtable sleuth, Hercule Poirot.

The book by the historian Christie was published in 1801, and rejoices in the kind of all-encompasing title so popular at the time: *An Inquiry into the Ancient Greek Game, Supposed to have been invented by Palamedes, antecedent to the Siege of Troy. With Reasons for believing the same to have been known from remote Antiquity in China, and also progressively improved into the Chinese, Indian, Persians and European Game Chess.* Dame Agatha, by contrast, preferred the terse and dramatic title, and although the one she has given to this story, 'A Chess Problem', may seem deceptively simple, it conceals a mystery that demands all Poirot's formidable skill. At the same time it reveals its author's knowledge of the game, for she played from her childhood, and to the end of her life continued to enjoy games with her husband, Sir Max Mallowan, as relaxation after a day's hard plotting. With her agile and ingenious mind she must have made a formidable opponent!

A classic case of chess leading to real-life bloodshed occurred in 1624 when a play called *A Game at Chess* by Thomas Middleton was staged at the Globe Theatre, London. The drama, which was about a controversial game between the Church of England and the Roman Catholic Church — won by the former — aroused heated passions among its audiences when it played before packed houses for an unprecedented nine days. According to contemporary reports, arguments and fights broke out among patrons belonging to the different religions, and a number of men and women were injured. So strong, indeed, were the protests about the political and religious implications of the play — led by the Spanish Ambassador to London whose predecessor was actually portrayed on the stage as the Black Knight — that the unfortunate Thomas Middleton was arrested and thrown into prison. There he wrote a petition in the form of a poem addressed to King James, in order to secure his release:

> A harmless game, coyned only for delight,
> 'Twas play'd betwixt the black house and the white,
> The white house won, yet still the black doth brag,
> They had the power to put me in the bag,
> Use but your royal hand, 'twill set me free,
> 'Tis but removing of a man — that's me —
>
> Thomas Middleton.'

Alfred Noyes (1880-1958), the second contributor in this section, with 'Checkmate', was a keen student of seventeenth-century theatrical and social history and wrote about the Thomas Middleton episode in his work, *The Loom of Years* (1902). Noyes played chess as an undergraduate at Oxford and continued to be a keen competitor when he lived in America from 1913-1923 as a lecturer and visiting Professor of Poetry at Princeton. Like Middleton, he, too, became involved in a controversy — although there was no bloodshed — when, shortly after being converted to Roman Catholicism, he published a study of Voltaire which was condemned by the Holy Office in Rome. He, too, fought the condemnation and won a retraction. Noyes' story concerns an author obsessed with playing classical games of chess, who suddenly finds himself in contest with an invisible opponent who all too clearly foreshadows tragedy. . .

'Professor Pownall's Oversight' is a favourite story of mine by Herbert Russell Wakefield (1888-1964), a writer of supernatural tales regarded by several experts as one of the great British ghost story writers of this century. The son of Bishop Wakefield of Birmingham, himself a noted Victorian chess-player, the young Wakefield was introduced to the game at home, developed his skills while at Oxford and consolidated them later in London where he worked as secretary to the newspaper tycoon, Lord Northcliffe. Although a number of collections of Wakefield's stories were issued during his lifetime, he has become strangely neglected of late. Perhaps 'Professor Pownell's Oversight', which describes how the bitter rivalry of two chess opponents leads to murder and then supernatural intervention, may help to focus attention again on his undoubted mastery of the genre.

'The Cat from Siam' is by the American journalist Fredric Brown (1906-1972) whose excellent short stories have only come to be really appreciated since his death. This is one of his typical stories of crime and violence, set against the background of a chess game interrupted by a sniper. It has been rescued from the pages of one of the pulp magazines to which Brown contributed, *Popular Detective* of September 1949, and will, I am sure, be enjoyed as much by lovers of crime fiction as by chess enthusiasts.

Another much admired American writer, Stanley Ellin (1916-) is the author of 'Fool's Mate' which has become something of a classic among lovers of mystery stories — and, I should add, among those chess-players already fortunate enough to have discovered it. Born in New York, Ellin graduated from Brooklyn College and took on a variety of jobs, including boilermaker's apprentice, steelworker, dairy farmer, teacher and newspaper promoter, before becoming a full-time writer at the end of the Second World War. He has subsequently won numerous awards for his novels and short stories, including the American 'Edgar' awards (named after Edgar Allan Poe) and the French Grand Prix de Litérature Policière, while his work has been much filmed (*The Big Night*, 1951 and *The House of Cards*, 1968, are two excellent examples) and screened on television in series such as the Alfred Hitchcock Hour. 'Fool's Mate', about a henpecked husband and his obsession with chess, which provides him with a very unusual solution to his problems, is Stanley Ellin at the top of his form.

Kenneth Gavrell (1958-) also has associations with the magic name of Hitchcock, for his story 'A Better Chess-Player' first appeared as the lead contribution in the November 1989 issue of the *Alfred Hitchcock Mystery Magazine*. It is a grim tale of imprisonment and cruelty in the same tradition as Stefan Zweig's 'The Royal Game', although the twist in the tail is in the very best Hitchcockian tradition. It makes a marvellous finale to the book.

A CHESS PROBLEM

Agatha Christie

Poirot and I often dined at a small restaurant in Soho. We were there one evening, when we observed a friend at an adjacent table. It was Inspector Japp, and as there was room at our table he came and joined us. It was some time since either of us had seen him.

'Never do you drop in to see us nowadays,' declared Poirot reproachfully. 'Not since the affair of the Yellow Jasmine have we met, and that is nearly a month ago.'

'I've been up north — that's why. Take any interest in chess, Moosior Poirot?' Japp asked.

'I have played it, yes.'

'Did you see that curious business yesterday? Match between two players of world-wide reputation, and one died during the game?'

'I saw a mention of it. Dr Savaronoff, the Russian champion, was one of the players, and the other, who succumbed to heart failure, was the brilliant young American, Gilmour Wilson.'

'Quite right. Savaronoff beat Rubenstein and became Russian champion some years ago. Wilson is said to be a second Capablanca.'

'A very curious occurrence,' mused Poirot. 'If I mistake not, you have a particular interest in the matter.'

Japp gave a rather embarrassed laugh.

'You've hit it, Moosior Poirot. I'm puzzled. Wilson was sound as a bell — no trace of heart trouble. His death is quite inexplicable.'

'You suspect Dr Savaronoff of putting him out of the way?' I cried.

'Hardly that,' said Japp dryly. 'I don't think even a Russian would murder another man in order not to be beaten at chess — and anyway, from all I can make out, the boot was likely to be

on the other leg. The doctor is supposed to be very hot stuff —
second to Lasker they say he is.'

Poirot nodded thoughtfully.

'Then what exactly is your little idea?' he asked. 'Why should
Wilson be poisoned? For, I assume, of course, that it is poison
you suspect.'

'Naturally. Heart failure means your heart stops beating —
that's all there is to that. That's what a doctor says officially at
the moment, but privately he tips us the wink that he's not
satisfied.'

'When is the autopsy to take place?'

'Tonight. Wilson's death was extraordinarily sudden. He
seemed quite as usual and was actually moving one of the pieces
when he suddenly fell forward — dead!'

'There are very few poisons would act in such a fashion,'
objected Poirot.

'I know. The autopsy will help us, I expect. But why should
anyone want Gilmour Wilson out of the way — that's what I'd
like to know. Harmless, unassuming young fellow. Just come
over here from the States, and apparently hadn't an enemy in
the world.'

'It seems incredible,' I mused.

'Not at all,' said Poirot, smiling. 'Japp has his theory, I can
see.'

'I have, Moosior Poirot. I don't believe the poison was meant
for Wilson — it was meant for the other man.'

'Savaronoff?'

'Yes. Savaronoff fell foul of the Bolsheviks at the outbreak of
the Revolution. He was even reported killed. In reality, he
escaped, and for three years endured incredible hardships in the
wilds of Siberia. His sufferings were so great that he is now a
changed man. His friends and acquaintances declare they would
hardly have recognised him. His hair is white, and his whole
aspect that of a man terribly aged. He is a semi-invalid, and
seldom goes out, living alone with a niece, Sonia Daviloff, and
a Russian manservant in a flat down Westminster way. It is
possible that he still considers himself a marked man. Certainly
he was very unwilling to agree to this chess contest. He refused
several times point-blank, and it was only when the newspapers
took it up and began making a fuss about the "unsportsmanlike
refusal" that he gave in. Gilmour Wilson had gone on challenging
him with real Yankee pertinacity, and in the end he got his way.

Now I ask you, Moosior Poirot, why wasn't he willing? Because he didn't want attention drawn to him. Didn't want somebody or other to get on his track. That's my solution — Gilmour Wilson got pipped by mistake.'

'There is no one who has any private reason to gain by Savaronoff's death?'

'Well, his niece, I suppose. He's recently come into an immense fortune. Left him by Madame Gospoja whose husband was a sugar profiteer under the old regime. They had an affair together once, I believe, and she refused steadfastly to credit the reports of his death.'

'Where did the match take place?'

'In Savaronoff's own flat. He's an invalid, as I told you.'

'Many people there to watch it?'

'At least a dozen — probably more.'

Poirot made an expressive grimace.

'My poor Japp, your task is not an easy one.'

'Once I know definitely that Wilson was poisoned I can get on.'

'Has it occurred to you that, in the meantime, supposing your assumption that Savaronoff was the intended victim to be correct, the murderer may try again?'

'Of course it has. Two men are watching Savaronoff's flat.'

'That will be very useful if anyone should call with a bomb under his arm.' said Poirot dryly.

'You're getting interested, Moosior Poirot,' said Japp, with a twinkle. 'Care to come round to the mortuary and see Wilson's body before the doctors start on it? Who knows, his tie-pin may be askew, and that may give you a valuable clue that will solve the mystery.'

'My dear Japp, all through dinner my fingers have been itching to rearrange your own tie-pin. You permit, yes? Ah! that is much more pleasing to the eye. Yes, by all means, let us go to the mortuary.'

I could see that Poirot's attention was completely captivated by this new problem. It was so long since he had shown any interest over any outside case that I was quite rejoiced to see him back in his old form.

For my own part, I felt a deep pity as I looked down upon the motionless form and convulsed face of the hapless young American who had come by his death in such a strange way.

Poirot examined the body attentively. There was no mark on it anywhere, except a small scar on the left hand.

'And the doctor says that's a burn, not a cut,' explained Japp.

Poirot's attention shifted to the contents of the dead man's pockets which a constable spread out for our inspection. There was nothing much — a handkerchief, keys, notecase filled with notes, and some unimportant letters. But one object standing by itself filled Poirot with interest.

'A chessman!' he exclaimed. 'A white bishop. Was that in his pocket?'

'No, clasped in his hand. We had quite a difficulty to get it out of his fingers. It must be returned to Dr Savaronoff sometime. It's part of a very beautiful set of carved ivory chessmen.'

'Permit me to return it to him. It will make an excuse for my going there.'

'Aha!' cried Japp. 'So you want to come in on this case?'

'I admit it. So skilfully have you aroused my interest.'

'That's fine. Got you away from your brooding. Captain Hastings is pleased too, I can see.'

'Quite right,' I said laughing.

Poirot turned back towards the body.

'No other little detail you can tell me about — him?' he asked.

'I don't think so.'

'Not even — that he was left-handed?'

'You're a wizard, Moosior Poirot. How did you know that? He *was* left-handed. Not that it's anything to do with the case.'

'Nothing whatever,' agreed Poirot hastily, seeing that Japp was slightly ruffled. 'My little joke — that was all. I like to play you the trick, you see.'

We went out upon an amicable understanding.

The following morning saw us wending our way to Dr Savaronoff's flat in Westminster.

'Sonio Daviloff,' I mused. 'It's a pretty name.'

Poirot stopped, and threw me a look of despair.

'Always looking for romance! You are incorrigible.'

The door of the flat was opened to us by a manservant with a particularly wooden face. It seemed impossible to believe that that impassive countenance could ever display emotion.

Poirot presented a card on which Japp had scribbled a few words of introduction, and we were shown into a low, long room furnished with rich hangings and curios. One or two wonderful ikons hung upon the walls, and exquisite Persian rugs lay upon the floor. A samovar stood upon a table.

I was examining one of the ikons which I judged to be of considerable value, and turned to see Poirot prone upon the floor. Beautiful as the rug was, it hardly seemed to me to necessitate such close attention.

'Is it such a wonderful specimen?' I asked.

'Eh?' Oh! the rug? But no, it was not the rug I was remarking. But it *is* a beautiful specimen, far too beautiful to have a large nail wantonly driven through the middle of it. No, Hastings,' as I came forward, 'the nail is not there now. But the hole remains.'

A sudden sound behind us made me spin round, and Poirot spring nimbly to his feet. A girl was standing in the doorway. Her eyes, full upon us, were dark with suspicion. She was of medium height, with a beautiful rather sullen face, dark-blue eyes, and very black hair which was cut short. Her voice, when she spoke, was rich and sonorous, and completely un-English.

'I fear my uncle will be unable to see you. He is a great invalid.'

'That is a pity, but perhaps you will kindly help me instead. You are Mademoiselle Daviloff, are you not?'

'Yes I am Sonia Daviloff. What is it you want to know?'

'I am making some inquiries about that sad affair the night before last — the death of M. Gilmour Wilson. What can you tell me about it?'

The girl's eyes opened wide.

'He died of heart failure — as he was playing chess.'

'The police are not sure that it was — heart failure, mademoiselle.'

The girl gave a terrified gesture.

'It was true, then,' she cried 'Ivan was right.'

'Who is Ivan, and why did you say he was right?'

'It was Ivan who opened the door to you — and he has already said to me that in his opinion Gilmour Wilson did not die a natural death — that he was poisoned by mistake.'

'By mistake.'

'Yes, the poison was meant for my uncle.'

She had quite forgotten her first distrust now, and was speaking eagerly.

'Why do you say that, mademoiselle? Who should wish to poison Dr Savaronoff?'

She shook her head.

'I do not know. I am all in the dark. And my uncle, he will

not trust me. It is natural, perhaps. You see, he hardly knows me. He saw me as a child, and not since till I came to live with him here in London. But this much I do know, he is in fear of something. We have many secret societies in Russia, and one day I overheard something which made me think it was of just such a society he went in fear.'

'Mademoiselle, your uncle is still in danger. I must save him. Now recount to me exactly the events of that fatal evening. Show me the chessboard, the table, how the two men sat — everything.'

She went to the side of the room and brought out a small table. The top of it was exquisite, inlaid with squares of silver and black to represent a chessboard.

'This was sent to my uncle a few weeks ago as a present, with the request that he would use it in the next match he played. It was in the middle of the room — so.'

Poirot examined the table with what seemed to me quite unnecessary attention. He was not conducting the inquiry at all as I would have done. Many of his questions seemed to me pointless, and upon really vital matters he seemed to have no questions to ask.

After a minute examination of the table and the exact position it had occupied, he asked to see the chessmen. Sonia Daviloff brought them to him in a box. He examined one or two of them in a perfunctory manner.

'An exquisite set,' he murmured absent-mindedly.

Still not a question as to what refreshments there had been, or what people had been present.

I cleared my throat significantly.

'Don't you think, Poirot, that — '

He interrupted me peremptorily.

'Do not think, my friend. Leave all to me. Mademoiselle, is it quite impossible that I should see your uncle?'

A faint smile showed itself on her face.

'He will see you, yes. You understand, it is my part to interview all strangers first.'

She disappeared. I heard a murmur of voices in the next room, and minute later she came back and motioned us to pass into the adjoining room.

The man who lay there on a couch was an imposing figure. Tall, gaunt, with huge bushy eyebrows and white beard, and a face haggard as the result of starvation and hardships. Dr Sava-

ronoff was a distinct personality. I noted the peculiar formation
of his head, its unusual height. A great chess-player must have
a great brain. I knew. I could easily understand Dr Savaronoff
being the second greatest player in the world.

Poirot bowed

'M. *le Docteur*, may I speak to you alone?'

Savaronoff turned to his niece.

'Leave us, Sonia.'

She disappeared obediently.

'Now, sir, what is it?'

'Dr Savaronoff, you have recently come into an enormous
fortune. If you should — die unexpectedly, who inherits it?'

'I have made a will leaving everything to my niece, Sonia
Daviloff. You do not suggest — '

'I suggest nothing, but you have not seen your niece since she
was a child. It would have been easy for anyone to impersonate
her.'

Savaronoff seemed thunderstruck by the suggestion. Poirot
went on easily.

'Enough as to that. I give you the word of warning, that is all.
What I want you to do now is to describe to me the game of
chess the other evening.'

'How do you mean — describe it?'

'Well. I do not play the chess myself, but I understand that
there are various regular ways of beginning — the gambit, do
they not call it?'

Dr Savaronoff smiled a little.

'Ah! I comprehend you now. Wilson opened Ruy Lopez — one
of the soundest openings there is, and one frequently adopted in
tournaments and matches.'

'And how long had you been playing when the tragedy happened?'

'It must have been about the third or fourth move when Wilson
suddenly fell forward over the table, stone-dead.'

Poirot rose to depart. He flung out his last question as though
it was of absolutely no important, but I knew better.

'Had he had anything to eat or drink?'

'A whisky and soda, I think.'

'Thank you, Dr Savaronoff. I will disturb you no longer.'

Ivan was in the hall to show us out. Poirot lingered on the
threshold.

'The flat below this, do you know who lives there?'

'Sir Charles Kingwell, a Member of Parliament, sir. It has been let furnished lately, though.'

'Thank you.'

We went out into the bright winter sunlight.

'Well, really, Poirot,' I burst out. 'I don't think you've distinguished yourself this time. Surely your questions were very inadequate.'

'You think so, Hastings?' Poirot looked at me appealingly. 'I was *bouleversé*, yes. What would you have asked?'

I considered the question carefully, and then outlined my scheme to Poirot. He listened with what seemed to be close interest. My monologue lasted until we had nearly reached home.

'Very excellent, very searching, Hastings,' said Poirot, as he inserted his key in the door and preceded me up the stairs. 'But quite unnecessary.'

'Unnecessary!' I cried, amazed. 'If the man was poisoned — '

'Aha,' cried Poirot, pouncing upon a note which lay on the table. 'From Japp. Just as I thought.' He flung it over to me. It was brief and to the point. No traces of poison had been found, and there was nothing to show how the man came by his death.

'You see,' said Poirot, 'our questions would have been quite unnecessary.'

'You guessed this beforehand?'

' "Forecast the probable result of the deal." ' quoted Poirot from a recent bridge problem on which I had spent much time. '*Mon ami*, when you do that successfully, you do not call it guessing.'

'Don't let's split hairs,' I said impatiently. 'You foresaw this?'

'I did.'

'Why?'

Poirot put his hand into his pocket and pulled out — a white bishop.

'Why,' I cried, 'you forgot to give it back to Dr Savaronoff.'

'You are in error, my friend. That bishop still reposes in my left-hand pocket. I took its fellow from the box of chessmen Mademoiselle Daviloff kindly permitted me to examine. The plural of one bishop is two bishops.'

He sounded the final *s* with a great hiss. I was completely mystified.

'But why did you take it?'

'*Parbleu*, I wanted to see if they were exactly alike.'

He stood them on the table side by side.

'Well, they are, of course,' I said 'exactly alike.'

Poirot looked at them with his head on one side.

'They seem so, I admit. But one should take no fact for granted until it is proved. Bring me, I pray you, my little scales.'

With infinite care he weighed the two chessmen, then turned to me with a face alight with triumph.

'I was right. See you, I was right. Impossible to deceive Hercule Poirot!'

He rushed to the telephone — waited impatiently.

'Is that Japp? Ah! Japp, it is you. Hercule Poirot speaks. Watch the manservant, Ivan. On no account let him slip through your fingers. Yes, yes it is as I say.'

He dashed down the receiver and turned to me.

'You see it not, Hastings? I will explain. Wilson was not poisoned, he was electrocuted. A thin metal rod passes up the middle of one of those chessmen. The table was prepared beforehand and set upon a certain spot on the floor. When the bishop was placed upon one of the silver squares, the current passed through Wilson's body, killing him instantly. The only mark was the electric burn upon his hand — his left hand, because he was left handed. The "special table" was an extremely cunning piece of mechanism. The table I examined was a duplicate, perfectly innocent. It was substituted for the other immediately after the murder. The thing was worked from the flat below, which, if you remember was not furnished. But one accomplice at least was in Savaronoff's flat. The girl is an agent of a Russian secret society, working to inherit Savaronoff's money.'

'And Ivan?'

'I strongly suspect that Ivan is the girl's confederate.'

'It's amazing,' I said at last. 'Everything fits in. Savaronoff had an inkling of the plot, and that's why he was so averse to playing the match.'

Poirot looked at me without speaking. Then he turned abruptly away, and began pacing up and down.

'Have you a book on chess by any chance, *mon ami*?' he asked suddenly.

'I believe I have somewhere.'

It took me some time to ferret it out, but I found it at last and brought it to Poirot, who sank down in a chair and started reading it with the greatest attention.

In about a quarter of an hour the telephone rang. I answered it. It was Japp. Ivan had left the flat, carrying a large bundle. He had sprung into a waiting taxi, and the chase had begun. He was evidently trying to lose his pursuers. In the end he seemed to fancy that he had done so, and had then driven to a big empty house at Hampstead. The house was surrounded.

I recounted all this to Poirot. He merely stared at me as though he scarcely took in what I was saying. He held out the chess book.

'Listen to this, my friend. This is the Ruy Lopez opening. 1 P-K4, P-K4; 2 Kt-KB3, Kt-QB3; 3 B-Kt5. Then there comes a question as to Black's best third move. He has the voice of various defences. It was White's third move that killed Gilmour Wilson, 3 B-Kt5. Only the third move — does that say nothing to you?'

I hadn't the least idea what he meant, and told him so.

'Suppose, Hastings, that while you were sitting in this chair you heard the front door being opened and shut, what would you think?'

'I should think someone had gone out, I suppose.'

'Yes — but there are always two ways of looking at things. Someone gone out — someone come *in* — two totally different things, Hastings. But if you assumed the wrong one, presently some little discrepancy would creep in and show you that you were on the wrong track.'

'What does all this mean, Poirot?'

Poirot sprang to his feet with sudden energy.

'It means that I have been a triple imbecile. Quick, quick, to the flat in Westminster. We may yet be in time.'

We tore off in a taxi. Poirot returned no answer to my excited questions. We raced up the stairs. Repeated rings and knocks brought no reply, but listening closely I could distinguish a hollow groan coming from within.

The hall porter proved to have a master key, and after a few difficulties he consented to use it.

Poirot went straight to the inner room. A whiff of chloroform met us. On the floor was Sonia Daviloff, gagged and bound, with a great wad of saturated cotton wool over her nose and mouth. Poirot tore it off and began to take measures to restore her. Presently a doctor arrived, and Poirot handed her over to his charge and drew aside with me. There was no sign of Dr Savaronoff.

'What does it all mean?' I asked, bewildered.

'It means that before two equal deductions I chose the wrong one. You heard me say that it would be easy for any one to impersonate Sonia Daviloff because her uncle had not seen her for so many years?'

'Yes?'

'Well, precisely the opposite held good also. It was equally easy for anyone to *impersonate the uncle!*'

'What?'

'Savaronoff *did* die at the outbreak of the Revolution. The man who pretended to have escaped with such terrible hardships, the man so changed "that his own friends could hardly recognise him," the man who successfully laid claim to an enormous fortune — is an imposter. He guessed I should get on the right track in the end, so he sent off the honest Ivan on a tortuous wild-goose chase, chloroformed the girl, and got out, having by now doubtless realised most of the securities left by Madame Gospoja.'

'But — but who tried to kill him?'

'Nobody tried to kill *him*. Wilson was the intended victim all along.'

'But why?'

'My friend, the real Savaronoff was the second greatest chess player in the world. In all probability his impersonator did not even know the rudiments of the game. Certainly he could not sustain the fiction of a match. He tried all he knew to avoid the contest. When that failed, Wilson's doom was sealed. At all costs he must be prevented from discovering that the great Savaronoff did not even know how to play chess. Wilson was fond of the Ruy Lopez opening and was certain to use it. The false Savaronoff arranged for death to come with the third move, before any complications of defence set in.'

'But, my dear Poirot,' I persisted, 'are we dealing with a lunatic? I quite follow your reasoning, and admit that you must be right, but to kill a man just to sustain his rôle! Surely there were simpler ways out of the difficulty than that! He could have said that his doctor forbade the strain of a match.'

Poirot wrinkled his forehead.

'*Certainement*, Hastings,' he said 'there were other ways, but none so convincing. Besides, you are assuming that to kill a man is a thing to avoid, are you not? Our impostor's mind, it does not act that way. I put myself in his place, a thing impossible for you. I picture his thoughts. He enjoys himself as the professor at that match. I doubt not he has visited the chess tourneys to study his part. He sits and frowns in thought; he gives the impression that he is thinking great plans, and all the time he laughs in himself. He is aware that two moves are all that he knows — and all that he *need know*. Again, it would appeal to his mind to foresee the events and to make Wilson his own executioner . . . Oh, yes, Hastings, I begin to understand our friend and his psychology.'

I shrugged.

'Well, I suppose you're right, but I can't understand anyone running a risk he could so easily avoid.'

'Risk!' Poirot snorted. 'Where then lay the risk? Would Japp have solved the problem? No; if the false Savaronoff had not made one small mistake he would have run no risk.'

'And his mistake?' I asked, although I suspected the answer.

'*Mon ami*, he overlooked the little grey cells of Hercule Poirot.'

Poirot has his virtues, but modesty is not one of them.

CHECKMATE

Alfred Noyes

When Everard Martin was left alone after dinner — a most excellent little dinner — he drank a thimbleful of Benedictine and lit a cigarette. He had put out two of the candles that had been burning badly, and the soft shaded light of the other two made him look rather younger than he was. His black velvet smoking-jacket, hardly distinguishable from the panelling behind him, made his face and hands emerge from the dark like those of a living Raeburn portrait. His rosy, clean-shaven, clear-cut face, with the curved beak and prominent chin, floating there among the faint blue wreaths of tobacco smoke, suggested the successful barrister rather than the novelist or playwright. But a close observer would have noted the stigmata of his profession (one might almost say, as of all the civilized moderns, the symptoms of his case) in the super-sensitive quickness of his nerves. It is a commonplace to say that civilised men have lost the alertness of the tiger or the Red Indian; but they have acquired a new quickness of the senses to a host of impressions of which the tiger and the Red Indian would be utterly unaware. And Everard Martin was far more keenly aware than the average human being. This was, of course, the secret of his work, the explanation of its quality.

It was noticeable in the strong nervousness of the hands, a quickness and grace of movement that did not for a moment convey the idea of restlessness or fidgetiness, but rather the delicacy of a finely adjusted, powerful machine, very steadily, tensely, controlled.

The door opened. Helen, his wife and Pauline, his daughter, in evening clothes and furs, appeared, waving good-bye to him. They stood there, framed in the brighter light of the hall — like a picture, touched with more significance than he knew.

Helen, one of those fragile Dresden-china women who never grow old, and seem only to gather a little more wistfulness in their faces with the passage of time, looked younger than Pauline tonight. Pauline had inherited her father's height, and something of his quick nervous temperament. This was evident enough in the sensitive red mouth, as it quivered into a smile; and in the deep eyes, that seemed always to be looking into a far country, a more constant world than ours.

'You won't change your mind, Popples, and come with us?' called Pauline. 'There are five seats in the box, you know.'

'Five? Who is to make the fifth of this party?'

'Maurice is to meet us there.'

'Oh, Maurice is to be there, is he?'

'You don't look altogether pleased about it. Why, Daddie, what is the matter?'

Pauline ran up to her father, placed two slender white hands on his shoulders and looked into his face. For a moment she had imagined that his usually ruddy face had lost its colour.

'I'm a little absent-minded tonight,' he said, 'thinking about my work, I suppose.'

'But you looked so desperately sad when I mentioned Maurice. You want me to be happy, don't you, Daddie?'

'More than anything in the world, dear. But tell me' — he took both of her hands — 'are you so absolutely sure that your happiness means — Maurice?'

'But, Daddie, what an extraordinary question to ask me just as we are rushing off to the opera. Should I be engaged to him if I didn't think so?'

His troubled grey eyes met the large dark sincerity of her own and fell.

'Now-a-days,' he muttered. 'Life is such a rush for you young people that one feels you can have very little time to make up your minds. Why, I don't suppose, you even know the colour of his eyes.'

'Grey, Daddie. Very like the colour of yours. Oh, yes. I know what you are thinking. An American girl told me this afternoon that she had been engaged sixteen times in five years and didn't write to break off the fifteenth engagement until she had been married for six weeks. She had clothes enough to fill three rooms in this house, and she told me that she was looking for a "dear little cottage" in the country. You are always telling me that I am a child of the age, but you must admit that I am fairly consistent. I don't do things of that sort, even if I laugh at them. But I suppose you have been saying all these things to test me. It's rather too bad, Daddie. If I hadn't seen through you it might have spoilt the evening. And we're late already. Won't you come with us?'

'No. I'm going to do some work.'

'The mystery book?'

'Yes. The mystery book. The *chef d'oeuvre.*'

'Ah, well. Good luck to it.'

She threw him a kiss, and the door closed upon her young beauty with the effect of a bright light going out, leaving Martin in the discreet and mellow dusk of the orange-shaded candles, to his own meditations.

There was every reason why these should be very pleasant. He was a very fortunate man. He was not yet forty-five; and, after a very brief struggle with the common adversities of the penniless young literary man, he had taken his place as one of the 'names' that counted. His novels were read as widely as good writing could hope to be read; and, despite the 'high-brow' and the prig, this did not mean that they were restricted to a small literary public.

Everard Martin's work, in fact, was in the major key and he had found the right way to the major audience. His plays held the stage in two continents and, best of all, his reputation, even among the coteries, was that of an artist. He was not merely successful. He had done something that was generally acknowledged to be worth doing, and yet he never seemed to be quite happy about it.

The external evidence of Martin's success was all around him. If ever they could afford him pleasure it must surely be now, when he was left, undisturbed, to enjoy a long and luxurious evening by his own fireside, to think over the difficulties he had surmounted, the many-bolted doors he had broken down, the literary battles he had fought and won; and to set a hundred memories a-swim in the blue wreaths of his own tobacco smoke.

When he had finished his cigarette, he rose, blew out the candles, and went to his book-lined study. This was his haven of quiet — amazingly still for any town house — where no sound but the ticking of the clock or the fluttering of the fire could ever intrude, unless by his own invitation. It was the pleasantest room in the house; and here, if anywhere, one might have expected the cloud to vanish from his brooding face.

If he had been asked to give any definite reason whatsoever for this 'cloud' he could not have done so; but, for many months now, he had been obsessed by that strange feeling of expectancy, the vague presentiment of approaching disaster which is some times found in the early stages of some merely physical trouble. But Martin was unusually healthy and fit; and the shadow was not to be dismissed by exercise.

More and more, lately, on entering his study, he had a sense that the room itself seemed to be waiting for something to happen. At one time, he attributed this merely to its work-room hush, its air of wanting him to sit at his desk and create. But, latterly, it had been more than this, and he could not explain it any more than he could explain why he had troubled Pauline with his doubts about Maurice. Maurice Lemoine was a very charming young artist who had already made a reputation for himself. He had lived most of his twenty-four and a half years in Paris, where his mother, the English widow of a Frenchman still lived. But his work had captured the London critics. He was far more English than French, and he intended to make his headquarters in London. Out of mere perversity, apparently, Martin preferred to regard him as more French than English; and, though, in other matters, Martin had a cosmopolitan mind, he had developed a slight prejudice against what he vaguely called 'international marriage' in the case of Pauline. This was probably nothing more than the usual moodiness of the male parent, deepened by the shadow of that other cloud which brooded over him so continually now.

For a moment or two, however, the cloud did disappear; while Martin stood, back to the fire, and looked at those warmly-coloured rows of old books, the best friends he had ever had, or was ever likely to have.

He took down a volume at random from the shelf that was nearest to him, opened it at random, and read the passage that had been marked in pencil by the friend who sent him the book, in his undergraduate days. It was curious, very curious, that he should have hit upon that passage. It gave him that strange sense — it comes upon even the most mechanically-minded of philosophers at times — of the presence in all our affairs of the Supreme Artist, the Creative Power that sustains the universe; touches our life with gleams of significant drama; and, if we have eyes to see, communicates with us constantly through each new combination of circumstances; so that all natural phenomena become symbolical hieroglyphics; and even light and darkness, the song of a bird, or the fresh buds on a tree at the door, have power to encourage, dissuade, or pierce with remorse. Every book, every picture, every human face, every forest and hill and meadow then is endowed with the magic quality that men once attributed to the verse of Virgil, when they opened his pages at random to look for guidance in their affairs.

How vividly that marked passage brought back the day when he had first read it, a day of terrible distress, on which those cool measured words had restored his self-control. It was a passage in one of Huxley's essays, a passage that had always haunted him; the famous comparison of life with a game of chess, played upon the chessboard of the world.

The player the other side is hidden from us. We know that his play is always fair, just and patient. But also we know, to our cost, that he never overlooks a mistake or makes the smallest allowance for ignorance. To the man who plays well the highest stakes are paid, with that sort of overflowing generosity with which the strong shows delight in strength. And one who plays ill is checkmated without haste, but without remorse.

He put the book back on the shelf; and, instead of going to his desk, where a neat pile of white paper awaited his pen, he decided to lose himself and his thoughts in his favourite recreation. He was reputed to be one of the most diligent and patient of contemporary writers; but those who affirmed it in press-paragraphs, and, in fact, even his immediate family, would have been astonished if they had known how spasmodic his writing had always been; how long the intervals when nothing was accomplished; and how often, when his study door was bolted to the world, he was sitting, not at his desk, but at the big shining chess board with its beautiful pieces of black and white Chinese ivory.

A wonderful game, chess! The king of games! Magical, glamorous with the memory of thousands of years. He liked to think that, when Britain was still the lair of woad-streaked savages these old ivory pieces were subtly moved by the delicate long-pointed fingers of intellectual beings, almond-eyed thinkers and philosophers, under a cherry-tree in a palace garden of old Cathay.

It was indeed always a pleasant moment when, with everyone else comfortably excluded, the curtains drawn, his old briar in his mouth, the whispering flames of the study-fire cheerfully reflected from the glass of the etchings and the warm leather bindings of his books, Martin sat in front of that big chessboard. To him it was more than the game of kings. It was the game of

Epicurean gods. The shining board was an image of the world. All the problems that confront one in life, political, artistic, ethnical, could be considered there, with the detachment of the immortals. It was the only game that could enthral the solitary student with as potent a spell as though an opponent sat opposite to him in the flesh. For, on this board, by his own fireside. he can play over the games of the masters. He can follow the fluctuations of their fortunes in their contests for world-primacy, as their moves are cabled from matches in distant countries. A few of those hieroglyphics in the *Times* so meaningless to the uninitiated, enable him to follow at his ease, on his own board, every subtlety of the finest games of contemporary players all over the world. He can analyse their moves, and examine every detail, every implication of their tactics and strategy. His pieces move exactly as their pieces moved. It is not a mere reproduction, a picture, or a shadow of the original game; but the very game itself.

Moreover, he can follow there the rise and fall of the generations. He can watch the arrival of the new master and the desperate struggle of the older and more romantic players to maintain their pre-eminence against the new, colder, more scientific methods. It was an image of life, even in this; and Martin never saw an older player going down before the ruthlessness of youth without something of the generous feeling which had marked him amongst the artists of his own profession as a 'conservative' and 'laudator temporis acti'.

He was not this at all; but he was always saddened by that curious cruelty of the mob which rejoices in the downfall of those whom it has crowned. 'There are dreadful things in human nature,' he used to say, 'and the suppressed smile at a friend's disaster is growing a little too common in the modern world.' So he was always, in playing over these games, a little tense with hope for the losing side; a little anxious that the age-worn master should at least come out of it with enough honour to justify the hero-worship with which he had been regarded. And, in all this, if one looks back at it in the light of what afterwards happened to himself, there is a suggestion for the psychologist that Martin's own subconscious mind was aware that the game of life was now setting against him.

And then, too, another thing that set the chess-player aloof with the immortals was the way in which he could play over the recorded games of the famous dead, exactly as they were played in life, recapturing every emotion, every excitement of the original players. He could take down from a bookshelf that volume of exquisite little masterpieces, the games of that Edgar Allan Poe of chess, that strange American master, Paul Morphy. Works of genius, poems, morbidly brilliant, those games, many of which Martin knew by heart, had advantage over other masterpieces for an artist who was a little tired of the world's way. They were conceived in symbols as remote as those of mathematics from the vexations of spirit that attend upon the art he practised, and yet had all the historic glamour that kings and queens, bishops and knights and pawns have lent to the oldest and subtlest of games, making of it a gorgeous living fairy-tale.

And then, last, there were his own memories. He could open a battered old note-book and fight over again his own old battles — as far back as his undergraduate days when he played for Cambridge University. Time was passing. The hieroglyphics in the note-book were already fading to that watery lilac colour which, till recently, he was wont to associate with the records of a much earlier generation. But, in playing over those games and re-tasting his victories and defeats, he recaptured the very faces of his young opponents; the colour of the eyes, yes, the very colour, even to the green specks in the grey; and, at certain moves, the expression of eagerness or annoyance; the nervous puffing of a pipe over a tense position; or — subdued as in life to the decorous hush of the chess club — a muttered 'damn'.

More than once, alone there in the evening, he had raised his eyes after a move, expecting to see his old friend Drummond on the other side of the board. He was a good player, Drummond; but he had not seen him for twenty-five years.

He lit his pipe and prepared to play over, from memory, that great encounter between Anderssen and Kieseritzki, known as the 'Immortal Game'. But he was not to play it that night.

He pushed out his white king's pawn, two squares; and then turned to put a log on the fire. When he looked at the board again he saw, with a slight start of surprise, that he had apparently moved the black king's pawn also; for that pawn, too, had been advanced two squares and confronted his own. Perhaps it was this that diverted him from his original intention; for, on his second move, he played out his king's knight; and he had hardly set it down before he saw — that the black queen's knight had also been advanced, to her bishop's third. He had certainly not moved it, and he had not seen it move.

He grew cold from head to foot. It was impossible of course.

He must have overlooked that black knight. It could not have been on its proper square to begin with. The black pieces, at night, when there are shadows on the board, do sometimes trick the eye. It was a mere accident that in its present position it happened to give the usual reply to his own move. But his hand trembled a little, when he moved the white king's bishop out, and he watched the board intently this time.

How it happened he did not know. There was no visible movement. Unless it happened during the unconscious winking of his eye-lids nothing had moved. Unless a piece could disappear like a shadow from one square and reappear like a shadow on another, nothing had moved. But the black king's knight had now been advanced to his bishop's third; and this, too, was a logical reply to Martin's last move; one of those mathematically correct replies to the Ruy Lopez that practised players make almost automatically.

For a minute or two he stared at the board as at an infernal machine, which it might be dangerous to touch. His mind was a whirl of bewildered ghosts of thought; the wraiths of his former philosophy. Fragments of familiar phrases echoed through his brain — *men of science* — *mechanism of the universe* — *the whole universe moving automatically* — *the mechanism of thought* — *laws of nature.* — *But laws were not forces; only a statement that in our experience certain phenomena always follow certain other phenomena.* — *The laws of nature explain nothing.* — *They do not explain why the universe moves* — *the laws of the game do not explain why the game is being played at all.* Fragments of verse, too, twisted and turned in the chaos of his mind, like little fiery nebulae, trying to solidify into ordered worlds again;

> Do we move ourselves? Are we moved, by an unseen hand, at a game
> That pushes us off from the board, and others ever succeed?

And all around that little rhythmic nucleus whirled the chaotic fire-mist of other thoughts, trying to compose themselves into a cosmos, a comprehensible whole.

Universal nature moved by universal mind. — The chessboard, a microcosm. — Battleships moved by wireless. Could a mind too, act on these material pieces from a distance? Material pieces? Composed of what? Atoms, electrons, centres of force, melting into 'thin air'. No — into something far more real than all phenomena. Even the so-called materialists, Huxley himself, in the book which he had been reading earlier in the evening, affirmed that all the phenomena of nature are, in their ultimate analysis, known to us only as facts of consciousness. Those pieces were called 'black', and these 'white', but the sensations of blackness and whiteness were not external realities. They were formed in the brain, through the mechanism of certain nerves. The object in itself at the other end of the mechanism was something different, something unknowable. — The moving Power on the other side of the veil of phenomena, that mist of our own sensations in which we are imprisoned, none could know, unless, looking inward.

But who, or what was moving those pieces through the impenetrable veils of Space and Time? Was it all *maya* — illusion?

The strangest fancies flashed upon him and vanished — Was he contending with some old almond-eyed owner of those pieces? Or was a dead college friend trying to communicate with him? Had there been some lesion in his brain? Had he himself been moving the pieces on both sides, without knowing it? Was he dreaming? Was he going mad?

His shaking hand went out again mechanically. He 'castled' his king. A moment later he saw that the reply of black was made; and, strangely enough, it pulled him together. It was the reply of a practised player who knew the latest analyses of the openings; and, by asserting the reign of reason to that extent, it gave him back his self-mastery. The bewildered panic of his nerves was succeeded by an abnormal calm and an intense intellectual curiosity, to which he rallied all the slumbering reserves of his spirit. He knew, instinctively, that this game was fraught with consequences of terrible importance to himself; and those connected with him. He remembered what Huxley had said of the famous picture in which Retzsch depicted Satan playing at chess with man for his soul. He sat there, a modern counterpart of that man and of Everyman. Modern, for his opponent was invisible; and perhaps he, too, might believe that instead of the mocking fiend, his opponent was 'a calm strong angel', who would rather lose than win. But always through his brain there was a warning echo. *'The player on the other side is hidden from us. We know that his play is always fair, just and patient. But also we know, to our cost, that he never overlooks a mistake.'*

He sat there, fascinated, spellbound. The game had become the only reality. It was the physical manifestation of his own relations with the universe. Everything else had become remote and unreal. The house was in a quiet street; and when a taxi-cab suddenly rattled past, it seemed a stranger sound to Martin than the witches' laughter of gulls among the remotest islands of the Hebrides. It seemed to come from an outside world with which he had little concern, and might soon cease to be concerned at all. He was at grips now with the inner realities; the imponderable things that move the world; the invisible, absolute, substantial powers to which sounds and colours and streets and taxi-cabs, and the distant glittering opera-house, where his wife and daughter (but not Maurice) were at this moment listening to the Pilgrim's Chorus, were merely shadowy appearances, external and superficial phenomena, a painted mask. He had forgotten this external world altogether. He bent over the board and concentrated his whole mind and will on it as he had never concentrated them on anything in his life hitherto, while the embers clicked on the hearth, and the little clock on the mantelpiece ticked unconcernedly — *life, death; life, death; life, death.*

* * *

At the end of an hour, the game appeared to be fairly even. Martin had been playing with the utmost caution; simplifying the position at every opportunity by changing pieces; avoiding all complications; and entering into no adventurous attacks. Their pieces were equal. He knew that, as in life, between scientific players of the game, success and even overwhelming victory can only come as the crowning result of an accumulation of small tactical advantages; and that these may, and often do, originate in one slight advantage in the position of a single pawn.

At the end of another half hour a single black pawn was 'passed' into just such a slightly advantageous position. This, as usual, led to other very slight, but definite, positional advantages, by a series of almost imperceptibly advantageous moves; and, then, suddenly, Martin discovered that one of his pieces was on the point of being trapped; and, in his endeavour to save the piece, he made a move which still further impaired his position. Like a general confronted with a choice between two evils, he weakened a good strategic position to prevent an army corps being captured elsewhere. He saved the army corps; but it was a mistake, for — if he had not been afraid of complications — he could have defended it, indirectly, by an attack elsewhere; and the mistake was not overlooked by the enemy.

Though, to the unpractised eye, from move to move, little seemed to happen, the aspect of the board had greatly changed during the last half hour. Nothing stirred in the room but the embers on the hearth, and the slow lifting of Martin's right hand, once every few minutes, to make his move. Each reply came soundlessly, imperceptibly, and immediately, changing very slightly the logical symmetry of the position, as by the shifting of a single grain of coloured glass in a kaleidoscope. But the cumulative result, as of the slight changes that through endless aeons evolve planets and armies and fleets and cities of men out of a fire-mist, was very great.

The end came without haste, but implacably and inevitably, as old age or death. Step by step, through a logical process, imperceptible from move to move, but steady as the stealing forward of the hour-hand on a dial, Martin's position was out-flanked. His king was forced into the open; hemmed round; driven back against his own pawns and checkmated.

He leaned back in his chair, staring at the board. Now that the game was ended, his tense concentration was succeeded by a curious calm, a relief like that of a man on trial for his life, when the verdict is finally given. For though he pinched the back of his left hand, digging his nails in till he brought the blood, to make sure that he was not dreaming, he knew that the position on the board was symbolical of something that had happened, irrevocably, in the larger field of his life. He knew, as birds know of the approach of thunder, that the unknown disaster was near, and that the invisible sword was upraised to strike him down, impossible as it seemed, in that sheltered fire-lit study. What unknown enemy of the body or the soul could enter there? He looked at the windows. They were high above the street and fastened securely.

A mad fear seized him for a moment. He rose hurriedly, darted across the room and locked the door. Then, with his forehead growing damp and cold, he unlocked a drawer in his desk, took out a revolver, slipped some cartridges into it, laid it beside the chessboard, and sat down again by the fire, to wait — for he knew not what?

Five minutes, ten minutes, fifteen minutes went by, and every tick of the clock was like a vital pulse of his own body. Then, making his heart leap like a trapped creature, the telephone bell beside his desk rang with what seemed to him a shattering violence in that expectant hush. He crossed the room, carrying his revolver with him, and took up the receiver.

'Yes,' he said, 'Who is it?'

The voice that replied — a woman's voice — he had not heard for twenty-five years, but he knew it at once, knew its every cadence, every tone, even the manner of the breathing. But oh, how could it happen! This chapter in his life had been torn out, and buried under the dust of all those dead springs and winters.

'Twenty-five years ago,' the voice said, 'you and I made a dreadful mistake; and now, God help us both, we must pay the penalty, though I hope His hand may fall less heavily on you and yours than it has fallen on me.'

'I don't know who it is. What is your name?' He whispered, lying desperately, out of sheer panic; but the unusual form of his reply was enough in itself to betray him.

'My name now,' answered the voice, 'is not the name by which you knew me; but you used to call me Diana.'

'It's impossible — I'

'Yes; I know. The name is no proof of my identity; but you remember, of course, the circumstances of our parting — the railway-platform where we walked, and how my crying upset you. You remember those lines you quoted when you were trying to persuade me that we should so soon and easily forget:

> For each day brings its petty dust
> Our soon-choked souls to fill;
> And we forget —

'How does it go on?' said the voice. 'I am forgetting even that, you see.' But it sounded to Martin as though it had been cut short by a sob.

He waited for a moment. Then, almost as if he were saying the lines to himself, he answered:

> 'And we forget because we must,
> And not because we will.'

'Yes; you know me now,' the voice answered. 'I had to make sure of that before I told you; and O, Everard, Everard, may God help you to bear it — Maurice is dead.'

'What in God's name, do you —'

'Maurice, my son Maurice, of whom you never knew; your son and mine, Everard. He is dead. I had to tell him tonight. He rushed away from me, leaving me unforgiven. He shot himself outside the opera-house, at your daughter's feet. They brought him here. Your wife and daughter came with him. They left me a few minutes ago. I don't know whether they understand yet. I am praying, on my knees, that God will help and comfort your poor girl; and forgive us for what we have done in our blindness. I can speak no more. I didn't know that we should ever speak to one another again. I am crying, Everard, crying from my heart.'

The voice ceased abruptly. Martin called her name, hoarsely.

'Diana! Diana! For God's sake!'

It was twenty-five years since he had spoken her name. He had almost forgotten it; and his voice rang out, in this quiet study of his latter years, like the voice of a stranger.

But he was cut off finally now; and, as he replaced the receiver, another sound came to him. He turned towards the window and listened. A motor-car — his own — was driving down the street.

He stood there, frozen, a listening statue. The car drew up at his front door. He heard the click of the lock; the quiet, dreadfully quiet entry of Helen and Pauline. There was no sound of voices as usual — only a shuffle of footsteps, as if the mother were supporting the daughter. But no voice — no word, no whisper! Not even a sound of weeping —

The front door closed. Footsteps — Pauline's, he knew — crossed the hall to his own locked door. The handle was turned and released. Then he heard a dull sound as of two pleading hands thudding with open palms against the upper panels of the door; and then, a long low sobbing cry that shivered through his heart like an arrow:

'O Daddie, Daddie, he's dead! He's dead!'

He moistened his lips, but he could not speak. He would have given his soul to be able to unlock the door; to take her in his arms and try to comfort her. But there was an end of all that now. Slowly, as if he were lifting an enormously heavy weight — for his will was cloven in two — he raised the revolver, thrust the muzzle into his gaping mouth and pulled the trigger.

The sharp report of the shot and the cries of the terrified women brought a heavy knocking and loud pealing at the front door, followed in a few minutes by the glint of dark helmets and uniforms, and the smell of London fog drifting in over the heads of the throng like a breath of the outer night. The study door was burst open upon a strange scene. It was one of the most cheerful and comfortable rooms, and Martin had chosen one of the ugliest means of killing himself there. He had fallen heavily backwards and looked as if he were wearing a crimson nightcap. Over his shattered skull, in front of the peacefully fluttering fire, stood the chess-table, on which the pieces of black ivory, undisturbed by his fall, still held the white king in their microcosmical checkmate.

PROFESSOR POWNALL'S OVERSIGHT

H. Russell Wakefield

A note by J.C. Cary, MD:

About sixteen years ago I received one morning by post a parcel, which, when I opened, I found to contain a letter and a packet. The latter was inscribed, 'To be opened and published fifteen years from this date'. The letter read as follows:

Dear Sir,

Forgive me for troubling you, but I have decided to entrust the enclosed narrative to your keeping. As I state, I wish it to be opened by you, and that you should arrange for it to be published in the *Chess Magazine*. I enclose five ten-pound notes, which sum is to be used, partly to remunerate you, and partly to cover the cost of publication, if such expenditure should be found necessary. About the time you receive this, I shall disappear. The contents of the enclosed packet, though to some extent revealing the cause of my disappearance, give no index as to its method.

E.P.

The receipt of this eccentric document occasioned me considerable surprise. I had attended Professor Pownall (I have altered all names, for obvious reasons) in my professional capacity four or five times for minor ailments. He struck me as a man of extreme intellectual brilliance, but his personality was repulsive to me. He had a virulent and brutal wit which he made no scruple of exercising at my and everyone else's expense. He apparently possessed not one single friend in the world, and I can only conclude that I came nearer to fulfilling this role than anyone else.

I kept this packet by me for safe keeping for the fifteen years, and then I opened it, about a year ago. The contents ran as follows:

The date of my birth is of complete unimportance, for my life began when I first met Hubert Morisson at the age of twelve and a half at Flamborough College. It will end tomorrow at six forty-five p.m.

I doubt if ever in the history of the human intellect there has been so continuous, so close, so exhausting a rivalry as that between Morisson and myself. I will chronicle its bare outline. We joined the same form at Flamborough — two forms higher, I may say, than that in which even the most promising new boys are usually placed. We were promoted every term till we reached the Upper Sixth at the age of sixteen. Morisson was always top, I was always second, a few marks behind him. We both got scholarships at Oxford, Morisson just beating me for Balliol. Before I left Flamborough, the Head Master sent for me and told me that he considered I had the best brain of any boy who had passed through his hands. I thought of asking him, if that were so, why I had been so consistently second to Morisson all through my school career; but even then I thought I knew the answer to that question.

He beat me, by a few marks, for all the great university prizes for which we entered. I remember one of the examiners, impressed by my papers, asking me to lunch with him. 'Pownall,' he said, 'Morisson and you are the most brilliant undergraduates who have been at Oxford in my time. I am not quite sure why, but I am convinced of two things; firstly, that he will always finish above you, and secondly, that you have the better brain.'

By the time we left Oxford, both with the highest degrees, I had had remorselessly impressed upon me the fact that my superiority of intelligence had been and always would be neutralised by some constituent in Morisson's mind which defied and dominated that superiority — save in one respect: we both took avidly to chess, and very soon there was no one in the university in our class, but I became, and remained, his master.

Chess has been the one great love of my life. Mankind I detest and despise. Far from growing wiser, men seem to me, decade by decade, to grow more inane as the means for revealing their ineptitude become more numerous, more varied and more complex. Women do not exist for me — they are merely variants from a bad model: but for chess, that superb, cold, infinitely satisfying anodyne to life, I feel the ardour of a lover, the humility of a disciple. Chess, that greatest of all games, greater than any

game! It is, in my opinion, one of the few supreme products of
the human intellect, if, as I often doubt, it is of human origin.

Morisson's success, I realise, was partly due to his social gifts;
he possessed that shameless flair for making people do what he
wanted, which is summed up in the word 'charm', a gift from
the gods, no doubt, but one of which I have never had the least
wish to be the recipient.

Did I like Morisson? More to the point, perhaps, did I hate
him? Neither, I believe. I simply grew profoundly and terribly
used to him. His success fascinated me. I had sometimes short
and violent paroxysms of jealousy, but these I fought, and on
the whole conquered.

He became a Moral Philosophy Don at Oxford: I obtained a
similar but inevitably inferior appointment in a Midland university. We used to meet during vacations and play chess at the
City of London Club. We both improved rapidly, but still I kept
ahead of him. After ten years of drudgery, I inherited a considerable sum, more than enough to satisfy all my wants. If one avoids
all contact with women one can live marvellously cheaply: I am
continuously astounded at men's inability to grasp this great and
simple truth.

I have had few moments of elation in my life, but when I got
into the train for London on leaving that cesspool in Warwick-
shire, I had a fierce feeling of release. No more should I have to
ram useless and rudimentary speculation into the heads of oafs,
who hated me as much as I despised them.

Directly I arrived in London I experienced one of those irresist-
ible impulses which I could never control, and I went down to
Oxford. Morisson was married by then, so I refused to stay in
his house, but I spent hours every day with him. The louts into
whom he attempted to force elementary ethics seemed rather
less dingy but even more mentally costive than my Midland half-
wits, and, so far as that went, I envied him not at all. I had
meant to stay one week; I was in Oxford for six, for I rapidly
came to the conclusion that I ranked first and Morisson second
among the chess-players of Great Britain. I can say that because
I have no vanity: vanity cannot breathe and live in rarefied intellectual altitudes. In chess the master surveys his skill impersonally, he criticises it impartially. He is great; he knows it; he
can prove it; that is all.

I persuaded Morisson to enter for the British Championship
six months later, and I returned to my rooms in Bloomsbury to

perfect my game. Day after day I spent in the most intensive study, and succeeded in curing my one weakness. I just mention this point briefly for the benefit of chess-players. I had a certain lethargy when forced to analyse intricate end-game positions. This, as I say, I overcame. A few games at the City Club convinced me that I was, at last, worthy to be called Master. Except for these occasional visits I spent those six months entirely alone: it was the happiest period of my life. I had complete freedom from human contacts, excellent health and unlimited time to move thirty-two pieces of the finest ivory over a charming chequered board.

I took a house at Bournemouth for the fortnight of the Championship, and I asked Morisson to stay with me. I felt I had to have him near me. He arrived the night before play began. When he came into my study I had one of those agonising paroxysms of jealousy to which I have alluded. I conquered it, but the reaction, as ever, took the form of a loathsome feeling of inferiority, almost servility.

Morisson was six foot two in height; I am five foot one. He had, as I impartially recognise, a face of great dignity and beauty, a mind at once of the greatest profundity and the most exquisite flippancy. My face is a perfect index to my character; it is angular, sallow, and its expression is one of seething distaste. As I say, I know my mind to be the greater of the two, but I express myself with an inevitable and blasting brutality, which disgusts and repels all who sample it. Nevertheless, it is that brutality which attracted Morisson, at times it fascinated him. I believe he realised, as I do, how implacably our destinies were interwoven.

Arriving next morning at the hall in which the Championship was to be held, I learned two things which affected me profoundly. The first, that by the accident of the pairing I should not meet Morisson until the last round, secondly, that the winner of the Championship would be selected to play in the forthcoming Masters' Tournament at Budapest.

I will pass quickly over the story of this Championship. It fully justified my conviction. When I sat down opposite Morisson in the last round we were precisely level, both of us having defeated all our opponents, though I had shown the greater mastery and certainty. I began this game with the greatest confidence. I outplayed him from the start, and by the fifteenth move I felt convinced I had a won game. I was just about to make my sixteenth move when Morisson looked across at me with that curious smile on his face, half-superior, half-admiring, which he had given me so often before, when after a terrific struggle he had proved his superiority in every other test but chess. The smile that I was to see again. At once I hesitated. I felt again that sense of almost cringing subservience. No doubt I was tired, the strain of that fortnight had told, but it was, as it always had been, something deeper, something more virulent, than anything fatigue could produce. My brain simply refused to concentrate. The long and subtle combination which I had analysed so certainly seemed suddenly full of flaws. My time was passing dangerously quickly. I made one last effort to force my brain to work, and then desperately moved a piece. How clearly I remember the look of amazement on Morisson's face. For a moment he scented a trap, and then, seeing none, for there was none, he moved and I was myself again. I saw I must lose a piece and the game. After losing a knight, I fought with a concentrated brilliance I had never attained before, with the result that I kept the game alive till the adjournment and indeed recovered some ground, but I knew when I left the hall with Morisson that on the next morning only a miracle could save me, and that once again, in the test of all tests in which I longed to beat him, he would, as ever at great crises, be revealed as my master. As I trotted back to my house beside him the words 'only a miracle' throbbed in my brain insinuatingly. Was there no other possibility? Of a sudden I came to the definite, unalterable decision that I would kill Morisson that night, and my brain began, like the perfectly trained machine it is, to plan the means by which I could kill him certainly and safely. The speed of this decision may sound incredible, but here I must be allowed a short digression. It has long been a theory of mine that there are two distinct if remotely connected processes operating in the human mind. I term these the 'surface' and the 'sub-surface' processes. I am not entirely satisfied with these terms, and I have thought of substituting for them the terms 'conscious' and 'subconscious'. However, that is a somewhat academic distinction. I believe that my sub-surface mind had considered this destruction of Morisson many times before, and that these paroxysms of jealousy, the outcome as they were of consistent and unjust frustration, were the minatory symptoms that the content of my sub-surface would one day become the impulse of my surface mind, forcing me to plan and execute the death of Morisson.

When we arrived at the house I went first to my bedroom to

fetch a most potent, swift-working, and tasteless narcotic which a German doctor had once prescribed for me in Munich when I was suffering from insomnia. I then went to the dining room, mixed two whiskies and soda, put a heavy dose of the drug into Morisson's tumbler, and went back to the study. I had hoped that he would drink it quickly: instead, he put it by his side and began a long monologue on luck. Possibly my fatal move had suggested it. He said that he had always regarded himself as an extremely lucky man, in his work, his friends, his wife. He supposed that his rigidly rational mind demanded for its relief some such inconsistency, some such sop. 'About four months ago,' he said, 'I had an equally irrational experience, a sharp premonition of death, which lingered with me. I told my wife — you will never agree, Pownall, but there is something to be said for matrimony: if I were dying I should like Marie to be with me, gross sentimentality, of course — I told my wife, who is of a distinctly psychic, superstitious if you like, turn of mind, and she persuaded me to go to a clairvoyant of whom she had a high opinion. I went sceptically, partly to please her, partly for the amusement of sampling one of this tribe. She was a curious, dingy female, slightly disconcerting. She stared at me remotely and then remarked, "It was always destined that he should do it." I plied her with questions, but she would say nothing more. I think you will agree, Pownall, that this was a typically nebulous two-guineas' worth.' And then he drained his glass.

Shortly afterwards he began to yawn repeatedly, and went to bed. He staggered slightly on entering his room. 'Good night, Pownall,' he said, as he closed the door, 'let's hope somehow or other we may both be at Budapest.'

Half an hour later I went into his room. He had just managed to undress before the drug had overwhelmed him. I shut the window, turned on the gas, and went out. I spent the next hour playing over that fatal game. I quickly discovered the right line I had missed, then with a wet towel over my face, I re-entered his room. He was dead. I turned off the gas, opened all the windows, waited till the gas had cleared, and then went to bed, to sleep as soundly as ever in my life, though I had a curiously vivid dream. I may say I dream but seldom, and I never before realised how sharp and convincing these silly images could be, for I saw Morisson running through the dark and deserted streets of Oxford till he reached his house, and then he hammered with his fists on the door, and as he did so he gave a great cry, 'Marie!

Marie!' and then he fell rolling down the steps, and I awoke. This dream recurred for some time after, and always left a somewhat unpleasant impression on my mind.

The events of the next day were not pleasant. They composed a testing ordeal which remains very vividly in my mind. I had to act, and act very carefully, to deceive my maid, who came screaming into my room in the morning, to fool the half witted local constable, the self-important local doctor, and carry through the farce generally in a convincing mode. I successfully suggested that as Morisson had suffered from heart weakness for some years, his own Oxford doctor should be sent for. Of course I had to wire to his wife. She arrived in the afternoon — and altogether I did not spend an uneventful day. However, all went well. The verdict at the inquest was 'natural causes', and a day or two afterwards I was notified that I was British Chess Champion and had been selected for Budapest. I received some medal or other, which I threw into the sea.

Four months intervened before the tournament at Budapest; I spent them entirely alone, perfecting my game. At the end of that period I can say with absolute certainty that I was the greatest player in the world; my swift unimpeded growth of power is, I believe, unprecedented in the history of chess. There was, I remember, during this time, a curious little incident. One evening after a long, profound analysis of a position, I felt stale and tired, and went out for a walk. When I got back I noticed a piece had been moved, and that the move constituted the one perfect answer to the combination I had been working out. I asked my landlady if anybody had been to my room: she said not, and I let the subject drop.

The Masters' Tournament at Budapest was perhaps the greatest ever held. All the most famous players in the world were gathered there, yet I, a practically unknown person, faced the terrific task of engaging them, one by one, day after day, with supreme confidence. I felt they could have no surprises for me, but that I should have many for them. Were I writing for chess-players only, I would explain technically the grounds for this confidence. As it is, I will merely state that I had worked out the most subtle and daring variants from existing practice. I was a century ahead of my time.

In my first round I was paired with the great Russian Master, Osvensky. When I met him he looked at me as if he wondered what I was doing there. He repeated my name as though it came as a complete surprise to him. I gave him a look which I have employed before when I have suspected insolence, and he altered his manner. We sat down. Having the white pieces, I employed that most subtle of all openings, the queen's bishop's pawn gambit. He chose an orthodox defence, and for ten moves the game took a normal course. Then at my eleventh move I offered the sacrifice of a knight, the first of the tremendous surprises I sprang upon my opponents in this tournament. I can see him now, the quick searching glance he gave me, and his great and growing agitation. Every chess-player reveals great strain by much the same symptoms, by nervous movements, hurried glances at the clock, uneasy shufflings of the body, and so forth: my opponent in this way completely betrayed his astonishment and dismay. Time ran on, sweat burst out on his forehead. Elated as I was, the spectacle became repulsive, so I looked round the room. And then, as my eyes reached the door, they met those of Morisson sauntering in. He gave me the slightest look of recognition, then strolled along to our table and took his stand behind my opponent's chair. At first I had no doubt that it was an hallucination due to the great strain to which I had subjected myself during the preceding months: I was therefore surprised when I noticed the Russian glance uneasily behind him. Morisson put his hand over my opponent's shoulder, guided his hand to a piece, and placed it down with that slight screwing movement so characteristic of him. It was the one move which I had dreaded, though I had felt it could never be discovered in play over the board, and then Morisson gave me that curious searching smile to which I have alluded. I braced myself, rallied all my willpower, and for the next four hours played what I believe to be the finest game in the record of Masters' play. Osvensky's agitation was terrible, he was white to the lips, on the point of collapse, but the Thing at his back — Morisson — guided his hand move after move, hour after hour, to the one perfect square. I resigned on move sixty-four, and Osvensky immediately fainted. Somewhat ironically he was awarded the first Brilliancy Prize for the finest game played in the tournament. As soon as it was over Morisson turned away, walked slowly down the room and out of the door.

That night after dinner I went to my room and faced the situation. I eventually persuaded myself, firstly, that Morisson's appearance had certainly been an hallucination, secondly, that my opponent's performance had been due to telepathy. Most people, I suppose, would regard this as pure superstition, but to me it seemed a tenable theory that my mind, in its extreme concentration, had communicated its content to the mind of Osvensky. I determined that for the future I would break this contact, whenever possible, by getting up and walking around the room.

Consequently on the next day I faced my second opponent, Seltz, the champion of Germany, with comparative equanimity. This time I defended a Ruy Lopez with the black pieces. I made the second of my stupendous surprises on the seventh move, and once again had the satisfaction of seeing consternation and intense astonishment leap to the German's face. I got up and walked round the room watching the other games. After a time I looked round and saw the back of my opponent's head buried in his hands, which were passing feverishly through his hair, but I also saw Morisson come in and take his stand behind him.

I need not dwell on the next twelve days. It was always the same story. I lost every game, yet each time giving what I know to be absolute proof that I was the greatest player in the world. My opponents did not enjoy themselves. Their play was acclaimed as the perfection of perfection, but more than one told me that he had no recollection after the early stages of making a single move, and that he suffered from a sensation of great depression and malaise. I could see they regarded me with some awe and suspicion, and shunned my company. It was also remarkable that, though the room was crowded with spectators, they never lingered long at my table, but moved quickly and uneasily away.

When I got back to London I was in a state of extreme nervous exhaustion, but there was something I had to know for certain, so I went to the City Chess Club and started a game with a member. Morisson came in after a short time so I excused myself and went home. I had learnt what I had sought to learn. I should never play chess again.

The idea of suicide then became urgent. This happened three months ago. I have spent that period partly in writing this narrative, chiefly in annotating my games at Budapest. I found that every one of my opponents played an absolutely flawless game, that their combinations had been of a profundity and complexity unique in the history of chess. Their play had been literally superhuman. I found I had myself given the greatest human performance ever known. I think I can claim a certain reputation for will-power when I say the shortest game lasted fifty-four moves, even with Morisson there, and that I was only guilty of most minute errors due to the frightful and protracted strain. I leave these games to posterity, having no doubt of its verdict. To the last I had fought Morisson to a finish.

I feel no remorse. My destruction of Morisson was an act of common sense and justice. All his life he had the rewards which were rightly mine; as he said at a somewhat ironical moment, he had always been a lucky man. If I had known him to be my intellectual superior I would have accepted him as such, and become reconciled, but to be the greater and always to be branded as the inferior eventually becomes intolerable, and justice demands retribution. Budapest proved that I had made an 'over-sight', as we say in chess, but I could not have foreseen that, and, as it is, I shall leave behind me these games as a memorial of me. Had I not killed Morisson I should never have played them, for he inspired me while he overthrew me.

I have planned my disappearance with great care. I think I saw Morisson in my bedroom again last night, and, as I am terribly tired of him, it will be tomorrow. I have no wish to be ogled by asinine jurymen nor drooled over by fatuous coroners and parsons, so my body will never be found. I have just destroyed my chessmen and my board, for no one else shall ever touch them. Tears came into my eyes as I did so. I never remember this happening before. Morisson has just come in —

A further note by J.C. Cary, MD:

Here the narrative breaks off abruptly. While I felt a certain moral obligation to arrange for the publication, if possible, of this document, it all sounded excessively improbable. I am no chess-player myself, but I had as a patient a famous Polish Master who became a good friend of mine before he returned to Warsaw. I decided to send him the narrative and the games so that he might give me his opinion of the first, and his criticism of the latter. About three months later I had my first letter from him, which ran as follows:

My Friend

I have a curious tale to tell you. When I had read through that document which you sent me I made some inquiries. Let me tell you the result of them. Let me tell you no one of the name of your Professor ever competed in a British Chess Championship, there was no tournament held at Pest that year which he states, and no one of that name has ever played in a tournament in that city. When I learnt these facts, my friend, I regarded your Professor as a practical joker or a lunatic, and was just about to send back to you all these papers, when, quite to satisfy my mind, I thought I would just discover what manner of chess-player this joker or madman had been. I soberly declare to you that those few pages revealed to me, as a Chess Master, one of the few supreme triumphs of the human mind. It is incredible to me that such games were ever played over the board. You are no player, I know, and, therefore, you must take my word for it that, if your Professor ever played them, he was one of the world's greatest geniuses, the Master of Masters, and that, if he lost them his opponents, perhaps I might say his Opponent, was not of this world. As he says, he lost every game, but his struggles against this Thing were superb, incredible. I salute his shade. His notes upon these games say all that is to be said. They are supreme, they are final. It is a terrifying speculation, my friend, this drama, this murder, this agony, this suicide, did they ever happen? As one reads his pages and studies this quiet, this — how shall we say? — this so deadly tale, its truth seems to flash from it. Or is it some dream of genius? It terrifies me, as I say, this uncertainty, for what other flaming and dreadful visions have come to the minds of men and have been buried with them! I am, as you know, besides a Chess Master, a mathematician and philosopher; my mind lives an abstract life, and it is therefore a haunted mind, it is subject to possession, it is sometimes not master in its house. Enough of this, such thinking leads too far, unless it leads back again quickly on its own tracks, back to everyday things — I express myself not too well, I know — otherwise, it leads to that dim borderland in which the minds of men like myself had better never trespass. We see the dim yet beckoning peaks of that far country, far yet near — we had better turn back!

I have studied these games, until I have absorbed their mighty teaching. I feel a sense of supremacy, an insolence, I feel as your Professor did, that I am the greatest player in the world. I am due to play in the great Masters' tournament at Lodz. We shall see. I will write you again when it is over.

Serge

Three months later I received another letter from him.

J.C. Cary, MD.

My Friend,

I am writing under the impulse of a strong excitement, I am unhappy, I am — but let me tell you. I went to Lodz with a song in my brain, for I felt I should achieve the aim of my life. I should be the Master of Masters. Why then am I in this distress? I will tell you. I was matched in the first round with the great Cuban, Primavera. I had the white pieces. I opened as your Professor had opened in that phantom tourney. All went well. I played my tenth move. Primavera settled himself to analyse. I looked around the room. I saw, at first with little interest, a stranger, tall, debonair, enter the big swing door, and come towards my table. And then I remembered your Professor's tale, and I trembled. The stranger came up behind my opponent's chair and gave me *just that look*. A moment later Primavera made his move, and I put out my hand and offered that sacrifice, but, my friend, the hand that made that move *was not my own*. Trembling and infinitely distressed, I saw the stranger put his arm over Primavera's shoulder, take his hand, guide it to a piece, and thereby make that one complete answer to my move. I saw my opponent go white, turn and glance behind him, and then he said, 'I feel unwell. I resign.' 'Monsieur,' said I, 'I do not like this game either. Let us consider it a draw.' And as I put out my hand to shake his, it was my own hand again, and the stranger was not there.

My friend, I rushed from the room back to my hotel, and I hurled those games of supreme genius into the fire. For a time the paper seemed as if it would not burn, and as if the lights went dim: two shadows that were watching from the wall near the door grew vast and filled the room. Then suddenly great flames shot up and roared the chimney high, they blazed it seemed for hours, then as suddenly died, and the fire, I saw, was out. And then I discovered that I had forgotten every move in every one of those games, the recollection of them had passed from me utterly. I felt a sense of infinite relief, I was free again. Pray God, I never play them in my dreams!

Serge

THE CAT FROM SIAM

Fredric Brown

We were in the middle of our third game of chess when it happened.

It was late in the evening — eleven thirty-five, to be exact. Jack Sebastian and I were in the living room of my two-room bachelor apartment. We had the chess game set up on the card table in front of the fireplace, in which the gas grate burned cheerfully.

Jack looked cheerful too. He was wreathed in smoke from his smelliest pipe and he had me a pawn down and held a positional edge. I'd taken the first two games, but this one looked like his. It didn't look any less so when he moved his knight and said, 'Check.' My rook was forked along with the king. There didn't seem to be anything I could do about it except give up the rook for the knight.

I looked up at the Siamese cat who was sleepily watching us from her place of vantage on the mantel.

'Looks like he's got us, Beautiful,' I said. 'One should never play with a policeman.'

'I wish you wouldn't do that, dammit,' Jack said. 'You give me the willies.'

'Anything's fair in love and chess,' I told him. 'If it gives you the willies to have me talk to a cat, that's fine. Besides, Beautiful doesn't kibitz. If you see her give me any signals, I'll concede.'

'Go ahead and move,' he said, irritably. 'You've got only one move that takes you out of check, so make it. I take your rook and then — '

There was a noise, then, that I didn't identify for a second because it was made up of a *crack* and a *ping* and a *thud*. It wasn't until I turned to where part of the sound came from that I realised what it had been. There was a little round hole in the glass of the window.

The *crack* had been a shot, the *ping* had been the bullet coming through the glass — and the *thud* had been the bullet going into the wall behind me!

But by the time I had that figured out, the chessmen were spilling into my lap.

'Down, quick!' Jack Sebastian was saying sharply.

Whether I got there myself, or Jack pushed me there, I was on the floor. And by that time I was thinking.

Grabbing the cord of the lamp, I jerked the plug out of the wall and we were in darkness except for the reddish-yellow glow of the gas grate in the fireplace. The handle of that was on Jack's side, and I saw him, on his knees, reach out and turn it.

Then there was complete darkness. I looked toward where the window should be, but it was a moonless night and I couldn't see even the faintest outline of the window. I slid sideways until I bumped against the sofa. Jack Sebastian's voice came to me out of the darkness.

'Have you got a gun, Brian?' he asked.

I shook my head and then realised he couldn't see me. 'No,' I said. 'What would I be doing with a gun?'

My voice, even to me, sounded hoarse and strained. I heard Jack moving.

'The question is,' he said, 'what's the guy outside doing with one? Anybody after you, pal?'

'N-no,' I said. 'At least, not — '

I heard a click that told me Jack had found the telephone. He gave a number and added, 'Urgent, sister. This is the police.' Then his voice changed tone and he said, 'Brian, what's the score? Don't you know anything about who or why — '

He got his connection before he could finish the question and his vice changed pitch again.

'Jack Sebastian, Cap,' he said. 'Forty-five University Lane. Forty-five University Lane. Somebody just took a pot-shot in the window here. Head the squad cars this way from all directions they can come from. Especially the campus — that's the logical way for him to lose himself if he's on foot. Start 'em. I'll hold the line.'

Then he was asking me again, 'Brian, what can I add? Quick.'

'Tell 'em to watch for a tall, slender, young man,' I said. 'Twenty-one years old, thin face, blond hair.'

'The hell,' he said. '*Alister Cole?*'

'Could be,' I told him. 'It's the only guess I can make. I can be wrong, but — '

'Hold it.' Whoever he'd been talking to at the police station was back on the line. Without mentioning the name, Jack gave the description I'd just given to him. He said, 'Put that on the radio and come back in.'

Again to me, 'Anything else?'

'Yes,' I said. 'Tell 'em to converge those squad cars on Doc Roth's place, Two-ten University Lane. Forget sending them here. Get them *there*. Quick!'

'Why? You think if it's Alister Cole, he's going for Doc Roth, too?'

'Don't argue. Tell 'em. Hurry!'

I was on my feet by now, trying to grope my way across the pitch black room to the telephone to join him. I stepped on a chessman and it rolled and nearly threw me. I swore and got my lighter out of my pocket and flicked the wheel.

The tiny flame lighted part of the room dimly. The faint wavering light threw long dancing shadows. On the mantel, the Siamese was standing, her back arched and her tail thick. Her blue eyes caught and held the light like blue jewels.

'Put that out, you fool,' Jack snapped.

'He isn't standing there at the window,' I said impatiently. 'He wouldn't stay there after we doused the light. Tell them what I said about Roth's, quick.'

'Hello, Cap. Listen, get some of the cars to Two-ten University Lane instead. Two-one-oh. Fast. No, I don't know what this is about either. Just do it. We can find out later. The guy who took a shot here might go there. That's all I know. So long.'

He put the receiver back on the hook to end argument. I was there by that time, and had the receiver in my hand.

'Sorry, Jack, I said, and shoved him out of the way. I gave Dr Roth's number and added, 'I'll keep ringing till they answer.'

I held the receiver tight against my ear and waited. I realised I was still holding up the tiny torch of the cigarette lighter and I snapped it shut. The room snapped again into utter darkness.

'You stay in here,' Jack said. 'I'm going out.'

'Don't be a fool. He's got a gun.'

There was a sharp knock on the door, and we neither of us moved until the knock came again, louder. Then we heard Professor Winton's high, nervous voice.

'Brian, was that a shot a minute ago? Are you all right?'

Jack muttered something under his breath and groped for the door handle. In the receiver against my ear I could hear Dr Roth's phone still ringing. He hadn't answered yet. I put my hand over the mouthpiece.

'I'm all right, Dr Winton,' I called out.

By that time, Jack had found the knob and opened the door. Light streamed into the room from the hallway outside, and he stepped through the door quickly and closed it behind him.

'Someone shot through the window, Doctor,' I heard him say, 'but everything's under control. We've called the police. Better get back inside your room, though, till they get here.'

Dr Winton's voice said something, excitedly, but I didn't hear what, because Jeanette Roth's voice, husky and beautiful, but definitely sleepy, was saying 'Hello,' in my ear. I forgot Jack and Winton and concentrated my attention on the phone.

I talked fast. 'This is Brian Carter, Jeanette,' I said. 'Listen, this is important. It's maybe life and death. Just do what I say and don't argue. First, be sure all the lights in your house are out, all doors and windows locked tight — bolted, if they've got bolts. Then don't answer the door, unless you're sure it's the police — or me. I'm coming over, too, but the police may get there first.'

'Brian, what on earth — ?'

'Don't argue, darling,' I said. 'Do those things, fast. Lights out. Everything locked. And don't answer the door unless it's me or the police!'

I hung up on her. I knew she'd do it faster that way than if I stayed on the line.

I groped my way through the dark room and out into the lighted hallway. The door to Dr Winton's room, just across from my apartment, was closed, and there was nobody in the hallway. I ran to the front door and out onto the porch.

Out front on the sidewalk, Jack Sebastian was turning around, looking. He had something in his hand. When he turned so light from the street lamp down on the corner shone on it, I could see that it was a long-barrelled pistol. I ran out to join him.

'From Winton. It's a target pistol, a twenty-two. But it's better than throwing stones. Look, you sap, get back in there. You got no business out in the open.'

I told him I was going to Roth's place, and started down the sidewalk at a trot.

What's the score?' he called after me. 'What makes you think it was that Cole kid and why the excitement about Roth?'

I saved my breath by not answering him. There'd be plenty of time for all that later. I could hear him running behind me. We pounded up the steps onto the porch of Dr Roth's place.

'It's Brian Carter — and the police!' I called out while I rang the bell.

Maybe Jack Sebastian wasn't exactly the police, in the collective sense, but he was a detective, the youngest full-fledged detective on the force. Anyway, it wasn't the time for nice distinctions. I quit leaning on the bell and hammered on the door, and then yelled again.

The key turned in the lock and I stepped back. The door opened on the chain and Jeanette's white face appeared in the crack. She wasn't taking any chances. Then, when she saw us she slid back the chain and opened the door.

'Brian, what — 'she began.

'Your father, Jeanette. Is he all right?'

'I — I knocked on his door after you phoned, Brian, and he didn't answer! The door's locked. Brian, what's *wrong?*'

Out front a car swung into the curb with a squealing of brakes and two big men got out of it. They came running up the walk toward us and Jack stepped to the edge of the porch, where light from a street lamp would fall on his face and identify him to the two men. It also gleamed on the gun dangling from his hand.

Jeanette swayed against me and I put my arm around her shoulders. She was trembling.

'Maybe everything's okay, Jeanette,' I said. 'Maybe your father's just sleeping soundly. Anyway, these are the police coming now, so *you're* safe.

I heard Jack talking to the two detectives who'd come in the squad car, and then one of them started around the house, on the outside, using a flashlight. Jack and the other one joined us in the doorway.

'Let's go,' Jack said. 'Where's your father's room, Miss Roth?'

'Just a second, Jack,' I said. I snapped on the hall lights and then went into the library and turned on the lights there and looked around to be sure nobody was there.

'You wait in here, Jeanette,' I said then. 'We'll go up and try your father's door again, and if he still doesn't answer, we'll have to break — '

Footsteps pounded across the porch again and the other detective, the one who'd started around the house, stood in the doorway.

'There's a ladder up the side of the house to a window on the second floor — northwest corner room,' he said. 'Nobody around unless he's upstairs, in there. Shall I go up the ladder, Sebastian?'

Jack looked at me, and I knew that he and I were thinking the same thing. The killer had come here first, and there wasn't any hurry now.

'I'll go up the ladder,' he said. 'We won't have to break the door now. Will you two guys search the house from attic to cellar and turn all the lights on and leave them on? And, Brian, you stay here with Miss Roth. Can I borrow your flashlight, Wheeler?'

I noticed that, by tacit consent, Jack was taking charge of the case and of the older detectives. Because, I presumed, he was the first one on the scene and had a better idea what it was all about.

One of the men handed over a flashlight and Jack went outside. I led Jeanette into the library.

'Brian,' she asked, 'do you think Dad is — that something has happened to Dad?'

'We'll know for sure in a minute, darling. Why make guesses meanwhile? I don't know.'

'But — what happened that made you call me up?'

Jack and I were playing chess at my place,' I told her. 'Someone took a shot through the window. At me, not at Jack. The bullet went into the wall behind me and just over my head. I — well, I had a sudden hunch who might have shot at me, and if my hunch was right, I thought he'd consider your father his enemy, too. I'm afraid he may be — mad.'

'Alister Cole?'

'Have you noticed anything strange about him?' I asked her.

'Yes. He's always scared me, Brian, the way he's acted. And just last night, Dad remarked that — '

She broke off, standing there rigidly. Footsteps were coming down the stairs. That would be Jack, of course. And the fact that he walked so slowly gave us the news in advance of his coming.

Anyway, when he stood in the doorway, Jeanette asked quietly, 'Is he dead?' and Jack nodded.

Jeanette sat down on the sofa behind her and dropped her head into her hands, but she didn't cry.

'I'll phone headquarters,' Jack said. 'But first — you and he were alone in the house tonight, weren't you, Miss Roth?'

She looked up and her eyes were still dry. 'Yes,' she said. 'Mother's staying overnight with my aunt — her sister — in

town. This is going to hit her hard. Will you need me here? I —
I think it would be best if I were the one to break it to her. I can
dress and be there in half an hour. I can be back in an hour and
a half. Will it be all right?'

Jack looked at me. 'What do you think, Brian? You know this
guy Cole and you know what this is all about. Would Miss Roth
be in any danger if she left?'

'You could figure that yourself, Jack,' I said. 'Cole was here,
alone in the house with her after he killed Dr Roth, and he had
all the time in the world because there hadn't been an alarm yet.
But let me go with her, though, just to be sure.'

He snorted. 'Just to be sure — of *what?* He *is* after you, my
fine friend. Until we get Cole under lock and key — and throw
away the key — you're not getting out from under my eye.'

'All right,' I said, 'so I'm indispensable. But everybody isn't,
and this place will be full of police in a few minutes. If I'm not
mistaken, that sounds like another squad car coming now. Why
not have one of the boys in it use it to drive Miss Roth over to
her aunt's?'

He nodded. 'Okay, Miss Roth. I'll stick my neck out — even
though Headquarters may cut it off. And Wheeler and Brach
have finished looking around upstairs, so it'll be okay for you to
go to your room if you want to change that housecoat for a
dress.'

He went to the front door to let the new arrivals in.

'I'm awfully sorry, Jeanette,' I said then. 'I know that sounds
meaningless, but — it's all I can think of to say.'

She managed a faint smile. 'You're a good egg, Brian. I'll be
seeing you.'

She held out her hand, and I took it. Then she ran up the
stairs. Jack looked in at the doorway.

'I told the new arrivals to search the grounds,' he said. Not
that they'll find anything, but it'll give 'em something to do. I
got to phone Headquarters. You stay right here.'

'Just a second, Jack,' I said. 'How was he killed?'

'A knife. Messy job. It was a psycho, all right.'

You say messy? Is there any chance Jeanette might go
into — ?

He shook his head. 'Wheeler's watching that door. He
wouldn't let her go in. Well, I got to phone — '

'Listen, Jack. Tell me one thing. How long, about, has he been
dead? I mean, is there any chance Cole could have come here

after he shot at me? I might have thought of phoning here, or getting here a minute or two sooner. I'd feel responsible if my slowness in reacting, my dumbness

Jack was shaking his head. 'I'm no ME,' he said, 'but Roth had been dead more than a few minutes when I found him. I'd say at least half an hour, maybe an hour.'

He went to the phone and gave the Headquarters number. I heard his voice droning on, giving them the details of the murder and the attempted murder.

I sat there listening, with my eyes closed, taking in every word of it, but carefully keeping the elation off my face.

It had gone perfectly. Everything had worked out.

Whether or not they caught Alister Cole — and they *would* catch him — nothing could go wrong now. It had come off perfectly.

I would never be suspected, and I stood to gain a million dollars — and Jeanette . . .

She came down the stairs slowly, as one approaching a reluctant errand. I waited for her at the foot of the staircase, my eyes on her beautiful face. There was shock there, but — as I had expected and was glad to see — not too much grief. Roth had been a cold, austere man. Not a man to be grieved for deeply, or long.

She stopped on the second step, her eyes level with mine and only inches away. I wanted to kiss her, but this was not the time. A little while and I would, I thought.

But I could look now, and I could dream. I could imagine my hand stroking that soft blonde hair. I could imagine those soft, misty blue eyes closed and my lips kissing the lids of them, kissing that soft white throat, her yielding lips. Then —

My hand was on the newel post and she put hers over it. It almost seemed to burn.

'I wish I could go with you, darling,' I said. 'I wish there was something I could do to help you.'

'I wish you could come with me too, Brian. But — your friend's right. And didn't you take an awful chance coming over here anyway — out in the open, with a madman out to kill you?'

'Jack was with me,' I said.

Jack was calling to me from the library. 'Coming,' I said, and then I told Jeanette, 'It's cool out, darling. Put a coat on over that thin dress.'

She nodded absently. 'I wish you could come with me, Brian. Mother likes you — '

I knew what she meant, what she was thinking. That things were going to be all right between us now. Her mother did like me. It was her stuffy, snobbish father who had stood in the way. Jack called again impatiently.

'Take care of yourself, Brian,' Jeanette whispered quickly. Don't take any chances, please.'

She pressed my hand, then ran past me toward the coat closet. I saw that one of the detectives was waiting for her at the door. I went into the library. Jack was still sitting at the telephone table, jotting things into a notebook. He looked very intent and businesslike.

Captain Murdock — he's head of Homicide — is on his way here,' Jack said. 'He'll be in charge of the case. That's why I wanted you to let the girl get out of here first. He might insist on her staying.'

'What about you?' I asked him. 'Aren't you staying on the case?'

He grinned a little. 'I've got my orders. They're to keep you alive until Cole is caught. The Chief told me if anything happens to you, he'll take my badge away and shove it up my ear. From now on, pal, we're Siamese twins.'

'Then how about finishing that chess game?' I said. 'I think I can set up the men again.'

He shook his head. 'Life isn't that simple. Not for a while yet, anyway. We'll have to stick here until Cap Murdock gets here, and then I'm to take you into the Chiefs office. Yeah, the Chiefs going down there at this time of night.'

It was after one when Jack took me into Chief Randall's office. Randall, a big, slow-moving man, yawned and shook hands with me across his desk.

'Sit down, Carter,' he said, and yawned again.

I took the seat across from him. Jack Sebastian sat down in a chair at the end of the desk and started doodling with the little gold knife he wears on the end of a chain.

'This Roth is a big man,' Chief Randall said. 'The papers are going to give us plenty if we don't settle this quick.'

'Right now, Chief,' Jack said, 'Alister Cole is a bigger man. He's a homicidal maniac on the loose.'

The Chief frowned. 'We'll get him,' he said. 'We've got to. We've got him on the air. We've got his description to every railroad station and airport and bus depot. We're getting out fliers with his picture — as soon as we get one. The state patrolmen are watching for him. We'll have him in hours. We're doing everything.'

'That's good,' I told him. 'But I don't think you'll find him on his way out of town. I think he'll stay here until he gets me — or until you get him.'

'He'll know that you're under protection, Brian,' Jack said. 'Mightn't that make a difference? Wouldn't he figure the smartest thing to do would be to blow town and hide out for a few months then come back for another try?'

I thought it over. 'He might,' I said, doubtfully. 'But I don't think so. You see, he isn't thinking normally. He's under paranoic compulsion, and the risks he takes aren't going to weight the balance too strongly on the safety side. He was out to kill Dr Roth and then me. Now I'm no expert in abnormal psychology, but I think that if he'd missed on his *first* killing he might do as you suggested — go away and come back later when things had blown over. But he made his first kill. He stepped over the line. He's going to be under terrifically strong compulsion to finish the job right away — at any risk!'

Jack said, 'One thing I don't get. Cole was probably standing right outside that window. We reacted quickly when that shot came, but not instantaneously. He should have had time for a second shot before we got the light out. Why didn't he take that second shot?'

'I can suggest a possibility,' I told them. 'I was in Alister's room about a week ago. I've been there several times. He opened a drawer to take out his chess set for our game, and I happened to notice a pistol in the drawer. He slammed the drawer quickly when he saw me glancing that way, but I asked him about the pistol.'

'He said it had been his brother's, and that he'd had it since his brother had died three years ago. He said it was a single-shot twenty-two calibre target pistol, the kind really fancy marksmen use in tournaments. I asked him if he went in for target shooting and he said no, he'd never shot it.'

'Probably telling the truth about that,' Chief Randall said, 'since he missed your head a good six inches at — how far would it have been, Jack?'

'About twelve feet, if he'd been standing just outside the

window. Farther, of course, if he'd been farther back.' Jack turned to me. 'Brian, how good a look did you get at the pistol? Was it a single-shot, the kind he described?'

'I think so,' I said. 'It wasn't either a revolver or an automatic. It had a big fancy walnut handle, silver trimmings, and a long, slender barrel. Yes, I'd say I'm reasonably sure it was a single-shot marksman's gun. And that would be why he didn't shoot a second time before we got the light and the gas-grate turned out. I think he could have shot by the light of that gas flame even after I pulled out the plug of the floor lamp.'

'It would have been maybe ten seconds, not over fifteen,' Jack said, 'before we got both of them out. A pistol expert, used to that type of gun, could have reloaded and shot again, but an amateur probably couldn't have. Anyway, maybe he didn't even carry extra cartridges, although I wouldn't bet on that.'

'Just a second,' Randall said. He picked up the phone on his desk and said, 'Laboratory.' A few seconds later he said, 'That bullet Wheeler gave you, the one out of the wall at Brian Carter's room. Got anything on it?' He listened a minute and then said 'Okay,' and hung up.

He said, 'It was a twenty-two all right, a long rifle, but it was too flattened out to get any rifling marks. Say, Jack, do you know if they use long rifle cartridges in those target guns?'

'A single-shot will take any length — short, standard, or long rifle. But, Brian, why would he carry as — as inefficient a gun as that? Do you figure he planned this on the spur of the moment and didn't have time to get himself a gun with bigger bullets and more of them?'

'I don't think it was on the spur of the moment,' I said. 'I think he must have been planning it. But he may have stuck the target gun in his pocket on the spur of the moment. I figure it this way: The knife was his weapon. He intended to kill us both with the knife. But he brought along the gun as a spare. And when he got to my place after killing Dr. Roth and found you there, Jack, instead of finding me asleep in bed, it spoiled his original idea of coming in my window and doing to me what he did to Roth. He didn't want to wait around until you left because he'd already made one kill, and maybe he remembered he'd left the ladder at the side of the house. There might be an alarm at any time.'

Randall nodded. 'That makes sense, Carter. Once he'd killed Roth, he was in a hurry to get you.'

Jack quit doodling with his penknife and put it in his vest pocket. 'Anything from the ME?' he asked.

Randall nodded. Says the stroke across the jugular was probably the first one, and was definitely fatal. The rest of the — uh — carving was just trimming. The ladder, by the way, belonged to a painting contractor who was going to start on the house the next day. He painted the garage first — finished that today. The ladder was lying on its side against a tree in the yard, not far from where Cole used it. Cole could have seen it there from the front walk, if he'd gone by during the day or during the early evening while it was still light.'

'Did the medical examiner say about when he was killed?' I asked.

'Roughly half an hour to an hour before he was found,' Randall said. He sighed. 'Carter, have you told us everything about Cole that you think of?'

'Everything.'

'Wish I could talk you into sleeping here, under protective custody. What are your plans for the next few days?'

'Nothing very startling,' I told him. 'This is Friday night — Saturday morning, now. I have to teach a class Monday afternoon at two. Nothing special to do until then, except some work of my own which I can do at home. As for the work I was doing with Dr Roth, that's off for the time being. I'll have to see what the Board of Regents has to say about that.'

'Then we'll worry about Monday when Monday comes,' Randall said. 'If, as you think, Cole is going to stay around town, we'll probably have him before then. Do you mind Sebastian staying with you?'

'Not at all.'

'And I'm going to assign two men to watch the outside of your place — at least for the next forty-eight hours. We won't plan beyond that until we see what happens. Right now, every police man in town is looking for Cole, and every state policeman is getting his description. Tomorrow's newspaper and the Sunday papers will carry his photograph, and then the whole city will be on the lookout for him. You have your gun, Sebastian?'

Jack shook his head. 'Just this twenty-two I borrowed from Winton.'

'You better run home and get it, and whatever clothes and stuff you'll need for a couple of days.'

'I'll go with him,' I said.

'You'll wait here,' Jack told me. 'It's only a few blocks. I'll be right back.' He went out.

'While he's gone, Carter,' Randall said, 'I want to ask a few things he already knows, but I don't. About the set-up at the university, the exact relationship between you and Roth and between Roth and Alister Cole, what kind of work you do — things like that.'

Dr Roth was head of the Department of Psychology,' I said. 'It's not a big department, here at Hudson U. He had only two full professors under him. Winton, who stays where I do, is one of them. Dr Winton specialises in social psychology.

'Then there are two instructors. I'm one of them. An instructor is somewhere between a student and a professor. He's taking postgraduate courses leading to further degrees which will qualify him to be a professor. In my own case, I'm within weeks of getting my master's. After that, I start working for a doctorate. Meanwhile, I work my way by teaching and by helping in the research lab, grading papers, monitoring exams — well, you get the idea.

'Alister Cole was — I suppose we can consider him fired now — a lab assistant. That isn't a job that leads to anything. It's just a job doing physical work. I don't think Cole had even completed high school.'

'What sort of work did he do?'

'Any physical work around the laboratory. Feeding the menagerie — we work with rats and white mice mostly, but there are also Rhesus monkeys and guinea pigs — cleaning cages, sweeping — '

'Doesn't the university have regular cleaning women?'

'Yes, but not in the lab. With experiments going on there, we don't want people who don't know the apparatus working around it, possibly moving things that shouldn't be moved. The lab assistants know what can be touched and what can't.'

'Then, in a way, Dr Roth was over both of you?'

'More than in a way. He didn't exactly hire us — the Board of Regents does all the hiring — but we both worked under him. In different capacities, of course.'

'I understand that,' Randall said. 'Then you could say Dr Roth's job was something like mine, head of a department. Your relationship to him would be about that of your friend, Sebastian, to me, and Alister Cole would be — umm — a mess attendant over on the jail side, or maybe a turnkey.'

'That's a reasonably good comparison,'I agreed. 'Of course I was the only instructor who worked directly under Dr Roth, so I was a lot closer to him than Jack would be to you. You have quite a few detectives under you, I'd guess.'

He sighed. 'Never quite enough, when anything important happens.'

There was a knock on the door and he called out, 'Yeah?'

The detective named Wheeler stuck his head in. 'Miss Roth's here,' he announced. 'You said you wanted to talk to her. Shall I send her in?'

Chief Randall nodded, and I stood up. 'You might as well stay, Carter,' he told me.

Jeanette came in. I held the chair I'd been sitting in for her, and moved around to the one Jack had vacated. Wheeler had stayed outside, so I introduced Jeanette and Randall.

'I won't want to keep you long, Miss Roth,' Randall said, 'so I'll get right down to the few questions I want to ask. When did you see Alister Cole last?'

'This afternoon, around three o'clock.'

'At your house?'

'Yes. He came then and asked if Dad was home. I told him Dad was downtown, but that I expected him any minute. I asked him to come in and wait.'

'Did he and you talk about anything?'

'Nothing much. As it happened, I'd been drinking some coffee, and I gave him a cup of it. But we talked only a few minutes — not over ten — before Dad came home.'

'Do you know what he wanted to see your father about?'

'No. Dad took him into the library and I went out to the kitchen. Mr Cole stayed only a few minutes, and then I heard him leaving.'

'Did it sound as though he and your father were quarrelling? Did you hear their voices?'

'No, I didn't hear. And Dad didn't say, afterwards, what Mr Cole had wanted to see him about. But he did say something about Mr Cole. He said he wondered if the boy was — how did he put it? — if he was all right. Said he wondered if maybe there wasn't a tendency toward schizophrenia, and that he was going to keep an eye on him for a while.'

'Had you noticed anything strange about Cole's actions or manner when you talked to him before he saw your father?'

'He seemed a little excited about something and — well, trying to hide his excitement. And then there's one thing I'd always noticed about him — that he was unusually reticent and secretive about himself. He never volunteered any information about his — about anything concerning himself. He could talk all right about other things.'

'Do you know if Cole knew your mother would not be there tonight?'

'I don't believe — Wait. Yes, he did. I forget just how it came into the conversation when I was talking with Mr Cole, but I did mention my aunt's being sick. He'd met her. And I think I said Mother was staying with her a few nights.'

'Was anything said about the ladder in your yard?'

'He asked if we were having the house painted, so I imagine he saw it lying there. It wasn't mentioned specifically.'

'And tonight — what time did you last see your father?'

'When he said good-night at about ten o'clock and went up to bed. I finished a book I was reading and went upstairs about an hour later. I must have gone right to sleep because it seemed as though I'd been asleep a long time when I heard the phone ringing and went to answer it.'

'You heard nothing until — I mean, you heard nothing from the time your father went to sleep at ten until you were wakened by the phone — which would have been at a quarter to eleven?'

'Not a sound.'

'Did your father usually lock the door of his room?'

'Never. There was a bolt on the door, but he'd never used it that I know of.'

Chief Randall nodded. 'Then Cole must have bolted the door before he went back down the ladder,' he said. 'Is there anything you can add, Miss Roth?'

Jeanette hesitated. 'No,' she said. 'Nothing that I can think of.' She turned and smiled, faintly, at me. 'Except that I want you to take good care of Brian.'

'We'll do that,' Randall told her. He raised his voice, 'Wheeler!' The big detective opened the door and Randall said, 'Take Miss Roth home now. Then take up duty at Forty-five University Lane — that's where Carter here lives. Outside. Jack Sebastian'll be inside with him. If the two of you let anything happen to him — God help you!'

Pulling the car to the curb half a block from my place, Jack said,

'That looks like Wheeler in a car up ahead, but I'm not taking any chances. Wait here.'

He got out and walked briskly to the car ahead. I noticed that he walked with his hand in his right coat pocket. He leaned into the car and talked a moment, then came back.

'It's Wheeler,' he said, 'and he's got a good spot there. He can watch both windows of your room, and he has a good view of the whole front of the place besides.'

'How about the back?' I asked him.

'There's a bolt on the back door. Cole would have trouble getting in that way. Besides, we'll both be in your place and your door will be locked. If he could get into the house, he's got two more hurdles to take — your door and me.'

'And don't forget me.'

'That's the hurdle he wants to take. Come on. I'll leave you with Wheeler while I case the joint inside before I take you in.'

We walked up to Wheeler's car and I got in beside him. 'Besides looking around in my place,' I told Jack, 'you might take a look in the basement. If he got in while we were gone, and is hiding out anywhere but in my place, it would be there. Probably up at the front end.'

'I'll check it. But why would he be there?'

'He knows that part of the place. Mr Chandler, the owner, turned over the front section of the basement to me for some experiments that Dr Roth and I were doing on our own time. We were working with rats down there — an extension of some experiments we started at the university lab, but wanted to keep separate. So Alister Cole's been down there.'

'And if he wanted to lay for you someplace, that might be it?'

'It's possible. He'd figure I'd be coming down there sooner or later.'

'Okay, but I'll get you into your apartment first, then go down there.'

He went inside and I saw the lights in my place go on. Five minutes later he came out to the car. 'Clean as a whistle,' he said. 'Wait till I get my stuff from my own car and we'll go in.'

He went to his own car half a block back and returned with a suitcase. We went into the house and into my place.

'You're safe here,' he said. 'Lock me out now, and when I come back, don't let me in until you hear and recognize my voice.'

'How about a complicated knock? Three shorts and a long.'

He looked at me and saw I was grinning. He shook his finger at me. 'Listen, pal,' he said, 'this is dead serious. There's a mad man out to kill you, and he might be cleverer than you think. You can't take anything for granted until he's caught.'

'I'll be good,' I told him.

'I've got more at stake on this than you have' he said, 'because if he kills you, you're only dead. But me, I'll be out of a job. Now let's hear that door lock when I go out in the hall.'

I locked it after him, and started to pick up the chessmen from the floor. The Siamese blinked at me from her perch on the mantel. I tickled her under the chin.

'Hi, Beautiful,' I said. 'How'd you like all the excitement?'

She closed her eyes, as all cats do when they're having their chins chucked, and didn't answer me.

I leaned closer and whispered, 'Cheer up, Beautiful. We're in the money, almost. You can have a silken cushion and only the best grades of calves' liver.'

I finished picking up the chessmen and went over to the window. Looking out diagonally to the front, I could see the car that Wheeler was sitting in. I made a motion with my hand, and got an answering motion from the car.

I pulled down the shades in both rooms and was examining them to make sure that one couldn't see in from the outside when there was a tap at the door. I walked over and let Jack back in after he'd spoken to me.

'Nothing down there but some guinea pig cages and what look like mazes. The cages are all empty.'

'They're rat cages,' I told him. 'And the things that look like mazes, strangely enough, are mazes. That's a sizable suitcase you brought. Planning to move in on me?'

He sat down in my most comfortable chair. 'Only suitcase I had. It isn't very full. I brought an extra suit, by the way, but it's not for me. It's for Alister Cole.'

'Huh? A suit for — '

'Strait-jacket. Picked it up at Headquarters, just in case. Listen, pal, you got any idea what it means to take a maniac? We'll take him alive, if we can, but we'll have to crease him or sap him, and I'll want some way of holding him down after he comes to.' He shuddered a little. 'I handled one of them once. Rather, I helped handle one. It took four of us, and the other three guys were huskier than I am. And it wasn't any picnic.'

'You're making me very happy,' I told him. 'Did you by any chance pick up an extra gun for me?'

'Can you shoot one? Ever handled one?'

I said, 'You pull the trigger, don't you?'

'That's what I mean. That's why I didn't get you one. Look, if this loonie isn't caught, and he makes a clean getaway, I'll tell you what I'll do. I'll get you a permit for a gun, help you pick one out, and take you down to the police range and teach you how to use it. Because I won't be able to stay with you forever.'

'Fine' I said. 'I'd feel happier with one right away, though.'

'Brian, people who don't know guns, who aren't expert with them, are better off without them. Safer. I'll bet if Alister Cole hadn't had a gun tonight, he'd have got you.'

'How do you figure that?'

'Simple. He looked in the window and saw me playing chess with you. If he'd had only the shiv, he'd have hidden somewhere until after I'd left and given you time to get to sleep. Then he'd have come in your window — and that would have been that. But since he had a gun, he took a chance with it. Not knowing how to squeeze a trigger without moving his sights, he over-shoots. And, I hope, ends his chances of getting you.'

I nodded, slowly. 'You've got a point,' I admitted. 'All right, I'll wait and learn it right, if you don't get Alister. Want to finish that game of chess?' I glanced towards Beautiful, now sound asleep, but still perched where she could overlook the game. 'I promise you that Beautiful won't kibitz.'

'Too late,' Jack said. 'It's after three. How long have you had that cat, Brian?'

'You should remember. You were with me when I bought her. Four years ago, wasn't it? Funny how a pet gets to mean so much to you. I wouldn't sell her for anything on earth.'

Jack wrinkled his nose. 'A dog, now, I could understand. They're some company to a guy.'

Moving my hand in a deprecating gesture, I laughed at him. 'That's because you're not used to such intelligent and aesthetic company. Next to women, cats are the most beautiful things on earth, and we rate women higher only because we're prejudiced. Besides, women talk back and cats don't. I'd have gone nuts the last few months if I hadn't had Beautiful to talk to. I've been working twelve to fourteen hours a day, and — that reminds me. I'd better get some sleep. How about you?'

'Not sleepy yet, but don't let me stop you. I'll go in the other room and read. What have you got that might give me some dope on Alister Cole. Got any good books on abnormal psychology?'

'Not a lot. That's out of our line here. We don't have courses in the abnormal brand. We work with fundamentals, mostly. Oh, I've got a couple of general books. Try that *Outline of Abnormal Psychology* on the top shelf, the blue jacket. It's pretty elementary, I guess, but it's as far as you'll cover in a few hours' reading anyway.'

I started undressing while Jack got the book and skimmed the table of contents. 'This looks okay,' he said. 'Chapters on dementia praecox, paranoia, waking hypnosis — Never heard of that. Is it common?'

'Certainly,' I told him. 'We've tried it. It's not really part of abnormal psychology at all, although it can be used in treatment of mental troubles. We've subjected whole classes — with their consent, of course — to experiments in automatic writing while under suggestion in waking state amnesia. That's what I used for my senior thesis for my BA. If you want to read up on what's probably wrong with Alister Cole, read the chapter on paranoia and paranoid conditions, and maybe the chapter on schizophrenia — that's dementia praecox. I'd bet on straight paranoia in Cole's case, but it could be schiz.'

I hung my clothes over the chair and started to pull on my pyjamas.

'According to Jeanette,' Jack said, 'Dr Roth thought Cole might have a touch of schizophrenia. But you bet on paranoia. What's the difference?'

I sighed. 'All right, I'll tell you. Paranoia is the more uncommon of the two disorders, and it's harder to spot. Especially if a subject is tied up in knots and won't talk about himself. A man suffering from paranoia builds up an air-tight system of reasoning about some false belief or peculiar set of ideas. He sticks to these delusions, and you can't convince him he's wrong in what he thinks. But if his particular delusion doesn't show, you can't spot him, because otherwise he seems normal.

'A schizophrenic, on the other hand, may have paranoid ideas, but they're poorly systematised, and he's likely to show other symptoms that he's off-balance. He may have ideas that other people are always talking about him, or trying to do him harm, and he's subjected to incoherence, rambling, untidiness, apathy — all sorts of symptoms. Cole didn't show any of them.'

'A paranoiac, then, could pretty well hide what was wrong

with him,' Jack said, 'as long as no one spotted the particular subject he was hipped on?'

'Some of them do. Though if we'd been specialists, I think we'd have spotted Cole quickly. But listen. Hadn't you better get some sleep too?'

'Go ahead and pound your ear. I'll take a nap if I get tired. Here goes the light.'

He turned it out and went into the next room. He left the door ajar, but I found that if I turned over and faced the wall, the little light that came in didn't bother me.

Beautiful, the cat, jumped down from the mantel and came over to sleep on my feet, as she always does. I reached down and petted her soft warm fur a moment, then I lay back on the pillow and quit thinking. I slept.

A sound woke me — the sound of a window opening slowly.

With me, as with most people, dreams are forgotten within the first few seconds after waking. I remember the one I was just having, though, because of the tie-up it had with the sound that wakened me.

My dream had changed that slow upward scrape of the window into the scrape of claws on cement, the cement of the basement. There in the little front room of the basement, Dr Roth was standing with his hand on the latch of a rat cage, and a monstrous cat with the markings of a Siamese was scraping her claws on the floor, gathering her feet under her to spring. It was Beautiful, my cat, and yet it wasn't. She was almost as large as a lion. Her eyes glowed like the headlights of a car.

Dr Roth cowered back against the tier of rat cages, holding a hand in front of him to ward off the attack. I watched from the doorway, and I tried to open my mouth to scream at her to stop, not to jump. But I seemed paralysed. I couldn't move a muscle or make a sound.

I saw the cat's tail grow larger. Her eyes seemed to shoot blue sparks. And then she leaped.

Dr Roth's arm was knocked aside as though it had been a toothpick. Her claws sank into his shoulders and her white, sharp teeth found his throat. He screamed once, and then the scream became a gurgle and he lay on the cement floor, dead, in a puddle of his blood. And the cat, backing away from him, was shrinking to her real size, getting smaller, her claws still scraping the cement as she backed away . . .

And then, still frozen with the horror of that dream, I began to know that I was dreaming, that the sound I heard was the opening of a window.

I sat up in bed, fast. I opened my mouth to yell for Jack. Someone stood there, just inside the window!

And then, before I had yelled, I saw that it was Jack who stood there. Enough light came in from the other room that I could be sure of that. He'd raised the shade. He was crouched down now, and his eyes, level with the middle of the lower pane, stared through it into the night outside.

He must have heard the springs creak as I sat up. He turned. 'Shhh,' he said. 'It's all right — I think.'

He put the window back down again then, and threw over the lock. He pulled down the shade and came over to the bed and sat down in a chair beside it.

'Sorry I woke you,' he said, very quietly. 'Can you go back to sleep, or do you want to talk a while?'

'What time is it?' I asked.

'Three-forty. You were asleep only half an hour. I'm sorry, but — '

'But what? What's been happening? Did you think you heard a sound outside?'

'Not outside the window, no. But a few minutes ago I thought I heard someone try the knob of the hall door. But when I got there and listened, I couldn't hear anything.'

'It could have been Alister Cole,' I said, 'if he got in the back way. Wheeler isn't watching the back door.'

'That's what I thought, even though I didn't hear anything back there. So I went to the window. I thought if I could attract Wheeler's attention, he'd come in the front way. Then I'd take a chance opening the hall door — with my gun ready, of course. If Cole was there, we'd have him between us.'

'Did you get Wheeler's attention?'

He shook his head slowly. 'His car isn't where it was. You can't even see it from the window. Maybe he moved it to a different spot where he thought he'd be less conspicuous, or could watch better.'

'That's probably it. Well, what are you going to do?'

'Nothing. Sit tight. If I stick my neck out into that hall, or go outside through the window, the edge is going to be with Cole. If I sit here and make him come to me, it's the other way round.

Only I'm through reading for tonight. I'm sitting right here by the bed. If you can sleep, go ahead. I'll shut up and let you.'

'Sure,' I said. 'I can sleep swell. Just like a lamb staked out in the jungle to draw a tiger for the hunters. That's how I can sleep.'

He chuckled. 'The lamb doesn't know what it's there for.'

'Until it smells tiger. I smell tiger.' That reminded me of my dream, and I told him about it.

'You're a psychologist,' he said. 'What does it mean?'

'Probably that I had a subconscious dislike for Dr Roth.' I told him. 'Only I know that already. I don't need to interpret a dream to tell me that.'

'What did you have against Roth, Brian? I've known there was something from the way you've talked about him.'

'He was a prig, for one thing,' I said. 'You know me well enough, Jack, to know I'm not too bad a guy, but he thought I was miles away from being good enough for Jeanette. Well — maybe I am, but then again, so's everybody else who might fall in love with her.'

'Does she love you?'

'I think so.' I thought it over. 'Sure, I practically know she does, from things she said tonight.'

'Anything else? I mean, about Roth. Is that the only reason you didn't like him?'

I didn't say anything for a while. I was thinking. I thought, why not tell Jack now? Sooner or later, he'll know it. The whole world will know it. Why not get it off my chest right now, while there was a good chance to get my side of it straight?

Something made me stop and listen first. There wasn't a sound from outside nor from the hallway.

'Jack,' I said, 'I'm going to tell you something. I'm awfully glad that you were here tonight.'

'Thanks, pal.' He chuckled a little.

'I don't mean what you think I mean, Jack. Sure, maybe you saved my life from Alister Cole. But more than that, you gave me an alibi.'

'An alibi? For killing Roth? Sure, I was with you when he was killed.'

'Exactly. Listen, Jack, I had a reason for killing Roth. That reason's coming out later anyway. I might as well tell you now.'

He turned and stared at me. There was enough light in the room so that I could see the movement of his head, but, not enough so that he could watch my face. I don't know why he bothered turning.

If you need an alibi,' he said, 'you've sure got one. We started playing chess at somewhere around eight. You haven't been out of my sight since then, except while you were in Chief Randall's office.'

'Don't think I don't know that,' I told him. 'And don't think I'm not happy about it. Listen, Jack. Because Roth is dead, I'm going to be a millionaire. If he was alive, I still might be, but there'd have been a legal fight about it. I would have been right, but I could have lost the same.'

'You mean it would have been a case of your word against his?'

'Exactly. And he's — he was — department head, and I'm only a flunky, a little better on his social scale than Alister Cole. And it's something big, Jack. Really big.'

'What?'

'What kind of rat cages did you find in the basement when you looked down there?' I asked him.

'What kind? I don't get you. I don't know makes of rat cages.'

'Don't worry about the make,' I said. 'You found only one kind. Empty ones. The rats were dead. And disposed of.'

He turned to look at me again. 'Go on,' he said.

Now that I'd started to tell him, I knew I wouldn't even try to go back to sleep. I was too excited. I propped the pillow up against the head of the bed.

'Make a guess, Jack,' I said. 'How much food do rats eat a year in the United States alone?'

'I wouldn't know. A million dollars' worth?'

'A hundred million dollars' worth,' I said, 'at a conservative estimate. Probably more than a million dollars is spent fighting them, each year. In the world, their cost is probably a billion dollars a year. Not altogether — just for one year! How much do you think something would be worth that would actually completely eliminate rats — both *Mus Rattus* and *Mus Norvegicus* — completely and once and for all? Something that would put them with the hairy mammoth and the roc and the dinosaurs?'

'If your mathematics are okay,' Jack said, 'it'd be worth ten billion bucks in the first ten years?'

'Ten billion, on paper. A guy who could do it ought to be able to get one ten-thousandth that much, shouldn't he? A million?'

'Seems reasonable. And somebody ought to throw in a Nobel prize along with it. But can you do it?'

'I can do it,' I said. 'Right here in my basement I stumbled across it, accidentally, Jack, in the course of another experiment. But it works. It works! It kills rats!'

'So does Red Squill. So does strychnine. What's your stuff got that they haven't?'

'Communicability. Give it to *one* rat — and the whole colony dies! Like all the rats — thirty of them, to be exact — died when I injected one rat. Sure, you've got to catch one rat alive — but that's easy. Then just inject it and let it go, and all the rats in the neighbourhood die.'

'A bacillus?'

'No. Look, I'll be honest with you. I don't know exactly how it works, but it's not a germ. I have a hunch that it destroys a rat's immunity to some germ he carries around with him normally — just as you and I carry around a few million germs which don't harm us ordinarily because we also carry around the antibodies that keep them in check. But this injection probably destroys certain antibodies in the rat and the germs become — unchecked. The germs also become strong enough to overcome the antibodies in other rats, and they must be carried by the air because they spread from cage to cage with no direct contact. Thirty rats died within twenty-four hours after I inoculated the first one — some in cages as far away as six feet.'

Jack Sebastian whistled. 'Maybe you have got something,' he said softly. 'Where did Roth come in on it, though? Did he claim half, or what?'

'Half I wouldn't have minded giving him,' I said. 'But he insisted the whole thing belonged to the university, just because I was working on an experiment for the university — even though it was in my own place, on my own time. And the thing I hit upon was entirely outside the field of the experiment. I don't see that at all. Fortunately, he didn't bring it to an issue. He said we should experiment further before we announced it.'

'Do you agree with that?'

'Of course. Naturally, I'm not going off half-cocked. I'm going to be sure, plenty sure, before I announce it. But when I do, it's going to be after the thing has been patented in my name. I'm going to have that million bucks, Jack!'

'I hope you're right,' he said. 'And I can't say I blame you, if you made the discovery here at your own place on your own time. Anyone else know about it?'

'No.'

'Did Alister Cole?'

'No, he didn't. I think, Jack, that this thing is bigger even than you realise. Do you know how many human lives it's going to save? We don't have any bubonic here in this country — or much of any other rat-and-flea-borne disease, but take the world as a whole.'

'I see what you mean. Well, more power to you, keed. And if everything goes well, take me for a ride on your yacht sometime.'

'You think I'm kidding?'

'Not at all. And I pretty well see what you mean by being glad you've got an alibi. Well, it's a solid one, if my word goes for anything. To have killed Dr Roth — no matter how much motive you may have had — you'd have had to have had a knife on a pole a block and a half long. Besides -'

'What?'

'Nothing. Listen, I'm worried about Wheeler. Probably he moved that car to another spot, but I wish I knew for sure.'

'It's a squad car, isn't it?' I asked.

'Yes.'

'With two-way radio?'

'Yes, but I haven't got a radio in here.'

'We got a telephone. If you're worried about Wheeler — and you're getting me that way too — why don't you phone Headquarters and have them call Wheeler and phone you back?'

'Either you're a genius or I'm a dope,' he said. 'Don't tell me which.'

He got up out of the chair and I could see he was still holding the gun in his hand. He went first to the door and listened carefully, then he went to the window. He listened carefully there. Finally, he pulled back the shade a crack to look out.

'Now you're giving me the willies, and I might as well get up,' I said. 'For some reason, I'd rather get killed with my pants on — if I'm going to get killed.' I looked at my cat. 'Sorry, Beautiful,' I said as I pulled my feet out from under the Siamese.

I took off my pyjamas and started putting on my shirt and trousers.

'Wheeler's car still isn't anywhere I can see,' Jack said.

He went over to the telephone and lifted the receiver off the hook. I slipped my feet into a pair of loafers and looked over.

He was still holding the receiver and hadn't spoken. He put it back gently. 'Someone's cut the wires,' he said. 'The line is dead.'

I said, 'I don't believe this. It's out of a horror programme on the radio. It's a gag.'

Jack snorted. He was turning round, looking from the window to the door. Got a flashlight?'

'Yes. In the drawer over there.'

'Get it,' he said. 'Then sit back in that corner where you're not in direct range from the window or the door. If either opens, bracket it with your flash. I've got my flash but I'm using it left-handed. Anyway, two spots are better than one, and I want to see to shoot straight.'

While I was getting the flashlight, he closed the door to the other room, leaving us in pitch darkness except for our flashes. I lighted my own way to the chair he'd pointed out.

'There's a window in that other room,' I said. 'Is it locked?'

'Yes,' he answered. 'He can't get in there without breaking that window. Okay, turn out that light and sit tight.'

I heard him move across the room to another corner. His flash light played briefly first on the door to the hallway, then swept across to the window. Then it went out.

'Wouldn't the advantage be with us if we kept the light on?' I asked.

'No. Listen, if he busts in the window, when you aim your flash at it, hold it out from your body, out over the arm of your chair. So if he shoots at the flash, he won't hit you. Our two lights should blind him. We should be able to see him, but he shouldn't be able to see us.'

'Okay,' I said.

I don't know how many minutes went by. Then there was a soft tapping at the window. I tensed in my chair and aimed the flashlight at the window without turning it on.

The tapping came again. An irregular series: *tap — tap — tap — tap*.

'That's Wheeler,' Jack whispered. 'It's the code tap. Cole couldn't possibly know it. Sit tight.'

I could hear him moving across the room in the darkness. I could see the streak of greyness as he cautiously lifted one side of the shade, then peered through the crack between shade and window. As quietly as he could, he raised up the shade and unlocked and raised the window.

It was turning slightly grey outside, and a little light came from the street lamp a quarter of a block away. I could recognise the big body of Wheeler coming through the window. Wheeler, and not Alister Cole.

I began breathing again. I got up out of the chair and went over to them. Wheeler was whispering.

' . . . So don't put down the windows,' he was saying. 'I'll come in that way again.'

'I'll leave it up to Brian,' Jack whispered back. 'If he wants to take that chance. Meanwhile, you watch that window.'

He pulled me to one side then, away from the open window. 'Listen,' he said. 'Wheeler saw somebody moving in back. He'd moved his car where he could watch part of the back yard. He got there in time to see a window going down. Alister Cole's inside the building. Wheeler's got an idea now, only it's got a risk to it. I'll leave it up to you. If you don't like it, he'll go out again and get help, and we'll sit tight here, as we were until help comes.'

'What's the idea?' I asked. If it wasn't too risky, I'd like it better than another vigil while Wheeler went for help.

'Wheeler,' Jack said, 'thinks he should walk right out of the door into the hall and out the front door. He thinks Cole will hear that, and will think I'm leaving you. Wheeler will circle around the house and come in the window again. Cole should figure you're here alone and come in that hallway door — and both Wheeler and I will be here to take him. You won't be taking any risk unless by some chance he gets both of us. That isn't likely. We're two to one, and we'll be ready for him.'

I whispered back that it sounded good to me. He gripped my arm.

'Go back to your chair then. That's as good a place as any.'

Groping my way back to the chair, I heard Jack and Wheeler whispering as they went towards the hallway door. They were leaving the window open and, since it was momentarily unguarded, I kept my eyes on it, ready to yell a warning if a figure appeared there. But none did.

The hallway door opened and closed quickly, letting a momentary shaft of light into the room. I heard Jack back away from the door and Wheeler's footsteps going along the hallway. I heard the front door open and close, Wheeler's steps cross the porch.

A moment later, there was the soft *tap — tap — tap — tap* on the upper pane of the open window, and then Wheeler's bulk came through it.

Very, very quietly, he closed the window and locked it. He pulled down the shade. Then I heard the shuffle of his footsteps as he moved into position to the right of the door.

I haven't any idea how long we waited after that. Probably five or ten minutes — but it seemed like hours. Then I heard, or thought I heard, the very faintest imaginable sound. It might have been the scrape of shoes on the carpet of the hall outside the door. But there wasn't any doubt about the next sound. It was the soft turning of the knob of the door. It turned and held. The door pushed open a crack, then a few inches. Light streamed over a slowly widening area.

Then one thing Jack hadn't counted on happened. A hand reached in, between the door and the jamb, and flicked on the light switch. Dazzling light from the bulbs in the ceiling almost blinded me. And it was in that blinding second that the door swung back wide and Alister Cole, knife in one hand and single-shot target pistol in the other, stood in the doorway. His eyes flashed around the room, taking in all three of us. But then his eyes centred on me and the target pistol lifted.

Jack stepped in from the side and a blackjack was in his upraised hand. It swung down and there was a sound like someone makes thumping a melon. He and Wheeler caught Alister Cole, one from each side, and eased his way down to the carpet.

Wheeler bent over him and got the gun and the knife first, then held his hand over Cole's heart.

'He'll be all right,' he said.

He took a pair of handcuffs from his hip pocket, rolled Cole over and cuffed his hands together behind him. Then he straightened, picking up the gun he'd put down on the carpet while he worked on Cole.

I'd stood up, my knees still shaking a little. My forehead felt as though it was beaded with cold sweat. The flashlight was gripped so tightly in my right hand that my fingers ached.

I caught sight of Beautiful, again on the mantel, and she was standing up, her tail bushy and straight up, her fur back of the ears and along the back standing up in a ridge, her blue eyes blazing. 'It's all right, Beautiful,' I said to her soothingly. 'All the excitement's over, and everything's — '

I was walking toward the mantel, raising my hand to pet her, when Wheeler's excited voice stopped me.

'Watch out,' he yelled. 'That cat's going to jump — '

And I saw the muzzle of his gun raising and pointing at the Siamese cat.

My right hand swung up with the flashlight and I leaped at Wheeler. Out of the corner of my eye I saw Jack stepping in as Wheeler ducked back. The corner of my eye caught the swing of his blackjack . . .

The overhead light was bright in my eyes when I opened them. I was lying flat on the bed and the first thing I saw was Beautiful, curled up on my chest looking at me. She was all right now, her fur sleek and her curled tail back to normal. Whatever else had happened, she was all right.

I turned my head, and it hurt to turn it, but I saw that Jack was sitting beside the bed. The door was closed and Wheeler and Cole were gone.

'What happened?' I asked.

'You tried to kill Wheeler,' Jack said. There was something peculiar about his voice, but his eyes met mine levelly.

'Don't be silly,' I said. 'I was going to knock his arm down before he could shoot. He was crazy. He must have a phobia against cats.'

Jack shook his head. 'You were going to kill him,' he said. 'You were going to kill him whether he shot or not.'

'Don't be silly.' I tried to move my hands and found they were fastened behind me. I looked at Jack angrily. 'What's wrong with you?'

'Not with me, Brian,' he said. 'With you. I know — now — that it was really you who killed Dr Roth tonight. Yes, I know you've got an alibi. But you did it just the same. You used Alister Cole as your instrument. My guess would be waking hypnosis.'

'I suppose I got him to try to kill me, too!' I said.

'You told him he'd shoot *over your head*, and then run away. It was a compulsion so strong he tried it again tonight, even after he saw Wheeler and me ready to slug him if he tried. And he was aiming high again. How long have you been working on him?'

'I don't know what you're talking about.'

'You do, Brian. You don't know it all, but you know this part of it. You found out that Cole had schizophrenic tendencies. You found out, probably while playing chess with him, that you could put him under waking hypnosis without his knowing it. And you worked on him. What kind of a fantasy did you build in

him? What kind of a conspiracy, did you plant in his mind, Dr
Roth was leading against him?'

'You're crazy.'

'No, *you* are, Brian. Crazy, but clever. And you know that
what I've just told you just now is right. You also know I'll never
be able to prove it. I admit that. But there's something else you
don't know. I don't have to prove it.'

For the first time I felt a touch of fear. 'What do you mean?' I
asked.

'You gave Cole his fantasies, but you don't know your own.
You don't know that — under the pressure, possibly, of working
too hard and studying too hard — your own mind cracked. You
don't know that your million-dollar rat-killer is *your* fantasy. You
don't believe me, now that I'm telling you that it is a fantasy.
You'll never believe it. The paranoiac builds up an air-tight
system of excuses and rationalisation to support his insane
delusions. You'll never believe me.'

I tried to sit up and couldn't. I realised then that it wasn't a
matter of my arms being tied. Jack had put the straitjacket on
me. 'You're part of it, then,' I said. 'You're one of those in the
plot against me.'

'Sure, sure. You know, Brian. I can guess what started it. Or
rather what set it off, probably only a few days ago. It was when
Dr Roth killed your cat. That dream you told me about tonight —
the cat killing Dr Roth. Your mind wouldn't accept the truth.
Even your subconscious mind reversed the facts for the dream.
I wonder what really happened. Possibly your cat killed a rat
that was an important part of an experiment and, in anger, Dr
Roth — '

'You're crazy,' I shouted. 'Crazy!'

'And ever since, Brian, you've been talking to a cat that wasn't
there. I thought you were kidding, at first. When I figured out
the truth, I told Wheeler what I figured. When you gave us a
clue where the cat was supposed to be, on the mantel, he raised
his gun and pretended — '

'Jack!' I begged him, to break off the silly things he was saying.
'If you're going to help them railroad me, even if you're in on
the plot — please get them to let me take Beautiful with me.
Don't take her away too. Please!'

Cars were driving up outside. I could feel the comforting
weight and warmth of the cat sleeping on my chest.

'Don't worry, Brian,' Jack said quietly. 'That cat'll go wherever you go. Nobody can take it away from you. Nobody.'

FOOL'S MATE

Stanley Ellin

When George Huneker came home from the office that evening
he was obviously fired by a strange excitement. His ordinarily
sallow cheeks were flushed, his eyes shone behind his rimless
spectacles and instead of carefully removing his rubbers and
neatly placing them on the strip of mat laid for that purpose in
a corner of the hallway, he pulled them off with reckless haste
and tossed them aside. Then, still wearing his hat and overcoat,
he undid the wrappings of the package he had brought with him
and displayed a small, flat, leather case. When he opened the
case Louise saw a bed of shabby green velvet in which rested
the austere black and white forms of a set of chessmen.

'Aren't they beautiful?' George said. He ran a finger lovingly
over one of the pieces. 'Look at the work on this: nothing fancy
to stick away in a glass case, you understand, but everything
neat and clean and ready for action the way it ought to be. All
genuine ivory and ebony, and all handmade, every one of them.'

Louise's eyes narrowed. 'And just how much did you pay out
for this stuff?'

'I didn't,' George said. 'That is, I didn't buy it. Mr Oelrichs
gave it to me.'

'Oelrichs?' said Louise. 'You mean that old crank you brought
home to dinner that time? The one who just sat and watched us
like the cat that ate the canary, and wouldn't say a word unless
you poked it out of him?'

'Oh, Louise!'

'Don't you "Oh, Louise" me! I thought I made my feelings
about him mighty clear to you long before this. And, may I ask,
why should our fine Mr Oelrichs suddenly decide to give you
this thing?'

'Well,' George said uneasily, 'you know he's been pretty sick,
and what with him needing only a few months more for retire-
ment I was carrying most of his work for him. Today was his

last day, and he gave me this as a kind of thank-you present. Said it was his favourite set, too, but he wanted to give me the best thing he could, and this was it.'

'How generous of Mr Oelrichs,' Louise remarked frigidly. 'Did it ever occur to him that if he wanted to pay you back for your time and trouble, something practical would be a lot more to the point?'

'Why, I was just doing him a favour, Louise. Even if he did offer me money or anything like that, I wouldn't take it.'

'The more fool you.' Louise sniffed. 'All right, take off your things, put them away right and get ready for supper. It's just about ready.'

She moved towards the kitchen, and George trailed after her placatingly. 'You know, Louise, Mr Oelrichs said something that was very interesting.'

'I'm sure he did.'

'Well, he said there were some people in the world who *needed* chess — that when they learned to play it real well they'd see for themselves how much they needed it. And what I thought was that there's no reason why you and I . . . '

She stopped short and faced him with her hands on her hips. 'You mean that after I'm done taking care of the house, and shopping, and cooking your hot meals, and mending and darning, then I'm supposed to sit down and learn how to play games with you! For a man going on fifty, George Huneker, you get some peculiar ideas.'

Pulling off his overcoat in the hallway, he reflected that there was small chance of his losing track of his age, at least not as long as Louise doted so much on reminding him. He had first heard about it a few months after his marriage when he was going on thirty and had been offered a chance to go into business for himself. He had heard about it every year since, on some occasion or other, although as he learned more and more about Louise he had fallen into fewer traps.

The only trouble was that Louise always managed to stay one jump ahead of him, and while in time he came to understand that she would naturally put her foot down at such things as his leaving a good steady job, or at their having a baby when times were hard (and in Louise's opinion they always were), or at buying the house outright when they could rent it so cheap, it still came as a surprise that she so bitterly opposed the idea of having company to the house, or of reading some book he had just enjoyed, or of tuning in the radio to a symphony, or, as in this case, of taking up chess.

Company, she made it clear, was a bother and expense, small print hurt her eyes, symphonies gave her a splitting headache and chess, it seemed, was something for which she could not possibly find time. Before they had been married, George thought unhappily, it had all been different somehow. They were always in the midst of a crowd of his friends, and when books or music or anything like that were the topics of discussion, she followed the talk with bright and vivacious interest. Now she just wanted to sit with her knitting every night while she listened to comedians bellowing over the radio.

Not being well, of course, could be one reason for all this. She suffered from a host of aches and pains which she dwelt on in such vivid detail at times that George himself could feel sympathetic twinges go through him. Their medicine chest bulged with remedies, their diet had dwindled to a bland and tasteless series of concoctions and it was a rare month which did not find Louise running up a sizeable doctor's bill for the treatment of what George vaguely came to think of as 'women's troubles'.

Still, George would have been the first to point out that despite the handicaps she worked under, Louise had been as good a wife as a man could ask for. His salary over the years had hardly been luxurious, but penny by penny she had managed to put aside fifteen thousand dollars in their bank account. This was a fact known only to the two of them, since Louise made it a point to dwell on their relative poverty in her conversations with anyone, and while George always felt some embarrassment when she did this, Louise pointed out that one of the best ways to save your money was not to let the world at large know you had any, and since a penny saved was a penny earned she was contributing as much to their income in her way as George was in his. This, while not reducing George's embarrassment, did succeed in glossing it with increased respect for Louise's wisdom and capability.

And when added to this was the knowledge that his home was always neat as a pin, his clothing carefully mended and his health fanatically ministered to, it was easy to see why George chose to count his blessings rather than make an issue of anything so trivial as his wife's becoming his partner at chess. Which, as George himself might have admitted had you pinned him down to it, was a bit of a sacrifice, for in no time at all after receiving the set of chessmen he found himself a passionate devotee of the game. And chess, as he sometimes reflected while poring over his board of an evening with the radio booming in his ears and his wife's knitting needles flickering away contentedly, would seem to be a game greatly enhanced by the presence of an opponent. He did not reflect this ironically; there was no irony in George's nature.

Mr Oelrichs, in giving him the set, had said he would be available for instruction at any time. But since Louise had already indicated that that gentleman would hardly be a welcome guest in her home, and since she had often expressed decided opinions on any man who would leave his hearth and home to go traipsing about for no reason, George did not even think the matter worth broaching. Instead, he turned to a little text aptly entitled *An Invitation to Chess*, was led by the invitation to essay other and more difficult texts and was thence led to a whole world of literature on chess, staggering in its magnitude and complexity.

He ate chess, drank chess and slept chess. He studied the masters and past masters until he could quote chapter and verse from even their minor triumphs. He learned the openings, the middle-game and the end-game. He learned to eschew the reckless foray which led nowhere in favour of the positional game where cunning strategy turned a side into a relentless force that inevitably broke and crushed the enemy before it. Strange names danced across his horizon: Alekhine, Capablanca, Lasler, Nimzovich, and he pursued tbem, drunk with the joy of discovery, through the ebony and ivory mazes of their universe.

But in all this there was still that one thing lacking: an opponent, a flesh-and-blood opponent against whom he could test himself. It was one thing, he sometimes thought disconsolately, to have a book at one's elbow while pondering a move: it would be quite another to ponder even the identical move with a man waiting across the board to turn it to his own advantage and destroy you with it. It became a growing hunger, that desire to make a move and see a hand reach across the table to answer it; it became a curious obsession so that at times, when Louise's shadow moved abruptly against the wall or a log settled in the fireplace, George would look up suddenly, half-expecting to see the man seated in the empty chair opposite him.

He came to visualise the man quite clearly after a while. A quiet contemplative man much like himself, in fact, with greying hair and rimless spectacles that tended to slide a bit when he bent over the board. A man who played just a shade better than himself; not so well that he could not be beaten, but well enough to force George to his utmost to gain an occasional victory.

And there was one thing more he expected of this man: something a trifle unorthodox, perhaps, if one was a stickler for chess ritual. The man must prefer to play the white side all the time. It was the white side that moved first, that took the offensive until, perhaps, the tide could be turned against it. George himself infinitely preferred the black side, preferred to parry the thrusts and advances of white while he slowly built up a solid wall of defence against its climactic moves. *That* was the way to learn the game, George told himself: after a player learned how to make himself invulnerable on the defence, there was nothing he couldn't do on attack.

However, to practise one's defence still required a hand to set the offence into motion, and eventually George struck on a solution which, he felt with mild pride, was rather ingenious. He would set up the board, seat himself behind the black side, and then make the opening move for white. This he would counter with a black piece, after which he would move again for white, and so on until some decision was reached.

It was not long before the flaws in this sytem became distressingly obvious. Since he naturally favoured the black side, and since he knew both plans of battle from their inception, black won game after game with ridiculous ease. And after the twentieth fiasco of this sort George sank back into his chair despairingly. If he could only put one side out of his mind completely while he was moving for the other, why, there would be no problem at all! Which he realised cheerlessly, was a prospect about as logical as an ancient notion he had come across in his reading somewhere, the notion that if you cut a serpent in half, the separated halves would then turn on each other and fight themselves savagely to death.

He set up the board again after this glum reflection and then walked round the table and seated himself in white's chair. Now, if he were playing the white side what would he do? A game depends not only on one's skill, he told himself, but also on one's knowledge of his opponent. And not only on the opponent's style of play but also on his character, his personality, his whole nature. George solemnly looked across the table at black's now empty chair and brooded on this. Then slowly, deliberately, he made his opening move.

After that, he quickly walked round the table and sat down on black's side. The going, he found, was much easier here, and almost mechanically he answered white's move. With a thrill of excitement chasing inside him, he left his seat and moved round to the other side of the board again, already straining hard to put black and its affairs far out of his mind.

'For pity's sake, George, what *are* you doing!'

George started, and looked around dazedly. Louise was watching him, her lips compressed, her knitting dropped on her lap and her manner charged with such disapproval that the whole room seemed to frown at him. He opened his mouth to explain, and hastily thought better of it.

'Why, nothing,' he said, 'nothing at all.'

'Nothing at all!' Louise declared tartly. 'The way you're tramping around, somebody would think you can't find a comfortable chair in the house. You know I . . . '

Then her voice trailed off, her eyes became glassy, her body straightened and became rigid with devouring attention. The comedian on the radio had answered an insult with another evidently so devastating that the audience in the studio could do no more than roar in helpless laughter. Even Louise's lips turned up ever so slightly at the corners as she reached for her knitting again, and George gratefully seized this opportunity to drop into the chair behind black's side.

He had been on the verge of a great discovery, he knew that; but what exactly had it been? Was it that changing places physically had allowed him to project himself into the forms of two players, each separate and distinct from the other? If so, he was at the end of the line, George knew, because he would never be able to explain all that getting up and moving around to Louise.

But suppose the board itself were turned round after each move? Or, and George found himself charged with a growing excitement, since chess was completely a business of the mind anyhow — since, when one had mastered the game sufficiently it wasn't even necessary to use a board at all — wasn't the secret simply a matter of *turning oneself into the other player* when his move came?

It was white's move now, and George bent to his task. He was playing white's side, he must do what white would do — more than that, he must feel white's very emotions — but the harder he struggled and strained in his concentration, the more elusive became his goal. Again and again, at the instant he was about to reach his hand out, the thought of what black intended to do, of what black was surely *going* to do, slipped through his mind like a dot of quicksilver and made him writhe inwardly with a maddening sense of defeat.

This now became the obsession, and evening after evening he exercised himself at it. He lost weight; his face drew into haggard lines so that Louise was always at his heels during mealtimes trying to make him take an interest in her wholly uninteresting recipes. His interest in his job dwindled until it was barely per-functory, and his superior, who at first had evinced no more than a mild surprise and irritation, started to shake his head ominously.

But with every game, every move, every effort he made, George felt with exultation he was coming nearer that goal. There would come a moment, he told himself with furious certainty, when he could view the side across the board with objectivity, with disinterest, with no more knowledge of its intentions and plans than he would have of any flesh-and-blood player who sat there; and when that day came, he would have achieved a tri-umph no other player before him could ever claim!

He was so sure of himself, so confident that the triumph lay beyond the next move each time he made a move, that when it came at last his immediate feeling was no more than a comfort-able gratification and an expansive easing of all his nerves. Some-thing like the feeling, he thought pleasurably, that a man gets after a hard day's work when he sinks into bed at night. Exactly that sort of feeling, in fact.

He had left the black position on the board perilously exposed through a bit of carelessness, and then in an effort to recover himself had moved the king's bishop in a neat defensive gesture that could cost white dear. When he looked up to study white's possible answer he saw White sitting there in the chair across the table, his fingertips gently touching each other, an ironic smile on his lips.

'Good,' said White pleasantly. 'Surprisingly good for you, George.'

At this, George's sense of gratification vanished like a soap bubble flicked by a casual finger. It was not only the amiable insult conveyed by the words which nettled him; equally disturb-ing was the fact that White was utterly unlike the man that George had been prepared for. He had not expected White to resemble him as one twin resembles another, yet feature for feature the resemblance was so marked that White could have been the image that stared back at him from his shaving mirror each morning. An image, however, which, unlike George's, seemed invested with a power and arrogance that were quite overwhelming. Here, George felt with a touch of resentment, was no man to hunch over a desk computing dreary rows of figures, but one who with dash and brilliance made great decisions at the head of a long committee table. A man who thought a little of tomorrow, but much more of today and the good things it offered. And one who would always find the price for those good things.

That much was evident in the matchless cut of White's clothing, in the grace and strength of the lean, well-manicured hands, in the merciless yet merry glint in the eyes that looked back into George's. It was when he looked into those eyes that George found himself fumbling for some thought that seemed to lie just beyond him. The image of himself was reflected so clearly in those eyes; perhaps it was not an image. Perhaps . . .

He was jarred from his train of thought by White's moving a piece. 'Your move,' said White carelessly, 'that is, if you want to continue the game.'

George looked at the board and found his position still secure. 'Why shouldn't I want to continue the game? Our positions . . .'

'For the moment are equal,' White interposed promptly. 'What you fail to consider is the long view: I am playing to win; you are playing only to keep from losing.'

'It seems very much the same thing,' argued George.

'But it is not,' said White, 'and the proof of that lies in the fact that I shall win this game, and every other game we ever play.'

The effrontery of this staggered George. 'Maroczy was a master who relied a good deal on defensive strategy,' he protested, 'and if you are familiar with his games . . . '

'I am exactly as well acquainted with Maroczy's games as you are,' White observed, 'and I do not hesitate to say that had we ever played, I should have beaten him every game as well.'

George reddened. 'You think very well of yourself, don't you,' he said, and was surprised to see that instead of taking offence White was regarding him with a look of infinite pity.

'No,' White said at last, 'it is you who think well of me,' and then as if he had just managed to see and avoid a neatly baited trap, he shook his head and drew his lips into a faintly sardonic grimace. 'Your move,' he said.

With an effort George put aside the vaguely troubling thoughts that clustered in his mind, and made the move. He made only a few after that when he saw clearly that he was hopelessly and ignominiously beaten. He was beaten a second game, and then another after that, and then in the fourth game, he made a despairing effort to change his tactics. On his eleventh move he saw a devastating opportunity to go on the offensive, hesitated, refused it and was lost again. At that George grimly set about placing the pieces back in their case.

'You'll be back tomorrow?' he said, thoroughly put out at White's obvious amusement.

'If nothing prevents me.'

George suddenly felt cold with fear. 'What could prevent you?' he managed to say.

'White picked up the white queen and revolved it slowly between his fingers. 'Louise, perhaps. What if she decided not to let you indulge yourself in this fashion?'

'But why? Why should she? She's never minded up to now!'

'Louise, my good man, is an extremely stupid and petulant woman. . . .'

'Now, that's uncalled for!' George said, stung to the quick.

'And,' White continued as if he had not been interrupted at all, 'she is the master here. Such people now and then like to affirm their mastery seemingly for no reason at all. Actually, such gestures are a sop to their vanity — as necessary to them as the air they breathe.'

George mustered up all the courage and indignation at his command. 'If those are your honest opinions,' he said bravely, 'I don't think you have the right to come to this house ever again.'

On the heels of his words Louise stirred in her arm chair and turned towards him. 'George,' she said briskly, 'that's quite enough of that game for the evening. Don't you have anything better to do with your time?'

'I'm putting everything away now,' George answered hastily, but when he reached for the chessman still gripped between his opponent's fingers, he saw White studying Louise with a look that made him quail. White turned to him then, and his eyes were like pieces of dark glass through which one can see the almost unbearable light of a searing flame.

'Yes,' White said slowly. 'For what she is and what she has

done to you I hate her with a consuming hate. Knowing that, do you wish me to return?'

The eyes were not unkind when they looked at him now, George saw, and the feel of the chessman which White thrust into his hand was warm and reassuring. He hesitated, cleared his throat, then, 'I'll see you tomorrow,' he said at last.

White's lips drew into that familiar sardonic grimace. 'Tomorrow, the next day, any time you want me,' he said. 'But it will always be the same. You will never beat me.'

Time proved that White had not underestimated himself. And time itself, as George learned, was something far better measured by an infinite series of chess games, by the moves within a chess game, than by any such device as a calendar or clock. The discovery was a delightful one; even more delightful was the realisation that the world around him, when viewed clearly, had come to resemble nothing so much as an object seen through the wrong end of a binocular. All those people who pushed and prodded and poked and demanded countless explanations and apologies could be seen as sharp and clear as ever but nicely reduced in perspective, so that it was obvious that no matter how close they came, they could never really touch one.

There was a single exception to this: Louise. Every evening the world would close in around the chessboard and the figure of White lounging in the chair on the other side of it. But in a corner of the room sat Louise over her knitting, and the air around her was charged with a mounting resentment which would now and then eddy around George in the form of querulous complaints and demands from which there was no escape.

'How *can* you spend every minute at that idiotic game!' she demanded. 'Don't you have anything to talk to me about?' And, in fact, he did not, any more than he had since the very first years of his marriage when he had been taught that he had neither voice nor vote in running his home, that she did not care to hear about the people he worked with in his office and that he could best keep to himself any reflections he had on some subject which was, by her own word, Highbrow.

'And how right she is,' White had once taken pains to explain derisively. 'If *you* had furnished your home it would be uncluttered and graceful, and Louise would feel awkward and out of place in it. If she comes to know the people you work with too well, she might have to befriend them, entertain them, set her blatant ignorance before them for judgement. No, far better under the circumstances that she dwells in her vacuum, away from unhappy judgements.'

As it always could, White's manner drove George to furious resentment. 'For a set of opinions pulled out of a cocked hat that sounds very plausible,' he burst out. 'Tell me, how do you happen to know so much about Louise?'

White looked at him through veiled eyes. 'I know only what you know,' he said. 'No more and no less.'

Such passages left George sore and wounded, but for the sake of the game he endured them. When Louise was silent all the world retreated into unreality. Then the reality was the chess-board with White's hand hovering over it, mounting the attack, sweeping everything before it with a reckless brilliance that could only leave George admiring and dismayed.

In fact, if White had any weakness, George reflected mourn-fully, it was certainly not in his game, but rather in his deft and unpleasant way of turning each game into the occasion for a little discourse on the science of chess, a discourse which always wound up with some remarkably perverse and impudent reflec-tions on George's personal affairs.

'You know that the way a man plays chess demonstrates that man's whole nature,' White once remarked. 'Knowing this, does it not strike you as significant that you always choose to play the defensive — and always lose?'

That sort of thing was bad enough, but White was at his most savage those times when Louise would intrude in a game: make some demand on George or openly insist that he put away the board. Then White's jaw would set, and his eyes would flare with that terrible hate that always seemed to be smouldering in them when he regarded the woman.

Once when Louise had gone so far as to actually pick up a piece from the board and bang it back into the case, White came to his feet so swiftly and menacingly that George leaped up to forestall some rash action. Louise glared at him for that.

'You don't have to jump like that,' she snapped. 'I didn't break anything. But I can tell you, George Huneker, if you don't stop this nonsense I'll do it for you. I'll break every one of these things to bits if that's what it takes to make you act like a human being again!'

'Answer her!' said White. 'Go ahead, why don't you answer her!' And caught between these two fires George could do no more than stand there and shake his head helplessly.

It was this episode, however, which marked a new turn in White's manner: the entrance of a sinister purposefulness thinly concealed in each word and phrase.

'If she knew how to play the game,' he said, 'she might respect it, and you would have nothing to fear.'

'It so happens,' George replied defensively, 'that Louise is too busy for chess.'

White turned in his chair to look at her and then turned back with a grim smile. 'She is knitting. And, it seems to me, she is always knitting. Would you call that being busy?'

'Wouldn't you?'

'No,' said White, 'I wouldn't. Penelope spent her years at the loom to keep off importunate suitors until her husband returned. Louise spends her years at knitting to keep off life until death comes. She takes no joy in what she does; one can see that with half an eye. But each stitch dropping off the end of those needles brings her one instant nearer death, and, although she does not know it, she rejoices in it.'

'And you make all that out of the mere fact that she won't play at chess?' cried George incredulously.

'Not alone chess,' said White. 'Life.'

'And what do you mean by that word "life", the way you use it?'

'Many things,' said White. 'The hunger to learn, the desire to create, the ability to feel vast emotions. Oh, many things.'

'Many things, indeed,' George scoffed. 'Big words, that's all they are.' But White only drew his lips into that sardonic grimace and said, 'Very big. Far too big for Louise, I'm afraid,' and then by moving a piece forced George to redirect his attention to the board.

It was as if White had discovered George's weak spot, and took a sadistic pleasure in returning to probe it again and again. And he played his conversational gambits as he made his moves at chess; cruelly, unerringly, always moving forward to the inescapable conclusion with a sort of flashing audacity. There were times when George, writhing helplessly, thought of asking him to drop the subject of Louise once and for all, but he could never bring himself to do so. Something in the recesses of George's mind warned him that these conversational fancies were as much a part of White as his capacity for chess, and that if George wanted him at all it would have to be on his own terms.

And George did want him, wanted him desperately, the more so on such an evening as that dreadful one when he came home to tell Louise that he would not be returning to his office for a while. He had not been discharged, of course, but there had been something about his taking a rest until he felt in shape again. Although, he hastily added in alarm as he saw Louise's face go slack and pale, he never felt better in his life.

In the scene that followed, with Louise standing before him and passionately telling him things about himself that left him sick and shaken, he found White's words pouring through his mind in a bitter torrent. It was only when Louise was sitting exhausted in her armchair, her eyes fixed blankly on the wall before her, her knitting in her lap to console her, and he was at his table setting up the pieces, that he could feel the brackish tide of his pain receding.

'And yet there is a solution for all this,' White said softly, and turned his eyes toward Louise. 'A remarkably simple solution when one comes to think of it.'

George felt a chill run through him. 'I don't care to hear about it,' he said hoarsely.

'Have you ever noticed, George,' White persisted, 'that that piddling, hackneyed picture on the wall, set in that baroque monstrosity of a frame that Louise admires so much, is exactly like a pathetic little fife trying to make itself heard over an orchestra that is playing its loudest?'

George indicated the chessboard. 'You have the first move,' he said.

'Oh, the game,' White said. 'The game can wait, George. For the moment I'd much prefer to think what this room — this whole fine house, in fact — could be if it were all yours, George. Yours alone.'

'I'd rather get on with the game,' George pleaded.

'There's another thing, George,' White said slowly, and when he leaned forward George saw his own image again staring at him strangely from those eyes, 'another fine thing to think of. If you were all alone in this room in this house, why, there wouldn't be anyone to tell you when to stop playing chess. You could play morning, noon and night, and all around to the next morning if you cared to!

'And that's not all, George. You can throw that picture out of the window and hang something respectable on the wall: a few good prints, perhaps — nothing extravagant, mind you — but a few good ones that stir you a bit the first time you come into the room each day and see them.

'And recordings! I understand they're doing marvellous things with recordings today, George. Think of a whole room filled with them: opera, symphony, concerto, quartet — just take your pick and play them to your heart's content!'

The sight of his image in those eyes always coming nearer, the jubilant flow of words, the terrible meaning of those words set George's head reeling. He clapped his hands over his ears and shook his head frantically.

'You're mad!' he cried. 'Stop it!' And then he discovered to his horror that even with his hands covering his ears he could hear White's voice as clearly and distinctly as ever.

'Is it the loneliness you're afraid of, George? But that's foolish. There are so many people who would be glad to be your friends, to talk to you and, what's better, to listen to you. There are some who would even love you, if you chose.'

'Loneliness?' George said unbelievingly. 'Do you think it's loneliness I'm afraid of?'

'Then what is it?'

'You know as well as I,' George said in a shaking voice, 'what you're trying to lead me to. How could you expect me, expect any decent man, to be that cruel!'

White bared his teeth disdainfully. 'Can you tell me anything more cruel than a weak and stupid woman whose only ambition in life was to marry a man infinitely superior to her and then cut him down to her level so that her weakness and stupidity could always be concealed?'

'You've got no right to talk about Louise like that!'

'I have every right,' said White grimly, and somehow George knew in his heart that this was the dreadful truth. With a rising panic he clutched the edge of the table.

'I won't do it!' he said distractedly. 'I'll never do it, do you understand!'

'But it will be done!' White said, and his voice was so naked with terrible decision that George looked up to see Louise coming towards the table with her sharp little footsteps. She stood over it, her mouth working angrily, and then through the confusion of his thoughts he heard her voice echoing the same words again and again. 'You fool!' she was saying wildly. 'It's this chess! I've had enough of it!' And suddenly she swept her hand over the board and dashed the pieces from it.

'No!' cried George, not at Louise's gesture, but at the sight of White standing before her, the heavy poker raised in his hand. 'No!' George shouted again, and started up to block the fall of the poker, but knew even as he did so that it was too late.

Louise might have been dismayed at the untidy way her remains were deposited in the official basket; she would certainly have cried aloud (had she been in a condition to do so) at the unsightly scar on the polished woodwork made by the basket as it was dragged along the floor and borne out of the front door. Inspector Lund, however, merely closed the door casually behind the little cortège and turned back to the living-room.

Obviously the Lieutenant had completed his interrogation of the quiet little man seated in the chair next to the chess-table, and obviously the Lieutenant was not happy. He paced the centre of the floor, studying his notes with a furrowed brow, while the little man watched him, silent and motionless.

'Well?' said Inspector Lund.

'Well,' said the Lieutenant, 'There's just one thing that doesn't tie in. From what I put together, here's a guy who's living his life all right, getting along fine, and all of a sudden he finds he's got another soul, another personality. He's like a man split into two parts, you might say.'

'Schizoid,' remarked Inspector Lund. 'That's not unusual.'

'Maybe not,' said the Lieutenant. 'Anyhow, this other self is no good at all, and sure enough it winds up doing this killing.'

'That all seems to tie in,' said Inspector Lund. 'What's the hitch?'

'Just one thing,' the Lieutenant stated: 'a matter of identity.' He frowned at his notebook, and then turned to the little man in the chair next to the chess-table. 'What did you say your name was?' he demanded.

The little man drew his lips into a faintly sardonic grimace of rebuke. 'Why, I've told you that so many times before, Lieutenant, surely you couldn't have forgotten it again.' The little man smiled pleasantly. 'My name is White.'

A BETTER CHESS PLAYER

Kenneth Gavrell

The penal compound stood on acres of cleared field at the edge of the jungle. It was enclosed by a high electrified fence topped with barbed wire. At fifty-yard intervals along the fence were guard towers with powerful searchlights and always-loaded machine guns. At night the compound was floodlit so that it was almost as bright as day. Nearly all of the prisoners, many of them very intelligent men, were there for political reasons, but in the eight years of its existence, no one had ever escaped the compound. It was thought that sprinkled among the prisoners were paid informants who immediately reported any escape plan they heard of to the colonel.

Colonel Buko was a tall, heavyset, well-muscled man of forty-two. He had a shaved head, a black moustache, and skin the colour of burlap. Immediately after taking command of the compound (shortly after its inception) he had had a sign erected over the entrance. The sign read ABANDON HOPE ALL YOU WHO ENTER HERE. Dante's *Inferno* was one of Colonel Buko's favourite books. The colonel had read widely; he also liked Celine, Dostoevski, and Yukio Mishima. He was an expert in chess and most other board games. With such interests, Colonel Buko did not much mind the steamy heat in which he passed his days at the isolated penal camp. Occasionally he found an opportunity to mitigate his boredom by an unusual act of cruelty. Perhaps he got some of his ideas from Dante.

On the day Gorshin was brought through the gates of the camp he vowed to escape. A short, dark, wiry man in his thirties, Gorshin was a university professor with a specialisation in Middle Eastern literature. He had been arrested for his political ideas. As in most such cases, his sentence was for an unspecified duration. Gorshin assumed that if the present government remained in power, he would spend the rest of his life in Colonel Buko's inferno.

From the day of Gorshin's arrival, Colonel Buko seemed to take a special interest in him. Both men were readers and both played chess. The colonel ascertained these facts at their first interview and invited Gorshin to a game that evening after food call and before lights out. Gorshin disliked the colonel at first sight, but he showed up at the designated time.

Colonel Buko won the first game in six minutes. Gorshin had never seen so good a player. The second victory took Colonel Buko almost twelve minutes.

'You don't play very well for a college professor.'

'I always thought I did.'

'Do you want some rice wine?'

'No, thank you.'

The colonel refilled his own cup. 'A man who cannot win at chess should not become involved in politics,' he said.

'Are you interested in politics?' Gorshin asked.

'If you live in this country, you must be interested in politics. I helped put the present government in power.'

'And this is how they rewarded you?' Gorshin said, sweeping his hand to indicate the sweaty compound beyond the mosquito screens.

The colonel emptied his cup. 'I enjoy my work,' he said.

'Why?'

'I enjoy power. In this compound, I have absolute power.'

'Have you ever had anyone escape?' Gorshin asked matter-of-factly.

'No one. Several have tried. If I hear even a rumour of an escape plan, I have the perpetrators shot immediately.'

'Without proof that the rumour is true?'

'Proof is not important here.'

'Nor is life, I take it.'

'Fewer vermin crawling on the face of the earth,' Colonel Buko said.

They played a third game of chess. The colonel won that also. Gorshin got up to leave.

'You will be locked in at nine o'clock,' the colonel said, 'until exercise call at five tomorrow morning.'

The professor nodded and said good-night.

'If I were you, I would not think of escaping,' Colonel Buko said. 'It's as bright as day out there. We have two guards in each tower, plus two at the gate, two at the electric station, and four more who patrol the compound. All are equipped with automatic weapons and all are very familiar with those weapons. I have seen to that.'

'I wouldn't dream of leaving you before I win a chess game,' the professor said.

He walked back across the yard to Hut 4, where he bunked with five other men. At nine o'clock sharp he heard the padlocking of the quonset hut's metal door and the interior lights suddenly went out. Gorshin lay on his bunk, which smelled of mould, and looked out of the barred windows at the two guards in the tower twenty yards away. They leaned on their machine guns, looking bored.

Gorshin was not much interested in his hut-mates. Two were students who had barely begun to shave, one was a former civil servant who Gorshin soon learned was as corrupt as those who had replaced him, one was a common and incorrigible thief, and the fifth an army major who had chosen the wrong side eight years earlier. Only the last, whose name was Rozazi, held the slightest interest for Gorshin. He slept in the bunk directly below, and Gorshin would sometimes talk to him between lights out and the coming of sleep.

The major was a man of ideals. He had thought the former government more decent than the present one. Apparently he had been naïve enough to think that right would triumph in the end. He'd had eight years to reconsider his idealism, but was still hopeful that the regime supported by men like Colonel Buko would one day be overthrown.

'Your memory is bad,' Gorshin said. 'The previous regime was not much better than this one.'

'Then why are you here?' Rozazi asked.

'Because I spoke too openly against this regime, not because I supported the other.'

'Someday we will have a democratic government, ' Rozazi said.

'Well, in the meantime we'd better get some sleep,' said Gorshin.

Each morning a siren shattered the silence at four-thirty while it was still dark outside. The hut lights would come on blindingly, and the six men would line up for turns into the tiny connected outhouse. Then they'd dress and be bunched up by the metal door by five o'clock.

The prisoners liked the morning exercise period. Colonel Buko wanted to keep them in good physical condition so that his compound would run efficiently. Each man had his work to do for nine hours of the day. The colonel had scheduled their activities as neatly as Benjamin Franklin:

5:00 — 6:00 a.m.	Physical exercise
6:00 — 6:30 a.m.	Showers and shaving in the large, common lavatory building
6:30 — 7.00 a.m.	Breakfast
7.00 — 11.30 a.m.	Work
11:30 — 1:00 p.m.	Lunch and relaxation
1:00 — 5:30 p.m.	Work
5:30 — 6:00 p.m.	Supper

The time between six and lights out was the men's own, but most of it was consumed with cleaning up the huts, outhouses, and personal bunk areas. Colonel Buko thought of his compound as a military installation and held military-style inspections every day.

On his second day in the camp, Gorshin was assigned to the laundry. This was considered by the men to be the least desirable of the work assignments. It meant sweating over vats of hot, soapy water heated by wood fires which were constantly kept burning from seven a.m. to late afternoon. Drying was done on long metal clothes-lines.

The men in Gorshin's hut had ranked the different types of work in the compound. The best jobs were in maintenance and repair, but these normally went to those with some experience. Second in preference was working in the huge compound garden which supplied most of the inmates' food. In addition to a large, inundated rice area, there were separate sections for Asian cabbage, squash, and tomatoes. Perhaps because excrement was used for fertiliser, the size of the vegetables was exceptional. An orchard provided lemons and oranges. The oranges were full of seeds, but very sweet. There were hog pens and chicken coops connected to the garden, and the same workers took care of the animals. Once or twice a month, beef and fish were brought to the camp from outside. Water was collected in rooftop metal tanks; the rainfall in the area was copious.

The various mess hall jobs were next in preference, followed by garbage disposal, which was done either by burning or burying, depending on the type of garbage. These workers were the only ones who ever left the compound, but always under heavy guard.

At the bottom of the list was Gorshin's laundry job. Most of the men there were newcomers like himself.

During his first few days in the camp, Gorshin observed everything carefully. He was looking for some means of effecting his escape. Nothing overhung the fence; in fact, nothing was built very close to it. The electric generators that provided the fence current were always under guard as the colonel had said. Guards seemed to be everywhere, and Gorshin's hut-mates told him that the guards were so afraid of Colonel Buko they were incorruptible.

It didn't look like it was going to be easy.

On his second evening, Gorshin was again invited to play chess with the colonel. This time there was a third man present: a gaunt, bearded, middle-aged officer who was introduced as Captain Sasin, the camp doctor. The doctor drank much rice wine while he observed the game, which Colonel Buko won in nine moves. The two military men chuckled.

'I understand you are a political prisoner,' the doctor said to Gorshin. 'Tell me, do you think it was worth it?'

'If you feel strongly about something, you have no choice,' said Gorshin.

'You have the choice of keeping silent.'

'No, you don't.'

'I'm afraid I wouldn't understand that,' Dr Sasin said.

Gorshin looked at him curiously. The doctor stroked his wispy beard, not at all discomposed by Gorshin's searching eyes.

'You see, I believe in nothing,' Dr Sasin said.

'Nobody can live without believing in something,' Gorshin said.

'Oh yes, they can.'

'You must believe in humanity.'

'No,' said Dr Sasin. 'Nor in inhumanity.'

'Then why are you a doctor?'

'Once, I suppose, I was capable of belief.'

'And what changed you?'

'I grew older. Now I perform my work as a machine performs its work. I am necessary, as a car mechanic or a garbage collector is necessary. I keep the men here healthy.'

'The morning exercise periods were Dr Sasin's idea,' Colonel Buko said. 'A very good idea. The men are so healthy that we don't even have a regular infirmary here.'

'Their health is as much your doing as mine, colonel. They know that there is no infirmary here.'

'Yes, it's important that the prisoners realise certain things,' Colonel Buko said. 'For example, that the smallest infraction of the rules will be severely punished. I've had several opportunities to show them that like a good parent I am absolutely consistent.'

'But men without hope may be capable of anything,' Gorshin said.

'In this camp, action is the same as inaction,' the colonel said. 'There is no hope either way. You saw the sign over the gate.'

'Well then, some men would prefer the illusion of hope to inaction,' Gorshin said.

'I trust you're not one of them,' the colonel said. 'If you were to try something foolish, I would have to shoot you. In fact,' he chuckled, 'I promise you that I would do it myself, with that pistol.' He pointed to his holstered Japanese revolver hanging from a hook on the wall.

'I will attempt to abandon all hope,' Gorshin said. He started to reset the pieces on the chessboard. The colonel took another sip of rice wine. The doctor lit a cigarette.

'Have you read Jack London's *The Sea Wolf*?' Colonel Buko asked Gorshin.

'No, I don't think so. Is that one of the few books the government still permits?'

'As a professor of literature, you would naturally object to censorship,' the colonel remarked understandingly.

'They thoroughly purged the university library,' Gorshin said, 'if you could still call it a university.'

'These things are necessary but unpleasant,' Colonel Buko said. 'I may be one of the few people left with a decent library.'

'Including banned books,' said Gorshin.

'Now how could a man in my position have banned books?' the colonel asked, smiling. 'In any case, you must read *The Sea Wolf*. I'll lend you my copy.'

'I'll be glad to take a look at it.'

'Piggishness and yeast,' Colonel Buko said. 'That's what life is: piggishness and yeast.'

He proceeded to take Gorshin's queen in six moves.

Apparently Colonel Buko felt he had learned enough about Gorshin, or else he'd become tired of winning so easily at chess, because the professor was not invited to the colonel's quarters a third time.

Gorshin was quite satisfied with this. He relished the modicum of leisure between supper and lights out. The laundry *was* the worst work assignment in the compound. A row of vats and clothes-wires under a corrugated zinc roof, it baked under the sun and steamed in the drenching rains. To work there meant to be perpetually soaked in sweat, and washing other people's clothes seemed to Gorshin the most disgusting job imaginable. He preferred scrubbing the outhouse attached to the quonset hut.

The men co-operated well in cleaning the hut and usually were able to rest by seven-thirty p.m. Perhaps because Gorshin was the most educated in the group, he became the centre of the talk during these leisure hours. One night he told them a story from his favourite literature, *The Thousand and One Nights*. It was a work the professor knew virtually by heart, and his stock of stories was as inexhaustible as Scheherazade's. As soon as his hut-mates discovered this, they, like the mythical sultan, would ask for one after another. Gorshin was gratified to see that the book he loved had lost none of its magic over the hundreds of years of its existence, even though all copies of it had been burned by the present government. It had been officially pronounced 'degenerate'. But Gorshin had managed to save his favourite edition as well as several other banned books by hiding them at a cousin's farm before they arrested him.

Dr Sasin, unlike Colonel Buko, seemed to have retained his interest in Gorshin's ideas. He would drop in frequently to talk to him — to pit his own nihilism against what he termed Gorshin's naïveté. One night he came in during one of the stories from *The Thousand and One Nights* and listened with apparent interest. He stayed for the one which followed. Thereafter he would make a point of being present to hear Scheherazade's fictions.

'You've never read the *Nights*?' Gorshin asked him just before lights out one night.

'No. Oh, a few of them when I was a child: Sinbad and Aladdin's Lamp. I didn't realise there were so many.'

'Volumes,' said Gorshin. 'My favourite edition is in fifteen leatherbound volumes.'

'To me that sounds like a lifetime of reading,' said the doctor.

'Not so long,' Gorshin said.

'I like to hear them because they remind me of when I was a

boy,' said Dr Sasin, startling Gorshin with his honesty, his lack of cynicism.

'I suppose we all like them for that reason,' Gorshin agreed. 'Did you believe in something then?'

'Don't we all?' said the doctor. 'Life looks very different to children. It looks like the *Arabian Nights:* magic, heroism, beautiful princesses . . . '

'Are you married?' Gorshin asked him.

'Never. I'm not the kind of man who marries. And you?'

'I was until a few years ago. My wife died.'

'Everything dies,' the doctor said.

'Ideas don't,' the professor said.

'In time they do.'

'*The Arabian Nights* have lasted a thousand years.'

'They will die, too.' Dr Sasin said.

Gorshin was beginning to formulate a plan of escape. Because of the rumours he'd heard, he was afraid to confide in his hut-mates, wondering if one of them might be Colonel Buko's informer. He didn't think it could be the students or Rozazi, the idealistic major, but the corrupt civil servant and the thief both looked like excellent candidates.

The former civil servant, Balim, was a soft, olive-skinned man with bad teeth and equally bad breath. He wasn't a bad hut-mate, however, since he was mainly concerned with getting along comfortably without any trouble for himself. His favourite line was 'I don't want any trouble.' But Gorshin wouldn't trust him a jot: Balim was the kind of man who'd sell his soul for some small creature comfort.

Kochi, the thief, was a weasel in every respect. He spoke in a whiny, wheedling way that got on Gorshin's nerves. Although they hadn't yet missed anything in the hut, Gorshin was pretty sure that one day they would.

As it happened, when Kochi finally did give in to his incorrigible propensities, no one in the hut was the victim. Instead he stole a basket of fresh tomatoes from the mess hall where he worked. He was caught, and Gorshin was given the opportunity to see Colonel Buko's manner of meting out justice. Both of Kochi's ears were cut off. After that he cried a great deal and kept to himself in his corner bunk, his face to the wall. Gorshin couldn't stand to look at him.

Three days after Kochi lost his ears, another prisoner in Hut 7 assaulted a guard who, he claimed, was constantly harassing him. Colonel Buko naturally saw this as a serious breach of camp discipline. By way of punishment, he had all of the prisoner's teeth pulled out. It took a long time, and the man's screams filled the compound and had a very chastening effect on the other inmates. It would be months before another breach of discipline.

Punishments like these convinced Gorshin that, in spite of his fondness for reading, the colonel was indeed the monster he claimed to be. Dr Sasin was called in to stop the bleeding and prevent infection after both punishments; he performed these duties impassively and made not one comment on the colonel's perversity.

'You seem very loyal to the colonel,' Gorshin remarked to him bitterly on the night of the toothpulling incident.

'I do my job as I'm told,' Dr Sasin said. 'I have no loyalties.'

'Not to your parents? Your profession?'

'Loyalty implies a system of values. But in this country there is no longer a system of values. Colonel Buko is quite correct: might makes right.'

'Yet you are one of the few men here I somehow feel I could trust,' Gorshin said.

'Don't believe it,' Dr Sasin said soberly. 'I am not a man to be trusted.'

Gorshin had all but worked out his scheme of escape. It awaited only the right conjunction of circumstances. Just the hope of escaping Colonel Buko's well-run hell lifted his spirits immensely. He was almost in a genial mood when the colonel sent for him again one evening.

'I thought you had tired of humiliating me at chess,' he said.

'I have,' said the colonel. 'I called you in to lend you the book we spoke of, London's *The Sea Wolf*.'

'Oh.'

The colonel slid the novel to him across his desk. 'You may learn something from that. Maybe it will make you a better chess-player.'

'Thank you,' Gorshin said. He tucked the book under his arm and returned to his quonset hut, where his fellow inmates were awaiting another instalment of *The Arabian Nights*. A few minutes after his return, Dr Sasin dropped by as had become his custom.

In the evenings following, Gorshin would read some pages from *The Sea Wolf* before he began his storytelling. The novel's hero was a titanic brute named Wolfe Larsen who, having come from hard beginnings, was convinced that life was a dog-eat-dog battle for survival whose ultimate meaning was absolutely nothing. To be strong was good, because the strong survived. Life was a fermenting yeast, a senseless hierarchy of voracious cannibalism. Gorshin could easily see why Colonel Buko liked the book, and even he had to feel a grudging admiration for the colossal rebel London had created. But it was a relief to turn afterwards to the gentler cynicism of Scheherazade's tales.

One evening, after he'd been in the camp almost six weeks, Gorshin decided the time had come. The key to his escape plan was the electric station, the generators that fed the floodlights and the electrified fence. A padlocked door and the ever-present pair of guards seemed to make the station invulnerable, but this evening the door was not padlocked because a maintenance man was working inside. What was needed was something to distract the guards, and Gorshin had already thought that out.

Because of his floodlights, Colonel Buko had placed no restrictions on the men's walking around the compound between supper and lights out. Gorshin had taken one confederate into his plan and this confederate had supplied him with a heavy monkey wrench, a can of lighter fluid, and a box of matches. With the monkey wrench stuck in his belt under his shirt and the matches and fluid in his pockets, Gorshin strolled casually across the open space between his hut and the laundry building where he worked. The laundry was never locked. Gorshin slipped inside and threw heaps of dried clothing against the wooden walls. He doused the piles liberally with lighter fluid and tossed several burning matches on each. In a few seconds the clothing was blazing, the greedy flames already licking the walls. Gorshin slipped out of the door and strolled towards the electric station, which stood close by.

No one appeared to have taken any notice of his actions. It wasn't long before the cry of 'Fire!' went up, and every eye in the area was on the flames leaping from the windows of the laundry. As Gorshin had expected, one of the guards at the electric station started running immediately towards the conflagration. The other hesitated, unsure whether he should leave his post even under these circumstances. Pointing excitedly and yelling like the others, Gorshin approached the second guard, a young corporal. The guard still hesitated. Gorshin reached inside his shirt, jerked out his monkey wrench, and struck the young guard solidly across the base of the skull. He fell as if hit by a bulldozer.

Everyone was shouting and running towards the blazing building and no one had noticed Gorshin's act. He heaved back the already half-open door of the station and pulled the guard's body through very quickly, kicking the door to behind him. The maintenance man, who was not Gorshin's confederate but one of Colonel Buko's most trusted inmates, turned to Gorshin with eyes dilated by surprise and fear. Gorshin took no chances and hit him also with the heavy wrench. His first blow only grazed the terror-stricken man, but his second sent the man to the dirt floor unconscious.

The professor had learned about generators while living for some months at his cousin's farm. All the electricity there had been produced by generator. In seconds Gorshin put the two machines out of commission, plunging the whole compound into sudden darkness, the only light coming from the fire. Before anyone could fully realise what had happened, Gorshin was out of the door and around the side of the electric station. He ran through the darkness along a route he had chosen very carefully, a route where buildings shielded his every step from the light created by the fire.

Gorshin's plan brought him to the bottom of the wooden lattice-work guard tower that rose beside the fence not far from his own quonset hut. The tower's structure made it a natural ladder, and Gorshin climbed up the inside quickly, out of sight of everyone including the two guards in the little shack above him. The tower was higher than the barbed wire-topped fence, and Gorshin was able to step onto the wire while still unnoticed by the guards above him. The wire gave beneath his thick-soled shoes, but Gorshin's clothes caught in it as he let himself down the outside of the fence. He tore his clothing from the barbs savagely, cutting himself in several places, and was soon scrambling down. In all the commotion, the guards above did not notice him at all.

He dropped the last six feet to the ground, landed on his feet, and started to run for the nearest wall of jungle. It was a clouded, moonless night, and travelling very close to the ground, Gorshin was nothing more than a swiftly gliding shadow. Just as he was about to enter the deeper darkness of the jungle, half a dozen lights blazed out at him from the trees. Gorshin was blinded by the lights and instinctively threw his hands up over his eyes. The lights rapidly closed the few yards' distance to him, and

Gorshin found himself in the hands of Colonel Buko's soldiers. The colonel stood with his hands on his hips grinning at the professor's amazed face. Beside the colonel stood Dr Sasin. Dr Sasin had been Gorshin's confederate.

'I warned you that you shouldn't trust me,' the doctor said.

His clothes in rags, his arms and legs bleeding, Gorshin stood in front of the colonel's desk. The colonel sat with his polished boots up on the desk, smoking a cigarette. Against a wall, in a comfortable chair, sat the doctor.

'Now that was quite exciting,' the colonel smiled. 'Did you really think you could convert Dr Sasin?'

'I'm glad that you enjoyed it,' Gorshin said bitterly.

'Why, I even helped you along with it!' Colonel Buko said. 'Didn't you notice how incredibly smoothly everything went for you? As if Divine Providence were at your elbow.'

'You could have eliminated all this charade,' Gorshin said.

'I could have, yes. But I wanted you to taste the illusion of success, of freedom attained — so that your final disappointment would be all the more crushing.'

'In the process, you lost your laundry building,' Gorshin said.

'Oh, that's nothing. Rebuilding it will give the prisoners something to do. You know I like to keep them busy.'

'Well, shoot me and get it over with,' said the professor.

'No, no, not tonight. I want you to think about it first. I'll do it tomorrow at noon. You remember what the experience of awaiting his own execution did to Dostoevski? Of course, he wasn't executed — a little joke of the Czar — but Dostoevski never got over it.'

'Will you play the same perverse joke?' Gorshin asked him.

'Oh no, I *will* shoot you. Go back to your hut now and get some sleep.'

Gorshin walked out the door and across the again-floodlit space that separated the colonel's quarters from quonset hut 4. Colonel Buko didn't even bother to send a guard with him.

At noon the next day Gorshin was standing ten yards from Colonel Buko's pointed pistol. He was not tied or blindfolded. He was drenched under a tropical downpour that had been falling in thick grey curtains for more than an hour. The colonel did not say anything, and Gorshin did not say anything either. The colonel sighted the pistol carefully and placed two bullets exactly where Gorshin's heart would be. Gorshin fell without a sound and lay in the mud in the rain.

Every two weeks a supply truck arrived at the compound from the capital two hundred and twenty miles away. The truck which arrived about a month after Gorshin's death contained a package addressed to Dr Sasin. He took it to his quarters before unwrapping it.

It was Dr Sasin who had pronounced Gorshin dead after the execution and who had supervised the burial of the body. He had also put the blanks in Colonel Buko's pistol and shown Gorshin how to release 'blood' into his shirt. In the package which the doctor opened in private were fifteen beautifully bound volumes of *The Thousand and One Nights*.

Weeks later, in another country, when Gorshin was asked why he hadn't simply escaped according to his original plan, he replied:

'First of all, I wasn't sure it would work, and secondly, it was preferable to be thought dead than to have escaped. They wouldn't look for a dead man.'

ACKNOWLEDGEMENTS

The editor and publishers are grateful to the following authors, agents and publishers for permission to use copyright stories in this collection: E.J. Carnell Literary Agency for 'The Dreams of Albert Moreland' by Fritz Leiber; Michael Joseph Ltd for 'The Three Sailors' Gambit' by Lord Dunsany and for the quotation from his autobiography *Patches of Sunlight*; Wm Heinemann Ltd for 'The Devil That Troubled the Chessboard' by Gerald Kersh; The Bodley Head for 'Pawn to King's Four' by Stephen Leacock; Cassell & Co for 'The Royal Game' by Stefan Zweig; Jonathan Cape Ltd for 'End-Game' by J.G. Ballard and 'Professor Pownall's Oversight' by H. Russell Wakefield; Avon Books for 'The Immortal Game' by Poul Anderson; The Estate of E.R. Punshon for 'The Haunted Chessmen'; Arkham House Publishers for 'Bishop's Gambit' by August Derleth; Aitken & Stone for 'A Chess Problem' by Agatha Christie; Hodder & Stoughton Ltd for 'Checkmate' by Alfred Noyes; Standard Magazines Inc for 'The Cat from Siam' by Fredric Brown; Curtis Brown Ltd for 'Fool's Mate' by Stanley Ellin; Davis Publications Inc for 'A Better Chess-Player' by Kenneth Gavrell; Times Supplements Ltd. for comments by John Fowles on Stefan Zweig, published in *The Times Literary Supplement*. While every care had been taken to clear permission for use of the stories in this book, in the case of any accidental infringement, copyright holders are asked to contact the editor care of the publishers.